I0612666

ANGEL'S FEATHER
A CASTOR'S GROVE YOUNG ADULT PARANORMAL ROMANCE

A.J. RENWICK

PLOTWORKS PUBLISHING

Copyright © 2023 Plotworks Publishing

Cover Copyright © 2023 Plotworks Publishing

All rights reserved.

No part of this book may be reproduced in any form or by any electronic or mechanical means, including information storage and retrieval systems, without written permission from the author, except for the use of brief quotations in a book review.

For inquiries, please contact ashley@plotworkspublishing.com.

Electronic ISBN: 978-1-960936-21-9

Print ISBN: 978-1-960936-22-6

1

EVANGELINA

Most people would be annoyed about transferring schools at the start of their senior year. Eva preferred to think of it as an opportunity to make new friends.

The crowded parking lot and narrow halls of Dashmoor High School possessed a unique charm. The building's gray and brown color-scheme wasn't drab, but reminiscent of the earth and clouds on a rainy day.

Eva forced a smile as she walked down the hallway. Several boys returned it, but their eyes swept toward the hem of her dress. Eva tugged it lower. She tried not to miss the purple plaid skirt and white button-down of her old uniform. Or her friends. Leah would've smiled back at a stranger, and Max never leered at girls and—

No, stop it. Don't think about them.

Otherwise, Eva's thoughts would turn to her brother. She needed to keep her composure and stay positive.

With that in mind, Eva took a seat near the front of the classroom. She smiled at a pair of girls as they walked past her. One nudged the other and whispered. Both snickered and continued glancing at Eva as they made their way to the back.

That couldn't be good.

Eva reached over her shoulder. The only feathers she felt belonged to her dress.

Phew.

"Interesting outfit for your first day of school." A large girl with gorgeous brown hair stopped beside the desk. She studied Eva's notebook with a pair of bright green eyes. "That your name?"

The brunette tapped the pink swirly letters at the top, which read *Evangelina Heaven*.

"Yes!" Eva responded a bit too quickly. But she couldn't help it. The brunette was the first girl to speak to her. "Everyone calls me Eva though. It's much shorter."

"Huh."

"What's your—?" Before Eva could learn the brunette's name, their teacher stormed in and ordered everyone to their seats.

Mr. Harris was a short man with a bald spot on the back of his head. He taught Grade 12 Advanced Functions and AP Calculus. Unfortunately, Eva had been forced to take the latter. Her math grades had been artificially inflated by Cassel's lax standards for the subject. Teachers at Dashmoor would care a lot more about numbers.

Eva struggled to keep up as Mr. Harris launched a slideshow providing definitions and explanations of limits. She wasn't used to taking her own notes. Her penmanship looked like chicken scratch.

With more than a little envy, she eyed the tablets of her classmates. Maybe she should ask her parents for one. It could help her blend in. And taking photographs seemed a lot easier than writing by hand. Before the end of the period, Eva's fingers had started to cramp.

The door swung open. A tall boy with long limbs strolled into the room. He kept one hand in his pocket while the other pushed back the black waves of hair falling in his face.

Wow.

Eva forgot about the slideshow. Judging from the whispers, the rest of the class did too.

The boy could've been a model. He had the height, the long limbs, and near perfect features, almost like an artist's sketch come to life. His smooth, golden-brown skin held a natural glow. Just talking to Mr. Harris, the boy's movements displayed an easy casualness that a camera would've loved. Perhaps he thought he'd walked into a photoshoot now because—though he looked about Eva's age—he couldn't be a student. Otherwise, he'd be over thirty minutes late!

"Welcome back, Nathan. So pleased you could join us," Mr. Harris said with obvious annoyance. He pointed to an empty seat near the front.

"Of course," the boy, Nathan, responded in a deep voice that carried the same sense of relaxed wryness as his posture. "Figure if I'm around for at least half the classes, I'll have a full year of work under my belt."

The other students laughed. Eva didn't understand the joke. But she decided to join in.

Unfortunately, she was a beat too late.

The class fell silent, and Eva's giggle hung awkwardly in the air.

From his place in the row ahead, Nathan turned to consider her.

Eva's breath caught. She'd hadn't noticed his eyes, but

they might've been his most striking feature: warm and dark, with thick lashes. They reminded Eva of a deer, sweet and almost shy, at odds with his angular features and aloof demeanor.

Hope flickered in her chest. Maybe Nathan was nice. Maybe they could be friends. Eva smiled and raised her hand in a wave.

Nathan snorted and turned away. Not so sweet after all.

Mildly embarrassed, Eva checked her shoulders. Still just her dress. Good. Eva relaxed for a second before realizing that she'd missed several slides.

———

Despite the spasms in her fingers, Eva felt a flutter of excitement as fourth period began. She'd never taken a French class before. But Dashmoor insisted that she needed a language credit.

Eva spotted a vacant seat at the back of the room. A freckle-faced boy in a backward blue baseball cap sat beside it. He leaned against the wall, eyes already closed.

"Mind if I sit here?" Eva inquired as she approached. Asking might've been the wrong move. She'd have been mortified if he said no. But so far, the boys at Dashmoor seemed nicer than the girls.

Baseball Cap opened one eye and grinned. "Not at all. But what're you doing in the back with us slackers?"

Us?

Eva glanced around, expecting another student to materialize in one of the vacant chairs. But of course, no one did.

"Don't you talk?"

"Oh. Yes!" Eva nodded, feeling embarrassed. She should know better than to look for someone invisible hiding in a chair at Dashmoor. "I need a break from taking notes." As evidence, Eva lifted her hand, showing him the way her fingers had cramped, tightening and bending into a claw.

"Yikes. That's why you should never work too hard." He grinned. "My name's Chris by the way."

"I'm Evangelina, but you can call me—"

He snapped his fingers before she could finish. "Blue Eyes."

"I was going to say Eva, but sure." Nicknames were a sign of friendship, right? And *Blue Eyes* was still fewer syllables than *Evangelina*.

Ms. Lyle, their French teacher arrived. She was a tall, thin woman with her lips downturned in a perpetual frown. She greeted the class, connected her laptop to a cable, and projected a slideshow onto the board.

"They're not very creative in their teaching style here, are they?" Eva whispered to Chris.

He gave her another grin. "Now you're getting it."

But Eva had been too hasty in her judgment. Ms. Lyle deviated from her slideshow after a few minutes, instructing them to pair up and practice the reviewed vocabulary in conversation.

"That assignment's not for us slackers, Blue Eyes," Chris informed Eva, turning toward her. Still speaking English, he asked, "So, where'd you transfer from?"

"Nowhere interesting," Eva said. It bordered on a lie, but people in the city considered Cassel snobbish and elite. Eva didn't blame them. The school catered to a narrow selection of the population.

"Mysterious," Chris said, rubbing the end of his rather pointed nose. "What do you think of Castor's Grove so far?"

"I love it!" Eva had lived in the city all her life, so her answer was technically true.

"Ahem." Ms. Lyle cleared her throat.

Eva jumped. She hadn't noticed the teacher approach, but Ms. Lyle now stood beside them, staring down her nose.

"That doesn't sound like French."

"Aw come on, ma'am," Chris said, rocking his chair as he shrugged. "It's the first day. Let us just chat for once, *sill-vooz-plate.*" He butchered the pronunciation so badly that it could only have been intentional.

Ms. Lyle smiled. She clapped her hands and turned toward the rest of the class. "Everyone, focus your attention here. Christopher and his new friend want to chat. Let's listen."

Eva took a deep breath as almost thirty chairs turned toward her.

Don't panic.

Ms. Lyle started with Chris. She asked him several questions about his family and hobbies, but Chris must not have understood. In a phony French accent, he proceeded to tell her about how he'd spent his summer perfecting his skills in a racing game. Other than *oui, oui* and *mademoiselle*, he spoke in English.

Eva laughed along with the rest of the class until Ms. Lyle silenced them.

"Charming. But you'll impress a lot more girls if you can speak the language. Right now, they're simply laughing at you." Ms. Lyle turned to Eva next. "*Ou alors êtes-vous impressionné par les garçons qui échouent en cours de français?*"

Eva stopped laughing. The question seemed like a trap, but she did her best to answer. "*Non, mademoiselle. Mais Chris a l'air sympa, et je suis hereux de me faire un ami.*"

Ms. Lyle's eyebrows rose. Her frown grew more pronounced.

Perhaps Eva should've thrown in an apology. Her response had clearly displeased the teacher.

Ms. Lyle fired off question after question. First about Eva's family, then pets, then books, then movies. Eva had no idea why the French teacher kept changing topic, but she continued to answer until the lunch bell rang.

No one in Room 4B moved.

"I'm sorry, what did you say your name was?" Ms. Lyle asked, switching back to English.

"Evangelina Heaven," Eva responded, shuffling in her chair and wishing the rest of the class would stop staring.

Ms. Lyle's eyes narrowed in immediate dislike. "You're the transfer from Cassel."

A lump rose in Eva's throat. She avoided looking at Chris, but she heard him whistle. Whispers broke out among the rest of the class.

"Your French is quite advanced." Ms. Lyle did not sound impressed. "Perhaps you should challenge yourself with a new language. Spanish maybe? Or German?"

Eva hesitated. But skirting the truth hadn't helped her before, so she admitted, "I'm fluent in those too."

The class grew louder. Snippets of conversation reached Eva's ears.

"...you really think..."

"...she's such a showoff..."

"...Why is she even here?"

Eva's throat tightened. She didn't know where to look. Her classmates stabbed her with glares or gaped with undeserved awe. They were right to question her presence. Eva shouldn't be there.

Except that my brother got arrested, and now my family are pariahs, and— oh no!

Eva felt it at once. No need to reach over her shoulder and check. She pressed her back further against the seat, heart pounding.

Ms. Lyle forced a tight-lipped smile. "My, my, I do hope we here at Dashmoor can find something to teach you, Evangelina. Class dismissed."

She didn't notice. No one has.

At least, they hadn't yet.

Eva grabbed her bag, slung it over her back, and bolted for the door. Her limbs bumped at least a dozen people as she ran down the hallway. Eva shouted apologies, but she didn't dare stop.

She needed to get to the bathroom before someone realized. Eva's wings had popped out.

2

NATHAN

"Dude, you should NOT have skipped French today," Chris said, slamming his tray onto the table. Brown mush, which the cafeteria passed off as mashed potatoes, dripped over the side of his bowl.

Nathan's stomach growled.

Jesus, he must've been hungry if that looked good.

Nathan grabbed the packet of peanuts from his pocket. Only half left. He'd have to ration them until he had a chance to go shopping. He poured three onto his palm and put the rest back.

"Why not?" Nathan asked, popping one of the peanuts into his mouth. "Don't tell me Lyle missed me."

Chris barked out a laugh. "Please. I don't even think she knows you take her class."

Nathan inclined his head in a fake bow. In the past four years, he'd missed a lot of classes at Dashmoor. But French was the only one he skipped on purpose.

"The new girl is in it," Chris said.

"Who?"

"Oh come on. You noticed her. She's hot."

Nathan knew who Chris meant. Even if she hadn't been attractive, the new girl would have been impossible to miss. Still, Nathan pretended to think for a moment. "Ah, you mean the overly cheery blonde who's dressed like she's going to a club."

Chris snapped his fingers. "That's Blue Eyes."

"I don't know what color her eyes are," Nathan lied. "She's wearing a white feather dress. Kind of hard to notice anything else." Other than her legs. Even if he hadn't studied the new girl, Nathan would have noticed those. But he blamed the dress for that as well. It wasn't exactly long.

"Yeah, I get it. She's not your type. None of them ever are after a couple weeks." Chris waved his spoon in dismissal, wasting flecks of mush. "But you'll never guess what Blue Eyes did in French class."

"Speak French?"

"Well, yes." Chris sounded disappointed. "But she didn't just sort of speak it. She's fluent."

"Wow. Are you telling me someone can speak two languages? Call the newspaper. Alert the media."

"Not two languages," Chris said, rolling his eyes. "Four. She said she speaks Spanish and German too."

The hairs rose on the back of Nathan's neck. He rolled his final peanut between his fingers and shrugged. "She's multilingual. So what?"

"You don't think that's impressive?" Chris laughed. "Seriously, what does a girl have to do to get your attention?"

"More than they have to do to get yours." Nathan smiled and ate his last peanut. He chewed it slowly. Without meaning to, he found his eyes flitting around the cafeteria, searching for a feathery white dress.

What is wrong with me?

Nathan blamed the girl's laugh. It had been sweet and warm, even if obviously nervous. He'd turned at once to find the source and assessed her: blonde hair, blue eyes, big smile that spread across her face and transformed her from pretty to stunning. He'd arrived at one word. Perfect. Her dress cemented the impression.

Nathan wanted nothing to do with perfection. The less he saw of the new girl, the better. Yet, he couldn't resist pressing Chris for more information. "So what? That's it? You seemed so excited. I thought you'd have more intel."

"So you are interested." A sly smile came over Chris' face, and he waved his spoon at Nathan.

"I didn't say that." Nathan grabbed the spoon out of his friend's hand and stole a bite of the brown mashed potato mush. He almost spat it back out. Starvation might be more palatable.

Likely noticing the disgust on Nathan's face, Chris laughed before suddenly stopping. He glanced at the table. "You didn't bring food today?"

"I'm watching my figure." Nathan stuck the spoon back in the mush. "So come on, tell me about the new girl. I'm sure you learned more."

Chris' eyes narrowed. He must've known that Nathan wasn't giving him a real answer. But one of Chris' best qualities was that he didn't ask too many questions.

"Maybe you figured out what she did in French, but that one was easy." Chris took another spoonful of lunch and continued talking with a mouth full of mush. "But you'll definitely never guess where she transferred from."

Curiosity seized Nathan's chest. He feigned a sigh, as though he were only accommodating his friend, and turned. With a belabored smile, Nathan said, "Tell me."

3
EVANGELINA

Eva locked herself in the nearest available stall and hung her backpack on the peg. If she twisted her head, she could see the edges of her wings. They formed an elongated heart down her back with the tops peeking over her shoulders.

Most Castors with wings could control when they appeared. But Eva's popped out whenever she felt overwhelmed. At Cassel, surrounded by fairies, elves, and other angels, it had been a cute quirk. Now, it was a magical disaster waiting to happen.

If enough of the humans at Dashmoor spotted her wings, they might realize what she was. And there was only one belief that all of the magical species of Castor's Grove shared.

"Secrecy is our salvation," Eva whispered the motto that she'd learned at Cassel. It was why Castors kept to themselves and stayed away from humans. But that would be impossible at Dashmoor. Unless Eva took up permanent residence in the bathroom stall.

She took a few deep breaths and ran her fingers over the

edge of her wings. The softness of the down tickled her skin. She loved the feeling, but she couldn't enjoy it for long.

Eva closed her eyes and imagined her wings vanishing. When she looked next, they were hidden again.

Thank you.

Eva sent up a silent prayer and sighed in relief. But maybe she shouldn't be too happy. She'd been at Dashmoor less than a day, and she'd already had trouble with her wings. That was a bad sign.

"No," Eva said, speaking aloud to herself once more. "I'll get better."

"Hello?" A confused voice came from outside the stall. "Are you okay in there?"

Eva jumped and grabbed her backpack. She hadn't realized someone else had come in.

"I'm fine. Just talking to myself," Eva admitted.

"In the bathroom?"

"I was just reassuring myself. I've had a weird first day." Eva double-checked her wings, exited the stall, and held out her hand to a short redhead standing beside the sinks. "I'm Eva. I'm new."

The redhead grimaced and glared at Eva's hand like it might bite. "I didn't ask." She vanished into another stall.

And just like that, Eva failed again at making a friend.

She sighed and left the bathroom with a sense of defeat. Why was it so difficult to connect to the girls at Dashmoor? Was there something fundamentally different about humans or was Eva just out of practice? Her core group of friends hadn't changed since she was six.

How can they all believe that Zeke is guilty?

Eva hugged the straps of her backpack closer as she walked to the cafeteria. She shouldn't waste energy getting angry with her old friends. It wasn't their fault. The Heavens had gone from admired and respected to under investigation in the space of a few days.

It would be better at Dashmoor. Even if her classmates thought speaking multiple languages signaled an expensive education, their gossip about Eva wouldn't include wild, unsubstantiated rumors about excommunication.

A chill shot down Eva's spine. The image of feathers falling from her wings flashed before her. She slammed it away fast.

Even without students flying, transforming, or casting spells, the cafeteria at Dashmoor managed to be loud and chaotic. Students weaved through the large room, balancing trays of strange-looking food that matched the school's gray and brown color scheme. People sat on benches and tables alike, and a pair of teens staged a sword fight with broomsticks. They'd gathered an audience, who chanted and cheered. Their voices rose and then vanished in the general din of conversation and music that pulsed through the room.

Eva searched for a friendly face in the chaos. There had to be at least one, didn't there?

Chris sat beside Nathan, the admittedly attractive boy who'd ignored Eva in math. Were they friends?

Eva smiled, raised a tentative hand, and braced for rejection.

To her unexpected delight, Chris grinned and waved her over.

Maybe Eva had made a friend at Dashmoor! Feeling suddenly more confident, she moved toward the two boys. But before she reached their table, someone grabbed her arm and pulled her away.

"Trust me. You don't want to sit at the Gross Ward table. You're better than that."

"Excuse me? That's incredibly rude," Eva objected as a strong pair of hands forced her into a seat at an empty table.

Her captor was the large still-nameless brunette who'd commented on Eva's dress.

"Don't be silly," the brunette said, taking the chair opposite. "It's a compliment."

"You shouldn't call people gross." Eva didn't know either of the boys well, but she felt the need to defend them all the same. "They're nice."

"No, they're Gross and Ward. Those are the names. Christopher Gross and Nathan Ward," the brunette explained, grinning as though more amused than annoyed by Eva's misunderstanding. "You have so much to learn. You're lucky I grabbed you."

Eva didn't feel lucky. She glanced back at Chris and Nathan. They'd forgotten about her and were engaged in their own conversation.

However, as though he sensed Eva watching, Nathan turned.

Sweet or not, he really was striking. It was the way the sharpness of his cheekbones and angular lines of his chin contrasted with the softness of his eyes. They met Eva's own as he tilted his head.

Oh no, I'm staring!

Eva snapped her face forward, feeling her cheeks heat.

The brunette giggled. "You think he's cute?"

"I suppose," Eva admitted. Afraid to give the brunette the wrong impression, she hurried to add, "But I'm not interested in him. I mean, I don't know him."

"You don't need to," the brunette assured, pulling her

lunch out of a brown paper bag. "Nate is hot. But he's not worth it, trust me."

Eva had watched enough movies about human schools to guess why another girl might caution her from taking an interest in their attractive classmate. "Are you into him?"

The brunette dropped her sandwich. Then, she threw back her head and laughed. It was unusually deep and rich. "Definitely not! I'm objectively acknowledging that he's attractive. There are definitely girls who've gone for him thanks to that alone, but he's tossed them all aside after about a week. He's a huge commitment-phobe. Which isn't automatically disqualifying, but I like men who are smart, who know about the world and can recite Shakespeare. Nate and Chris were supposed to graduate last year, but they missed so many classes, they had to repeat. And not to shame them, but Dashmoor's not exactly competitive, you know?"

Eva unpacked the lunch she'd brought from home. She dipped the carrots into the dressing and crunched as she listened to the brunette, who seemed set on providing an overview of every Dashmoor senior. After finishing her description of Nathan and Chris, she moved onto the girls who'd first laughed at Eva, then a pair of kids at the table beside them, then a boy who came over to try to talk to them.

It wasn't until the brunette stopped to take a bite of her sandwich that Eva finally managed to ask, "But who are you?"

"Mm." The brunette's eyes widened. She hurried to swallow, coughing slightly before holding out her hand. "Sorry, I do have a tendency to just talk and skip important first steps. I'm Beatrice Blackwell."

Eva's hand went limp. Beatrice either didn't notice or didn't care. Grip tight, she forced the handshake.

It was an odd coincidence. The Blackwells were a prominent coven of witches. But there were humans with the surname too. Beatrice Blackwell must have been one of them. Because, surely, a Blackwell witch wouldn't also be attending Dashmoor High.

4
EVANGELINA

Halo was waiting for Eva when she arrived home. She scooped the fluffy white cat into her arms and snuggled him against her face. He mewled in protest before settling. Now that he was no longer a kitten, Halo liked to pretend that he didn't enjoy being held. But Eva knew the truth.

"I'm home!" she shouted.

No response came.

A spark of hope fluttered in Eva's chest. Had her mother finally left the house? Maybe the Sanctum found evidence proving Zeke's innocence. Magdalena could be at the prison collecting her son now.

Eva rested both Halo and her backpack by the bottom of the steps. The cat followed her as she went toward the kitchen.

"I made a friend today," Eva said, hoping she was talking to no one. "Her name's Beatrice."

The silence that greeted Eva was delightful. But her smile vanished when she entered the kitchen. Not only was her mother home, her father was there as well.

Cyrus and Magdalena Heaven stared at one another from opposite ends of the kitchen. He wore his usual gray suit. She'd draped herself in a silky peach robe. The muscles twitched on their faces. Their fingers fluttered in almost microscopic gestures.

Eva watched the motions, trying to guess what each meant. It was no use. Her parents had been bonded for over a quarter of a century. They could communicate without words in a manner that was beautiful and romantic. And incredibly frustrating for their children.

Magdalena's eyes flicked to Eva. She shook her head.

Cyrus glanced at Eva next. Then, he turned back to his wife, eyes serious. He nodded.

Are they fighting about me?

Had someone noticed her wings at school after all? Her parents might've gotten a call from the Sanctum. It would be another strike against their family.

Eva was about to launch into an apology when a deep, falsely cheery voice caught her off guard.

"If it isn't the girl of the hour?" Farrah, Cyrus' assistant, stepped from behind the refrigerator. She'd pulled her wild, dark curls into a high ponytail and paired her purple glasses with a matching blouse.

Eva's smile returned. In the wake of her brother's arrest, her father's employees had vanished one-by-one: new jobs, sudden resignations. All were too polite to offer the truth. They thought Zeke was guilty, and they wanted to jump ship before their names became associated with the Heavens.

Farrah was different. Young and idealistic, she'd proved more loyal than others who'd worked for Cyrus for years. Farrah claimed she'd stayed for selfish reasons. Once everything resolved, she'd reap the rewards of Cyrus' gratitude.

But Eva suspected Farrah was just a good person. The assistant had become a daily visitor over the past few weeks, and she'd agreed to help with Zeke's case. Eva loved Farrah for that alone.

"Your first day of school might be about to get even better," Farrah said, waving a brown envelope. Her smile stretched too wide, and her eyes bored into Eva as though afraid to accidentally make eye-contact with anyone else in the room.

Magdalena and Cyrus had definitely been fighting.

But it couldn't have been about Eva. The envelope in Farrah's hand bore Zeke's full name: *Ezekiel Heaven.* It looked like official correspondence from the Sanctum.

Magdalena's hands flew upward. She huffed toward the ceiling, "Fine. Show it to her. See what she says."

The shadow of a smile flashed across Cyrus' face. Whatever their argument, he'd won.

Farrah must've been on his side. She looked relieved as she stepped forward and offered the envelope to Eva. "This came for your brother today."

"Like some sort of cruel joke," Magdalena added. She sighed, turned from the rest of them, and began to straighten the appliances on her kitchen counters.

Eva took the envelope. The seal had been broken, but she could see the remains of the golden wax. Whatever this was, it had come from the Inner Sanctum of Archangels.

For a brilliant, fleeting moment, Eva imagined it was an official pardon, clearing Zeke's name. But the tension in the room told her otherwise.

Nervous, Eva pulled the letter free. She scanned it: *To Ezekiel Heaven... your service has been requested by The Fates... etc. etc.,* signed by *Greatness Mikhail Auclair.*

That title signified a prince of the Inner Sanctum. They

were the highest ranked among the angels on earth. While archangels managed operations, the princes conversed directly with the Fates. They acted as the ultimate authority on earth and determined how each angel could best serve. Now, a prince had responded to her brother's guardian angel application.

"Zeke's been accepted?" Eva's eyes widened. The hope she'd dismissed earlier returned in full force. "Does that mean they're going to let him out so he can perform his assignment?"

Magdalena let out a choking sob. She raised her hand, covered her mouth, and disappeared into the pantry.

"Eva, you're too old to ask such a silly question," her father scolded. He rubbed a hand over his forehead, where more wrinkles seemed to have appeared overnight. "Ezekiel stole for his own personal gain. From a charity of all things. They're not going to release him."

"But it's a misunderstanding. Zeke is innocent," Eva insisted, clenching her jaw to hide how much her father's comment upset her.

"So help me," Cyrus muttered. He sighed, and his voice softened. "Whether he's innocent or not doesn't matter. It's a question of what the Sanctum believes.'

"Then why are you showing me this?" Eva waved the letter, and tears filled her eyes. It was a silly thing to cry about, but she couldn't help it.

Zeke had dreamed about becoming a guardian angel. Like most things involving the Fates, the selection process was shrouded in mystery. He'd applied years ago. No one had been expecting a response to come now.

"We think you could take his place," Farrah said, answering before Cyrus could.

Eva blinked, clearing the water from her eyes as she

considered her father's assistant. Farrah tugged a loose curl, her expression anxious. But she had to be joking.

"You want me to become a guardian angel?" Eva shook her head. "I'm in high school."

"You're eighteen," Farrah said. "That's the only requirement. And they must want someone in this area, or your brother wouldn't have been accepted."

"But they requested Zeke. I've never even submitted an application."

"We can send one in," Farrah said. "My mother used to work in the Guardian Division. I have some contacts. I think if you write that you're volunteering as a substitute for your brother since he's—you know, incapacitated, we can get you in."

Eva chewed the inside of her lip. She didn't know enough about the process or Farrah's contacts to argue semantics. Maybe proximity was the most important factor in becoming a guardian angel. But even if the Inner Sanctum accepted Eva's application, there was a crucial thing missing.

"I don't want to be a guardian angel."

"If it's because of the risks, we can—" Farrah started, but Eva cut her off.

"That's not it." Eva knew that being a guardian angel could be dangerous. It involved protecting someone marked by the Fates and guiding them down the right path. Sometimes that went against the interests of powerful groups. She'd heard stories about demons attempting to ruin guardian angels and injure their charges, but those instances were rare. Zeke had reassured Eva of that when he'd first applied. So it wasn't fear that made her hesitate now. "I don't want to steal Zeke's dream."

"Oh." Farrah tugged on her loose curl and glanced to her boss for assistance.

"This isn't about dreams," Cyrus said, sighing as he stepped forward. He took Eva's hands in his as though they were praying. "It's not noble, but we have to think about optics. Having a guardian angel in the family will look good. You'd be serving the Fates, showing everyone that we haven't lost sight of our purpose here. The Heavens haven't all fallen to earthly temptations."

Like money. Like Zeke.

Eva wriggled her hands free. She clasped them to her chest, feeling her heart ache. "If I become a guardian angel, would it make it easier to clear Zeke's name?"

Cyrus' eyes closed. His head bowed toward the floor.

"It certainly wouldn't make it harder," Farrah said. She stepped forward, but kept enough of a distance so as not to intrude. "Eva, the truth is that we were discussing having you apply for a guardianship position anyway. This is a sign. I think you should take this opportunity."

Eva's throat felt dry. She considered the possibility of becoming a guardian angel for the first time. Could she guide someone in accordance with God's plan? She couldn't even control her own wings.

But she was an angel. That meant she had to at least try to do the right thing. Anything that could help Zeke had to be right, and she trusted Farrah.

Eva licked her lips and forced a smile. "Let's put through the application then."

5
NATHAN

Where is it?

Nathan flung the last of his shirts into the mess on his floor. Empty shelves stared back at him. There was no sign of the red box.

"Perfect." Nathan muttered a curse, then began tossing his clothing back into the closet. He was too furious to worry about folding. Socks and underwear were shoved together; a pack of half-used tissues ended up with his shorts. It didn't matter. Who cared how tidy his clothes were if there was no money?

Nathan groaned and banged his head against the edge of the wall. All of his savings had been in the red box. He should've hidden it better. Kay Ward sniffed out cash like a pig hunted truffles.

If only Nathan's mother would use that ability to find a rich man instead of the pathetic losers she seemed drawn to. The cycle was always the same. Kay would attempt to play *Mom* for a few weeks, then she'd meet a new man, and vanish until it inevitably ended in disaster. This time, she'd taken Nathan's savings. He hated to imagine what she was doing with them.

"I'm hungry," a small voice said from the door.

Nathan's brother, Daniel, stepped into the room. Black curls stuck to his forehead, and he hugged a raggedy old teddy bear. His head tilted as he surveyed the pile of clothing on the floor.

"Are you doing laundry?" Daniel asked.

The machine in their apartment was broken. They didn't have change to spare at the laundromat across the street. But how did you say that to an eight-year-old?

"Yeah, I might put in a load when I go grab us dinner," Nathan lied. "You want something specific?"

It was a stupid question. What would Nathan do if his brother requested lobster?

Thankfully, Daniel shook his head. "Is Mom joining us tonight?"

"She's staying with a friend for a bit. You know how foggy her head gets. She needs a break sometimes." That was Nathan's euphemism for *Mom would rather get high than take care of her kids.* "I'm sure she'll be back soon."

"That's okay. It's quieter when one of you is away."

Nathan winced. He and his mother did argue a lot, but Dan wasn't supposed to hear them. The apartment needed better sound proofing.

"Can I come with you to get dinner?" Dan asked. "I'm feeling up to it."

That was nice to hear for a change. Nathan smiled and ruffled his brother's hair. "Mrs. Taylor downstairs can watch you. I'm not going anywhere fun. Promise."

Daniel narrowed his eyes. "Where are you going?"

"It's going to be a surprise," Nathan said.

For both of us.

There had to be somewhere to get food with zero cash-on-hand.

"Go grab your pain-killers," Nathan instructed.

"But I'm feeling—"

"Just in case."

Daniel sighed, but he turned around to do as he was told.

That was at least one win for the day.

Nathan ran his hand through his hair, feeling the grease beneath his fingers. It needed washing, but of course, there was no shampoo.

Priorities. Food first, then basic hygiene.

Nathan pulled his phone from his pocket. He couldn't afford a decent plan, and Kay was too cheap to pay for Wi-Fi. Luckily, they'd hacked their neighbor's years ago.

Nathan walked into the corner of his room where the reception was best and called Chris via a messaging app. His friend answered after only two rings. Game music played in the background.

"Sup dude?" Chris always managed to sound happy.

Nathan tried to copy his friend's nonchalant tone. "Sup! I got a favor to ask."

The music stopped as Chris paused his game. "You want to know more about the new girl, don't you?"

"Absolutely not."

Evangelina Heaven was the last thing Nathan wanted to think about right now. The multi-lingual former Cassel student was a walking reminder of just how shitty his life was.

"I... uh..." Nathan struggled to get the words out. He hated himself for asking, but options were limited. "I need to borrow some money."

Chris would be well within his rights to refuse. Nathan still owed him from last time this had happened.

"Sure. I probably have a bit somewhere lying around," Chris said. "You okay, dude?"

Nathan couldn't tell his friend the truth. Chris lived with both his parents, and his house had a garage. He wouldn't understand.

"My mom's refusing to give me my allowance," Nathan lied. "She's annoyed I showed up late on the first day."

Silence followed for a couple seconds, then Chris laughed. "Oh man, my parents always do that. I get it dude. No problem."

"Thanks. Think I can come for it now?"

"Course."

"Thanks," Nathan repeated. He wished he had something better to say. "You know I'm good for the cash, right?"

"No doubt." Chris paused. "It would be fine if you weren't though."

"Yeah, thanks." Nathan hung up before his friend could say anything more. Begging was pathetic but being pitied felt worse.

"I'm ready," Daniel announced. He'd returned with a to-go bag filled with an assortment of medications. He'd learned how to pack one for himself when he was four. "Aren't you going to gather your clothes?"

Nathan's brow furrowed. Then, he remembered that he'd lied about doing laundry. For someone who suffered with migraines, Daniel's memory remained unaffected.

"Maybe tomorrow," Nathan said. "I think my clothes look great right there. Kind of like a very artsy carpet, no?"

"No," Daniel's response was quick.

"Wow. When I'm a famous artist, you're going to be so

embarrassed that you dismissed my talents." Nathan rubbed his knuckles on top of the eight-year-old's head.

Daniel laughed and pushed him away. "I think you should stick to cooking."

"Professional gaming is my calling actually. I just need Eric to get better Wi-Fi so I stop getting kicked off," Nathan joked, gesturing to the wall they shared with their neighbor.

"Last week, you said you were going to become a professional basketball player," Daniel reminded him.

Jesus, there was the kid's memory again. Did he keep track of all the nonsense Nathan invented?

"Why limit myself to one when I have so many talents?" Nathan said.

Despite being eight, Daniel could be a smart ass when he wanted. Nathan suspected his younger brother had a quip lined up, but the high-pitched trill of the doorbell drew both their attention."

"Mom?" Daniel guessed.

Not unless Kay had forgotten her key. Which she might have. She'd done it before.

But their mom had left that morning. She wouldn't be back so soon. More likely, the person outside was one of her exes.

"Go back to your room," Nathan said. When his brother didn't move, he added, "Don't worry. I'm not going to slip out and leave you home alone."

That comforted Daniel enough that he listened.

Once his brother's door shut, Nathan crept to the kitchen and grabbed a knife. Their mom's exes weren't normally aggressive, but he preferred to be careful.

Holding the knife handle tight, Nathan pressed his eye

to the peephole. A figure in a large purple robe stood outside.

What the hell?

Had one of his mom's exes joined some sort of freakish cult?

The robed figure tossed back their cowl, and a round-faced middle-aged blonde stared at him. Nathan was quite certain he'd never seen her in his life.

But she clearly knew him.

"I know you're in there, Nathan Ward," the woman said, and he could hear the smugness in her voice. "I've come to make you an offer."

6

EVANGELINA

By lunch on Friday, Eva had almost forgotten about the application to become a guardian angel. She'd been too busy trying to find a way to enjoy Dashmoor.

The classes were nothing like what she'd taken at Cassel. Eva could daydream through French, and Biology was much easier when you didn't need to learn the physiology of fairies, werewolves, mermaids, and every other species that called Castor's Grove home. But Calculus made her head spin, and history sounded completely different when you removed all awareness of magic.

Eva wouldn't have minded the challenge, but her classmates took particular delight in seeing her struggle. They snickered whenever she asked a question or got confused. Even the teachers smiled when they corrected her mistakes.

The only two people who didn't seem to judge Eva for having attended Cassel were Chris and Beatrice.

The self-proclaimed slacker invited Eva to sit beside him whenever Beatrice wasn't around. It would've been a relief were it not for his friend. Eva got the distinct impression that Nathan Ward hated her even more than the rest of her classmates. He ignored her whenever she tried to make conversation, but sometimes, she'd catch him staring at her.

Like right now.

Eva and Nathan locked eyes across the crowded cafeteria. Her hands flew to her shoulders, but her wings remained hidden.

Nathan shot her a look of such disdain that a casual observer would've thought he was the one who'd caught Eva staring. The expression sharpened the angles in his face.

"Ignore him, Eva," Beatrice said.

"But he keeps looking at me like he's waiting for me to do something," Eva insisted. Though maybe that was her imagination.

"He probably just thinks you're hot. I'll bet he's glaring at you like that to seem standoffish, but really he's fallen madly in love." Beatrice launched into a tirade of theories about what was going on inside Nathan's mind. Some of the suggestions made Eva giggle. A few made her blush. All were absurd.

Beatrice spoke as though she were paid per word. It had confused Eva at first, but she was starting to appreciate the constant chatter. It drowned out some of the snarky comments from the rest of the school.

An alert trilled like a bird on Eva's phone. She recognized the tone. It was a message from The Sanctum

"...and Nate's following some—Ooh. That's not your normal alarm. What is it?" Beatrice asked, changing topic mid-sentence. Her eyes burned with curiosity. "Something special? A text from a boy? You can tell me."

"It's about my brother," Eva said. That was the only reason The Sanctum had messaged the Heavens recently.

Beatrice leaned over as if trying to see Eva's phone. "You've never mentioned your brother before. Younger or older?"

"Older brother," Eva admitted. She shifted position so that her new friend couldn't see the screen. Opening the email at school would be too risky, but she saw the subject line: *New Guardian Position Assigned.*

Eva's breath caught. Did that mean the Inner Sanctum had accepted her application?

"I have an older brother," Beatrice continued. "Albert graduated last year. He's an absolute pain. Got in trouble all the time."

"You've mentioned him before," Eva said, shoving her phone back into her pocket. "And his friend, Oliver."

Eva hoped to change the topic. She suspected Beatrice had a crush on Oliver given how frequently the brunette mentioned him.

However, Beatrice had latched onto this new information about Eva.

"What's your brother like?" Beatrice asked.

"Zeke's the best."

Beatrice's eyebrows quirked up. "Really? He's never done anything wrong?"

Eva's chest tightened. The conversation seemed eerily familiar. Her friends at Cassel had pressed her in a similar manner before they'd begun to avoid her entirely.

"No, never," Eva insisted. She steeled herself, waiting for a rebuttal.

Beatrice pursed her lips. She remained silent for an unusual length of time. Then, she smiled and took the first bite of her sandwich. "Well, if that ever changes, you can trust me with the truth."

―――――

When school finished that afternoon, Eva took the subway downtown. Her fingers tapped against her knee as she read the email for the hundredth time.

She'd been accepted for the position of guardian angel. Her charge had been selected. And at the bottom, in no uncertain terms, it instructed: *Report immediately to Irena Elysium.* The address of her office in the Sanctum's Headquarters followed.

Eva refreshed the email. Reread it. The name remained the same.

But it had to be an error.

Irena Elysium had been up for the position of Archangel at the same time as Eva's father. Cyrus got the promotion. Irena had been assigned as a karmic angel instead. Her role in the Justice Division of the Sanctum involved tracking criminals and ensuring that proper punishments were meted out to those who succumbed to earthly temptations.

She'd be the prosecutor at Zeke's trial.

Why would I need to report to her?

Either Eva's charge was a criminal of some sort, or Irena had requested this. Neither option was reassuring.

Eva stepped off the subway at the corner of Medway and 75th Street. She walked west toward the Sanctum Headquarters, mind spinning with worst case scenarios.

What if this was a trap so Irena could spy on the Heavens? What if her charge was a bank robber and they set Eva up to implicate her in the crime? No, that couldn't happen. The Fates would have assigned her task.

But why have Irena supervise her instead of someone in the Guardian Division?

Eva was so lost in her thoughts that it didn't even occur to her that she was close to Cassel until she spotted a pair of familiar faces. Leah and Max Celand approached from the opposite side of the street. Despite a drastic difference in height, the two shared the same square faces, with broad cheeks and button noses. Leah's ponytail bounced between her shoulders. Max's curls fell loose around his forehead. Both wore their Cassel uniforms, and their hands swung in wild gestures the way they always did when they argued.

The sight felt so familiar that Eva almost smiled. Her hand raised of its own accord to wave to them.

What am I doing?

Eva shouldn't have come down this street. Her friends would be meeting at Magic Maeve's. Despite its name, the burger joint was human-operated and decorated in a wonderfully horrendous lime green and fluorescent red. The food was cheap and greasy, and no one named Maeve worked there. Eva and her friends loved it. She'd gone with them every Friday.

Leah's eyes widened. She turned from her brother mid-argument and spotted Eva with her hand half raised. Unlike the kids at Dashmoor, Leah waved back. Which might've been worse. The gesture felt awkward and foreign. Only a month ago, she would've raced forward and pounced on Eva to give her a hug.

Max at least smiled. He stepped past the entrance to Magic Maeve's, approaching Eva. "How are—Are you coming in?" Max gestured to the door.

"I don't think that's—" Leah hurried forward, glaring at her brother, but she cut off as her eyes landed on Eva. "Not that we don't want you to, or anything. Just, I figured you were going somewhere else."

"I am," Eva assured her, forcing a massive smile. "I'm a guardian angel now. I'm about to get my assignment."

"Really?" Leah looked genuinely relieved. "That's great! I had no idea you wanted to be a guardian angel."

"I didn't."

"Oh."

A painful silence hung between them.

Max broke it, offering Eva another smile. "I'm sure you'll be amazing. If you have time after you can join us."

"She won't have time," Leah said. She grabbed her brother's arm, offered Eva an awkward wave goodbye, and tugged Max toward the diner's entrance. Through the window, Eva could see the twins resume bickering as they walked to the back table where the rest of their friends sat.

Eva watched for a moment through the smudged glass, memories of recent conversations surfacing in her mind. Her friends had called Zeke a criminal, suggested he'd always been a borderline heretic, and said the Heavens should've seen this coming. When Eva told them that she'd thought about transferring to a human school, she'd hoped they might apologize for being unnecessarily cruel, for not listening to her. Instead, they'd all agreed—even Max. Eva should escape the unwanted notoriety that her brother had brought and return when it all died down.

But when would that be?

Eva didn't know, but in that moment, it didn't matter what her friends had said about Zeke. She would've given anything to be at that booth with them, planning a trip to go flying on the coast or placing bets on who would win the Castor's Cup. Eva wanted her old life back.

7
EVANGELINA

Irena Elysium sat in a high-backed office chair that rose like a throne behind her head. On first glance, it would have been easy to mistake the karmic angel for a Mrs. Claus-like figure. Irena's plump physique gave her round, rosy cheeks. Wisps of blonde curls framed her temples.

But closer inspection revealed the pains the karmic angel took to dispel any notions of softness. She wore an austere black suit with pointed shoulder pads. She painted her lips a dark red that bordered on purple and matched the single splash of color—a small rug—in an otherwise industrial office. Her metal shelves and desk featured corners sharp enough to stab.

Eva considered both the office and the karmic angel through a massive window. Unlike at Magic Maeve's, the glass was clean enough to make the barrier almost invisible.

Irena leaned forward, pressing her elbows onto her desk. Her chin rested on the tips of her fingers as her eyes latched onto Eva with chilling precision.

A water nymph guarded a small desk outside the door. Though she must have been in her thirties, butterfly clips styled her shockingly bright blue hair. Trails of water coursed like rivers across the visible portion of her arms, gathering into pools on the back of her hands. An identification card labeled her as Irena Elysium's assistant.

"Sorry, I have to let her know you're here first." The nymph had a sweet voice, yet she blocked Eva with a slender arm.

"But she can see me." Eva pointed through the glass to where Irena continued to stare.

"Sorry," the nymph apologized again, then lifted her phone. She held up a finger. The nail matched her hair.

On the other side of the glass, Irena answered the call.

"Miss Heaven is here to see you, Ma'am... Yes...Yes...Very good, Ma'am." The nymph put down the phone and offered Eva an apologetic smile. "Ms. Elysium will be with you in a moment."

Eva chewed the inside of her cheek. She wanted to argue. It was obvious that Irena wasn't busy.

"Chocolate?" the nymph offered. She pushed a glass bowl across her desk.

Eva pursed her lips. It was tempting to decline in protest, but it wasn't the nymph's fault that her boss was being cruel. And Eva appreciated anyone who kept treats readily available.

"Thanks." Eva grabbed one from the top. "Is Irena often *busy* when people arrive?"

The nymph gave a nervous giggle. "Ms. Elysium is a good person. I've been with her for, I think, five years now? She can be a bit... particular... but she means well."

Eva had her doubts, but she didn't want to argue, so she unwrapped the chocolate instead. It had a rich orange filling. The flavors paired together well. Eva might consider mixing them into a cake.

"Yum! That's good, Thanks..." Eva glanced at the assistant's identification tag.

The nymph must have caught her searching for a name. She supplied it herself, "I'm Maddie. Here, have another."

Eva accepted a second chocolate. This one had a gooey toffee center.

Irena chose then to open her office door. Perhaps she'd been waiting for Eva to have her mouth full.

"You kept me waiting, Miss Heaven," Irena said. Her scowl looked out of place with her plump cheeks.

No, you kept me waiting.

Eva hurried to finish the toffee so she could point that out.

Irena continued to take advantage of Eva's inability to respond. "You were instructed to come immediately. That was at midday. It's now almost four. Madeline is being far too generous rewarding your tardiness with sweets."

Like a chastised child, Maddie took the chocolate bowl and hid it beneath her desk.

"I was at school," Eva explained as the toffee finally dissolved. "This was the fastest I could get here."

Irena sniffed. "A poor excuse. A guardian angel can't ignore her charge because of school."

Then maybe a high schooler was a poor choice for the position.

Eva kept that thought to herself. Farrah had called in favors, and the Inner Sanctum had agreed. Eva didn't want to look unappreciative. Not when Irena would be looking for reasons to criticize.

"I trust you know that I would never approve of this under normal circumstances," Irena continued. "Remember where your priorities lie. We've come to this realm to protect and serve its inhabitants. Not get straight As."

"I think that's already impossible thanks to calculus."

Maddie giggled. Irena remained unimpressed.

"You can count on me, Ma'am!" Eva tried again, plastering a big smile on her face to psyche herself up. She meant it. However strange the situation, Eva had been chosen to be a guardian angel. It was a significant role. If she impressed the Sanctum, maybe things would turn around. At least Farrah seemed to think it was a possibility.

"Hmm." Irena's gaze flicked over Eva. Her nose wrinkled in distaste. "Come into my office, Miss Heaven. We'll discuss your assignment."

Air conditioner blasted into Eva's face as she stepped through the door. Irena must've been the first cold-blooded angel to come to Earth.

The karmic angel crossed to her desk and pulled an antiquated-looking phone from one of the drawers.

"Aren't you lucky. They used to print everything." She dropped the heavy chunk of metal into Eva's hand.

So lucky.

Older angels didn't approve of sarcasm. Eva forced a smile instead and tapped the screen. Nothing happened.

"Do I need to charge it?" she asked.

Irena clicked her tongue. She reached out a manicured hand and pressed a small black button near the top. The screen turned white.

"Touch it now," Irena explained, in a tone that suggested she thought this should be obvious. "It should have the information on your charge."

"Who is my charge?" Eva asked as she tapped. The white screen vanished. Pixel-by-pixel an image appeared: a strikingly handsome face, with a strong nose and sharp cheekbones. Deceptively sweet eyes stared at her through thick lashes. Waves of black hair framed the expression. It was the type of photograph that appeared in magazine advertisements.

Eva's breath caught. Her eyes felt glued to the image.

"He's a student at Dashmoor High School. A sign that this assignment was meant for you," Irena said. "Perhaps you recognize him?"

Eva nodded. Of course, she did. She'd been assigned to be the guardian angel of Nathan Ward.

8

NATHAN

"Mind if I sit here?"

Nathan held back a groan at the sound of Eva's voice. Her chipper positivity was the last thing he needed first period on a Monday. He raised his hand, cupping it to his temple so that he resisted the urge to look at her. Most people would've taken his silence as a *no*.

Of course, Eva wasn't most people.

"Thanks!" she said, still far too cheery.

The chair scraped against the floor as she dragged it out to sit. Her backpack dropped with a heavy thump.

Damn. What has she got in there?

Nathan glanced at the pale blue bag. Eva's legs formed the background. Somehow, his focus shifted to her crossed ankles, then roved higher.

Eva wore the same ridiculously fancy feather dress that had attracted everyone's attention on the first day. It had to be a violation of Dashmoor's dress-code. The hemline barely covered her, leaving the smooth skin of her thighs exposed.

No wonder Chris won't shut up about how hot she is.

The moment the thought crossed his mind, Nathan pulled his eyes from Eva's legs. He didn't want her to catch him and get the wrong impression. Nathan had no interest in Eva, and, since her arrival, he'd been doing his best to ignore her.

Admittedly, his best was terrible.

Eva was distracting.

That might've been the one consensus among the senior students of Dashmoor. Given Eva's outfits and over-eager smiles, the girls assumed she was looking for attention. The boys debated if it was intentional, but either way it worked. Eva attracted jealous glances and overly enthusiastic stares. It didn't help that she'd attended Cassel. The exclusive nature of the downtown private school gave her an aura of mystery that intimidated her classmates.

But it was more than all that.

Eva was a blinding beam of sunshine. Her smile radiated with the optimism of someone unaware that the world wasn't all puppies and teddy bears. She'd lived a perfect life, and her very presence shoved that fact in everyone else's face.

Or maybe I'm just jaded and bitter.

So far, despite the warning he'd received from his cloaked visitor, Eva had paid Nathan little attention. He didn't know if he appreciated or resented that.

But she's asked to sit by me now. Why?

Eva pulled a notebook from her bag. A sparkly gold unicorn flashed on the cover.

"You know that's a notebook for a little kid, right?" Nathan said, unable to resist.

"It probably is," Eva agreed, giggling as though he hadn't just insulted her. "But it makes me smile."

Nathan stifled a groan. Eva's image must've appeared next to the definition of toxic positivity.

As she looked at the notebook, she was indeed smiling. It lit up her face, making her skin glow. Her eyes crinkled in genuine happiness, drawing Nathan's attention to the brilliant blue. No surprise Chris had homed in on the color.

Jesus, on top of everything, why does she also have to be attractive?

"That's weird," Nathan said, putting as much disgust into his tone as he could manage. He pulled out his own notebook, which had an appropriately bland brown cover, and assumed that would be the end of their conversation.

But a moment later, Eva tapped his shoulder.

"What?"

"Do you want a cookie?" Eva pulled a massive glass container from her bag and unclipped the top. "I made them myself."

The scent of cinnamon wafted into the air. Nathan glanced down at the offered baked goods. Was this what Eva did? Bribe strangers into trusting her with food?

Nathan wanted to see if a refusal would finally wipe the smile off her face. But the cookies smelled good. His desire to be petty grappled with his desire for food. Ultimately, Nathan's stomach won.

He grabbed a cookie from the top and shoved it in his mouth.

"Do you like it?" Eva asked.

It was delicious. Nathan grabbed another three before Eva could close the container. Then, cookie still in his mouth, Nathan shrugged. "It's a'ite."

"Thanks!"

Nathan ground his teeth. Did she take everything as a compliment?

"I really like to bake," Eva said, twisting a strand of blonde hair around her finger. "I think I'm pretty good at it. Is there anything you like to do? Something you're secretly great at?"

Nathan's ears prickled at the word. The memory of his round-faced visitor returned. He grabbed another two cookies and offered a small smile. "Sorry to disappoint, but the only thing I'm great at is looking out for myself."

9
NATHAN

Over the next few days, Nathan continued to replay the visit from the mysterious cloaked woman in his mind.

———

The middle-aged woman could've been with Social Services. Only, the purple cloak that obscured her body gave the sense of something arcane. Nathan wasn't willing to let her into the apartment with Daniel inside, but he couldn't risk ignoring her either. So, he stepped into the hall.

"Who are you?" Nathan asked. "A friend of my mother's?"

"I met her a few months ago. Not sure I'd call us friends." The woman's nose wrinkled. She had an almost girlish voice, younger than the wrinkles around her eyes suggested. "But you and I could be."

"I don't even know your name."

"You can call me your Godmother."

Nathan snorted. He didn't have a godmother. "Are you a fairy?"

"Close enough."

"And why are you at my apartment, G?"

Her brow furrowed for a moment before she figured out that he'd abbreviated the ridiculous moniker. She smiled. "To discuss Evangelina Heaven. She's your new classmate. Have you met her yet?"

"No," Nathan lied quickly.

"You will. She'll want to make you great."

The claim seemed absurd. G must've shown up at the wrong door.

"I'm the last person she'd take an interest in."

"So you do know her." G's smile turned smug, like she'd caught Nathan in a lie.

"I've seen her," Nathan conceded. "My friend thinks she's hot."

"Friend? If you wanted to pursue her that could work too. But you'd need to be very committed."

Nathan's neck heated at the implication. He coughed and glanced behind him at the door, relieved that he'd made Daniel go hide. Wherever the hell this conversation was headed, he didn't need his brother to overhear. "I think you should leave. Whatever you're up to, I—"

"Relax, that was a joke." G giggled. "But you're right. I'm up to something. And I'll make it worth your while if you help."

Nathan crossed his arms and leaned against the wall. Under different circumstances, he'd have gone back into the apartment, slammed the door and locked this mad woman outside. But he had himself and Daniel to take care of, and no money. "I'll bite. What's in it for me?"

G's lips curled into an almost coquettish smile. "How'd you like to get paid?"

"In cash," Nathan quipped. "But what do I have to do?"

"I told you, Eva will want to make you great. Whatever she tries, you mustn't let her."

10

NATHAN

Unfortunately, the list of Eva's many annoying qualities included persistence.

Every class they shared, she sat right beside Nathan, chattering in his ear until the teacher arrived. She followed him to lunch. She waited outside to say goodbye to him after school.

It was horrible.

Partly because Nathan might not have been as immune to Eva's charm as he'd hoped. It took effort to hate someone so nice. Especially when the someone in question had legs designed to make guys drool. Nathan had to constantly remind himself that Eva was up to something.

By Thursday, it seemed safest to avoid her. Instead of eating in the cafeteria, Nathan convinced Chris to hang out elsewhere. His friend chose under the bleachers in the gym. There were only two reasons Dashmoor students went there.

A pair of juniors appeared to be trying to eat one another's faces in one corner. Nathan kept his back to them, watching Chris roll his joint instead.

"She's hot, and she's into you," Chris said before licking the paper. "Most guys would kill to have that problem."

Nathan wished it were that simple. If Eva's interest had been romantic, he could've gotten her to shut up. She wouldn't be able to talk if he—Nope! Nathan shook that image from his head fast. It didn't help that one of the juniors behind them had started to moan. Honestly, the younger kids did not understand bleacher etiquette.

"You know Aidan tried to hit on her? Told her she was a ten, but he was the one who could make her scream."

"Jesus," Nathan muttered. That was a terrible line. "What'd she say to that?"

"She told him that it was wrong to assign a numerical value to another person, but that she was certain he would grow into a wonderful man as he gained self-confidence and empathy."

Nathan snorted.

"I think she meant it though," Chris said, taking out his lighter and holding the flame to the end of his joint. He took a pull and leaned back. "Maybe it's for the best you're not interested. Eva doesn't seem like the casual relationship type, and I think your record for keeping a girl is two weeks."

"I don't have time for a relationship."

"I know. How is your brother?"

Nathan shrugged. He hated being asked about Daniel. His friends had only met his brother a few times, and that had been because Nathan couldn't leave a little kid alone in a death trap of an apartment. A few of the guys had asked questions when Nathan showed up to play games with an eight-year-old in tow. Chris never had. That was why he'd always been Nathan's favorite, even before they'd both had to repeat senior year.

But Chris was smarter than people thought, and it didn't take a genius to figure out Daniel was sick. The poor kid wheezed when he got excited, and Nathan had to carry him if they walked too far.

"Guess Dan's okay if you're here. That's good," Chris said. He held out the joint. "Take it."

"You don't have to share." Nathan wasn't much of a smoker. He couldn't afford to be.

Chris shoved the end of the blunt into Nathan's mouth. "It's no fun getting high alone."

Nathan inhaled and let the smoke fill his lungs. Then he returned the joint. "Ever thought about doing something else with your time?"

"Of course." Chris grinned and flicked his gaze to the juniors, who continued to sloppily make out in their corner. "But we don't all have Eva showering us with attention."

"She's annoying."

"She's *nice*." Chris exaggerated the word as he sent the joint back. "You should try it sometime."

"I'm nice," Nathan objected before taking another pull.

"Not to her. You're a total jerk. I don't know why she likes you."

"Exactly. She's up to something."

Chris laughed. It was loud enough that the juniors untangled their limbs to shush him.

"Damn, dude," Chris said, shoulders trembling as he suppressed his laugh. He reached for the joint. "Maybe you shouldn't have any more because that's paranoid even for you."

Chris might think different if G had showed up at his door.

———

Nathan arrived at English class purposefully late. But, of course, Eva had saved him a seat. He would've begged someone to swap, but the vacant desk was at the front, and an unimpressed Mrs. Shepherd pointed him toward it.

Don't look at Eva.

Nathan pretended not to see her smile as he sat.

"Now that everyone is present," Mrs. Shepherd said, shooting Nathan a glare as though she'd waited to begin on his account. "You can start finding quotes on survival and resilience for your essay. I'll be back in a minute."

Someone coughed into their hand near the back of the class and said, "Diarrhea."

The joke earned them a few chuckles and a withering look from Mrs. Shepherd before she stepped out.

Once the door closed, the class broke into immediate chatter. Eva leaned closer to Nathan.

"Your eyes are red," she said. "Are you sick?"

"Yup."

Someone behind them laughed.

Eva shot whoever was eavesdropping a disapproving look. But she must've known why Nathan's eyes were red. She couldn't be that naïve.

"Do you want to work together to find quotes?"

"Nope." Nathan folded his arms on the desk and slumped his chin onto them.

Missing the obvious hint, Eva pulled her chair closer. Her knee brushed Nathan's leg. She'd worn her feather dress again. It threatened to slide even higher on her thighs.

In fact, at his current angle, if Nathan tilted his head—

"You know, I just realized something!" Eva leaned in. Her breath tickled his ear, sending a shiver over his skin as she whispered, "I've never seen you write anything in any of our classes."

Nathan sprang up and dragged his chair a few inches back. His neck felt hot. Eva had to be hoping to have an effect getting close to him like that. But she continued speaking as if she had no idea.

"Is it because you have a really great memory?" Eva clasped her hands before her and smiled hopefully, almost as though she was begging.

It was cute.

No, not cute. Manipulative.

Nathan needed to remember that instead of getting distracted by Eva's growing smile. She was probably using her looks to throw him off on purpose. Whatever weird game this was, he couldn't let her get the upper hand.

"You caught me, Eva," Nathan said, running his fingers through his hair for a moment. Then, he reached out and took her hands in his.

The contact caught her off guard. Her eyes flashed down, and her cheeks turned pink. Good. Let her be flustered.

Nathan brought his lips close to her ear the way she'd done to him. Her hair smelled like lavender. He almost lost himself in the scent, before reminding himself that he'd once used a medicated brand shampoo that he'd scrounged from a neighbor's garbage. That might be his only option again if he didn't keep G happy.

"The truth is, I'm illiterate," Nathan whispered. He pulled away just as Mrs. Shepherd returned and ordered everyone back to their seats. Hopefully, the sarcastic comment would put Eva off harassing him for the rest of class.

But the moment their English teacher looked away, Eva scooted closer again. "I'm sorry. I had no idea," she whispered. "Do you want—I mean, I could teach you. If you'd like."

Nathan almost fell off his chair. Eva had to be messing with him. She couldn't have believed him. "You want to teach me to read and write?"

"Only if you want," Eva said. There was no hint of mockery in her tone. She was one hundred percent genuine.

Wow. Either Nathan came across even dumber than he realized, or Eva was more gullible than Daniel. Whichever it was didn't matter. The misunderstanding presented a brilliant opportunity.

Nathan pushed his desk forward and stood. The motion drew everyone's attention.

"Did you guys hear that?" Nathan asked, turning to look at each of his classmates in turn. "Evangelina offered to teach me how to read and write. She thinks I'm illiterate. That's how dumb she thinks we are at Dashmoor!"

The outburst wouldn't have worked against anybody else. Calling a second-time senior illiterate hardly qualified as an all-encompassing insult against the school. But half the seniors were looking for reasons to hate their attractive, multi-lingual transfer student. They turned on Eva at once, booing and jeering.

"No, I—That's not—" Eva struggled to defend herself. Her entire face turned pink, and she turned to Nathan. "You said—"

"Nathan, sit down!" Mrs. Shepherd stepped in before Eva could say more. The English teacher quieted the rest of the class and refocused them on finding quotes. But it didn't matter. The damage was done.

Eva buried her face in her hands, and Nathan felt a twinge of guilt. Was she about to cry?

No way. Nathan had been a little mean, but Eva

couldn't really care what the students at Dashmoor thought of her.

A tear streaked down her face. Eva wiped her cheeks. Then she jumped up and shot out of the room.

Shit.

Maybe Nathan had taken things too far.

11

EVANGELINA

That night, Eva stood in her kitchen, pressing her weight down onto either end of a wooden rolling pin. The pie dough wouldn't budge. It was frozen solid. Eva groaned.

Halo gave a disapproving mewl from his spot on the floor.

Great. Even my cat thinks I'm annoying.

Eva sighed and eased off the rolling pin. Baking normally cheered her up. But tonight, it was feeding her anger.

Why was Nathan Ward such a massive jerk?

All week, she'd been so nice to him. She'd brought him cookies and cake and muffins. He'd taken all her baked goods, and how had he repaid her? By making an absolute fool of her in their English class!

Her wings had popped out. Again. It was so frustrating!

Eva slapped her palm against the dough imagining it was Nathan's stupid face. It wasn't very angelic behavior, but she didn't care.

"How am I supposed to make someone like him great?" Eva demanded, turning to the only other creature in the room for response.

Halo hissed, stood, and turned his tail to her before jumping onto the kitchen counter. He ran across, almost knocking over half the supplies.

Eva hurried to catch a glass bowl before it shattered on the floor. Her eye caught on something shiny in the corner of the kitchen: her new guardian phone, if the ancient-seeming device could even be called that. It was difficult to believe she'd been given the *updated* version.

Maybe it has the answers.

Eva brushed the flour off her hands and onto her apron before reaching for the device. She tapped the screen.

Nathan appeared: warm eyes, beautiful lashes, a half-smile on his stupid, perfect face. Why did he get to be handsome? His outside should reflect the jerk within.

I'm the one who thought he was illiterate.

Embarrassment heated Eva's cheeks. But it wasn't fair. She'd only believed that because he'd said it! And it had sort of made sense. Eva had never seen him write, and it would've been a clue about how to approach her new job.

"What am I supposed to do for Nathan?" Eva asked the archaic device.

The guardian phone didn't have apps like a regular one. Eva had tried to find them and gotten frustrated before she realized that it responded to her voice. Irena could've mentioned that instead of just saying the device was *intuitive*. Then Eva wouldn't have wasted an hour just to find basic information like *Name: Nathan Ward. Age: 19. Species: Human.*

Files appeared on the screen as though the phone

needed to manually search them. Eva waited. Finally, it produced an image of a piece of paper with what she assumed to be the answer to her question: *Guide him to greatness.*

The phone was as helpful as Eva's cat.

"I know that's the general goal. That's what Irena said when she gave me the assignment," Eva said. "But what does it mean?"

The phone didn't even bother searching.

Eva tried a different approach. "What is Nathan great at?"

A new page appeared. It read: *Nathan Ward is great at...*

"Making the rest of the school hate me?" Eva suggested.

To her surprise, the phone began filling that in.

"No, don't write that!" Eva tried to stop it, but she had no idea how. The device had a mind of its own. At least she hadn't voiced her other theory.

But, as if it could read her thoughts, the phone added a second bullet point beneath the first so that the screen read:

Nathan Ward is great at:

- *Making the seniors at Dashmoor High hate Evangelina Heaven*
- *Being hot*

"Handsome. I thought handsome," Eva argued, shaking the phone to get it to comply. The screen didn't update.

"Having fun with your new toy?"

Eva dropped the device face down on the counter as her mother appeared.

Several loose strands fell from Magdalena's messy bun. The hem of her silver robe swept the floor.

"I don't think Irena would appreciate it being called a toy," Eva said.

"Never mind what Irena would and wouldn't like. Just get it off my counter." Magdalena gestured to the guardian phone like it was a live newt.

Eva complied, mostly because she didn't want her mother lifting the phone and reading what it had written in its files. However, instead of holding the device in her hands, she summoned her wings and tucked it among her feathers. They'd always been useful for carrying small items in an emergency. The phone, with its unnecessary bulk, just managed to qualify.

Magdalena ran her fingers over the countertop where it had been. "I don't know when this house started to get so dirty."

Eva did. It had started shortly after Zeke's arrest, when their mother had been *temporarily excused* from her position in the Local Charity Division. Magdalena had imprisoned herself at home and begun to obsess over every imperfection—real and imagined.

"Do you want to volunteer at the Soup Kitchen this weekend?" Eva suggested. "I know you're not in charge, but I'm sure we could—."

"Zola's running things," Magdalena said, waving her hand in dismissal.

"Oh." Eva hadn't realized. Her mother had complained about Zola Astrum on-and-off for the past five years since she'd joined her division. Magdalena considered her co-worker's style too harsh for local charity work. "Sorry, Mom."

"Zola's completely ill-equipped, of course. She'll question everyone in line to check that they're really starving and that there's no fraud," Magdalena said with a bitter laugh. "But Irena's star is rising, and—for all her posturing about fairness—I've no doubt she advocated for her friend. Otherwise, Victoria should've been in charge." She paused. "Have you heard from Max and Leah recently?"

Eva didn't want to lie, but she didn't feel like discussing her friends either. She shrugged, grabbed the rolling pin, and resumed her attempts to soften the dough.

"I always thought you and Max would end up together."

Eva's cheeks heated. "I told you there was nothing there."

"Yes, but you were so young when you dated."

"We barely dated."

"Why do you keep making desserts this week? Honestly, you'd think you'd become a baker and not—" Magdalena's voice broke in a sudden sob.

Eva spun, surprised by the response. But she'd seen her mother breakdown multiple times over the past month. "I'm sorry. I know you didn't want me to take Zeke's place."

"Oh, sweetheart, it's not that. It's just—Your father is grasping at straws. He thinks if one of his children is seen upholding angelic values then maybe he won't look guilty."

"But he's not guilty."

"Of course not! Your father would never condone theft."

"Exactly, and neither would Zeke," Eva said. She pressed her finger into the dough. She still couldn't dent it. "Why can't we forget the optics and go visit him?"

Magdalena sighed. "It's a complicated thing Eva. We're under investigation too. The Sanctum might misinterpret a visit."

"You mean Irena might," Eva muttered though Farrah had said the same thing. "I just really miss him."

"I know, baby." Magdalena stroked Eva's feathers. "Now let your dough defrost in the fridge, and go upstairs, so I can clean."

12

EVANGELINA

A knock interrupted Eva's painful attempts to find a derivative.

Thank God!

In her haste to close the calculus book, Eva startled Halo who'd been sleeping beside it. He leaped from the desk, almost knocking over her lamp. It was an incredibly tacky piece of décor with unicorns frolicking around the base. Zeke had presented it to her for her sixteenth birthday, perhaps as a joke. But he'd given her a unicorn themed gift every year since she became obsessed with them as a kid.

As though her brother were in the room, Eva heard his voice tease her: *Crazy that your taste hasn't changed since you were five.*

A sad smile spread across Eva's face. Nathan had made a similar comment about her notebook. She'd chosen to interpret it as a positive sign from the universe in that moment. Clearly not.

"Come in!"

Eva's father stepped into her bedroom. He still wore his suit.

"I just talked to your mother," Cyrus said. Eva hadn't heard them, so she suspected the conversation had been mostly silent. "You want to visit your brother."

"Of course I do." Eva swiveled her desk chair toward her father. "Don't you?"

"Sometimes." Cyrus massaged his temples, pulling the skin on his forehead tight. His eyes flicked to the guardian phone on Eva's desk. "How's your new job?"

"I think Irena is setting me up to fail," Eva admitted.

Cyrus dropped his hands, and the wrinkles burrowed back into his forehead, deeper than before. "They should never have agreed to let her oversee a guardian angel. I don't care if her assistant used to work in the department. It's completely outside her usual purview. And I doubt Irena will ask for help if she gets stuck."

"I could file a complaint."

"No." Her father's refusal came fast. "Irena might be exacting, but crossing her wouldn't end well. And she wouldn't purposefully compromise an assignment from The Fates. How is your charge?"

He meant Nathan. Eva considered her response carefully before answering, "Difficult."

"Were you assigned to keep him out of trouble? Farrah promised me your task wouldn't be dangerous."

"I'm guiding him to greatness," Eva assured her father.

Some of the tension eased from Cyrus' face. "Must be a talented boy."

"He is not."

"Talented or a boy?"

It was the closest thing to a joke her father had made in

a long time. Eva smiled. "I don't know. Does nineteen count as a boy?"

"When you're my age," Cyrus said. His eyes narrowed. "He's not attractive, I hope?"

"Really, Dad?" Eva avoided glancing at the guardian phone. She'd need to make sure her father never saw Nathan's photo. Or the note that the device had added.

But part of Eva appreciated the comment. It felt like a glimpse of her father's old self.

"I'm just saying." Cyrus held up his hands in mock surrender. "I notice you took down the picture of you and Max."

"Me, Max, *and Leah,*" Eva stressed. The twins' father had taken several of them together last year at the Cassel Ball. He was the Sanctum's official photographer, and he'd chaperoned the dance. They had an entire album dedicated to the event—and almost every other party Mr. Celand had attended—at their house.

Cyrus continued, "It would be dangerous to bond with a human. Especially now. The optics..."

He trailed off, but Eva understood what he meant. The Sanctum didn't forbid angels from dating other species, even humans. But serious relationships often ended poorly.

Angels mated for life, forming the type of bond that other species attempted to replicate through marriage contracts. It was the sort of connection that could make someone sacrifice their life, literally and metaphorically.

Although they lived on Earth, angels remained heavenly beings. They didn't have the luxury of succumbing to the little vices that others enjoyed, or a feather would drop. And, as the Sanctum taught: *lose one, lose them all.* Without their feathers, angels couldn't fly. They'd be trapped on

Earth, unable to return to their realm when their bodies here grew too old to continue.

Mating with a human often marked the first step in a fall from grace and inevitable excommunication. Luckily, given Nathan's personality and general awfulness, Eva wasn't in any danger.

"That won't be happening," she reassured her father.

"Good." Cyrus smiled, but the tension had returned, tightening his shoulders and making his wrinkles more pronounced. "You're going to guide this boy, Eva. You're going to succeed. We need you to."

Perhaps satisfied that he'd impressed upon her the importance of her assignment, Cyrus kissed his daughter's forehead.

Eva forced a smile until he left. Her chest felt tight. She grabbed the guardian phone and touched the screen. "Can I do this?"

No message appeared. The device didn't seem to know the answer either.

13
EVANGELINA

On Friday, Eva woke up with Halo on her chest. She scooped the cat into a hug. He was so sleepy, he forgot to complain and went immediately to purring. An excellent sign!

"Today's going to be the day, Halo," Eva informed him. "I'm going to figure out what Nathan Ward is good at."

After her father's talk with her the previous night, Eva had been on the verge of a meltdown. If he thought her assignment was crucial, she believed him. But Eva had no idea how to make Nathan great, and the guardian phone only kept showing her the note she'd accidentally added.

How did Nathan being attractive help anything? Was Eva supposed to turn him into a model? That didn't seem like the kind of talent The Fates would be interested in.

After screaming into her pillow for a few minutes, Eva had calmed herself enough to think. She was an angel. Her purpose was to help others. The Fates wouldn't have assigned her a task she couldn't achieve. They'd know her capabilities better than she would.

And there it was—Eva's solution! She'd been

approaching things from the wrong direction. Nathan hated her and had no interest in sharing anything about himself. But other people must have noticed his talents.

———

"You're still interested in Nathan?" Beatrice raised an eyebrow in disbelief. She'd taken the seat next to Eva at the front of their art history class, and they'd fallen into conversation while waiting for Mr. Shannons to arrive.

Eva's cheeks grew hot. She glanced around to make sure none of the other seniors were paying attention. Although Eva had pulled her chair close, Beatrice's voice was loud.

"Not *interested*," Eva explained. She knew the connotations that carried. "Curious about. I mean, he must be good at something."

Beatrice tapped her chin, frowned, and shook her head. "I'm coming up blank."

"Art? Sports? Just one subject?" If the Fates had foreseen potential greatness in Nathan, there had to be a reason.

"Nuuh-thing." Beatrice exaggerated each syllable and pointed to her lips. "Nathan is attractive, but unless that's a talent, he's got zilch. He'll probably knock up some poor girl, drop out of high school, and waste his life working a dead-end job."

"That seems a bit harsh."

"Seriously? After what he did to you yesterday?"

Eva chewed the inside of her cheek. Beatrice wasn't in the same English class, but news had spread, and she'd cornered Eva to discuss it that morning.

"That was partly my fault," Eva admitted.

"You're way too good for Nathan Ward," Beatrice continued, taking out her laptop and setting it on the desk.

"You're like a ten, and he's like a zero. Unless you're the kind of girl who goes for looks alone, but you aren't, so I don't know why you keep asking about him. Seriously, like, I'm trying to wrap my head around it, and nothing I come up with makes sense." Suddenly, Beatrice leaned in and whispered, "Are you here because of him?"

Eva's mouth opened. She didn't know how to respond. The question was absurd. But Beatrice's intense gaze suggested more was being implied, something the brunette didn't risk saying aloud.

———

After a double period hearing about the impressionists, Eva had European History. But it wasn't Napoleon she was hoping to learn about. She crossed both sets of fingers as she entered the classroom.

Please be there. Please be there.

Eva peeked around the doorway and was immediately disappointed. How did you find someone who only attended class half the time?

"Going in, Blue Eyes?"

At the sound of Chris' voice, a smile spread across Eva's face. She spun toward the hallway.

And her eyes landed on Nathan. He leaned in the corridor like he was posing for a photoshoot: a single strap of his backpack over one shoulder, his foot pressed against the wall. His lashes caught the light from overhead, giving his eyes a rich, warm glow.

Eva stared a fraction longer than she intended.

Nathan opened his mouth, probably to tell her to leave him alone.

I wish that was an option.

Eva grabbed Chris' arm and turned her smile to him. "I'm so happy you're here!"

"Me?" Chris' eyebrows rose to meet the edge of his backward blue cap. He grinned, making no attempt to resist Eva as she guided him to the back row.

Nathan strolled in a second later. Without acknowledging Eva, he took the vacant seat on Chris' other side.

"I'm happy you're here too, Blue Eyes," Chris said, still grinning at her. "Your history skills as good as your French ones? Cause I'm always looking to bum answers."

"I wouldn't copy mine," Eva admitted, offering him an apologetic smile as she pulled out her notebook. She waited to hear if Nathan would comment on the unicorn cover again, but he seemed to be ignoring her. Good, she didn't want him to be part of this conversation.

Unfortunately, Chris did. He pointed his thumb toward his friend and said, "No worries, I got Nate here today. I can always copy from him." Chris pulled a pencil from his pocket, leaned over Nathan's shoulder, and pretended to copy imaginary notes.

Eva was almost afraid to get her hopes up. "Is Nate good at history?"

To her surprise, Nathan himself responded. "Not to brag, but I was this close"—he held his forefinger and thumb so they were almost touching—"to passing last year."

Nathan put his hands behind his head and rocked his chair back, smirking as though *almost* passing was a great accomplishment. He had to be messing with Eva again. But she wasn't going to fall for the same setup twice.

"You know, Nate doesn't seem to think he's good at anything," Eva said, turning her attention back to Chris. "What do you think? Is he utterly devoid of talent?"

Nathan stopped rocking his chair. "Yes, I am."

Luckily, Chris ignored him. "Nate's got tons of talents."

Eva crossed her fingers and offered a silent prayer. She needed Chris to have suggestions that were better than the guardian phone.

"There's his incredible historic knowledge," Chris said. "And his sniper skills are on point. I can't tell you how many times he's gotten me by hiding behind a barrel."

Eva's eyes widened in horror before she clued in. Chris was talking about video games. Anything requiring modern technology suffered frequent breakdowns around too much magic. As such, video games hadn't been popular at Cassel. Eva considered them a very human form of entertainment and felt momentarily relieved that she'd recognized the reference.

"And he can dunk," Chris continued. "Dude is a beast on the court."

He'd officially lost Eva. "Sorry, what?"

"Basketball. Nate's great," Chris explained. "As am I. We were going to play at lunch today. You should check us out."

"Yes! I'd love to!" Eva squeezed the edges of her desk to keep herself from leaping up and hugging Chris from excitement.

This had to be it! People loved sports! Becoming a professional athlete would be an incredible opportunity for someone like Nathan. Some might even say a *great* opportunity. Eva just needed to step into her role as his guardian angel and guide him to it.

14

EVANGELINA

Eva's dreams were quickly dashed when she went to the gym. She knew nothing about sports, but even she could see that professional basketball was not in Nathan's future.

"He's terrible," Eva said, turning to Beatrice, who'd offered to come. They sat side-by-side on the bleachers watching a match between eight of the boys.

"I told you so," Beatrice said.

"No, you said he was maybe a bit above average. He's not even that."

Since the boys had started playing, Nathan had failed to score even once. Someone stole the ball every time he dribbled. When he passed to his teammates, his throws went wide. The one time it seemed like he'd make it to the hoop, Nathan managed to kick the ball away with his foot. He couldn't have played worse if he tried!

"Is it making you upset?" Beatrice asked, resting her hand on Eva's shoulder. Her fingers combed through the feathers on the jacket, almost as though she were searching for something.

"Of course it is," Eva admitted. She shifted, forcing Beatrice to lower her hand. "I thought he was going to be good at this. But you were right. Nathan is destined for failure and a dead-end job. He's completely useless. I've never met someone who literally has nothing going for them besides their looks, but here he is. He's not just mediocre. He's worse than that."

"Damn girl." Chris' voice was low.

Oh no!

Eva's hand sprang to her mouth. In her frustration, her voice must have grown louder than intended. All eight boys had stopped playing and stood staring at her from the court. Including Nathan.

He stood near the edge, dark waves framing his face. A light sheen of sweat made his skin glisten, and he studied her with his soft eyes.

Eva needed to apologize. What could she even say?

I didn't mean it! Beatrice is the one who thinks you're going to end up a dead-beat father, not me. At least, I said you were attractive!

Not that. Something else. But before Eva could figure out the right words, Nathan looked away. He pulled his phone from his pocket, raised his hand to Chris, and turned to the door.

What did that mean? Had Eva upset him so much that he was leaving?

Nathan might've been a jerk, but he didn't deserve to hear Eva insult him like that. She hadn't even meant all of it. She'd been frustrated and venting.

Eva sprang up to go after him, but just as she did, she became aware of most of the room staring. Guilt and embarrassment crashed into her. And just like that, her wings appeared. The feathers tickled the back of her neck.

Perfect.

"I have to go." Eva grabbed her bag and ran backward out the gym doors, ignoring Beatrice's protests.

———

"There you are."

Eva jumped at the unexpected voice. Her wings fluttered out, hitting against the edges of the bathroom stall.

Beatrice waved at her over the partition. The brunette must have climbed onto the toilet in the adjacent stall.

This is very bad.

When a human saw something magical, it was vital to douse them with amnesiac powder. But the stuff was government regulated. Eva had already used her quarterly allowance. It would be another strike against her family if she had to put in an early request for more.

"I've never seen an angel's wings before," Beatrice said. Her green eyes glinted in the fluorescent light.

Eva stepped back. She wasn't calm enough to hide her wings again, but she tucked them in and pressed her back against the opposite wall. Humans fell into various states of shock at the sight of an angel's wings. But neither overwhelming awe nor panicked hysteria could account for the hunger in Beatrice's expression.

"You are a witch!"

"Of course," Beatrice said. "It wasn't a secret."

"You didn't say you were," Eva argued, but she was annoyed with herself. She'd recognized the name Blackwell, then dismissed it. "What are you doing here?"

"I followed you when I saw that your wings had—" Beatrice squeezed her hands into fists then spread her fingers wide. Her eyes remained on Eva's feathers.

Eva did not like that. She took a few slow, deep breaths and got her wings to vanish.

Disappointment flashed across Beatrice's face.

"I meant, what're you doing at Dashmoor?" Eva asked.

"Learning, obviously," Beatrice said. With the feathers out of sight, her eyes appeared normal again. "Not everyone can afford to send their children to a Castors-only high school. Some of us have to slum it with the humans. But why are you here? I figured you'd transferred because of your brother's arrest, but you're way too interested in Nathan."

Eva's eyes widened. Learning Beatrice was a witch had been like being slapped in the face by a fish she'd just pulled out the water. Eva should have seen it coming. But this new revelation caught her off guard.

"You've known who I was this whole time!" Eva accused.

Beatrice had never claimed to be human, but she'd asked about Eva's brother like she had no idea who Zeke was.

"You've just been pretending to be my friend."

"Of course not. We are friends," Beatrice said. "Why else would I be here?"

"Seriously?"

Angel feathers were incredibly powerful ingredients for potions. Witches prized them. But they were almost impossible to obtain.

Given their potency, and the catastrophes their misuse could cause, relinquishing a feather would mark the beginning of a fall from grace. But if you were caught, the Sanctum wouldn't wait. They'd give a push. Excommunication. They stripped the feathers from any angels found guilty of serious crimes before they could begin to shed.

The individual in question would become an irin—a feath-erless angel, flightless and doomed to suffer the mortality of their human body when it succumbed to age.

"Yes, seriously," Beatrice said. "I like you."

Eva chewed the inside of her cheek. She liked Beatrice too. And maybe, just maybe the witch wasn't trying to steal a feather. Eva wanted to believe that. Because she desper-ately needed a friend right now.

———

"You're Nate's guardian angel, right? There's no other reason you'd care so much about him." Beatrice twisted a lock of hair around her finger and leaned against the door. They'd come out of the stalls, so she could guard the bath-room's entrance while Eva explained. The witch had no qualms about shooing the younger girls who tried to enter.

Technically, Eva shouldn't reveal information about her assignment, even to another Castor. But Beatrice had guessed, and Eva had never been a good liar. Plus, it was a relief to be able to talk to someone. Eva's mother had no interest. Her father would grow more anxious if she told him the truth. And Zeke wasn't an option.

So Eva spilled her guts to the witch in the Dashmoor bathroom.

Beatrice listened as patiently as she could, which meant interrupting a handful of times instead of a hundred. Once Eva finished, however, the witch launched into a list of questions.

"The Fates are your version of an oracle, right? They prophesy things?"

"They see glimpses of possible futures. The princes commune with them and use their wisdom to direct us so that we can best guide God's plan," Eva explained, but Beatrice wasn't listening for an answer.

"What if they misunderstood something they foresaw? Maybe they made a mistake and there's someone else you should be guarding. I mean, Nathan Ward doesn't exactly scream *destined for greatness.*"

On that point, Eva agreed. But the Fates didn't make mistakes. "Who else could they have meant?"

"Uh, hello? Me!" Beatrice waved her hand. "I'm talented and definitely destined for greatness. Maybe there was a mix-up, and you should be guarding me."

"That would be a pretty big mistake," Eva said.

But there could have been a smaller one, somewhere along the way. Beatrice continued to list the many talents she possessed that qualified her for greatness while Eva considered the idea. She'd already suspected something strange had occurred to make Irena her direct superior. What if it was more than just the karmic angel pushing her way in?

The Fates didn't make mistakes, but Eva doubted the three women programed the guardian phones themselves. The Sanctum loved paperwork and bureaucracy. Her assignment might have passed through dozens of hands before reaching Eva.

A dove's coo trilled in the middle of the bathroom, loud enough to quiet even Beatrice.

"Another alarm?" the witch asked.

Eva gave her an apologetic look and hurried to retrieve the guardian phone. The device certainly knew how to get attention. It displayed a message on its screen: *Report to Irena Elysium immediately. Situation update required.*

15

EVANGELINA

Eva kept her head low as she hurried through downtown. If someone saw her, they might think she was skipping school, which would be false. Eva had gone to Principal Davis and gotten permission to leave due to a family emergency. But she still felt like she was breaking a rule. The principal would assume she'd returned home, not gone traipsing through the city to get an update that probably could have been delivered as a text.

Unless this new information was too serious to send in writing.

What if Beatrice had been right? What if Nathan wasn't supposed to be Eva's charge?

She tried not to get her hopes up as she entered the Sanctum Headquarters.

Irena's office was located on the fifth floor. Since flying inside the building was prohibited, Eva stepped onto the elevator.

"Wait!" A slender hand slipped through, holding the doors. Farrah entered. She'd missed a button on her shirt, and papers threatened to spill from her shoulder bag. "You got the news about your brother's trial?"

"There was an update?" Eva scrambled to find her real phone. She must have missed the alert while she'd been on the subway.

"They've set a date," Farrah said. "We have less than a month."

The elevator doors closed, and classical music started to play. A screen within displayed positive reminders: *Breathe and relax. Everything happens for a reason. It's all part of the plan.*

Eva read and reread that last message, trying to find solace in the belief. As a child, she'd been taught that angels came to earth to help its inhabitants. They guided them in accordance with God's plan. Eva had never doubted that before.

But if the plan had been predetermined, why did the Fates see only possibilities in their visions? Why were people held accountable for their actions? Why had Zeke been arrested? Why did they have less than a month to prepare a defense for him?

"Why do bad things happen to good people?" Eva whispered, hearing her brother's voice in her mind. Zeke had always posed borderline-heretical questions. As a child, Eva had worried he'd start to drop feathers.

"Oh, Eva, that's—" Farrah grabbed her hand and squeezed.

Eva felt a momentary panic. She hadn't intended Farrah to overhear. The last thing she wanted was to alienate the one person who hadn't abandoned her family. And Eva knew the answer. Her mother used to recite it to Zeke in a couplet, hoping it would sink in: *God's plan is beyond what we can conceive. We see threads, not the rug they weave.*

But Farrah didn't parrot the sentiment. Instead, still squeezing Eva's hand, she sighed. "That's an excellent question."

The elevator dinged as it stopped on the fifth floor. Farrah stepped out, but Eva hesitated, staring at the back of the assistant's wild curls.

Farrah's response had been atypical for an angel. But she'd probably wanted to offer support instead of judgement.

So why am I questioning her?

That was exactly how Zeke would've responded. And he was a good person, not a true heretic and definitely not a thief. He'd be found innocent in his trial, and everything would work out for the best.

Eva believed in the plan.

"Your shirt needs fixing," she said, hurrying after Farrah. She helped her with the buttons before they rounded the corner.

Irena stood outside. She'd opted for a burgundy suit and a dark eyeliner to counter her round cheeks and loose cherubic curls. She leaned over her assistant's desk. whispering something to the blue-haired nymph. Maddie turned, spotted Farrah and Eva, and waved. Irena saw them and did not.

The karmic angel beckoned Eva into her office, leaving the two assistants to converse outside. Maddie hugged Farrah like an old friend. Perhaps they'd bonded instead of embracing the rivalry of their employers. The two would have more paperwork to exchange now that there was a date for the trial. Eva wished she could've stayed outside to listen to the logistics. There might've been something she could do to help.

But Irena shut the door and took a seat behind her desk. Eva glanced around for another chair. There wasn't one.

"You wanted to speak with me, Miss Heaven."

"Uh... no, Ma'am," Eva said, shifting her weight. "My guardian phone said there was a situation update."

"I'm aware," Irena said, sounding exasperated. "Given that you're the guardian, that means you have an update for me. I'm told the device must have sensed it. So what is it? I haven't got all day."

Seriously? What did the device think Eva wanted to share? She couldn't tell Irena that she'd publicly insulted Nathan and caused him to run off.

The alarm had cooed when she'd been talking to Beatrice.

"Oh!" Eva clapped her hands together. That had to be it. Maybe she was right after all. "I think there's been a mistake!"

"I beg your pardon?"

"With my charge." Seeing the way Irena's lips tightened, Eva hurried to explain, "Or with what I'm supposed to help him with. It's a very vague instruction, and he's not really inclined to greatness in any particular way, so maybe—"

"The Fates don't make mistakes, Miss Heaven."

"Of course not! But maybe a clerical mix-up—" Eva stopped talking as Irena's nostrils flared.

"You know, Miss Heaven, when Farrah informed us that you'd volunteered to take your brother's assignment as a guardian angel, I was impressed by your tenacity. I volunteered to oversee the task because I thought, of all your family, you at least deserved a chance. But you continue to disappoint. Arriving late. Doubting the Fates. You're not coming across well in my report at all."

Eva's chest tightened. What kind of report was Irena writing? Was it standard practice for supervisors to make notes on guardian angels?

"I wasn't late today," Eva said in a pathetic attempt to defend herself. "I got here as fast as I could."

"And now you're lying." Irena banged her desk. Her eyes grew wide and furious, as though the innocuous comment was the worst thing Eva had said. "Lies are a slippery slope for an angel, Miss Heaven. You would do well to remember that given the precarious nature of your situation."

Eva got the sense that they were no longer speaking about her guardian angel assignment. "You mean because of Zeke?"

"Obviously." Irena crossed her arms and leaned back in her seat. "To speak bluntly, Miss Heaven, your brother was caught embezzling money from ParadiseShared, a charitable organization that supports orphanages in Southeast Asia. It's difficult to think of a more deplorable act. And it was only possible because your father vouched that his son could be trusted with the Sanctum's finances. Both must share the blame. Then, there is your mother. As your father's mate, she's guilty by association."

Eva wanted to argue, but Irena must have sensed it for she bulldozed on, making an interruption impossible.

"Oh yes, Miss Heaven. All three of them are guilty. Which makes you the only untainted member of your flock. It will be at my discretion whether to request clemency for you."

A chill went through Eva. She'd never considered—but she should have. Angelic law understood families to be interconnected in a manner different to earthly species. Perhaps because they weren't born in the traditional way. Angels chose their parents, flying to earth in the bodies of newborn babes and waiting on doorsteps. Their flock became a cohesive, interconnected unit, greater than the sum of its individual parts. Growing up, Eva had always found that concept beautiful. The Heavens were a team who celebrated and shared in one another's victories. But if one faltered...

"What punishment are you going to suggest?" Eva whispered.

"For your family, our laws are clear. We can't have their feathers dropping everywhere while they lose themselves to the vices of this world."

Eva's chest tightened. Irena wanted to turn all her family into irin, make them flightless, condemn them to death.

"For you, I'm undecided. Some might consider me unnecessarily cruel should I have you penalized to such an extent. But should you fail your assigned task as a guardian angel, I shall take it as a clear sign that you should be preemptively stripped of your feathers as well."

16

EVANGELINA

"You're making a mess of my kitchen again," Magdalena said. She shuffled toward the counter wearing only a pair of gray sweatpants and a pajama shirt. Blonde hair tangled around her shoulders, and no makeup hid the shadows beneath her eyes. Not only had Magdalena stopped leaving the house, she'd also begun avoiding the windows. They all had.

When Eva had returned home on Friday, she'd found a reporter from *Castors Daily,* the city's major magical newspaper. He hadn't been alone for long. Writers from lesser magazines had been popping up all weekend. Everyone wanted a statement about Zeke's trial.

"I'm making a lemon meringue," Eva said. She held up the spoon. Whipped egg white dropped in a perfect peak from the back.

Magdalena opened the fridge and pointed to an upside-down pineapple cake, cinnamon cookies, and a row of peach tartlets. "And who do you plan on giving all this to? There's no one here to eat it."

"There's another reporter outside," Cyrus grumbled. An

old plaid bathrobe hung open around his shoulders, and his beard had grown wild and unruly during his weekend sequestered indoors. "Take it to him. See if it'll make him go away."

"I could."

"Don't you dare." Magdalena raised a finger in warning. "We don't feed vultures. I'd rather you dump it."

A silence descended on the room. Magdalena cherished every scrap of food and constantly reminded her children how lucky they were to have it. She used to take all Eva's extra treats to the Sanctum's homeless shelter.

"I didn't mean that," Magdalena said. She rubbed her head. "I'm just tired of the kitchen being such a mess, that's all."

"I can clean it," Eva offered.

Her mother brushed her away. She began gathering supplies that Eva still needed and taking them to the sink. "You never do a good enough job."

That wasn't fair. Eva looked to her father for support.

Cyrus glanced at her over a stack of papers that Farrah had brought for him that morning. "What're you even doing here? You should be with your charge."

Eva's chest tightened. Since Friday afternoon, she'd done her best not to think about Nathan. It sent thoughts spiraling into dark, featherless places where the words *irin* and *excommunication* echoed in her mind.

Zeke was innocent. His trial would prove it. Couldn't Eva just trust the plan?

"I figured you all needed me here," Eva said, dipping her finger into the meringue and stealing a taste.

"The only thing your mother and I need is for you to do a good job as a guardian angel. Whatever it takes, you need to succeed."

It won't save you from Irena's wrath.

But Eva couldn't bring herself to say that aloud, so instead, she hugged her father's shoulders and reassured him. "I'll see my charge at school, and I'll guide him all day. I promise."

———

But on Monday, there was no sign of Nathan at Dashmoor High. He didn't show for any of his classes.

"Do you think he's sick?" Eva asked Beatrice when they sat down for lunch.

The witch poked her fork into a gelatinous gray lump of food, which she'd purchased from the school's cafeteria. The glob jiggled. "I wouldn't worry about it, Eva. Nate skips school all the time."

"But isn't that illegal? If you miss enough?"

Beatrice shrugged. She prodded the glob again before eyeing Eva's spread of pastries. "Are you going to eat all those?"

Eva pushed a piece of pineapple upside-down cake toward the witch.

Beatrice grinned and buried her fork into it. She closed her eyes as she chewed. When she'd finished, she scooped her fork into the lemon meringue and grabbed a peach tartlet. "Did you bake all these? There's so much! When did you have time to leave your house this weekend?"

"I didn't," Eva admitted.

"Oh my gosh. That's my foot in my mouth again. What a stupid comment." Beatrice slapped her palm against her face. A fleck of peach filling landed on her forehead. "Of course, you were hiding in your house this weekend. I saw the articles about your brother's trial. The press is definitely having fun. Guess it's not often we see an angel as a villain. Any idea why he did it?"

Eva's eyes narrowed. "He didn't."

"Really? I swore I read that he'd confessed. Let me see if I can find it. Hold on…" Beatrice rummaged through her bag and produced a copy of *Witch Whisper*, a notoriously unreliable gossip magazine. She flipped to a page with a massive picture of Zeke.

Whoever had selected the image had been going for a specific angle on the story. Blond curls twisted on Zeke's head. The glossy paper made the blue shine in his eyes. But there were hints of a not-so-perfect angel. Light stubble grew on his heart-shaped jaw, and there was a mischievous quality to his smile.

At least they didn't find the picture of him pouring flour on my head and laughing.

That had been eight years ago, when they'd made a cake for their mother's birthday.

"*Witch Whisper* will make anything up to get readers," Eva said, barely glancing through the article. She waited for Beatrice to argue the way her former friends had.

"They definitely will," Beatrice agreed. "Pretty sure that's why they dedicated a whole page to his photo. You didn't mention your brother was hot. Mine looks like a brick."

"Ew. Zeke isn't hot." Eva shut the magazine before Beatrice made any more comments. "You're clearly seeing things."

The word *hot* reminded Eva of someone else. Her eyes swept across the cafeteria, half expecting Nathan to have appeared in his usual spot beside Chris.

"Have the reporters been camped outside your house?" Beatrice asked. "I read that they've been hounding your family for a statement. I doubt they'd be fooled by an impression, but I could brew something to help you sneak out unnoticed. I'm a whiz at potions. A natural savant some might say."

Eva smiled. She had a feeling the *some* in question referred to Beatrice herself. "Do you know how to do that? I thought your coven specialized in large-scale magical protections."

"Admittedly, transformation is more a Rookwood thing, and the Wyrmwoods specialize in invisibility. Sophie would probably lend me her scarf if I begged. But I think I could figure out how to disguise you with the right ingredients. There are those faceless ones among the demons. Maybe if I got one of their heads and skinned—"

"I'm an angel," Eva reminded her, cutting the witch off before her description went somewhere dark. "I can't use a potion with a demon's face as an ingredient. Or pieces of anyone's bodies. And I don't endorse you purchasing stuff like that."

"Let me think then." Beatrice waved off the objection without seeming to take offense. She took another bite of cake, then leaned across the table. "I could turn the reporters into frogs."

"I can't condone that either."

"It wouldn't be permanent," Beatrice said. "But I'll think of something I can do. We're friends. We help each other. I scratch your back, you scratch mine, that sort of thing."

"Sure," Eva agreed, but she was only half listening. "You don't think Nathan's skipping school because he's upset about what I said on Friday, do you?"

Beatrice rolled her eyes. "Trust me, Nate is fine. He'll probably show up tomorrow like nothing ever happened."

But Nathan didn't appear the next day or the one after that, and by the end of the week, Eva was getting anxious.

Unfortunately, Chris had taken her outburst against his friend personally. He refused to give her any indication about why Nathan wasn't at school, or share his number, or any details. Eva tried to explain that she wanted Nathan's address so she could apologize to him in person, but Chris claimed to have no idea where his friend lived.

The whole thing was a disaster. Eva had done more than fail as a guardian angel, she'd lost her charge. What if Nathan actually was destined for greatness and some demon had abducted him?

Each day Zeke's trial loomed closer. Irena would demand a report again soon. An entire week of Nathan's absence was all Eva could take before her insides tied themselves into a knot the size of a fist. Her mind raced with worst case scenarios.

She had to find Nathan. There was one last thing she hadn't tried.

After the device ordered her to report to Irena last week, Eva had wrapped it in a scarf and shoved it to the bottom of her backpack. She checked it only very quickly at night, afraid it would send another message or worse, reveal something horrible about Nathan. But it had done neither.

Friday afternoon, when she returned home, Eva barely scratched Halo's head before running upstairs. Once she reached her room, she locked the door, sat on her bed, and unwrapped the guardian phone. Nathan's face appeared on the screen.

"Do you know where he is?" Eva asked the device.

Nothing happened.

"Do you know if he's in trouble?"

Still no response.

Eva groaned. Why did they even bother issuing these things? She had the sudden urge to chuck it across the room.

"Do you at least know where he lives?"

Files flickered across the screen. An address appeared. It was only about ten blocks north of Eva's house. She could walk there, search for Nathan, and get back before dinner.

Perfect!

17
NATHAN

Nathan took a whiff of the pan as he tossed the garlic in with the rest of the vegetables. They sizzled nicely in the butter.

He grinned. This was what cooking was supposed to be like.

Nathan dipped his spoon into the sauce and tasted it. *Perfect.*

Amazing what a difference having all the ingredients made.

"Dan, you got to try this." Nathan scooped some into a ladle and carried it to the small bedroom near the back of the apartment.

Daniel lay on their mother's bed, arms resting over the sheets, which were tucked around his waist. He'd suffered another attack this week and barely moved. But the color was finally returning to his cheeks.

Nathan held the ladle to his brother's lips. Daniel sampled diligently.

"What do you think?"

A ghost of a smile flittered on Daniel's face. "Your food is always good."

"Yeah, but this is great, right? I added real parmesan." Nathan waved his hands in only semi-exaggerated excitement.

The doorbell wheezed. Nathan's chest tightened.

"Do you think that's mom or your new friend?"

Nathan wouldn't call G a friend, but he wouldn't call the cloaked, middle-aged woman his godmother either. She'd checked in earlier that week. Daniel hadn't seen her, only heard her voice and drawn his own conclusions.

Could she be back already?

"Keep quiet while I check," Nathan patted his brother's foot before leaving the room. He grabbed his usual knife from the kitchen, then pressed his eye to the peephole.

Standing in the hallway, wearing a wet dress that hugged every part of her, and holding what appeared to be a cake, was the last person Nathan wanted to see.

How the hell had Evangelina Heaven found where he lived?

———

"Hello? Nate, are you in there?" Eva called to him through the door.

Nathan remained glued to the spot, unable to look away. What was he supposed to do? G hadn't given him instructions on how to handle a situation like this.

Even though Eva had a cake, Nathan was tempted to turn her away. They had a sufficient amount of food in their kitchen for a change.

But Eva was soaking wet and shivering. She'd walked to Nathan's house. In the rain.

Dammit.

Nathan opened the door.

"Thank goodness! I was so worried." Eva's face lit up at the sight of him. When she smiled that big, it made her glow with an unearthly beauty that could've stopped traffic.

It certainly stopped Nathan's brain for a moment.

Eva sniffed and leaned forward, crossing the boundary of the door so that half of her at least was officially in his apartment. "Are you cooking something?"

"Shit!"

Nathan ran into the kitchen. He hadn't turned off the stove. If his sauce kept bubbling, it would lose too much liquid and burn. He twisted the knob on the burner, moved the pot, and gave the sauce a quick stir. It couldn't have been more than a couple seconds, but by the time he returned, Eva had let herself in.

The apartment door was closed. A white purse and a cake in a fancy glass display squashed onto the coffee table that doubled as a television stand. And Eva stood beside his couch.

Rain had smoothed the waves from her hair and stretched it almost to her waist. The feathers of her dress clung to her curves. Her legs stretched from the stained rug beneath her white sneakers up to the distant hem.

Nathan tried not to stare. But a girl shouldn't look like that after running through a torrential downpour. She ought to look like a drowned rat. It would at least make it easier to ignore her presence while they waited for the rain to stop.

Eva craned her head in every direction, not being shy about the fact that she was inspecting—and probably judging—the apartment.

Nathan waited for her to offer some condescending descriptor like *cozy* or *quaint*.

"Do you live here alone?"

Nathan's eyebrows rose. Why would she ask that? He considered the space and realized he'd left clothes folded on the couch, including a pair of his boxers. Nathan leaned forward and repositioned them beneath a shirt. "My mom's away for a bit."

"What about your dad?"

Nobody ever asked him that. They all just took the hint when Nathan didn't mention a father. But Eva stared at him expectantly.

Nathan sighed and turned away. "He's dead."

"Nate, I'm so sorry. I didn't know." Eva reached out and grabbed his hand.

Her skin was so soft.

The contact caught Nathan off guard. He had no idea how to respond. He pulled his hand back and crossed his arms. "What're you doing here, Eva?"

"I came to apologize about what happened on Friday," she said, casting her eyes toward the cake balanced next to the television before meeting Nathan's own. "What I said about you was stupid and childish. I didn't mean any of it."

Nathan ran his hand through his hair, trying to remember what she'd said. He'd been so focused on Daniel the past week, he'd barely thought about Dashmoor. As he searched his brain, however, the memory of the basketball game returned. He almost laughed.

"Of course you meant it. I was terrible." Purposefully so. Nathan had a deal to keep. He couldn't look competent in front of Eva.

"At basketball, yes," she admitted. "But that doesn't

mean you're less than mediocre at everything. I should never have said that. I was just frustrated."

"It's fine. I forgive you." Honestly, Nathan had forgotten she'd said that. Eva must have looked insane to everyone else. Why would she get angry about Nathan's lack of talent?

I wish I knew myself.

But G was cagey, and Nathan couldn't ask Eva directly. Not if he wanted to keep getting paid. And he did! So Nathan needed Eva out of his home before she undermined that.

Water trickled down the glass pane of the apartment's small corner window.

"Do you want me to call a car or someone to pick you up or something?" Nathan offered.

"No, it's fine. I walked." Eva was looking around the apartment still, making no indication that she was ready to leave. "Something smells really good in here. Are you making dinner? Can you cook?"

Shit.

Before Nathan could lie and claim incompetence, he was foiled by his own brother.

"He's the best chef in the world," Daniel said, creeping into the light. He'd chosen the worst moment to recover his energy. Nathan had told him to stay in bed. Instead, Daniel clutched his teddy bear in one hand and steadied himself against the wall with the other. Despite looking like he might fall over at any moment, a smile spread across his face. "I thought I heard a girl. Are you Evangelina?"

Nathan's ears pricked. How the hell did his brother know that?

Surprise flashed across Eva's face for a second, but then

her glowing smile returned, and she nodded. "You can call me Eva though. What's your name?"

"Daniel, but you can call me Dan. My brother talked about you with his friend."

Behind Eva, Nathan raised his hand. He shook his fingers frantically before his neck, trying to mime to his brother to stop talking.

Daniel didn't seem to be paying attention. He was too busy smiling at Eva. "You should stay for dinner. I'll show you where we keep the plates."

18

EVANGELINA

There was no room for a proper dining table in the apartment. Instead, the three of them ate side-by-side on the brown couch. Eva and Nathan sat on opposite ends. Daniel acted as a buffer between them.

Eva twirled her fork around the vegetarian pasta, stomach grumbling in delight. She brought it to her lips and almost cried.

Daniel hadn't been lying. Nathan was an incredible cook.

Could this be his talent?

Eva savored each bite, listening to the chattering eight-year-old beside her. Daniel questioned her enough to learn that she had a cat and an older brother, but he was more eager to share about his own life.

Daniel started with his parents.

"I don't remember Dad. He died when I was two. But Nate remembers him, don't you?"

"Yeah. He was an asshole."

Eva's eyebrows rose. Surely, Nathan hadn't meant to say that in front of a child.

But Daniel didn't seem fazed by the expression. He nodded as though this was a normal response and continued, "Mom was happier when Dad was alive though."

Nathan grunted, which Eva interpreted as assent.

"She gets overwhelmed now. We stress her out," Daniel said. Then, he shifted topic to his teddy bear, whose official name was Sir Cough Stopper, but he went by Coffee for short.

Eva shook the bear's hand in a solemn introduction, and Daniel moved on to his brother. He seemed to hold Nathan and his bear in equally high esteem.

"He made me magic soup once," Daniel informed her.

Nathan tapped his brother's knee. "Stop. Eva doesn't want to hear about that."

"I absolutely do."

"It was magic because there was almost no food in the house, so Mom said there was no way we had enough ingredients to make me any. But then, Nate did it! And nobody knows how, but it was the best soup we ever ate. Do you remember what you put in it?"

Nathan shook his head.

"And another time," Daniel continued. "When the TV broke and I was stuck in bed with nothing to do, Nathan dressed up like a superhero and acted out the rest of a show for me. You have to remember that, right? You had mom's tights and a pair of underwear on top—why're you hiding your face with a pillow?"

Eva took another bite of pasta to stop herself from giggling as Daniel attempted to tug the throw cushion from his brother's hands. Nathan held tight. Daniel laughed, seeming to enjoy the tug-of-war. Until his giggles turned into a sudden, deep-throated cough.

Nathan dropped the pillow at once, panic filled his eyes.

"Shit. Dan, I'm sorry." Nathan patted his brother's back. "I should've just let you get it. Lean back. I'll get you some water."

Nathan leaped up, carrying his brother's cup to the kitchen.

Eva's heart stopped as she watched him. Nathan Ward wasn't just handsome, he was sweet. He knew how to cook. And he wasn't skipping class to get high. He was taking care of his younger brother.

The dark chill of disease clung to the air around Daniel. Eva had sensed it the moment he entered the room. But it didn't take an angel to know he was sick.

Daniel coughed and wheezed. Mid-sentence, he'd pause to gasp for breath. When he shifted position, he'd wince like his muscles ached, and he'd eaten only a few bites of pasta before Nathan had started spoon feeding him sauce.

"Do you hurt?" Eva whispered.

Daniel had recovered his breath enough to give her a small, sad smile and answer, "Always."

Eva had expected the response, but it broke her heart just the same.

Healers existed among the angels. They had a natural affinity for helping the sick and understanding intuitively what those in distress needed. Some could perform miracles.

But only when the princes instructed it.

The average angel didn't commune with the Fates. They had no way to divine God's plan, and large-scale interference could prove disastrous.

Eva was no healer. She'd shown some slight aptitude when working with children at Cassel, but she couldn't work miracles. To even try would be an infraction of the Sanctum's rules, not something she should risk.

But Eva could sense Daniel's illness, aching through his bones and into his very soul. No child should carry something like that.

She reached forward, placed her hand on Daniel's forehead, inhaled, and closed her eyes. Warmth radiated from her palm. Eva became one with it, spreading her magic throughout the child's body.

The sickness hissed at her touch. It gathered into a dark, cold mass and flung Eva back into her own body.

"Thanks for trying," Daniel said. "It felt a little good."

Eva brushed the dark hair from his forehead to mask her surprise. Had he felt her trying to heal him?

———

After managing to swallow two bites of cake, Daniel fell asleep on the couch with his head on Eva's lap. She stroked his dark curls before Nathan lifted his little brother and the stuffed bear and carried both to bed.

Eva took the plates to the sink. There was no dishwasher, so she scrubbed by hand.

"You don't have to do that."

Eva turned to see Nathan leaning in the doorway. His head tilted as it often did when he studied her, mimicking the picture on the guardian phone's screen. The device hadn't done justice to his appearance by describing him as merely *hot*. Nathan's eyes had a depth that made Eva's breath catch.

And they were alone. In his kitchen.

Eva spun back to the sink, feeling her cheeks growing

hot. She couldn't think of Nathan like that. He was a human. She was his guardian angel.

"You didn't tell me you were such an incredible cook," Eva said, resting a now clean plate onto a narrow drying rack. She grabbed the frying pan from the stove. It still had some sauce. Eva dipped her finger in. "You're better than great. You're amazing. I could eat this every day."

Eva turned to him as she sucked the sauce from her finger, savoring the taste of the herbs.

Nathan's eyebrows rose. He stared at her.

"What?"

"You have to know what goes through a guy's head when you do that." Nathan's voice was blunt, without a hint of embarrassment.

It took Eva a second to clue in. She pulled her hand away and washed it under the running water. Her face felt hot again.

"I have no idea what you mean," Eva lied.

"Uh-huh."

"I was just complimenting your cooking."

"It's pasta pomodoro." Nathan shrugged. "Anyone could make it."

"Not like that. People would pay to eat what you just cooked. Have you ever thought about doing something with your talent?"

Nathan snorted. "Like what? Something great?"

The question startled Eva. But of course Nathan knew she was trying to find something he was great at. She'd harassed him about it for a week, and not subtly.

"You could work in a restaurant," Eva suggested. "I could help you with an application if you wanted. Or you could open your own place. You might already be talented enough, and that would be a pretty great—"

Nathan grabbed Eva's wrist and spun her toward him. Everything she'd wanted to say vanished from her mind. Nathan brought his face close. His breath tickled her cheeks. It smelled like pear and ginger. The flavors of Eva's cake. That's what he'd taste like if—

Don't think that. Don't think that.

Eva's heart pounded.

Still holding her wrist, Nathan raised his free hand and pressed a finger against her lips. The contact sent a shiver through Eva. Her face must've been red. Nathan had accused her of being suggestive. What was this? Did he want to see how bright she could blush?

"You can help me clean up, but we are not talking about me doing anything great. Understood?"

Eva nodded.

"Good." Nathan stepped to the side, positioning himself in front of the dish rack. He grabbed a towel from a drawer and began drying.

"But I do have one question."

Nathan glared at her from the corner of his eye. He kept drying the dishes. But he didn't say no.

So Eva asked, "What's wrong with your brother?"

19
NATHAN

Why would she ask about Daniel?

Eva stared at Nathan, all innocent blue eyes and loose blonde waves. But she obviously had an angle. No one just showed up with a cake and then started cleaning your kitchen. And they definitely didn't do it in clinging dresses that showed off their legs while suggestively licking sauce off their fingers.

Nathan's eyes drifted to Eva's lips.

No, get a grip!

It didn't matter how attractive Eva was. Nathan knew better. Whatever game she was playing, he didn't intend to become a pawn.

"Nothing's wrong with Daniel," Nathan lied as he put the first plate into the cupboard and began drying the next. "What's wrong with your brother?"

"He's in jail."

Nathan dropped the plate.

"Good thing you guys use plastic," Eva said. She bent over, lifted the fallen plate, and began washing it again. Her hands moved in smooth circles over the dish.

Nathan didn't know what to say. He'd intended the question as a petty retort, designed to shut her up. She'd mentioned an older brother earlier. Nathan assumed he'd be off delivering food to starving orphans or performing some other magnanimous deed.

Was Eva messing with him? Paying him back for convincing her he was illiterate?

"It's not like that," Eva said, catching him staring. "Zeke didn't do anything wrong. Some funds went missing from where he works, and they think he took them. But he didn't. It's a huge mistake."

"Yeah." Nathan snorted. He'd heard that before. "It was a mistake when my parents got arrested too."

Eva passed him the plate she'd just washed. "Your parents were arrested?"

Shit. Daniel had revealed enough personal information during dinner. Nathan hadn't intended to offer more. But he couldn't take it back, so he nodded and waited for the inevitable: *what were they arrested for?*

"I'm sorry." Eva sprang toward him.

Nathan hadn't been expecting it. He stumbled back, colliding with the nearby wall as Eva's arms wrapped around his waist. Her body pressed against him, soft and warm in all the right places. The lavender scent still lingered in her hair.

He wanted to hug her back, to hold her against him. But it was too dangerous. Because Eva didn't just feel perfect, she felt right.

Gently, Nathan pushed her away.

"Where's your mom now?" she asked.

Nathan's instinct was to inform her that it was none of her business. But Eva's eyes shone with tears, and her brow pulled low with genuine concern.

She's not lying about her brother.

Which meant all the assumptions Nathan had made about Eva's perfect life were wrong.

"My mom's not in jail," Nathan admitted. "She's with her boyfriend of the month getting high."

"I'm sorry," Eva apologized again, but at least she didn't hug him this time. "That's worse."

"No kidding." Getting locked up was outside of your control. Kay chose to disappear and let her sons fend for themselves. "But she thinks we're doomed anyway. Cursed to lives of pain and anguish."

Might as well find some false sense of happiness where you can. His mother's voice echoed in his head. *Make sure there's always something in it for you.*

"That's silly," Eva said. "No one's destined for a horrible life."

The comment caught Nathan off guard. Eva must've known precisely how possible it was for someone, or an entire family, to be cursed. Yet, there was no hint of sarcasm in her voice.

"Did you come here because you were worried about your brother?" Nathan asked.

"Of course not. I came to apologize. I had no idea your parents had been to jail. Do you have a container? I can't bear to throw away the rest of your sauce." Eva held up the pot.

She really doesn't know, does she?

Nathan grabbed a zip lock bag from a drawer and passed it to her.

Eva smiled as she poured the sauce in. "It would be a sin to dump anything this delicious."

The compliment was so genuine, Nathan found himself starting to smile too.

His phone, buzzing in his pocket, put a quick end to that. He pulled it out. No Caller ID.

Shit.

"Do you need to take that?" Eva asked.

"Uh, no." Nathan stepped backward and into the doorway. The raindrops had evaporated from the window. The weather had probably cleared up ages ago.

Why hadn't he kicked Eva out immediately then?

"It's late. You should head out. Just keep the sauce," Nathan said.

Eva seemed taken aback by the abrupt dismissal, but she followed him to the door. "Tell Dan it was nice to meet him. I like him. He's sweet."

"I'll tell him," Nathan promised.

He should've slammed the door the moment Eva went through, but a gnawing guilt made him hesitate.

"You were right about Daniel. He is sick. I was just being an ass because I don't like talking about it. Truth is, no one knows what's wrong."

"Thank you for telling me."

Nathan shrugged as though it weren't a big deal. In reality, he had no idea why he'd shared so much. He'd never been honest with Chris, and they were friends. Nathan didn't even like Eva.

Or, maybe he did.

It was lucky that Eva waved goodbye and walked away, or Nathan didn't think he would've shut the door. He'd have spent the entire night staring at the girl with the beautiful legs and glowing smile, who had the nerve to look every inch like an angel.

20

EVANGELINA

Eva missed her cake stand about halfway home. Normally that wouldn't matter. But her mother rearranged the kitchen daily now. Magdalena might have a fit when she noticed it missing.

But who cared?

Nathan Ward wasn't a less-than-mediocre slacker. He was clever and sweet and talented.

Eva clung to her bag of pomodoro sauce, spinning with it as she walked through Ladybug Park and toward her house. The red flowers lining the path swayed, sending a sweet scent into the breeze.

It made Eva think of Nathan's breath, hot against her cheek and smelling like pears and ginger.

Which would be great flavors for him to experiment with in the future. That was why that memory had popped into Eva's mind. Because her only focus was making Nathan great.

And she finally understood how!

Giggling and giddy, Eva collapsed onto the park bench opposite her house. She pulled the guardian phone from her purse. For once, she wanted to see what the device had to say.

"I know what Nathan is great at now," Eva informed it with a grin. "He's going to be a chef, so you can delete your previous notes."

The phone flipped through its folders. It hadn't replaced anything, but it had added to its list.

Nathan Ward is great at:

- *Making the seniors at Dashmoor High hate Evangelina Heaven*
- *Being hot*
- *Cooking*
- *Taking care of his brother*
- *Making Evangelina Heaven blush*

Eva stared at that last bullet point. It was even worse than the second one. Why did it mention her by name?

"You have to delete that last one. Please?"

The phone was unaffected by her politeness.

"It's very misleading," Eva said. "I only blushed because he kept getting close to me and—I mean, you know. You wrote the second bullet point yourself."

Nothing changed.

Eva groaned and shoved the device back into her purse before someone spotted her arguing with a hunk of metal.

It didn't matter anyway. If the device showed that list to Irena, Eva could explain. She blushed easily. It didn't mean anything.

Neither did the fact that memories of Nathan grabbing her wrist and spinning her toward him kept flickering into Eva's mind as she walked to her house.

A light shone behind the white curtains.

It was almost midnight. Her parents should be asleep. Maybe they'd forgotten to turn it off.

Eva crept in. Voices rose from the kitchen. Her parents were arguing. Aloud.

"Testify and say what?" Cyrus demanded. "If I defend him, I'll look guilty. Condemn him, and they'll question why I vouched for him in the first place."

"He's our son, Cyrus."

They were talking about Zeke's trial.

Eva tiptoed toward the kitchen.

"And he's damned us," Cyrus said. "Magda, you have to accept—"

"Then let us all be damned, Cyrus."

They fell silent as Eva stepped from behind the corner.

Cyrus and Magdalena stood on opposite ends of the kitchen. Her silver pajamas matched his house slippers. But they'd never appeared less in-sync.

"You're back!" Magdalena hurried across the tiles and wrapped her arms around her daughter. "Let's go upstairs. I want to hear about school."

"You ought to ask about her job," Cyrus snapped.

Magdalena's face tensed; anguish flashed in her eyes. She grew depressed whenever Eva's guardianship came up. "I have no delusions about her assignment, Cyrus."

Ouch. Had Eva been so obvious that she'd been struggling this past week?

"It's going really well actually," Eva said as she disentangled from her mother's embrace. "I think the Fates have a plan for my charge."

"Of course they do," Cyrus' response was quick. "Never doubt the plan, Eva."

"I don't," Eva assured him, but there was something

frantic and desperate in her father's tone. Was he taking his own advice? "You should testify at Zeke's trial, Dad. You're an archangel. The judge might listen if you tell him Zeke's innocent."

Fury flashed in Cyrus' eyes. He exchanged a look with his wife. Eva couldn't understand the meaning.

"Irena is coming after us either way," Eva said, resting her purse on the counter. "She told me. She wants to see all of us...punished." Eva couldn't bring herself to say the real word.

Another look passed between her parents.

"We know, baby," Magdalena said, reaching an arm out. She stroked Eva's hair, twisting the wave into a curl the way she'd done when Eva was little.

Cyrus stepped forward. His jaw set. "She's not coming after *all* of us."

"We're a family, Cyrus." Magdalena met her husband's gaze across the kitchen counter. "We stick together."

Suddenly, it clicked to Eva. They were talking about her. "You know that Irena offered to spare me if I succeed in my assignment?"

"Of course she will. She'll have no choice," Cyrus said, eyes flashing to Eva. "Why do you think I had Farrah pull so many strings? You are this family's last hope. You're barely eighteen. No one has a bad word to say about you. If you prove yourself, they'll spare you, and you can—"

"She can do what, Cyrus?" Magdalena interrupted. "Be treated like a pariah within the Sanctum? Never speak to us again?"

"She can eventually clear my name," Cyrus snapped, and his voice trembled with the desperate wish. He grabbed his wife's hands, touch gentle despite his tone. "And yours."

"And Zeke's?" Eva guessed, rubbing her temples. She'd

known her father thought proving herself would help clear the Heavens name, but she hadn't realized he thought it was their family's only chance.

What about Zeke's trial? What about trusting the plan?

Magdalena burst into tears. She pulled her hands from her husband and buried her face.

Cyrus closed his eyes. "Eva, your brother is guilty. He confessed. You must have seen it. The news is in every paper."

Beatrice's *Witch Whisper* article flashed in Eva's mind. She shook her head. "They're making stuff up to get it to sell."

"They're not," Cyrus said. He grabbed Eva's shoulders, forcing her to meet his gaze. "Ezekiel stole that money. Your brother can't be saved. But you still can be."

21

NATHAN

The sound of his phone woke Nathan. He bounded from the couch where he'd passed out and scanned the eerily tidy apartment.

"It's an unknown caller," Daniel said. He'd curled on the floor at the end of the couch. "Should I answer?"

"No, don't. It's probably a scammer." Nathan plucked the phone from his brother, silenced it, and shoved it into his pocket. "What're you doing with my phone anyway, you little brat?"

Nathan tussled Daniel's hair affectionately, careful not to be too rough.

"Playing games," Daniel said. He glanced toward the passageway. "Did Eva leave?"

"What? Of course, she did." Nathan laughed awkwardly, rubbing the back of his head. "Why would you think she was still here?"

"Because you were on the couch. I thought you'd given her your bed."

Right, that made sense. Nathan felt immediately ridiculous. What had been hoping to hear? That Daniel thought

Eva had been flirting with Nathan last night and assumed they'd hooked up?

He's a kid. He's not Chris.

"Can you make me a smoothie?" Daniel pulled himself off the rug and slumped onto the couch. Dark circles surrounded his eyes, and his lips looked dry and cracked. He was often too tired to chew in the mornings.

Nathan opened the fridge, pulled out the already sliced fruits, and added them to the blender. His phone buzzed by his hip. Another unknown caller.

It had to be G calling to talk about Eva.

So what? Cooking a decent meal isn't anything great. I'm still doing what she asked.

Nathan turned on the blender and answered. Hopefully Daniel couldn't hear.

"Finally. I was worried you were ignoring me," G said on the other end. "A little bird told me you had a visitor last night."

Jesus, she already knew? Nathan pressed his phone closer. "You keeping tabs on me?"

"Eva's feeling confident about her assignment," G said, ignoring the question. "Should she be?"

"Course not. She's just an eternal optimist."

"We have a deal, remember? I'm your benefactor. Eva may be pretty, but she can't offer you money. It would be against her rules."

"But it's not against yours? What kind of weird bet do you two have?"

The giggle on the other end would've been better suited to a younger woman. "This week's payment will be in your mailbox. Keep avoiding greatness, Nathan."

"Don't worry. Been managing that all my"—She hung up, leaving Nathan to finish lamely—"life."

He shoved his phone into his pocket and turned off the blender. Guilt twisted in his stomach. Nathan poured the smoothie into a large plastic cup, stuck in a straw, and took a sip in an effort to quash the feeling.

It didn't matter how nice Eva was. It didn't matter that she'd baked him a cake, or that she smelled like lavender, or that he'd enjoyed having her in his apartment last night. Nathan's only job was to look out for himself and his brother.

"Your smoothie, my liege!" Nathan plastered a grin on his face as he carried the drink out.

Daniel smiled and took the cup in both hands. He didn't sip.

"Do you like Eva?" he asked.

"Absolutely not." Nathan forced a laugh, then regretted it. The sound made it seem like he was lying.

Thank God our new benefactor didn't ask me that.

"I like her," Daniel said. "She tried to heal me."

Nathan sat beside his brother. "Eva wouldn't have done that."

"She did," Daniel insisted. "I felt it when she put her hands on me. She's an angel."

Well, shit. That much was obvious. She looked, dressed, and acted the part. And with a name like *Evangelina Heaven*, even an eight-year-old could piece it together.

"You should like her," Daniel insisted.

He wasn't going to drop this, was he? Nathan sighed, ran a hand through his hair and leaned back on the couch while he waited for his brother to drink what he could manage and share the rest.

"I don't *not* like Eva," Nathan admitted. "I just—that's not how I meant it. I like Eva. More than I should."

"Because she's an angel?"

And because the only reason we can afford food is because I agreed to foil her plan.

"We're angels too."

Daniel's words hit Nathan like a bucket of ice. His skin went numb. He corrected his brother, "Mom was an angel."

"So were you."

"Well, I don't remember. And we're nothing now."

"We must be something, otherwise, why would we have wings?"

"Dan, don't—" Nathan tried to stop his brother, but he was too late.

Daniel had forced himself from the couch. He closed his eyes, and a moment later, they appeared on his back.

Wings was a generous descriptor. Calling them bones would be more apt. They shone with an eerie, ivory sheen, clacking against one another whenever Daniel stretched them. The sound raked across Nathan's soul. He closed his eyes.

"Put them away, Dan."

"Why? I like them. I think they're kind of pretty."

"Dan, I'm telling you. There's no room to have them out here."

The horrible clatter came as the bones folded. When Nathan opened his eyes again, Daniel had hidden them and slumped back onto the cushions. Smoothie sloshed over his cup onto the rug.

"Mom hates them too," the eight-year-old said, sounding morose as he passed the cup to Nathan. "I saw her staring at them in the mirror and crying once. Do you think that's why she hates being around me?"

I know what's wrong with your brother, Kay's voice whispered, anxious and on the verge of laughter the way it got whenever she was high. *He shouldn't exist.*

Nathan's stomach clenched. He shoved the thought aside.

"Mom hates being around me, not you," Nathan lied, smudging the fallen smoothie into the carpet with his foot. The pink blended with the already present patchwork of stains. "And it's not personal. She's been on a downward spiral since Dad died."

"Because they were soulmates."

Nathan snorted. *Co-dependent* was his preferred term. But as disastrous as Kay and Shane had been as parents, they had loved each other. "Yeah, soulmates."

"You should find a soulmate too," Daniel said. "Maybe Eva."

Nathan almost dropped the smoothie.

"Don't be an idiot," he said, forcing a laugh. Nathan wasn't sure if he was talking to his brother or himself.

Irin didn't mix with other angels. It was strictly forbidden. If Eva ever learned the truth about Nathan, she'd do more than drop whatever plan for greatness she had. Eva would never speak to him again.

22

EVANGELINA

E va passed the weekend in a fog. Her body moved through familiar motions, but even awake, her mind was lost in nightmares about Zeke.

He was guilty.

Eva had gotten a picture of the *Witch Whisper* article from Beatrice and finally read the entire thing. It painted Zeke as some sort of *sexy rebel*—the writer's words, definitely not Eva's—for its readers to romanticize, like there was something appealing about an angel with a wicked side. Gross as the angle, however, the facts were clear.

Zeke had stolen from a charity. He'd used his role in the finance division to reroute payments intended for Paradise-Shared into his personal account. And he'd confessed. He'd told the Sanctum exactly how he'd done it. And why.

Not for the money. Cyrus' position provided the Heavens with more than sufficient funds. Zeke had done it because he wanted to see the response.

It sounded absurd. Until an almost forgotten memory resurfaced in Eva's mind.

———

Zeke marched into the kitchen. He'd just returned from a date. "Some bad things are supposed to happen, right?" he said. "If you believe in the plan, you have to accept that."

"I suppose." Eva glanced up from the puff pastry dough she'd been folding, hesitant to offer more. Zeke often set traps with his questions, and she wasn't up for sparring against her brilliant brother in some verbal mind game she was too dumb to even know they were playing.

"So how do we decide which bad things people get punished for?" Zeke asked, fiddling with the buttons on the cuff of his sleeve. "What if people are just playing their role and we should leave them? We shouldn't take offense to anything."

———

Eva had laughed off her brother's comment as the result of another terrible date. But what if, even then, Zeke had been planning to test his theory. He'd always been clever. Did he want to see if he could get away with a crime?

It felt so petty. Especially when his decision could drag his family down with him.

———

"Are you even listening to me?" Beatrice leaned across the cafeteria table and tapped Eva's arm with a tube of lip gloss. The witch had spent the past several minutes debating between two colors.

"I like the red," Eva offered, prodding the beige mass on her plate with a plastic fork. She'd barely thought about food all weekend, but hunger had caught up to her, and she'd made the mistake of purchasing lunch from the Dashmoor cafeteria. Monday's special claimed to be vegetarian pasta. If there were vegetables, however, they'd been hidden by the chewy, under-cooked noodles, which stuck together in an unappealing lump.

"Red. Bold. I like it. What happened to all your baked treats?" Beatrice shifted topic without pausing. "Gave up on Nate returning to school?"

"I already made up with Nate," Eva said as she attempted to separate her noodles. "I went by his house on Friday. Did you know he could cook?"

"You had dinner with Nate?"

Eva's face heated. "It wasn't like that. He just happened to have made dinner when I got there."

"And he invited you to stay?"

"I said it wasn't like that."

"Yeah, but you're blushing."

Eva covered her cheeks with her hands. Beatrice sounded like the guardian phone.

"Is that why you've been so weird today? Did some-thing happen between you and Nate?"

"I wish," Eva said.

Beatrice's eyebrows rose.

Eva realized too late how her comment had sounded. She'd been answering the witch's first question, not the second. "No, I didn't mean—I wish I was focused on Nathan because that's my job. I've been distracted by my brother."

For once, Beatrice waited for Eva to say more.

"Zeke is guilty." It was the first time Eva had said the words aloud. They tasted like bile.

Beatrice nodded, expression unchanged. The news

didn't surprise her. Unlike Eva, the witch had read all the articles.

"So what're you going to do about it?" Beatrice asked.

Eva's brow furrowed. Did the witch somehow know the stakes of Eva's position as Nathan's guardian angel?

But Beatrice kept talking, "I mean, your whole family is set to be punished, right? That's how your system works. Your brother commits a crime, they take all your wings so you can't fly off and die in the sky when you're old."

"We fly back to our true home in the heavens," Eva corrected. Her mouth felt like sand. The only article she'd managed to read was the one in *Witch Whisper*. Were the more official papers really reporting all that?

"Sure," Beatrice acquiesced, but her tone made it clear she thought otherwise. That shouldn't surprise Eva. Most witches were pagans who worshiped a three-part goddess. They believed in angels but not in the traditional sense.

Eva had avoided theological conversations with the witch so far. Conversion wasn't her purview.

"I could help you flee if you wanted," Beatrice said, leaning closer suddenly. "My family has an escape route out of the city. We'd set you and your parents up with new identities. Money. The works."

Eva's eyes widened. Was the witch seriously suggesting that the Heavens become fugitives?

She shook her head. "The Sanctum would find us."

"Not with the connections we have. Trust me." Beatrice took Eva's hand. The witch's smile looked warm and genuine. "Of course, we'd need a feather or two as payment."

She said it so casually.

Eva pulled her hand back. Suddenly, Beatrice's smile

seemed more shark-like than sweet. "You want one of my feathers."

"Helping people disappear isn't exactly cheap. The feather would pay for some of the supplies. And admittedly, there'd be a small profit for us, but it's not much of an ask all things considered. You'll probably lose your feathers if you stay anyway. Why not sell them first? Do you know how powerful they are in our potions? They make magic permanent. I could do something amazing if I had one."

Or something horrific.

In a witch's hands, an angel feather was as likely to create an abomination as a miracle. Eva would bear the responsibility for whatever occurred. And the sin of plucking one feather would cause the rest to fall out on their own. Then what? More witches stealing feathers. More disasters laid at Eva's feet.

"Are you actually my friend?" Eva asked. "Or were you just looking for a way to get a feather?"

Please say you weren't.

"Both things can be true," Beatrice said.

But they couldn't.

"A friend wouldn't ask me for a feather," Eva said. She stood, grabbed her bag, and walked out of the cafeteria, ignoring Beatrice's shouts.

23
NATHAN

I t was Wednesday by the time Daniel had recovered enough to return to school. That meant Nathan could finally do the same. He felt both eager and anxious walking into Dashmoor.

What is wrong with me?

Nathan shouldn't want to see Eva. But he'd spent the past few days wishing she'd turn up at his apartment again. And it wasn't because he wanted cake.

He needed to get his head on straight. Eva was an angel with an ulterior motive. Admittedly, it probably wasn't anything sinister, but he had to think about Daniel.

Nathan arrived at his history class and spotted the white feathers in the corner of the room.

Eva had chosen a desk at the front. She sat with her chin on her hand, lips slightly parted.

Nathan's heart quickened in anticipation of her greeting. Whenever Eva saw him, she smiled in a way that made her entire person seem to glow.

But Eva didn't look up.

Nathan hated that it bothered him. He'd spent a week

aiming to have her ignore him. This should've felt like a victory. It definitely made his job easier.

"Dude, you're back!" Chris wrapped his arm around Nathan's neck. The height difference forced Nathan to lean down as his friend led him to the back of the class.

Eva finally noticed him. She offered a small, tentative smile then turned back to the front, leaving Nathan grinning like a dolt at the back of her head.

What the hell?

Nathan thought they'd left things on good terms on Friday. Was she angry about how abruptly he'd kicked her out? Or was it something worse?

What if Eva had found out what he really was?

"Did I miss something?" Chris' eyes flicked between Nathan and Eva. "I thought we hated her now."

"I don't hate Eva." Nathan dropped his bag onto a desk in the back row, then sat and stretched his legs into the aisle. He purposefully positioned himself so that his back was toward the angel, yet he kept glancing over his shoulder. "Does she seem sad today?"

"Think she and Beatrice had a fight. Eva sat alone at lunch yesterday and got swarmed by the football team."

Something unpleasant twisted in Nathan's chest. "The entire football team?"

"I didn't count to check," Chris said. His eyes narrowed. "Are you jealous?"

"No." Nathan just didn't like the idea of the football team circling Eva like a pack of hungry wolves. He glanced back, hoping to find her looking at him. But Eva's attention was elsewhere.

Good. G would be thrilled. Maybe she'd pay extra.

Nathan pulled his history book out as Mrs. Matthews entered. "Did I miss anything while I was gone?"

"You mean in class? No idea." Chris shrugged. He pulled out a laptop, but when he loaded the screen, it was full of searches for cars. Now that class had officially begun, he leaned over, lowering his voice. "Eva pretty much ignored everyone yesterday. But she spent all of last week trying to get your number. Or your address. Think she had a vision of showing up at your house to apologize."

"I know. She showed up at my door on Friday." Nathan realized too late that it was the worst thing he could have said.

"What?" Chris' voice boomed through the classroom. Everyone turned to him.

Mrs. Matthews cleared her throat, looking unimpressed. "Something you'd like to share with the class, Mr. Gross?"

"Just can't believe how long it took the French to get their shit sorted, Ma'am. I mean, you kill all the aristocrats. You think you'd have a plan."

The comment earned a few muffled laughs and a sigh from Mrs. Matthews. She turned back to the slideshow and continued presenting.

Nathan suspected he'd gotten these notes already. History was the one class he actually enjoyed. But he pretended to write so that he could avoid Chris' gaze.

"How did Eva find you? I don't even know where you live."

That was a good question. Nathan assumed The Sanctum had a file somewhere in their mysterious headquarters that contained all kinds of unflattering information on Kay and Nathan Ward.

But Eva didn't know what he was.

"So what happened?" Chris nudged him.

"She apologized and stayed for dinner. With Daniel,"

Nathan hurried to add before Chris jumped to any false conclusions.

"So she met your brother."

Nathan stopped writing and looked at his friend. "Why're you saying it like that?"

"We were friends for two years before you felt comfortable bringing Daniel around."

"Well you didn't show up unexpectedly at my house," Nathan pointed out, going back to writing. "What? Are you jealous?"

"No, just curious what happened at that dinner to make you do a one-eighty."

Nathan had no idea what his friend meant by that, so he ignored the comment, hoping Chris would drop the topic.

He didn't.

"You like her."

Nathan dropped his pen and glared. "No, I don't. I told you, she's not my type. Eva's too perfect."

"Oh yeah, I hate when I find a girl perfect."

Chris' sarcasm barely registered. Nathan had remembered something. Eva's life wasn't perfect.

She sat in the front of the class, but her pen wasn't moving. It wasn't like her not to take notes. Something was clearly wrong.

Nathan had been being a self-centered asshole to assume it had to do with him. Because had he thought about it, he'd have recognized the expression on Eva's face. It was one he wore most of the time.

Eva was worried about her brother.

24
EVANGELINA

"Mind if I sit?"

Eva jumped. Her eyes flicked up from the bowl of cafeteria sludge.

Nathan leaned against her table. Black waves hid the edges of his face, emphasizing his eyes. He smiled, and his lashes fluttered.

Eva stared, her mind suddenly blanking on anything besides the memory of his breath against her cheeks.

"I'm going to trust that if you were cool with the whole football team joining you, I can sit."

Eva nodded frantically and pushed a chair out for Nathan. She could feel the blush rising to her cheeks. The guardian phone had a point. How had she gone from worrying about Zeke to gaping at Nathan in less than a second? Eva needed to get ahold of herself.

"How do you know about that?" Eva asked, cluing in suddenly on Nathan's comment. He hadn't been at school yesterday. She'd been absent-minded, but that wouldn't have escaped her notice. "Are people talking about it? I didn't know they wanted that table, I swear. It wasn't even in a good spot."

Nathan's eyebrows rose. "You think those guys sat at your table because they liked its location?"

"That's what they said."

Nathan's shoulders trembled. He was clearly holding back a laugh.

"What's funny about that?" Eva didn't get it. She'd spent most of the meal debating if to leave. The footballers were nice, but they'd felt the need to include her in their conversation when she would've preferred to be left to her thoughts.

"Nothing," Nathan said. "I brought you something."

He pulled a large cloth bag from within his backpack and passed it to Eva. She looked inside, and her face lit up. Nathan had brought her cake stand.

"Thank you!" Eva hugged the glassware to her chest. Her mother had been muttering about it having vanished for the past several days. Not that Magdalena had complained to Eva directly.

The Heaven household had been walking on eggshells around one another since Friday. Eva's parents had both tried to talk to her, but she'd shut down. Her father wanted to saddle her with the weight of being their family's salvation. Her mother would risk Eva's existence if it meant they stayed together. It was all too much.

"It is yours, you know," Nathan said.

"I know." The glassware displayed the Heaven family crest on its base: silver gates with golden light emanating beyond. Eva rested the cotton bag carefully beside her own. "I really appreciate you returning it."

"You must have a really low opinion of me if you're that relieved I gave you back your own dish." A smile curved

Nathan's lips. It might've been mocking if his eyes didn't soften it into something playful.

Eva's gaze lingered on Nathan's lips a beat longer than necessary.

She needed to get it together. It didn't matter what either of her parents wanted. Eva had accepted the position as Nathan's guardian angel. She owed it to him to complete her assignment.

I should have gone to see him again instead of hiding in my room.

And it wasn't just Nathan she should have returned to check on.

"How's your brother?" Eva asked, moving her spoon around the supposed pumpkin soup without lifting any to her mouth.

Nathan hesitated. Eva wondered if he'd deflect. It was clear he wasn't accustomed to discussing his brother.

"Dan's doing better," Nathan said, unpacking a plastic container with his lunch. He opened it, and the scent of thyme and lemon rose into the air, making Eva's mouth water. "Kid's on an upward swing for now. So that's good. But you stole my line. I came to ask about your brother."

A lump rose in Eva's throat. She'd almost forgotten that she'd told Nathan about Zeke.

"Eva, are you okay?"

She liked the way Nathan said her name. He lingered on the 'a' at the end, and the scent of thyme on his breath washed over her. Funny thing to notice now.

"I'm fine," Eva said. "My brother's in prison. He's guilty."

What more was there to say?

Nathan didn't react to her acknowledgement of Zeke's guilt. That fact seemed to surprise no one besides Eva.

"But how is your brother?" Nathan asked, tilting his head and studying Eva through the shadow of his hair. "Like, is he doing okay?"

"He's—I don't know." Eva admitted. "I haven't spoken to him since summer."

Zeke had said his boss needed him to go in late, but to save him a slice of blueberry pie. The Powers, the Sanctum's seldom-used internal soldiers, had been waiting in the office. They'd captured and arrested him. News had reached the Heavens in the middle of dessert.

Eva had set aside a slice of pie for her brother anyway. She'd assumed it was a misunderstanding and that Zeke would return soon. Magdalena had thrown it out a few days after, much to Eva's annoyance. But now she understood.

She knew he wasn't coming back.

"They won't let you visit him?" Nathan sounded horrified, but then their eyes met. He must have seen the guilt in Eva's expression. Nathan scoffed. "No, of course, you're choosing not to visit."

Judgement crept into his tone. It stung Eva more than she'd expected. Once she could stay close enough to guide him, what did it matter what Nathan's opinion of her was?

"He's guilty," Eva said, as though that made it better.

"He's your brother."

"I know that! But my parents and Farrah all think—" Eva's voice grew louder than she'd intended. Water pooled in her eyes. She tried to blink it away before she started crying and drew attention. Then her wings would pop out and—

"I'm sorry. Forget I said anything." Nathan's fingers closed around her wrist. His voice was soft, gentler than Eva had heard it before. "Do you want to share?"

Nathan shoved his fork into a roasted potato and pushed it toward her.

Eva hesitated before taking the fork, but the food looked too good to pass up. She took a bite. It was like a little explosion of flavors in her mouth. She licked the coating of oil from her lips.

Nathan leaned his head against his chin, studying her again.

"You think I should go visit him, don't you?"

Nathan's brow lowered as though caught off guard by the question. He ran his hand through his hair. "Does it matter what I think?"

No. Yes. Maybe?

"You'd visit your brother," Eva said. "It would never happen, of course, because Dan's a sweetheart, but if he ever got arrested, you'd be there for him."

"It's different though, isn't it?" Nathan said softly. He ran his hand through his hair. "I'd visit Dan. But he might not visit me. Depends how badly I messed up. I don't think I'd want him to come if it could be bad for him though."

"Zeke messed up pretty bad," Eva admitted. "He stole from an orphanage because he wanted to see how people would react."

"Curious motivation," Nathan noted, taking the fork from Eva's hands so he could take a bite of his own lunch. "What reaction was he hoping for?"

Eva shrugged. She had no idea.

25
NATHAN

Nathan might have made a serious miscalculation when he'd joined the angel for lunch on Wednesday. Because somehow, even though he'd been a bit of an ass, it had been enough to make Eva think they were friends.

Even scarier, she might have been right.

Now that she wasn't nagging him about his capabilities, Nathan enjoyed Eva's company. She sat with him and Chris in class and joined them for lunch.

By Friday, she'd invited them to study with her in the library during her free period.

Considering the rest of Dashmoor, the library was an oasis. Yellow lights warmed a carpeted floor and several wooden desks. Rows of shelves held books, some more interesting than others. The school had even hired a stereotypical librarian, an older woman who wore her hair in a bun and spent her time shushing students.

But there was one part of the library where talking was allowed. Sectioned off at the back of the room, several armchairs formed a semi-circle around a stone fireplace: The Study Lounge. The chimney had long been sealed, but the aesthetic alone made it popular enough that the space could only be used by juniors and seniors who made reservations in advance.

"Who was it that said he wouldn't be caught dead in The Study Lounge?" Chris asked, shooting Nathan a sly grin as they followed Eva toward the back of the library. "Something about it being pathetic to fight over an armchair where a bunch of other kids had drooled?"

Nathan pushed his hair back, so he could glare at his friend.

Chris kept grinning. "Guess it was someone who hadn't met Eva. I don't have to stick around. Just say the word."

"She invited us both," Nathan insisted, wishing his friend would lower his voice. Eva was only a few feet away. So far she seemed oblivious, but Chris' comments were becoming increasingly obvious.

Eva hurried them forward with an excited wave. Nathan had little experience with study sessions. He suspected that Chris had even less. But Eva took delight in pulling out all their notes. She had colorful tabs and highlighters and a unicorn eraser.

"I can't believe you didn't pass history. This essay is incredible, Nate," Eva said. She actually smiled as she read the scratchy, handwritten assignment he'd done in class last year.

Is there anything she can't find joy in?

But Eva's smile had an infectious quality. Nathan's lips twitched. He leaned back in the armchair, which was more comfortable than he cared to admit, and spread his arms in what he liked to think was a suave shrug. "I attended about forty-eight percent of classes and ended up with forty-eight percent. Many people would consider that a hundred."

Chris snorted.

"I think you'd have ended up with a significantly better grade if missing too many classes didn't cap your final results at an automatic fail," Eva said, still looking at the essay. "You're a really good writer."

Nathan pushed his hair back, trying to look unaffected by the compliment. No one ever said anything good about his assignments. Even when he got decent grades, the comments from his teachers bordered on scolding. The feedback on the essay in Eva's hands declared it, *A rare show of effort, Mr. Ward.*

Unlike Nathan and Chris, Eva had settled on the floor with her back against the stone fireplace. As she read, she stretched her legs, and her dress shifted, creeping higher to expose more of her thighs. The sight put unwanted thoughts in Nathan's head, like what it would be like to slip his hand between them.

"See something you like in Eva's notes?" Chris' voice was heavy with innuendo.

Shit. Nathan had been staring. He pulled his eyes from Eva's legs and flashed his middle finger at his friend. It was a quick gesture. He didn't think Eva would approve if she saw. But, despite his reaction, Nathan wasn't annoyed, embarrassed admittedly, but he needed Chris to call him out.

Nathan couldn't think of Eva like that. She was an angel.

And he was a featherless asshole who'd accepted a bribe to mess with her.

What am I doing trying to be friends with her?

But Eva was sweet, and she'd been so sad on Wednesday. And, maybe, Nathan hadn't wanted an entire team of guys to try comforting her.

"Do you mind if I copy your essay to study from for our test next week?" Eva asked.

"Sure. Copier's over there." Nathan pointed to the far corner of the library.

Eva shot him another one of her brilliant smiles before heading toward it. She looked good walking away.

"Damn, you have it bad," Chris said. "You might be the one who starts drooling in the armchair. When are you going to ask her out?"

"I told you, she's not my type," Nathan said, lowering his voice. Eva should've been far enough away that she wouldn't hear, but he still wished Chris would save his comments for when she wasn't in the same room.

"I never thought I'd see you too shy to ask out a girl," Chris continued, clearly ignoring what Nathan had said before. "Is it because you want to ask her out on an actual date instead of just suggesting she meet you under the bleachers? She was all over you less than a week ago. She's not going to say no."

"I don't want to ask her out," Nathan hissed. "Now shut up. She's coming back."

Chris' grin made it clear that he didn't believe any of that. But there was no way to make him understand. If Nathan tried to explain that he couldn't date Eva because she was a literal angel, he'd sound like a lovesick fool.

"Did you get through okay?" Nathan asked as Eva returned. He wanted to slap himself immediately after. What sort of stupid question was that?

"I don't think I know how to use the photocopier," Eva admitted, chewing her bottom lip.

Maybe not a stupid question after all.

Had it been another girl, Nathan would've assumed her helplessness to be performative or a jab at him for asking. But Eva had attended a school with magic. Cassel probably hired witches that poofed duplicates into existence.

"Don't worry, Blue Eyes," Chris said. "Nate can help you."

Not if I want to get paid.

Nathan should've volunteered Chris instead.

But Eva clasped her hands and hit him with a smile that could've lit the entire room. "Really? Thanks, Nate!"

Nathan's heart skipped. How could he say no to a smile like that?

He pushed himself up from the low armchair and followed her to the corner of the library where the old copier sat gathering a sheen of dust. Most things were online.

"Let me see the essay." As he reached for it, Nathan's phone buzzed. His heart stopped. His body froze.

It had to be G. She was checking up on him.

"Do you need to get that?" Eva pointed to his pocket.

"It can wait. We gotta get you that essay."

Eva pulled the paper away, a slight frown on her face. "But it could be about your brother."

Dammit. She was right.

Guilt twisting in his stomach, Nathan took out his phone. He tapped the screen. A message appeared.

It was from Chris: *Ask her out.*

Nathan was going to strangle him.

"Everything okay?" Eva sounded genuinely concerned.

"Spammer," Nathan lied without hesitation. "Let's make some copies."

He grabbed the essay before she could take it away, and

placed it in the machine. Nothing happened when he told it to copy.

"How is Dan?" Eva asked. "Is he still on that upward swing?"

"Yeah. But that's how he normally is. Good for a few weeks, then bad for a few." Nathan discovered the problem with the copier fairly quickly. It was out of paper. "Just gotta make the most of the good ones."

"Do you go out sometimes when he's good? Other than to school, I mean."

"I do have something of a life, Eva, yes." There was spare paper in the drawer at the bottom of the copier. Nathan bent down to retrieve it. And only at that moment did he realize what Eva had just asked. "Why?"

"I wondered if you were doing something this weekend."

Was Eva asking him on a date? For a split second, Nathan started to smile. Then, his mouth clamped shut and pulled into a tight, straight line. This wasn't a good thing. It was disastrous.

The only thing worse than him falling for Eva would be her falling for him.

"Uh, I don't know," Nathan said, avoiding her eyes as he fed the paper into the machine. "Probably busy. Gotta see."

"Oh." Eva sounded disappointed.

Nathan pressed the button. The copier began printing this time.

"I was going to go visit my brother."

Nathan's head snapped toward her. Whatever he'd expected, it wasn't that.

God, I'm an idiot. Did I really think she was asking me out?

Eva's interest in him had never been romantic. She had

feathers. She could fly. Nathan was the only one at risk of falling.

"That's a big deal," Nathan acknowledged. He rubbed the back of his head, uncertain what more to say.

"I know." Eva clasped her hands as though she were praying, and she looked up at Nathan with bright, hopeful eyes. "That's why I was hoping you'd come with me."

26

EVANGELINA

"You made it!" Eva rushed toward Nathan as he approached the bus stop. Without thinking, she wrapped her arms around his waist.

He stumbled, and for a moment, she worried he'd trip over the grate in the sidewalk. But then his arms rose. They hovered over Eva's back for a moment. Nathan squeezed and pulled away.

It was very quick. But it was definitely a hug.

He smells different.

Normally the scent of herbs and spices lingered on Nathan's clothing. Today, his red sweatshirt carried a woodsy scent. Eva liked it, but it wasn't laundry detergent.

"Are you wearing cologne?" she asked.

Nathan pushed his hair back. "You don't realize when an entire football team is hitting on you, but you notice that."

A wry smile flashed on Nathan's lips, but his eyes flicked toward the bus stop, almost like he was embarrassed to hold her gaze. With his sharp, near-perfect features, the expression was charming enough to make Eva's heart race.

Was Nathan suggesting that he'd put on the cologne because of her?

No, no, that was crazy. She and Nathan were friends now; at least Eva thought they were. But he'd wanted nothing to do with her just a couple weeks earlier. He wouldn't put on cologne to impress her.

I wouldn't mind if he did though.

Eva's cheeks heated. She turned so Nathan wouldn't see that she'd started blushing for no reason.

"I wasn't sure if you'd come," Eva admitted, fiddling with the sleeve of her feather jacket as she watched cars pass on the road.

Nathan leaned against the bus stop. "How could I not when you mentioned a prison in the Cursed Woods."

Eva glanced around. They'd met half-way between their homes in a semi-residential area. A few people were outside, but no one stood close enough to eavesdrop. Humans weren't supposed to know about Ironvault. Eva shouldn't even have risked telling Nathan.

"I'm not making it up, I swear," she whispered, drawing an x over her heart.

"I know."

The bus pulled up at the corner where they stood. The doors opened.

"Shall we?" Nathan gestured for Eva to enter first.

But she froze.

The significance of the decision pressed against Eva like a weight. Her father would be furious. Irena might count it as a strike against her if she found out. And Zeke...

Eva didn't know how her brother would react. Was he angry his family hadn't visited? Or was he repentant for his crime? What would he say to her? What would she say to him?

Nathan rested his hand on Eva's back, right between where her wings connected to her shoulder blades when visible. Even through her jacket, she could feel the warmth of his palm.

It freed Eva from her sudden stasis. She turned to him.

"We don't have to go," Nathan said. "Whatever you want to do, I'm here." He smiled. It was warm and genuine. The kind of smile that could make a girl's heart melt.

Eva's brain certainly did, because her response slipped out, "Do you know what goes through a girl's head when you look at her like that?"

Nathan's eyebrows rose. Somehow, it was still Eva who felt her face heat.

"Thank you for being nice," she said, putting her hand forward to stop the bus door from closing. "But I need to see my brother."

———

Eva and Nathan sat together near the back of the bus. The proximity of the seats meant they pressed against one another at every turn. Eva tried, and failed, not to notice Nathan's muscles each time she fell against his chest. She didn't want to be attracted to her charge.

But at least it provided a momentary distraction from her thoughts about Zeke. Eva kept playing through possible scenarios in her mind. None went well.

Her leg brushed against Nathan as they went over a speed bump. His eyes flicked down, then immediately back to the window. He cleared his throat. "Why'd you ask me to come today?"

Ah, the dreaded discussion about the impending meeting. Eva's stomach turned as she admitted, "I guess I knew that I'd chicken out if I tried to go by myself."

"But why *me*?"

An excellent question, and one Eva had been turning over herself since she'd gotten the nerve to talk to Nathan on Friday. She'd wanted someone for moral support, and her options were limited. Her parents wouldn't approve, and Beatrice had been added to the list of former friends.

But Eva hadn't included Chris. She'd only asked Nathan. It wasn't just because he was her charge.

"I feel like you get it. Like you're not judging. Or not judging more than I deserve," Eva struggled to explain. "And—well—I don't know. I trust you."

Nathan's face froze as though her words had momentarily stunned him. Maybe they had. Nathan was sweeter than he pretended, but he didn't open up easily. Eva sharing so much might have made him uncomfortable.

Silence consumed them. Zeke crept back into Eva's thoughts. What if he didn't want to see her? She'd been so hung up on her own feelings, she hadn't considered—

"I brought snacks," Nathan declared suddenly. He pulled a plastic bag from the pocket of his sweatshirt. Within were dried slices of apple that had been coated in some sort of powder. They looked homemade.

Eva took a bag of mini chocolate chip cookies from her purse and waved it. "So did I."

"You started baking again?"

"They're store-bought. You noticed that I stopped baking?"

"You spent a week trying to bribe me with pastries, remember?" Nathan laughed. It sounded almost nervous. Then he held up his apples. "Want to trade?"

"Store-bought cookies for something you made? That's a pretty terrible deal for you."

"Eh, I'm not that picky. And anyway, you have to catch it." Nathan took a single apple chip out of his bag. He angled his body so that his back was to the window, and pulled back his hand as much as he could. "Open your mouth."

Eva did as instructed.

Nathan tossed the apple piece at her. It bounced off her chin and fell on her lap.

"Poor form." He shook his head. "You could've ducked and grabbed it."

"I still got it," Eva objected. She lifted it and popped it into her mouth. Sugar and cinnamon mixed with the apple. It was delicious. She smiled as she chewed.

"That's cheating. You can't eat what you don't catch. You're worse than Dan."

"You play this game with your brother?" Eva asked, pulling a cookie out of her container. She had to lean back so that half of her was in the aisle, but no one was close enough to object.

Nathan opened his mouth expectantly. It was only a short distance. But the movement of the bus messed with Eva's throw. The cookie hit his nose before falling onto the floor.

"Wow, you have terrible aim." Nathan grabbed the cookie. He dusted it off on the sleeve of his sweatshirt, blew on it, and popped it into his mouth.

"Ew. Wait! I thought we weren't supposed to eat what we didn't catch."

"That would be so wasteful. Why would you do that?" Nathan grinned. "You need to be more appreciative of your food."

The comment made Eva giggle. "You should meet my mother. The two of you would get along."

Nathan's laugh sounded unusually high. He coughed, nodded, and tossed another apple slice. It went straight into Eva's mouth.

"Good aim," she said.

"I have a lot of practice," Nathan admitted. "Dan prefers liquids most days, but he's very entertained watching me struggle to catch popcorn."

"Do you do that dressed in tights and boxers too?"

"I cannot let Dan talk to people," Nathan muttered. He tossed another apple slice without warning. "You can't be laughing, or the food will hit your face."

"Sorry," Eva apologized, but she was still smiling. She couldn't help it. She knew what Nathan was doing. "You're distracting me on purpose, aren't you you?"

"Don't be ridiculous. I just like showing off my amazing skills." Nathan grinned. It was a smile that showed all his teeth. "Unless you want to talk?"

Eva shook her head and, for a heartbeat, she lost herself in the depth of his eyes. Nathan wasn't just the most attractive boy she'd ever met, he was also the sweetest.

27
EVANGELINA

Eva clutched her purse as they approached the edge of the Cursed Woods. The wind groaned as it swept through the trees. Strange birds cooed within. Even knowing that the stories were false, a shiver ran down her spine.

"How far should I come with you?" Nathan studied the woods. The muscles pulsed in his arms, almost as though he were preparing for a fight. He glanced at Eva. There was nothing wry or disinterested in his expression. He looked almost protective.

Maybe he should be the guardian angel.

Eva had never stepped foot in the Cursed Woods before. She'd have felt better with Nathan by her side. But that wasn't realistic. Magic cloaked the woods to keep humans from exploring too deep. Nathan would lose his nerve if he tried to enter.

"Here is good. I'll find you at the Vampire's Lair when I'm done," Eva said. The themed restaurant was one of several businesses that attempted to profit off the haunted reputation of the woods. Eva wasn't a fan, but it was an iconic and obvious meeting point.

"I'll be waiting," Nathan said. He gave her one last breath-taking smile. "Don't worry, Eva. You got this."

———

A little over a mile into the Cursed Woods, the trees gave way to a high wall of smooth onyx. Colors shimmered off the dark stone, casting a rainbow of light on the surrounding forest floor. The effect was the result of the many enchantments that hid the woods hitting against the magical repellant of the prison.

Eva's chest tightened as she approached a pair of twisted alabaster gates. Beyond was Ironvault itself, a black windowless building with a single door.

"Name?" A troll stepped before the gates to block Eva's entrance. He was twice her height and three times her width. Only a fur pelt, tied around his hips, shielded his blue skin from the elements. Eva was very grateful for its presence.

"I'm Evangelina Heaven," she said, stopping before the guard and extending her hand.

The troll narrowed his already beady eyes, grunted, and raised a large, spiked club over his shoulder. "Species?"

No one usually asked that after hearing her name. Eva summoned and unfurled her wings. The white feathers picked up the rainbow of magical light reflecting from the walls.

"Don't get many of your kind here." The troll chuckled. "Come to pray for the souls of the unrepentant?"

"No, I'm here to see my brother," Eva said, feeling suddenly uncertain. "It's visiting hours now, isn't it?"

She'd called ahead on Friday evening and spoken to the warden, a werewolf who'd been surprisingly kind despite his gruff voice. She thought he'd said Sunday between twelve and three. But no other visitors appeared to be present.

"Might be visiting hours. I can never remember." The troll scratched the red stubble on his chin. "Let me just check you're cleared."

He reached behind his back, tucked his fingers underneath his pelt and brought out a clipboard.

Eva tried not to think about where it had been hidden.

"Yup, right there." The troll tapped his thumb, and then returned the clipboard to wherever it stayed. "Olivia will take you."

He shouted to someone through the gate, and a girl appeared wearing a significantly more official uniform. Olivia kept her clothes wrinkle-free, her brown hair cropped short, and her expression serious. Nothing betrayed her species, but Eva would guess werewolf. Most law enforcement officers were.

Olivia offered a curt greeting, searched Eva's purse, and patted her down before escorting her past the alabaster gates and through Ironvault's single door.

Eva followed the guard down a long corridor with dim yellow lights swinging overhead. Their steps echoed in the narrow passage. Eva tried not to think about what dangerous prisoners might be sealed within the surrounding iron cells.

"Meeting room's here." Olivia opened a door. The space beyond featured a small metal table with two chairs on opposite sides.

Olivia instructed Eva on how to sit and where to keep

her hands before walking to the door. "Your brother will be here soon. His cell is only a few floors down."

They imprisoned him under the Earth.

Even knowing the prisoners had no windows, it seemed unnecessarily cruel.

Eva tapped her fingers against the table. Her heart pounded. What was she going to say?

There was no time to figure it out. Footsteps grew louder in the passageway beyond. Then Zeke stepped into the room.

Spending over a month imprisoned had changed him. His skin had paled; his cheeks sunk in. A layer of blond stubble clung to his jaw. His blue eyes had turned lifeless and glassy. But at the sight of Eva, Zeke's old, mischievous smile appeared.

"You're here," he said, and his haunted expression returned.

The guard who'd escorted Zeke shoved him into the remaining seat. Eva's hands remained free. Zeke's had to be locked to the table, then his ankles to the floor.

Eva watched the process, mute as waves of emotion crashed through her. Excitement, sadness, anger. She didn't know what she was supposed to feel.

"You shouldn't have come, Eva. This isn't a good idea," Zeke said. "Do Mom and Dad know? Are they okay?"

Something inside Eva snapped. How could he ask that?

"Of course they're not okay, Zeke. None of us are okay," Eva said, forgetting for a moment about the guards listening by the door. "You stole from the Sanctum thanks to the job Dad helped you get. They want to take your feathers. They want to take all of our feathers. Mom and Dad are fighting. Out loud. Dad made me become a guardian angel because he thinks that'll save us somehow, and Mom keeps cleaning the kitchen."

"Probably because you're making a mess with all your stress baking," Zeke said. Then he flashed a smile.

Eva couldn't believe it. Was he trying to make a joke?

"You stole form an orphanage, Zeke! And everyone knows you did. You confessed."

"I wasn't going to deny it. Electronic trail makes me easy to catch." Zeke's tone was so casual, so indifferent. It wrenched in Eva's chest like a knife. "Let's not talk about that. Did you say you were a guardian angel?"

Eva shook her head. She wasn't letting him change the topic. She'd come all this way. He didn't get to escape what he'd done.

Or why.

"What reaction were you hoping for, Zeke?" Eva asked, hands curling into fists on the table. "Were you testing if the plan would punish you for doing something wrong? Are you satisfied now? Why couldn't you just have faith without—"

"I did have faith," Zeke snapped, and for the first time, his voice grew tense, and Eva could hear the pain. "I was trusting the plan."

"No outbursts," Olivia ordered from the door.

Eva barely glanced at the guard. She leaned closer to her brother. "What do you mean? Did you want to get caught?"

Zeke hesitated. "You won't believe me."

"Probably not. I barely believe any of this is happening."

His shoulders shook in a slight chuckle. "When you're trying to convince someone into giving you information, Eva, you're supposed to at least lie and act like you'll be on their side."

"Angels don't lie."

"You haven't met enough of us."

"So you won't tell me the truth? After I came all this way."

"How about this, I'll tell you I'm not the villain. So if you trust the plan, you don't need to know. Because I should be fine, right?"

Eva felt like she was a kid again, listening to her brother talk in circles and catching only half of what he meant. It made her head spin and her chest ache. She shouldn't have come.

"Forget the plan, Zeke. We might all lose our feathers because of you!" Eva pushed back her chair and stood.

"Wait!" Zeke's voice was so small and desperate.

Eva's chest squeezed. His eyes looked glazed and mostly dull, but deep beneath, a spark of brightness flickered that familiar blue that matched her own, a hint of her brother. He'd taught her how to tie her shoe, showed her how to make the best smores, held her hand when they crossed roads.

"I didn't steal from a charity," Zeke said. "Paradise-Shared doesn't support orphanages. It's a front."

Eva's eyebrows rose. "What are you talking about?"

"If you're staying you have to be seated," Olivia barked.

Eva returned to her position. She placed her hands flat on the table and leaned closer. Zeke did likewise.

"Someone approached me," he said. "She offered me money in exchange for a feather, but I thought it was odd."

"Why? Witches approach angels for feathers all the time."

"It wasn't a witch. It was this old angel, Adelaide Glory. I recognized her face from those farewell images the

Sanctum likes to display. She was almost a hundred, scheduled to fly into the clouds in a few days. Didn't make sense for her to be after a feather, so I played along."

"You gave away a feather?"

"I pretended to be interested, so I could find out more," Zeke corrected. "She wired partial payment upfront. I traced it back to an account connected to ParadiseShared and did some digging. The organization looks legitimate, but there's something off. Different sites and studies mention it, but they all read like they've been written by the same person. I took everything to my boss, but he didn't believe me."

"So you decided to catch the criminals yourself?" Eva couldn't believe it. "That's the opposite of trusting the plan! What did you think would happen? That you'd uncover some conspiracy and be a hero?"

"Honestly, that would've been my preferred outcome, yes. But I figured my arrest would at least force the Sanctum to investigate ParadiseShared."

Eva's chest tightened. Tears pooled in the corners of her eyes. "They're not. All Irena is doing is coming after us."

"I'm sorry. That wasn't my intention." Zeke's eyes grew heavy as he stared at his shackled wrists. He looked like Atlas, bowed by the weight of the world.

Eva squeezed his fingers quickly before the guards could see. "I know. What else can you tell me about the angel who approached you?"

"Not much," Zeke said. "She kept herself bundled up. And I thought her voice was weird. But earthly bodies do strange things as they age. Anyway, I wouldn't waste time looking for Adelaide. She flew up before my arrest. But someone flagged my transaction and reported it faster than I'd expected."

Eva's brow furrowed. "You think someone was specifically keeping tabs on the ParadiseShared account?"

"And whoever it was turned me in," Zeke confirmed. "If I were looking for the real criminal, I'd start there."

28

NATHAN

As soon as Eva vanished into the woods, Nathan took out his phone. He'd kept it together, but throughout the bus ride, his guilt had threatened to burn him from within. Every time Eva smiled at him, when she lit up with that glow, Nathan's chest ached. Her voice kept whispering in his mind: *I trust you. I trust you. I trust you.*

Why? Nathan had done nothing to earn Eva's trust. But he wanted to. Just like he wanted to deserve Eva's smile.

"I have become pathetic," Nathan informed whatever creature might've been listening near the edge of woods. But, pathetic or not, his fingers flew across his phone: *Can't do this. I'm out.*

Nathan sent the message through an app that G had used to contact him before. It might've been the worst fiscal decision he'd ever made. But eating cheap packets of ramen noodles, using garbage shampoo, and losing his phone plan would be better than feeling like shit every time Eva smiled at him. Nathan could borrow money for the necessities for Daniel until their mother returned. Kay always did eventually. And she usually brought food, courtesy of whatever man she'd left, as an apology.

Nathan's breaths came easier as he left the Cursed Woods and returned to the surrounding commercial strip.

The Vampire's Lair was a nightmare of a restaurant themed around an old urban legend. The story claimed a vampire had risen in the Cursed Woods and stalked the perimeter, drinking the blood of anyone foolish enough to come near. Given the location of Ironvault, there was probably some truth to the story.

But the myth was no excuse for the restaurant's décor. Heavy black curtains cascaded from the ceiling, encircling round booths. The intention was likely to offer customers' privacy, but in effect, the room appeared full of velvet mosquito nets.

The curtains were far from the worst of the aesthetic choices. A massive chandelier, designed to resemble vampire fangs provided most of the light. Hideous gothic knickknacks on display ranged from plastic bats to ceramic fortune tellers. A life-size, knock-off Count Dracula greeted potential customers by the door.

Nathan selected a booth near the front, leaving the curtains open so that he could see when Eva arrived.

A waiter with a powdery white face and a mop of red curls approached. Fake blood dripped from his neck, and his name tag read *Ivan the Undead*. He raised one arm straight in the air, dropped the menu before Nathan, and moaned, "Be careful, sir. You've entered the lair of the vampire. Order at your own risk."

"Please don't do the voice," Nathan requested, flicking his eyes down to the menu. Half the items included the word blood. "Do you have anything less themed?"

Ivan grinned, relaxing out of his zombie character and

bending his arms like a normal person. "Wrong place, dude. I'd say try somewhere else, but pretty much everything in this area has that problem."

"It's fine. I'm meeting someone here." Nathan flipped through the laminated pages. The menu was unnecessarily long and the prices high. Nathan had just bailed on his only source of income. "I'll just have water while I wait."

He passed the menu back to the unimpressed waiter.

29
EVANGELINA

E va hadn't brought a notebook. She hadn't expected to uncover a secret conspiracy. But she did her best to commit everything her brother said to memory before starting to say goodbye.

But Zeke squeezed her fingers quick. "Stay a bit longer. We have another twenty minutes?"

He looked to Olivia for confirmation.

"Twenty-two," she agreed.

"My charge is waiting for me," Eva said, but seeing the desperate, anxious look in her brother's eyes kept her glued to the chair.

How many visitors had Zeke gotten since his arrest? A few reporters? Maybe Farrah as she worked on the case?

"Yeah, you mentioned you were a guardian angel now," Zeke said. "Dad's attempt to save you. And himself, of course. Typical. Who said angels couldn't be selfish?" He smiled as though it were a joke. But it wasn't.

"That's not fair. Dad's scared. And it's better than Mom wanting us all to lose our feathers together."

Zeke winced. "I'm sorry. You're right. One of us should

get to keep their feathers, and it should be you. You don't deserve to be punished."

"That's not..." Eva's voice trailed. Her eyes closed. She rested her cheek against the top of one of her folded wings. She couldn't imagine life without feathers; she didn't want to be cursed to die on earth.

But she didn't want to spend an eternity without her family either.

"None of us should be punished," Eva said. "You didn't do anything wrong"

"How'd you become a guardian angel?" Zeke obviously wanted to change the subject. "I applied years ago. Did they flag me for potential heresy? I gather Irena's been keeping tabs on me for some time. Had me on some karmic angel watch list."

Eva scoffed. She could believe that. But Irena hadn't been to blame in this case. "Your application came through actually. Farrah pulled some strings, and I took your place."

"Seriously?" Given everything happening in his life, missing the chance to be a guardian angel shouldn't have fazed Zeke, but his shoulders slumped lower. "Who's Farrah? Not Dad's new assistant? I thought she was my age."

Eva's eyebrows rose. "Don't you know Farrah? She's working on your case. I thought she came to meet with you."

"Yeah. Once."

"Did you tell her about everything with ParadiseShared?"

Zeke glanced away. "I might have been annoyed that Dad hadn't come himself."

Which meant he'd been a complete jerk and done

himself no favors. It was a miracle Farrah hadn't jumped ship with everyone else.

"How'd she get the Sanctum to allow for a substitute guardian angel?" Zeke pressed, perhaps sensing that Eva had been about to scold him.

"Think it helps that the charge is a student at my new high school. I was already in the perfect position almost like—" Eva cut herself off. She'd almost said it was *part of the plan.* That would be a cruel jab that Zeke didn't need right now. "I'm sure you'd be doing a better job than I am."

"It's not dangerous, is it?"

Eva shook her head. "I'm guiding him to greatness."

"Wow. Must be some charge. What's he like?"

Memories flashed through Eva's mind. Nathan carrying his brother to bed, offering her a bite of his roasted potatoes, distracting her on the bus ride. She recalled the taste of Nathan's pasta pomodoro, thought about the way his eyelashes fluttered when he smiled.

"He's perfect," Eva said, though maybe that was a beat too far. Not even angels were perfect. "I mean, he's already great. Honestly, I'm not sure what more I'm even supposed to do."

"You have a crush," Zeke said, using the sing-song voice he'd always used to tease her. It was the most like himself he'd sounded since Eva arrived.

"I don't—" she started to object, but her cheeks grew hot. Her brother wasn't wrong. "Maybe, I do. So what? It doesn't matter."

"Are you guiding him to greatness with your tongue down his throat, then?" Zeke mimed a ridiculous, rather sloppy caricature of what that might look like.

Eva swore she heard a giggle. But when she glanced over her shoulder, the guards both stared at the wall.

"Don't be gross. We're angels," Eva objected. She wanted to kick her brother under the table to get him to stop, but that would get her in trouble. And, despite the shackles on his limbs and small, dark room, Zeke teasing her felt almost normal. When he grinned, the spark returned to his eyes.

"Angels can kiss people, Eva. Be glad I didn't ask if you were guiding him by a different appendage."

One guard, Olivia, definitely snorted that time.

"Nothing like that is happening," Eva hurried to clarify that for both her brother and the guards. "Nathan's human."

"Oh he has a name?" Zeke kept grinning. "What does it matter if he's human? It's not illegal to date outside your species. Unless the Sanctum's laws have changed, in which case I have a lot more crimes to atone for."

"He's my charge."

"Thought your job was finished and he was already great?"

Eva's brow furrowed. Could that be true? Maybe her role as a guardian angel had been about her and not Nathan. Maybe what she'd really needed to do was recognize how incredible he was. It would be unusual, but the Fates gave strange assignments at times.

But that wouldn't change anything.

"Nathan's not immortal though. I mean, he'll die eventually, and I'll fly back to our realm when the time comes and what? Just never see him again? That sounds horrible. Besides, bonding with a human has a tendency to go poorly. And given our current situation, the optics..." Eva left it hanging.

She expected some moment of contrition. After all, the

reason Eva needed to be extra careful was a direct result of Zeke's actions. Instead, her brother laughed.

It was warm and rich, and somewhat of a relief to hear. Until Zeke spoke. "You always jump like ten steps ahead. You're worried about bonding when you haven't even kissed him?"

Eva hated that her hands had to stay on the table. She wanted desperately to bury her face because she was certain it was red.

Zeke had a point. Eva didn't even know if Nathan liked her, and she'd skipped ahead to imagining how it would be when he died at the end of their marriage.

"Remember when you thought you and your friend Max were destined to be soulmates," Zeke continued. "How'd that go?"

They'd dated for a month. Then Max had kissed Eva at a dance, and it had felt like kissing her cousin.

"You know what I'd do if I was you?" Zeke asked, leaning closer.

"Go on several dates that ended in disaster and then complain to my sister while she's trying to bake?"

Olivia giggled again. Eva appreciated that it wasn't at her expense this time.

"Hey, when I'm an irin, and you can't talk to me, you're going to miss hearing all those stories," Zeke said. His voice was still light and teasing. But the spark dimmed in his eyes, leaving a haunted expression.

"Zeke, don't—" The tears returned. Eva closed her eyes, trying to hold them back. She would miss her brother's stories, and she'd miss him, and her parents. Every day for eternity if they lost their feathers.

That couldn't happen. Eva wouldn't let it.

She sniffed and forced a smile. "Fine, tell me what you'd do?"

30
NATHAN

Nathan tapped his fingers against his glass, leg bouncing up and down. His eyes flicked between the window and his phone.

He'd been at the Vampire's Lair for over an hour. Waiting. Both for Eva's return and for a response from his benefactor.

How is G going to react when she sees I've quit?

Nathan shouldn't have rushed to send the message. If she got angry, she might go back to the apartment. She could hurt Daniel.

I'm being paranoid.

Daniel wasn't in the apartment. Mrs. Taylor, a sweet older lady who lived on the floor below, had agreed to watch him. And G hadn't seemed violent. If anything, her round face and curls suggested the opposite.

Ivan the Undead returned. He did his zombie-schtick until Nathan ordered some French fries, the cheapest thing on the menu.

Knockoff Dracula cackled as the door opened.

Eva stepped into the Vampire's Lair. No one would

guess she'd walked over a mile through the dense forest. No twigs or leaves stuck in her hair. No sweat coated her skin. Her feather jacket remained white. She looked perfect, if slightly nervous.

Her eyes landed on Nathan. In an instant, she relaxed. A huge smile spread across Eva's face.

Time stopped. The echoes of Nathan's heart thumped in his ears.

She's beautiful

That wasn't the issue though. Nathan knew other attractive girls. This was different.

He liked Eva. A lot.

And that was very, very dangerous.

Eva ran over. Instead of taking the chair opposite Nathan, she slid into the curved semi-circular bench that surrounded half the table.

The curtains shut behind her.

Eva wrapped her arms around Nathan's neck. Despite her visit to Ironvault, her hair still smelled like lavender. Nathan closed his eyes and breathed in the scent for a second before he realized what he was doing.

Shit. Shit. Shit.

Whatever his feelings, this had to be platonic.

"You seem happy," Nathan said, extracting himself from her hug. "Things went well with your brother?"

"Sort of." Eva shrugged and leaned back on the seat. "Zeke is different, but he hasn't changed. Does that make sense?"

"A bit."

"He's always been smarter than me, and kind of an idiot at the same time." Eva's smile was small and sad. She addressed her statements to her purse, fiddling with the zipper. "But Zeke is a good person. He shouldn't be in there."

"Probably not," Nathan agreed. He didn't know Eva's brother, or the situation, but from the little he knew about Ironvault, it was a hellhole. Magical convicts had to be kept isolated, with as little access to their powers as possible. His mother never spoke about her time there, but sometimes she'd whisper in her sleep about the black walls. Kay had spent only a couple nights, not a month.

Eva turned to him. There was something curious in her eyes. "My brother wanted to give me advice about you."

That caught Nathan off guard.

"Still trying to figure out how to make me great?" he guessed, laughing nervously.

Since accepting that he and Eva were friends, Nathan had done his best to avoid the topic of greatness. He'd prefer not to know what vision of Eva's he was thwarting. But now that Nathan had officially dropped G as his benefactor, there was no risk in finding out.

Eva inched closer, still staring at him with that curious expression. "I think I'm done with that actually."

Ouch. Not that Nathan could blame her when he'd gone to great efforts to prove his lack of capability. He should've kept taking the money after all.

"Probably wise," Nathan said. "It was a hopeless cause." He forced another laugh, far too aware of Eva's leg pressing against his own.

"No, you're just already great," Eva said. She reached out and rested her hand on Nathan's cheek.

Warmth radiated from her fingertips. The skin where she brushed his cheekbone tingled. Nathan's breath caught.

It wasn't like he'd never had girls touch his face. Shit

they'd touched a lot more. But never with quite such an effect.

What is Eva doing?

Nathan should push her away, laugh, and tell her she'd clearly lost it if she thought he was great. But Eva's eyes shone with sincerity, and her whole body glowed in the curtained booth. The effect was quite literally stunning.

"Why'd you put on cologne to meet me?" Eva asked. Her eyes fluttered to her purse, then back to him. The expression was shy, but that curious look was still in her eyes.

Nathan finally recognized it. He'd seen girls look at him like that before, though perhaps not as sweetly. And given her sudden proximity, and her fingers on his skin, it seemed an obvious guess.

"Do you want to kiss me, Eva?"

Nathan didn't know what came over him, but instead of retreating, he found himself leaning closer as he asked. Their legs pressed against one another, then their chests, until their faces were barely an inch apart. Nathan smelled the lavender in her hair once more.

He held his breath, waiting for her to answer or to push him away and tell him he'd lost his mind.

She did neither.

Eva closed the small space between them. Her lips pressed softly onto his. The kiss was light, sweet, angelic. She tasted like sugar and cinnamon and everything Nathan wanted.

Then she pulled away, lips parted and blue eyes shining up at him with a look that managed to be hungry and soft and desperate all at once.

And just like that, Nathan's concerns about keeping things platonic vanished.

31
EVANGELINA

Zeke should never be trusted to offer romantic advice. He'd told Eva to *just go for it*. Most likely, she'd kiss Nathan and realize that she'd built everything up in her head. Then she could stop worrying about falling in love with a human.

But Zeke had been wrong. Eva had made a serious mistake. Because kissing Nathan was nothing like kissing Max.

The feeling of Nathan's lips on hers had sent a shiver through Eva's entire body. A heat had risen in her chest. And she'd known that, if he wanted to, Nathan could set her entire soul on fire. People talked about having their hearts stolen, but it wouldn't be theft. Eva would rip hers out and give it to Nathan if she wasn't careful.

But this couldn't happen. At least not now. Not while Zeke's trial—and her family's fate—loomed in the background. Eva couldn't risk—

Her thoughts vanished as Nathan pulled her back toward him.

The fire Eva had feared sparked in her chest as his lips

found hers again. Nathan's hand slipped into her hair. The other wrapped around her waist, holding her against him. His body was all limbs and muscles. The heat radiating from him made her tremble.

This couldn't be anything. Not now. Maybe not ever.

But if Eva only got to kiss Nathan once, it might as well count.

His fingers tangled in her hair and crept lower, following the curves of her hips. She traced the lines of his face, feeling the smooth, freshly-shaved skin along his jaw. Her elbow knocked the table. Eva had a faint awareness of her legs complaining about their current angle, but she was too intoxicated by the scent of Nathan's cologne to care.

At some point, he must have scooped her and moved her so that she was on top of him. Because Eva was an angel. Uncomfortable or not, surely, she wouldn't have subconsciously repositioned herself to straddle Nathan.

His fingers brushed over her thighs. She could feel them through her jeans. The scent of his cologne made her giddy. His tongue met hers. He pulled at her lower lip, and a sound escaped Eva, soft and high, somewhere between a whimper and a moan.

A trill came from her purse. The guardian phone.

Eva ignored it. She didn't want to take her lips from Nathan because the moment she did, she knew what would happen.

The curtain that had half closed when Eva entered stirred.

"Here are your—" a boy's voice began. "Oh snap."

And, just like Eva feared, reality crashed back in.

32
NATHAN

Eva sprang off Nathan faster than he'd thought possible. He caught a glimpse of her face turning bright red before she covered it, looking for all the world like she wanted to sink into the seat.

Nathan bit back a smile. He had to assume that making out in dark restaurant booths was not typical behavior for the angel. It wasn't exactly common for him either. He'd seen how his mother's love for his father had consumed her. Even after she'd lost her feathers, hell even after his death, Kay had never looked at anyone else the way she'd looked at Shane Fisher.

Nathan hadn't intended to let that happen to him. He'd fooled around with girls at school, sure, but he'd never let it get serious, never let himself get attached.

This was different. Kissing Eva felt like lightning coursing through his veins, setting his skin alight everywhere her fingers brushed. She'd moaned against his lips, and it had been the best sound Nathan had ever heard.

She likes me.

There was no way Eva went around making out with guys she didn't like, not like that.

But that made everything about this infinitely worse.

Ivan the Undead cleared his throat. He'd pulled back the curtain and arrived with Nathan's fries. If catching people making out in the booth bothered him, the waiter didn't show it.

"Shockingly common here," Ivan said, resting down the fries. "Though most people close the curtains the whole way. Can't say I understand the appeal of being able to see the décor outside. But my girlfriend seems to love this place too. Warning you in advance I'm coming back with another menu."

The waiter shut the curtain. Nathan leaned over and pulled it back open before he did something stupid again.

Eva stared at him. Their kiss had done more to affect her appearance than her trek through the Cursed Woods. Eva's cheeks remained flushed, her lips swollen, and her hair was finally messy.

Nathan liked it. He liked the fact that he'd caused it even more—No, he didn't.

I can't look at her.

Nathan searched desperately for a distraction, or at least something to say. But there was only one thing that kept coming to his mind.

I have to tell her.

Eva had just kissed an irin. That had to be sacrilegious for an angel.

Nathan opened his mouth, tried, and failed to find the words. Luckily, the sudden cooing of a bird saved him.

Eva grabbed her purse and produced a large, clunky device.

"Is that a phone?" Nathan asked, relieved to have something to focus on that wasn't Eva or the pounding in his chest when he looked at her.

"Something like that." Eva shoved the device back into her purse before he could catch more than a glimpse. "I'm sorry, but I have to go downtown. Like, right now, which is horrible because you waited all this time for me. But you could come, maybe? I liked having your company on the ride before."

Her voice was high and nervous. She kept glancing from Nathan to her purse to the door.

Nathan wanted desperately to say yes. But that desire was precisely the problem.

"I shouldn't," he said. "It's already getting late, and I've got to get back for Daniel."

"I understand." Eva smiled in a way that suggested she genuinely meant it. She grabbed her purse and smoothed down her hair. Her face was still flushed. "I'm really sorry. We should talk later."

Nathan nodded, but his stomach threatened to dispel his earlier snacks. He knew what talk meant.

He'd finally have to tell her the truth. And Eva was going to hate him when he did.

33
EVANGELINA

Eva arrived at Irena's office out of breath. Even angels had physical limitations. But every time she'd attempted to walk after getting off the subway, the guardian phone had started chirping again.

This time, Eva had little doubt what the device wanted her to report.

The entire ride over, her kiss with Nathan had replayed in her mind. It was a good thing he hadn't taken Eva up on the offer to accompany her. If Nathan had been beside her, with his fluttering lashes and wry smiles, Eva might have lost her resolve and kissed him again.

Was that what the phone expected her to say?

I kissed my charge to see if I was in danger of falling for him. Turns out, I already have. Also, we got caught by the waiter.

Eva would evaporate from embarrassment before she got all of that out. And that would be the best ending she could hope for. Because if Irena heard the truth, she might pluck Eva's feathers herself.

"You're here!" Maddie leaped up as Eva approached. The nymph was taller than she appeared when sitting on her stool, but naturally thin. Her arm almost knocked over the bowl of chocolates on her desk.

"Send Miss Heaven in." Irena's voice boomed through a system on her assistant's phone. "Now!"

Maddie squeaked and gave Eva an apologetic look.

Eva hurried through the glass door and into the office. But she didn't see what Irena could be upset about this time. True, Eva had ignored the guardian phone's first chirp, but that couldn't have added more than a few seconds to her journey. Irena just had an unrealistic sense of how long public transportation took in Castor's Grove.

"I'm sorry for keeping you waiting," Eva said, hoping that a preemptive apology might soothe the karmic angel's mood.

It did not. Irena stood before her desk, back straight and arms crossed. The shoulder pads of her dark green suit rose like horns, and her teeth ground with such fury that Eva could hear the enamel scraping from across the room.

"I imagine that you're waiting for an update? I have one," Eva said. She'd thought about what she could say on her trip over—at least when she hadn't accidentally started fantasizing about Nathan. And maybe she did have something else worth mentioning.

Irena arched a thin brow.

"I think I've succeeded in my task."

Irena's teeth-grinding stopped. "I beg your pardon?"

"My charge, Nathan Ward," Eva explained, words coming faster than she intended, "is an incredibly talented cook. He's an excellent brother. He's considerate. There's nothing I can do to improve him. He's already great, and I think the Fates are testing our ability to recognize it. My job is done."

Irena stared in a slack-jawed disbelief. Then, suddenly,

a laugh burst forth. It was bold and deep and so powerful that her whole body shook from the force.

That was unexpected. Eva didn't think she'd ever heard Irena laugh before.

"I can't tell if you're trying to be clever, or if you're just foolish, Miss Heaven." Irena wiped a tear from the corner of her eye. Despite her fit of laughter, her voice remained sharp. "Even I know that if your work as a guardian angel was finished, you wouldn't still have the phone."

"What?" Eva's eyebrows rose. Irena hadn't mentioned that. Would the device implode when Eva completed her assignment?

"You haven't succeeded at anything. All you've done is once again fail to comport yourself in a manner befitting your station."

Oh no. A cold dread crept over Eva. Irena knew about the kiss.

"It's not technically against the law," Eva said, addressing the defense to her sneakers.

"Just because something isn't illegal doesn't mean it isn't ill advised. Honestly, I thought I'd explained your situation clearly last time. Then I hear that you completely disregarded my warning and visited your brother. I cannot imagine what possessed you."

Eva's brow furrowed. "You're upset because I spoke with Zeke?"

"Your brother stole hundreds of thousands of dollars. He's twelve days from excommunication. And you go visit him. How will that information look to the judge?"

"Like I'm a sister who cares about her brother?"

Irena's nostrils flared. "No, it will look like you're an angel who condones immorality."

"But that's not true," Eva struggled to defend herself. She hadn't expected Irena to know about her visit to Zeke. "You're the prosecutor. You don't have to spin it like that."

"On the contrary, Miss Heaven. It is my job to present it in the worst possible light."

Eva didn't understand what was happening. Why would the guardian phone have wanted her to report a visit to her brother to Irena?

It wouldn't.

"Did you send an alert to the guardian phone so that I would come here, and you could lecture me about visiting Zeke?"

Irena bristled, straightening her jacket. "It is within my purview as your supervisor on this assignment to send alerts through the phone as well."

"But shouldn't they pertain to guardian angel business?"

"I'd say jeopardizing your position by visiting a criminal falls under that descriptor," Irena snapped, but there was something defensive about her tone.

She'd exploited a gray area. Given the condescending manner in which Irena lectured about timeliness and honesty, her using a loophole to control Eva's movement felt particularly grating.

"Do you even know what Zeke's defense is?" Eva asked, finding herself more annoyed than repentant.

Irena's eyes narrowed. "I certainly hope you're not suggesting that there's an acceptable reason to steal money that the Sanctum had allocated for charity, Miss Heaven."

"No, of course not," Eva said. She shouldn't expect empathy or help from Irena. The karmic angel had been tracking Zeke. She'd compiled suspicions of heresy, evidence of his theft, and notes on his confessions, including any claims he put forth on his behalf. She should already know to look into ParadiseShared.

So why wasn't she?

34
EVANGELINA

"She wasn't too harsh, was she?" Maddie grimaced as she saw Eva's expression. "Don't take it personally. She's like that sometimes. But truly, she means well."

Eva didn't think Irena had any kind intentions, but she smiled. "How did someone as nice as you end up working for her?"

"I worked for a friend of hers before, and I think I impressed Ms. Elysium. She offered me a job," Maddie said.

"She poached you?"

"I wanted to transfer. My previous boss moved to a smaller department. There's not a lot of upward mobility for non-angels in the Sanctum. Best we can do is hope to be an assistant somewhere interesting. The karmic department suits me." Maddie gave a nervous giggle. "I'm probably not as nice as you think."

There was something guilty in her tone. Was it because of her boss, or something else?

"Can I have a chocolate?" Eva asked.

"Of course!" Maddie pushed the bowl to the edge of her desk. "Take as many as you want."

"Thanks!" Eva pretended to search for a specific chocolate. "Ms. Elysium was really upset that I visited my brother. Do you know how she found out?"

Maddie splashed her fingers into the pool of water that naturally sat on the back of her hand. The guilt grew increasingly obvious in her expression.

"Does the guardian phone have a tracking ability?" Eva guessed

Maddie confessed at once. "I'm so sorry. Ms. Elysium told me to watch for if you went to Ironvault. I had to tell her! It's my job."

"I understand," Eva promised, keeping her voice soft. "Is there anything else she has you monitoring?"

"Like what?" Maddie's brow furrowed. She lowered her voice. "I know I've helped Farrah a bit more than I should, but I'm really not supposed to share information about your brother."

"No, I'm sorry. I don't want to get you in trouble," Eva said. She'd been thinking about the list on the guardian phone. But if Irena had seen that, she'd likely have called Eva in ages ago. "Thanks for the chocolate."

Eva pulled one from the bowl and flashed the orange wrapper toward the assistant.

The elevator waited on the fifth floor. Eva stepped inside. She didn't push the button that would take her to the exit on the ground floor. If Eva was already in the Sanctum, there was something else she needed to investigate.

———

A queasy feeling turned in Eva's stomach the moment the elevator passed beneath the earth. The buildings of the Sanctum Headquarters shared a single, massive subterranean level. Primarily, the space stored mountains of old paperwork and other seldom used, but necessary supplies. However, Cyrus had been temporarily *relocated* while they searched for a smaller office for him now that his staff had downsized.

In reality, the Sanctum wanted the archangel hidden so that his colleagues didn't have to suffer the guilt of interacting with him while they determined his fate.

Eva passed a pair of dark prison cells set in one of the distant walls. She refused to turn and acknowledge the shimmering metal door. Zeke would have spent a night or two within before his official charge came. It was unnecessarily cruel making Cyrus walk past them every day.

Whispers of conversation came from behind a large pile of boxes.

"And you're absolutely certain?" Farrah's voice was soft.

A male voice, which Eva didn't recognize, responded. "Already told Ms. Elysium I was."

Eva drew closer and found her father's assistant standing beside a short man with graying hair and a small, upturned nose.

Half of Farrah's dark curls had tangled. Fingerprints smudged her glasses, and her shirt had come untucked from her pencil-neck skirt. At the sight of Eva, she jumped and hurried forward.

"What're you doing here? Your dad's already gone home."

That wasn't a good sign. Cyrus had been finding tasks to distract himself with busywork. If he'd run out, he might start cleaning the kitchen alongside his wife.

"I came to see you, actually," Eva said.

The unfamiliar man watched her. His sharp green eyes sat a bit too close together over a hooked nose, giving him the appearance of a bird of prey that had donned a brown bowler hat and matching suit.

"Hyde Leonard." He introduced himself with a pointy-toothed smile and extended his hand. "Defense Attorney. You must be Evangelina Heaven."

Mr. Leonard dragged Eva's name out, turning it into a sort of song. She didn't care for it, but she shook his hand.

"I didn't think Zeke had a defense attorney," Eva said. They weren't typically used in angelic courts for fear their presence aroused the judge's suspicion. If the accused had a clear conscience and trusted the plan, why should they need someone else to speak for them? Farrah had taken charge of the paperwork and mundane details of Zeke's case, but she wouldn't say anything in court unless called upon.

"Might want to look into hiring one," Mr. Leonard said, offering another smile. "I'm an acquaintance of your father."

Something about the attorney's demeanor made Eva quite certain that was a lie.

"That won't be necessary, thank you, Mr. Leonard," Farrah said, shooting him a look from the corner of her eye. "I appreciate you meeting with me."

The dismissal was clear, but Mr. Leonard didn't leave. His eyes continued to study Eva. "You're a pretty thing. Jury would love you. Shame it's an angelic court. I've heard your judges aren't so easily swayed."

Eva pulled the edges of her jacket tighter. The attorney's gaze made her uncomfortable, but she didn't want to be rude either. He might've been trying to offer her a compliment.

"No, never mind. Can't put her on the stand," Mr. Leonard declared, chuckling and turning to Farrah. "She'd never be able to lie. Emotions are written on her face. You're going to have to be able to take an old man ogling you a bit without panicking out in the real world, sweetheart."

That last bit of advice was addressed to Eva again.

Farrah muttered something to the ceiling before plastering on a smile. "Thank you for your advice. Eva won't be testifying. No one wants her anywhere close to Zeke's trial."

"Smart move," Mr. Leonard agreed.

Eva fought to keep her face expressionless. She preferred to give people the benefit of the doubt, but she didn't like Mr. Leonard or his assessment of her.

And she didn't like what Farrah had said either.

"I think I might be very helpful for Zeke's trial, actually," Eva said. "We need to talk about ParadiseShared."

———

Eva waited until Mr. Leonard had left before giving a full overview of her visit with Zeke. Well, the parts relevant to his case. She omitted mentioning her brother's curiosity about her guardian angel job.

Farrah sat behind the fold-out table that had become her desk. Despite being shoved into a basement, she cared enough to have a second chair for visitors.

Eva felt both more relaxed and more animated sitting to tell her story. Her hands moved as she explained. It was difficult not to get excited. This could be the breakthrough Zeke's case needed.

Farrah's face was unreadable until the end at which

point she sighed, stood, and crossed to a filing cabinet a few feet away. She grabbed a large stack of papers and returned, dropping them before Eva with a thud.

"The Sanctum keeps meticulous records," Farrah said. "There are no secrets or conspiracies. Any information on the charity is here."

Eva's eyes widened at the mountain of paperwork. "You already read through all of this?"

Farrah nodded. "Your brother may not have shared his theories with me, but Maddie let me see some of Irena's files. Zeke flagged the company to several angels in his department and gave the same story about Adelaide Glory to the Powers who arrested him. But there's no proof for any of it. Adelaide was an archangel with an impeccable record. She may have signed off on ParadiseShared, but it was investigated and assessed separately. Plus, the charity has a web presence, images, reviews. Your brother's right that many of them sound similar, but I'd guess that's a translation issue."

"Why aren't you reading the originals?"

"Because none are available," Farrah admitted, rubbing her temples. "It's an international agency. Everything online about them has already been translated to English."

Eva's chest tightened. Had Zeke made a mistake?

No, her brother might've been a moron when it came to relationships, but he was brilliant otherwise.

"Zeke's not wrong about this. There's evidence here," Eva said, gesturing to the massive stack of paperwork. "We just have to find it. Who turned him in? We can start with that."

Farrah's eyes flashed to the stack of files, which reached almost to her head. She drummed her fingers against the fold-out table.

"It's in the records, right?" Eva pressed, not under-standing Farrah's silence. "You must've come across it."

"It is in there," Farrah agreed. She licked her lips, then pulled at her frizzing hair. "And it's not a secret. You'll find it if you look, so you might as well know."

Eva's breath caught. What had Farrah uncovered?

"It was me, Eva. I'm the one who turned in your brother."

35
EVANGELINA

"No, that's not possible," Eva said. She waited for her father's assistant to laugh or say that was a lie.

But Farrah didn't.

Eva shook her head. She couldn't believe it. This whole time, she'd thought Farrah had been the one member of her father's staff who'd stuck by them out of loyalty. She'd thought Farrah genuinely cared about them. But that hadn't been it at all.

"Are you helping us because you feel guilty?" Eva's voice sounded small and scared. She wanted Farrah to say no, to say that she was doing it because she believed the Heavens, even Zeke, were good people.

"Of course, I feel guilty," Farrah said, leaning over the table. Dark circles showed beneath her eyes. She needed to sleep. "I noticed suspicious movement in the accounts, so I flagged it. But I wasn't trying to get your entire family excommunicated. Especially not an innocent kid."

"I'm not a kid," Eva snapped. Her body trembled. She'd really thought Farrah believed in them.

How naïve am I?

"Why were you even checking the ParadiseShared account?" Eva demanded. "That wasn't your job." Cyrus oversaw finances for environmental initiatives outside of the city. His assistant would only need to look into a charity if directly ordered.

"I overheard something, so I—" Farrah cut off. She pulled her fingers through her curls, but it only made them wilder. "I thought your brother had made a mistake. Not that he'd stolen money on purpose. I just wanted to impress the Sanctum by catching it. It's not like my dream was to stay your father's assistant."

Eva's eyes narrowed. "Who did you overhear?"

"Irena," Farrah admitted. "She'd already caught the discrepancy. If I hadn't called it in, she would have. I thought that would be worse. Honestly, I—" She broke off, breath suddenly ragged.

But was her distress an act?

"So what, you just happened to overhear Irena Elysium talking to herself about turning in Zeke?"

"No, she was on the phone. Outside the Sanctum."

"That's convenient."

"Are you accusing me of something, Eva?"

Was she? Zeke assumed that whoever had turned him in had been keeping tabs on the ParadiseShared account. But what if Farrah was telling the truth? Zeke hadn't considered that he'd already attracted the Sanctum's suspicion.

Eva's stomach twisted. Her skin crawled. She needed air. She needed the sky. "I can't be down here."

She turned and fled.

———

Farrah caught Eva just as she reached the elevator. The assistant had her large bag flung over one shoulder. She stopped the door from closing and stepped inside.

"Let me a give you a lift home," Farrah offered.

Eva crossed her arms. "I can take a bus."

"So help me," Farrah muttered, staring at the ceiling. "Your eyes are red and puffy. You went from talking to your brother to dealing with Irena to getting upset with me." She sounded apologetic about that last part. "I can't let you walk off on your own."

"Follow me then." Eva sounded like a petulant child. She didn't care. Her chest ached. Everything felt confused.

Farrah muttered something again. It almost sounded like a curse, but an angel wouldn't do that. She pulled a stack of papers out of her bag. "If you come with me, you can look through these. It's everything I could fit in here on ParadiseShared."

———

Eva shifted her legs, trying to get comfortable in the small car as she flipped through the documents. Pages showed proposals for funding, applications for grants, and approval letters all related to ParadiseShared. For an individual person, the numbers discussed might've constituted a small fortune. But given the scope of the Sanctum's wealth, the donations could've been offered without much scrutiny.

"How's your guardian angel assignment going?" Farrah attempted small talk as she fiddled with the car's cooling system. It appeared to have two settings: ice box and sauna. She'd settled on the former.

Eva shrugged, trying not to think of Nathan. She

focused on the documents instead. Farrah had circled Adelaide Glory's name each time it appeared. That had to mean she hadn't completely dismissed Zeke's claims.

"Maddie mentioned you got one of the new guardian devices. My Mom had a prototype when I was a kid," Farrah said. "Can I see it?"

Eva pulled the clunk of metal out of her purse and waved it without looking up. According to the files, Adelaide Glory had overseen the Sanctum's Global Charitable Division. Once ParadiseShared had been vetted, her stamp of approval was the only one needed to secure the donations. Everyone else who'd signed documents would have been following her orders.

But what would an archangel, set to ascend in only a few days, want with one of Zeke's feathers?

"This is cool," Farrah said, a bit too enthusiastically given the guardian phone's design. She took the device from Eva and tapped the screen. Nathan's picture appeared. "Wait! Is that your charge? No one mentioned he was so— uh, photogenic."

Eva pulled her hair over her face, hoping to hide any hint of a blush. She really didn't want to get distracted by Nathan's *photogenic-ness* right now. Her focus needed to be on Adelaide Glory.

"If an archangel sinned and started losing their feathers, do you think they'd risk trying to ascend? They wouldn't be able to fly."

"I think they'd manage with only a few feathers missing." Farrah's eyes flicked between the guardian phone and the traffic ahead. She kept tapping, perhaps hoping the device would do something.

"But it wouldn't just be a few feathers," Eva said. "It would be all of them."

Farrah snorted. "Only if you believe the propaganda."

Eva looked up from the documents. Farrah's attention had returned to the road now that the light had turned green. "You think someone losing their feathers could ascend?"

"No, of course not. I just meant that I don't think losing one or two feathers means you're doomed to become an irin," Farrah tried to explain, staring through the windshield. "Not even angels are perfect. We can slip. It doesn't mean we're destined to fall."

"That's heresy," Eva whispered, or close to it at least. This suddenly felt like a conversation with her brother.

"It's reality. I've seen it," Farrah said. She stared at the road, but her eyes appeared glazed, like she'd lost herself suddenly in a memory.

Does she mean—?

Eva must've been misunderstanding. "You've seen an angel lose one of their feathers?"

"Three. One for each stab."

Eva blinked. Farrah had to be messing with her. "Angels don't stab people. And you can't lose just some of your feathers."

Farrah's smile grew sad. She lifted her hand and pressed the guardian phone to Eva's head. "Give me a feather, or I shoot."

"A bullet won't hurt an angel."

"But what if it was pointed at someone else. What if it was a kid? Would you be wrong to give away a feather?"

Eva pursed her lips, shuffling the papers to keep them from slipping from her lap as they stopped again. Zeke used to pose hypotheticals to her all the time.

He really should've spoken more to Farrah when she visited him. They might get along too well.

"It's an absurd scenario," Eva objected, crossing her arms over the papers. She stared out the window, partly to hide the fact that she had no idea how to respond. A feather could be corrupted and used to create a new plague. Thousands could die. But did that mean Eva would sacrifice a child in the moment?

"You're right. I'm sorry." Farrah rested the guardian phone in the car's cup holder under the radio. "I just think that maybe those us who come here aren't as pure as we believe. Like, maybe we're the angels who need to learn, just like the humans. So, one mistake shouldn't be a death sentence. That's why—I really wouldn't have reported your brother if I'd realized, Eva. And if there was a way to save him—"

"I could testify," Eva said. The idea had been shifting through her mind ever since Mr. Leonard claimed it would be a bad idea. "I could support Zeke's claims about ParadiseShared, or I could at least provide a character witness to prove that he believed he was doing the right thing."

Beep.

Eva's eyes flicked to the guardian phone. That was a different noise. Maybe it had been the car.

Farrah's lips pursed. She turned toward Ladybug Park, approaching the Heavens' residence. "Last time I saw you meet with Irena, you ran out close to tears. She'll eat you alive."

"Not if she thinks I'm doing a good job as a guardian angel."

"Are you?" Farrah parked in the driveway. "What's your charge great at so far?"

In the cup holder, the phone's screen remained visible.

The infuriating device evidently didn't distinguish between voices because it flashed at once to the answer.

"Don't look at that!" Eva sprang for the phone without remembering to disconnect the seatbelt. Papers flew from her lap onto the floor. She grabbed the device just as the belt jolted her back. Her eyes went to a new bullet point at the bottom of the list.

No, no, no, no, no.

"Gee, you're doing that good a job, huh?" Farrah evidently had no problem with sarcasm. She rolled her eyes, unbuckled, and bent over to gather the papers Eva had dropped. "Are you going to help?"

"Uh huh." Eva's her eyes remained glued to the device. Why had it felt the need to create an official record that declared Nathan Ward great at kissing?

I am so dead if Irena sees this.

Criminal offense or not, there was no way the Sanctum encouraged guardian angels to make out with their charges.

Beep. The phone vibrated in Eva's hand. Something flashed in the top of the screen. A little red circle with numbers within. Eva had missed it before. She pressed it, and the display grew bigger.

Farrah shoved the papers onto Eva's lap. "Look, unless you've built an incredible amount of good will with Irena, I don't see how—" She broke off as she saw the phone's screen. "That's a countdown. That means your assignment is going to end—"

"In twelve days," Eva finished. "Exactly when Zeke's trial takes place."

And the phone had started beeping when Eva mentioned testifying. That couldn't be a coincidence.

36
NATHAN

On Monday afternoon, Nathan found himself at a cafe waiting for Evangelina for the second time in two days.

At least there was no theme at The Purple Porcupine. Other than a few cushions and a single painting, the cafe hadn't taken its name too seriously. Given that it was only a block away from Dashmoor, it also kept its prices low enough to entice students.

Of course, even affordable was outside of Nathan's budget now. He ordered the cheapest thing on the menu, a black coffee, and pulled out his history textbook. His eyes raced over the lines without reading them.

He should bail, pretend to get sick. It would only be half a lie. Nathan's stomach was in knots.

But he couldn't leave. Mainly because Chris had taken it upon himself to guard the door. Nathan's friend slouched near the window, baseball hat poking out from behind his bag. Sweat slicked his hair to his forehead while further back the strands sprouted upward like weeds.

Why'd he have to be there when Eva invited me?

Chris claimed he was just in the mood for cake, but it was obvious that he thought Nathan was so much of a wuss he'd run from a date with a girl if he didn't have a chaperone.

Which was partly true. But only because Nathan knew that, while Eva might like him now, it wouldn't last long.

He attempted reading once more. The caffeine did nothing to calm his nerves. Nathan tapped his foot, and his knee slapped the underside of the table. There was always a downside to long legs.

His phone buzzed. A familiar sense of dread shot through Nathan. But it was unfounded. G had already accepted—or rejected, it was open to interpretation—Nathan's resignation: *You'll be back. Whatever romance you're envisioning won't happen. She'll never talk to you again if you tell her the truth, and you're not the type to trick her into your bed. Call me when you remember I'm your best option.*

Nathan didn't know which aspect of the reply chilled him more: the correct assumption that he'd fallen for Eva, or the certainty that he'd betray her again.

This new message came from Chris: *The eagle has landed.*

Nathan's brow furrowed. What did that mean?

"Do you know Chris is sitting by the door?" Eva's voice almost made Nathan knock over his coffee. She pulled out a chair and sat on the opposite side of the table. Blonde hair fell in loose waves over her shoulders. Beneath the feather jacket, a blue top emphasized the brightness of her eyes.

Nathan's heart raced. He felt a brief twinge of regret that he hadn't chosen a booth. Eva might've sat beside him like at The Vampire's Lair, and maybe she would've—

No, dumbass, you specifically didn't choose a booth.

"Chris is a regular here. He really likes the cake," Nathan

said, engrossing himself in the menu to avoid staring at the angel before him. "Do you want some cake? My treat."

Idiot. Why was he offering to pay? Even if he managed to get a part-time job for the next few weeks while Daniel was on the upswing, he'd still struggle to cover their expenses. And buying Eva cake wouldn't make her any less horrified to learn she'd kissed an irin.

"That's so sweet," Eva said. A smile started to spread across her face. But she cut it short, shook her head, and looked down at her own menu. "I should pay. I really owe you for yesterday. Especially when I had to bail. You're such a good friend."

She stressed the last word. Hard.

There was something anxious about her expression. Eva chewed the inside of her lip, and her fingers twisted in her lap.

Is she hoping I challenge the label?

Eva was an angel. She wouldn't have kissed a *friend* the way she had Nathan. Which meant she'd be looking for something real, a serious relationship.

For the first time in his life, Nathan wanted that too. But he was going to blow everything up before it began.

"Look, there's something I really need to say." Nathan took a deep breath. "I've been thinking about it since you kissed me, and—"

"I'm so sorry that was a mistake!" Eva cut him off, words tumbling from her mouth so fast that it took Nathan a moment to process them all. "I was just really emotional and confused after talking to my brother. And I wasn't thinking straight about what I was doing. I am so sorry!"

By the time Nathan understood, it felt like he'd been slapped across the face.

Eva was an angel. She wouldn't lie. And she'd said kissing him was a mistake.

The past twenty-four hours, Nathan had been racked with guilt because he'd thought the truth was going to break her heart. Turns out, it was only going to break his.

Because Eva didn't like him. Everything Nathan had felt when they'd kissed had been one sided. He should've known. An angel wouldn't fall for someone like him.

Nathan's chest tightened. He wished he'd pretended to be sick and left. Chris could judge all he wanted.

Eva's rejection stung worse than if she'd shouted and slapped Nathan in the face for deceiving her. At least if she'd cried or screamed, it would've meant she'd felt something.

Nathan couldn't let her see how much her words had affected him. He forced a laugh. "Don't worry about it, Eva. That kiss didn't mean anything."

"It didn't?" Eva sounded surprised and oddly hurt.

"Of course not," Nathan said, pushing his hair back and shrugging. "You think you're the first girl I've made out with on a whim? Honestly, I was worried that you were the type who'd overinterpret something like that. I'm glad we're on the same page."

"Good thing I'm not that type. That would be embarrassing," Eva agreed, staring at the painting of a porcupine in sunglasses that hung on the wall. Her lips pursed and trembled for a moment before she added, "Is that what you were going to tell me?"

Nathan hesitated. Even if Eva didn't like him, didn't he still owe her the truth?

"Yeah, that was it," Nathan lied, and the guilt returned to his stomach.

"Oh. Good, I guess." Eva stared at the floor, before glancing back up. "We're still friends though, right?"

Her eyes glistened, sweet and sad and oh-so-trusting. The guilt wriggled in Nathan until he felt like he'd swallowed a jar of worms. He took a sip of coffee, hoping it would calm him. It didn't. But it wet his throat enough for him to respond, "Of course."

"Great." Eva's smile returned, though she didn't light up quite as much as usual. "Because I have an idea."

In her excitement, she reached across the table and grabbed Nathan's hand.

The lightning he'd felt before danced across his skin. Nathan's heart pounded. Eva's fingers radiated warmth, just like when she'd brushed his cheek.

Eva's cheeks turned pink. She pulled her hand back and twisted her hair into a curl, not quite meeting Nathan's eyes as she explained, "You're an amazing chef, and the cafeteria food is abysmal at Dashmoor. What if we cooked lunches and sold them at school? We could send the proceeds to the children's ward of the Castor's Grove Hospital. Or a different charity, if you'd prefer."

"That sounds like I'd be doing something great."

"Right? And I already got approval from Principal Davis!" Eva grabbed her notebook and started showing Nathan the ideas she'd already started jotting down.

She'd missed the suspicion in his tone.

Nathan studied her as she went through her plan. Subtlety was not a skill Eva possessed. Her eyes lit up with excitement not only when talking about helping sick children, but when she discussed the role Nathan would play in it.

Whatever strange game Eva was playing, she still wanted to use Nathan as a pawn.

Why?

Nathan couldn't understand it. Eva acted almost like—but that was impossible. An irin would never be assigned a guardian angel. She must've made a bet. It wasn't angelic behavior, but neither was climbing on top of him in a restaurant booth. Or maybe he'd lifted her. But she certainly hadn't protested.

The thought of being manipulated as part of some bet made Nathan bristle. Noble as Eva's plan sounded, he had his own sick kid to worry about financially. He should say no.

But that would be playing into G's hands. It would prove that everything she'd thought was correct.

"So what do you think?" Eva clasped her hands underneath her chin. Her eyes grew big and hopeful. She smiled.

And the whole world seemed to stop.

Eva was so annoyingly beautiful. How could Nathan refuse?

37
EVANGELINA

The moment Mr. Shannons instructed his students to get into pairs after lunch on Wednesday, Eva turned desperately around the room. She'd been at Dashmoor for weeks now. Someone had to want to pair up with her.

Joey, one of only three boys who took Art History, caught Eva's eye before being grabbed by the girl beside him.

A chair scraped across the floor, moving closer to Eva.

"I'll be your partner," Beatrice said.

"No, that's fine. I'd really prefer..." Eva looked around again. There really was no one else.

Beatrice must have known it. She was already pulling her desk over and getting out her notes. "We're not doing our presentation on Dali. That's way too obvious. What about—Ooh. Those aren't Art History notes."

Eva slammed her folder shut. She'd recently learned, thanks to Chris, that the Dashmoor teachers posted their notes to an online platform, and her attention in class had waned. Between her role as a guardian angel and her brother's impending trial, Eva had enough going on.

"Are those to do with your guardian assignment?" Beatrice guessed, leaning in and whispering. "Your apple turnovers were amazing. And so was Nathan's rice dish. You were right about him being a great cook. But is selling lunch together part of your plan, or are you just looking for an excuse to spend time with him?"

Eva's cheeks heated.

"Nate's making money for charity," Eva whispered. "That's great."

Beatrice grinned, perhaps pleased that she'd gotten a response. "But you don't need to be selling pastries with him. He could do it by himself."

Farrah had made a similar observation when she'd helped come up with the plan. Evidently, Eva had blushed in response and earned herself a lecture on the seriousness of Zeke's trial being linked to her guardian assignment. She couldn't get *distracted* because her charge looked good.

"I'm guiding him," Eva insisted, searching her folder for what little she'd written about the surrealists. Her notes had grown increasingly scattered.

"Sure," Beatrice said, stretching the word. "You're also staring at Nathan like you want to do—well, not very angelic things to him."

Eva brushed her hair forward so that it hid her face. She knew her cheeks had turned red yet again. But that was not a fair accusation! Maybe she'd gotten distracted a few times while serving lunch, but she and Nathan were squashed between a trio of folded tables. Their bodies kept bumping against one another, and every time Nathan's fingers grazed Eva, her mind flashed back to The Vampire's Lair. She remembered how he'd touched her thighs, how he'd tasted, how his lips had felt against hers.

"You don't need to be embarrassed," Beatrice said. "He's totally looking at you the same way."

"No, he's not," Eva muttered. Nathan had made that abundantly clear.

When they'd met at the Purple Porcupine, Nathan had said their kiss meant nothing. And Eva had felt like she'd watched him take her heart and crush it in his palm.

But she should've expected it. Eva had gotten caught up in her feelings and forgotten that Nathan hooked up with girls all the time. He wasn't thinking about a relationship in terms of a human lifetime or an angelic eternity. He wasn't thinking about a relationship at all.

Which was good. Eva couldn't afford to fall for a human right now. She'd abandoned all romantic notions of Nathan.

At least, she was really trying to.

"Did something happen between you two?" Beatrice pressed.

Had they been friends, Eva might have told the witch. Instead, she flipped through her folder, trying to find anything she'd written on a surrealist.

"Hey!" Beatrice reached out and stopped her. "Why did you write down Hyde Leonard's name?"

Eva tightened her grip so that the witch couldn't pull out the page. During English, she'd tried to brainstorm a list of people who could be connected to ParadiseShared. She didn't know if, or where, the defense attorney fit. Farrah had admitted only that Mr. Leonard had claimed to have pertinent information, but that it had proven to be nothing.

"I wasn't going to give your feather to him," Beatrice

said, managing a rare whisper. "If that's what you were worried about. He already dominates the market. I'd never help him further."

"What market?"

"For angel feathers obviously. Rumor is, he's got a source inside the Sanctum who gets them for him. One of you all."

Eva's heart stopped. Zeke had said that Adelaide Glory approached him for one of his feathers. Could she be connected to Hyde Leonard?

"I don't know much else. I could find out for you though, if you like."

"For a price?" Eva guessed.

"Friends trade favors," Beatrice insisted.

"What about doing our presentation on Frida Kahlo?"

Beatrice pouted at the change in topic, but soon launched into a list of lesser-known surrealists for them to research instead. Occasionally, she attempted to steer the conversation back toward feathers and favors, but Eva refocused Beatrice each time.

Tempting as it would be to find more information on Hyde Leonard, Eva had a different lead on ParadiseShared to explore. Adelaide Glory had signed off on the charity, but it had been vetted by another angel first. When Eva found that name among the documents, she'd almost dropped them in the middle of English. Because she knew the angel in question: Victoria Celand, Leah and Max's mother.

Eva had spent half her weekends at their house. It might be time to visit again.

38

EVANGELINA

Eva stood before a familiar, blue-painted doorway. Her hand trembled as she raised it. Had she ever knocked on the Celands' door? In all her memories, Leah had been there, and they'd entered together.

But things were different.

Eva took a deep breath and knocked before she lost her nerve.

A moment later, Max answered. His pale gray shirt matched his eyes. He'd undone the top few buttons, revealing the muscles beneath. Over the past few years, Max had started visiting the gym, and his efforts showed. He'd always been cute, now most girls would swoon.

Eva tried to feel something. Thoughts of Nathan's wry smile mocked her attempts. Why did she have to like him? Having feelings for Max would be so much easier.

"Are you going to invite me in?" Eva suggested, offering her biggest, most optimistic smile.

"I shouldn't," Max said, but a smile fluttered across his face. He leaned forward and glanced out. Once he saw the street was empty, he stepped aside.

Eva ran into the house before he could change his mind.

"Who is it?" Leah shouted. Her footsteps pounded down the staircase, and she appeared a moment later in a pair of shorts and a bright green hoodie. Her mouth opened at the sight of Eva, but she covered quickly with a smile. "You're here! That's—How's your guardian angel job?"

"Great!" Eva forced a smile. "Is your mom home? I was hoping to speak to her."

———

Eva sat at the table in the Celand kitchen, tracing the rim of a teacup with her thumb. Max and Leah's voices traveled from upstairs.

"You know we all agreed to keep our distance—"

"She just showed up. I figured she had a reason."

"Oh please! You took one look at her in that dress and decided—."

Eva had been pretending not to hear, but she tugged the end of her feather dress lower. "It's the best outfit for hiding my wings."

Victoria Celand offered a kind, but amused smile. She sat on the other side of the kitchen table, holding her teacup in her thin hands. Her broad cheeks and stormy eyes matched almost exactly with her children. "Don't pay attention to the twins. It's good to see you again, Eva."

"Really?" Maybe Eva shouldn't have been so suspicious of the sentiment. Victoria had been like a second mother to her. "Didn't you tell Leah and Max to stay away from me?"

"Of course not. I mean—not from you. It's different with your parents. But your mother understands, I'm sure. How is she?"

"Keeping busy," Eva said.

"Zola's making an absolute mess of things," Victoria offered, twisting the string of her teabag around her finger. "Seems to think she's leading a military unit instead of a local charity department. Honestly, twelve years we've worked together, and she's never changed."

"I actually came in relation to your previous job," Eva said. "You were affiliated with the charity that Zeke stole from, ParadiseShared. I wanted to apologize on my family's behalf."

Victoria rested down her teacup, reached out, and took Eva's hand. "Aren't you the epitome of an angel? I'll be certain to mention that to Irena if she comes snooping around again. But it's really not necessary." Victoria withdrew her hands and took a sip of her tea. "I don't even remember the charity."

"Really?" Eva raised her own cup, trying to hide the eagerness in her expression. She'd prefer her friends' mother not be implicated in fraud, and if Victoria didn't remember the charity, that might be proof of a conspiracy. "You vetted it when you worked in the Global Charity Division. ParadiseShared is headquartered in Thailand. They work with orphanages around the region?" Eva tightened her grip on the cup, waiting to see if any of that jogged Victoria's memory.

"I remember our trip to East Asia," Victoria conceded. "But I reviewed and vetted so many different charities. I wish I could remember them all. They do good work. And I do appreciate you wanting to apologize. Your brother's theft was a terrible thing. But I'm not the one who's been hurt by his actions."

"So you don't remember meeting anyone from ParadiseShared? And if a judge asked you about it, you'd say that you had no recollection of the charity even existing?"

Victoria leaned back. "This is sounding less like an apology."

"No, it is. It's just—"

Leah was still shouting at Max upstairs. "Eva's *my* friend. I'm looking out for her. You dated her for less than a month, and then she dumped you."

"That was a mutual decision!"

Victoria's eyes flicked upward. She sighed and raised her voice to drown her children. "If I signed the approval paperwork, I'm sure I vetted the charity. My assistant from the time might know. I can give you her name."

"That would be incredible!"

Victoria nodded. She wrote the name on a piece of paper. "I really thought your mom had sent you to find out how we were managing without her."

"You could call and tell her. The number's still the same."

Victoria offered the paper with a small, sad smile. "*You* are welcome to visit again. But whatever you're up to, I'd rather not help any further. The last thing any angel needs is to be mixed up with what's happening to your brother."

———

Eva hadn't stepped off the Celand property before the familiar trill sounded in her purse. Instead of walking to the subway station, she hailed a cab to the Sanctum Headquarters. Then, Eva skipped the elevator and raced up the five flights of steps. If her success as a guardian angel was linked to Zeke's trial, she needed to impress Irena.

For once, Eva might've had a shot.

Maddie looked up from her computer and smiled as Eva approached. "Ms. Elysium's in a good mood this time.

What were you doing when the alarm went off? You must've been onto something pretty great with your charge."

Eva chewed the inside of her lip. Had she been thinking about Nathan when the alarm sounded? No, only Zeke and the trial. "Are you sure Irena didn't call me in again?"

Maddie shook her head.

"Miss Heaven, you're here. In a punctual manner." Irena stepped out of her office to greet Eva for a change. The karmic angel did appear to be in a better mood. Even the shoulder pads on her navy suit seemed less angry and pointed. "Come in. I want a full update."

Eva tried not to fidget as she stood before Irena's desk, describing how the past week had gone with Nathan. She stuck to the facts. If she went into detail, she'd say something she shouldn't and end up making it obvious that she'd fallen for her charge.

But how could she not?

Despite his rejection Nathan continued to be sweet, and charming, and unbearably attractive. Eva wanted to just be friends, but even going grocery shopping with him on Tuesday, she'd gotten all giggly and excited. It had only gotten worse from there.

The guardian phone had noticed and added to its list. *Nathan Ward is great at distracting Evangelina Heaven.* At least the device hadn't said with thoughts of what.

"This is all very impressive, Miss Heaven," Irena said at the end of the report.

Eva's lips twitched. She fought to keep herself from smiling from sheer surprise. Irena had never complimented her before.

"You intend to continue this endeavor until your assignment concludes on Friday?"

"Yes, but it's my hope that Mr. Ward will continue raising money for the hospital beyond the scope of my time with him."

Irena nodded. "You're making a commendable effort, Miss Heaven. You'll be a fine addition to the Sanctum when you're older."

If she'd thought Irena wouldn't shove her off in under a second, Eva would have hugged the karmic angel. "Will you say that to the judge?"

Irena's usual scowl returned. "I do wish you'd heed my advice against testifying."

"But will you tell the judge that you think I'm doing a good job?"

"If you still are on Friday, then yes. I won't lie," Irena said. "Does the device think you're on the right track?"

Eva frowned. She didn't think the clunk of metal *thought* anything. If it did, it probably only mused about what else it could add to its increasingly embarrassing list.

Irena clicked her tongue. "Ask the device, Miss Heaven. I'm told it was assigned to you for a reason. The magic controlling it knows more than either of us about the end goal of your work."

Eva lifted the guardian phone. Nervous what it might show, she asked the question fast. "Am I on the right track to guide Nathan Ward to greatness?"

For once, the device gave Eva a simple answer. In big, bold letters it lit the screen with one word: *YES*.

39
NATHAN

"Dude, you missed the most epic campaign," Chris' voice came through the speaker.

Nathan had propped his phone on a roll of paper towels in the corner of the kitchen. He needed both hands to chop carrots for the soup bubbling on his stove. Daniel stood beside him on a small footstool. The eight-year-old had been designated sous-chef, which made him much more willing to help stir.

"Don't tell me you're cooking. It's Sunday!" Chris continued.

Nathan paused to trade a grin with his brother.

"You totally are," Chris groaned.

"I had to cook like ten chickens in my oven," Nathan explained over the sound of his brother giggling. "It takes time. And this is important."

"Uh huh." There was the sound of chips being crunched on the other end. "Like you're super invested in feeding our classmates all of a sudden. When are you going to just admit you like Eva and ask her out on a proper date so you can go back to fighting zombies with me?"

Daniel's laughter stopped. His eyebrows rose, and a smile spread across his face like he knew he'd heard something he wasn't supposed to.

Nathan dropped his knife, grabbed his phone, and hurried to take Chris off the speaker.

"It's not like that," Nathan said, holding the phone to his ear. "I like cooking, and it's for a good cause. And I've told you already that Eva's not into me."

"Bullshit. Everyone knows you guys like each other. It's all over your faces. Have you seen the way she smiles at you?"

Nathan's heart pounded at the image. This past week, spending so much time with Eva, it had been easy to lose himself in a fantasy where she returned his feelings. But he was only deluding himself.

"That's just how Eva smiles," Nathan said, wiping his hand on a kitchen towel before grabbing his knife again. He was acutely aware of his brother eavesdropping.

"And I guess you can't see the way you stare at her," Chris continued as though Nathan hadn't spoken. "But your eyes get all soft and mushy."

Nathan chopped the last of the carrot with unnecessary force. He did not like that descriptor. "You're imaging all of that. We're just friends. And I have a soup to prepare."

"Put some aside for me," Chris said. "And whatever Eva's making for dessert."

"Only if you stop telling me to ask her out." Nathan ended the call just in case Chris had been about to argue.

"For what it's worth, I really like your new job," Daniel said, staring at the liquid bubbling in the pot

Nathan grinned and tousled his brother's hair. "You like it because it means different food every night."

To be fair, Nathan appreciated that aspect too. It was

easy to make a couple extra meals for Daniel and himself when he prepared the food to sell.

Nathan grabbed two spoons from the drawer. He dipped one into the chicken broth, then raised it to his lips. It needed rosemary. He grabbed a pinch, stirred it, and offered the next taste to his brother.

"What do you think, sous chef?"

Daniel sipped the broth and smiled. "Yum."

"Excellent." Nathan dropped the spoons into a growing pile in the sink. The one downside of cooking so much was the washing up.

"It's not as good as the cupcakes you brought home on Friday though. The ones that Eva made," Daniel added, with a cheeky grin.

"All right, sous chef, you can take dish duty then."

Daniel laughed, apparently pleased by the punishment. He pushed his stool from the stove over to the sink while Nathan roughly chopped some chard.

"Is Eva going to come over for dinner again?" Daniel asked.

"Not unless she shows up uninvited."

"Why don't you invite her? Since you like her."

Nathan finished chopping the chard before narrowing his eyes at his younger brother, who was smirking in delight. Daniel evidently saw no need to hide that he'd heard what Chris had said on the phone.

"Eva's an angel. She's not allowed to hang out with us," Nathan explained, ignoring the last part of his brother's comment. He poured the chopped vegetables into the soup pot, then carried a stack of bowls, the chopping board, and the knife to the sink.

Daniel frowned at the new dishes that had been added to his pile. "But you're already hanging out with Eva."

The kid had a point there. Nathan had spent Tuesday grocery shopping with Eva after school, and it had been fun. He'd tried to teach her how to juggle apples then laughed at how hopeless she was. The rest of the week, they'd sat next to each other in most classes and been together all lunch. Friday, he'd gotten sauce on his face. When Eva giggled, he'd grabbed her wrist and held her so that he could wipe some onto her nose as well. Her face had come dangerously close to his. He'd felt the pulse quicken in her wrist, and her lips had parted in a manner that had sent Nathan's mind spiraling in dangerous directions.

No wonder Chris thinks something is going on.

"Eva's really nice," Daniel continued, scrubbing the bowl as he talked. "I think she'd want to spend time with us, even if she did know that we weren't proper angels."

"It's not about her being nice," Nathan said, uncertain how to explain it to a kid. He went back to the stove to check the broth. "Angels are strange with things like that. They think hanging out with irin signifies that they're embracing the immorality of Earth."

Daniel scratched his head, getting soap suds in his hair. "What's immorality?"

"Doing the wrong thing."

"Is that what Mom did when she decided to marry Dad?"

Nathan almost dropped the spoon. He hadn't expected that question.

Kay Ward's decision to marry a human wasn't the reason she'd been excommunicated from the Sanctum. That had happened later when she'd used her powers to help him swindle several businessmen. Nathan had been a baby during that particular scandal, but his father had loved to tell the story. Shane Fisher had been exceptionally proud of how his beloved partner had sacrificed her wings to make them temporarily rich.

For as long as Shane lived, Kay had been proud too. It was after his death that she'd grown distraught. Then Daniel had been born, and everything got worse.

Nathan would never say that aloud to his brother. He shook his head and stirred the soup. "No, Mom was right to marry Dad. They were really in love."

"Are you in love with Eva?"

Nathan did drop the spoon this time. The bubbling yellow liquid swallowed the metal. That question was—Where had—? Nathan turned to his brother. "What on Earth made you ask that?"

"Because if you were in love then it wouldn't be wrong for you to be together. Even if she is a proper angel…" Daniel's voice started to fade, growing soft and slow, like he was drifting away.

Nathan grabbed a ladle to fetch the fallen spoon from the soup. He didn't know how to respond to anything his brother was saying. It was obviously ridiculous.

"Ah!" Daniel screamed and something clattered against the sink.

Nathan abandoned his efforts to recover the spoon.

Daniel hunched over, holding his hand beneath the tap. The water turned red as it swirled around the drain. Blood glinted on the edge of the chopping knife.

"Shit, Dan." Nathan grabbed a clean towel from a drawer and wrapped his brother's hand. The knife had sliced deep into the palm.

"I'm sorry," Daniel said. His voice was tired and strained. "It got so heavy. I couldn't hold it."

"It's not your fault. I shouldn't have given you a knife." Nathan cursed himself internally.

"But I felt good." Daniel slumped against Nathan as though all the strength had suddenly drained from his body.

It probably had. That was the problem. Daniel could go from good to terrible in a matter of seconds.

Nathan scooped his brother into his arms. "Good thing you're so light. Let's get you to bed."

"It's not a good thing," Daniel whispered, and his body trembled, the muscles twitching and convulsing in something akin to a miniature seizure. "I hate being like this."

Nathan kissed the top of Daniel's head and brushed his hair away from his eyes. "I'll bring you my phone. You can play games in bed. Way better than washing dishes."

Daniel grumbled, unconvinced. But the moment his head hit the pillow, his eyes started to droop. Phones and dishes were both out of the question.

Nathan might not make it to school tomorrow after all. What would he do with all this food? Could Eva collect it. He considered the dilemma as he returned to the kitchen.

Knock. Knock. Knock.

Nathan froze, broth-covered spoon in hand. A chill went through him.

"Let me in, Nathan," G's voice called with an almost girlish lilt. "I have an offer you won't be able to refuse."

Somehow, Nathan doubted that. He set the pots to simmer, grabbed a knife, and cracked the door, keeping the deadbolt locked.

In the hallway beyond, the round-faced woman smiled. Short curls twisted around her ears and neck. Her purple cloak hid anything more, but when she lifted her hand and waved, there was something in it, an envelope of some kind?

"I told you I was done," Nathan said. "Don't come back here."

"Aww, all because an angel was willing to kiss you? Don't choose a girl over your brother. I have something that can help him." G flashed the envelope again. "I just need one little favor from you in return. It'll be the last one. Promise."

40

EVANGELINA

Eva fought with the first of the three stubborn plastic tables, trying to pull the folded legs loose so it would stand. Principal Davis had been generous with allowing them to borrow school equipment, but he drew the line at making any staff help. Which was normally fine, except that Nathan wasn't at school yet. He'd messaged to tell Eva he'd be arriving late. Something must have happened with Daniel that morning.

A few of the guys entering the cafeteria glanced her way. Eva would've accepted help, but they might have been afraid to approach. Nathan had scared off the ones who'd offered to set up with her the first day. He'd insisted they all had ulterior motives. Eva preferred to think that some of the Dashmoor boys were just nice, but she hadn't hated Nathan wanting them gone.

Eva's phone rang. She stopped fighting with the table and hurried to grab it from her backpack. Her immediate concern was that Nathan wouldn't make it after all.

But it wasn't his number. Victoria Celand's former assistant was finally returning Eva's call from yesterday.

"Hello, is this Greta Snow?" Eva asked, holding the phone with her shoulder so she could resume her battle with the table.

A small, uncertain voice—which Eva's research told her belonged to an older fairy with green wings—responded, "Yes. Who is this?"

"Victoria Celand gave me your number," Eva said, skipping the fairy's question for fear that hearing the name *Heaven* might cause her to hang up the phone. "I'm calling about a charity that she vetted while you were her assistant: ParadiseShared. Do you remember anything about it?"

"Sure. The one in Thailand."

"Yes!" One of the table legs came loose with a sudden pop. Eva stumbled back, keeping the phone pressed to her ear. "Did you go with her to see it?"

"Oh yes, that's why I remember. She was supposed to take the day off, and I'd planned to leave early. But then she showed up dressed like she was going to tea, with gloves on her hands and a bee in her bonnet. She insisted."

"What was the charity like? Do you remember who you met with?" Eva asked, fighting with the second leg.

"Oh, I didn't go into the meeting. She had me wait in the lobby. Seemed a nice enough place. She was all set to start me on the paperwork when she came back."

"So you didn't see the charity or meet anyone yourself? Wasn't that unusual?" Eva clarified, straightening the table and setting her boxes of peach tartlets on top. Someone approached, but she didn't turn to see who.

"It might've been odd elsewhere, I suppose," Greta said. "But I don't speak Thai. I couldn't understand a thing people in the lobby said or the words on the signs. But, as I said, Ms. Celand liked it. Now, what did you say your name was again?"

"Thank you so much, Greta!" Eva hurried off the phone.

"Who's Greta?" Beatrice's voice came from behind Eva. "And why are you talking to her about a charity? Does this have to do with your brother?"

"That's really not—" Eva started, but her objection faltered as she turned.

Beatrice wore a pink shirt, hair pulled back into a high ponytail. She leaned forward, one hand each on a table. She'd unfolded the other two while Eva was distracted.

"Thank you," Eva said, chewing the inside of her lip. "That's actually very helpful."

"I'm always helpful," Beatrice said, flipping her ponytail and grinning. She grabbed a folded white sheet.

Eva took the other end. Together, they covered all three of the tables. Once that was done, Eva thanked the witch again before going to fetch the plates and bowls from the ladies in the cafeteria.

Beatrice followed. "Are you trying to give the money back to the charity your brother stole from? Is that what you and Nathan are donating to? Is that why you don't want to take me up on my offer to help you run away? Because I don't think returning the money is going to save the rest of your family."

That had been so many questions and such an off-base guess. Eva glanced behind her. "You have no idea what you're talking about."

"You're up to something regarding your brother," Beatrice insisted. "I looked into Hyde Leonard like you asked by the way. I can trade you for information."

"I didn't ask—" Eva started to argue but thought better of it. She lowered her voice as they stepped past the cafeteria doors. "I'm not giving you a feather for information on Hyde Leonard."

The silverware waited on a cart near the edge of the kitchen. Beatrice grabbed the handle before Eva could.

"I got Sophie to ask around to see if anyone knew anything. There are conflicting rumors, but Hyde definitely has an angel on the inside. Maybe more. Apparently, she wears a big purple cloak to hide herself. One of the Rookwood girls claims to have seen her face and swears Hyde's connect is an old archangel. But Sophie says that she's not the most reliable."

Eva tried not to gape. She had no idea who Sophie was, but Hyde's connect had to be Adelaide Glory. It fit perfectly with Zeke's story. "Did you learn anything else?"

"I did actually." Beatrice grinned as she pushed the cart out of the kitchen and through the cafeteria. Without slowing, she stuck her hand in the pocket of her jeans and produced a piece of paper. The witch waved it. "This is an official response from Hyde about purchasing a feather."

Eva reached for it.

Predictably, Beatrice pulled it away.

"I'm not giving you a feather for it," Eva whispered. They'd reached the trio of foldout tables they'd set out. Eva took the first stack of plates from the cart and set them out.

"Tell me what you're doing with your brother's case?"

Eva hated how the witch always wanted something in exchange. But she did want to see the letter. "I think my brother was set up. ParadiseShared wasn't a real charity."

Beatrice dropped a stack of bowls onto the table with a thud. "ParadiseShared, as in *P-S*?"

"I guess."

"Ooh. Okay, you definitely want to see this." Beatrice

pulled out the letter and unfolded it, pressing it flat on the table.

The message itself was only a price with Mr. Leonard's name scribbled beneath. Below that, in typeface, someone had added *PS*.

Beatrice tapped the letters. "I thought it was a typo. Like, maybe Hyde meant to add a postscript but didn't. But what if it's your charity? P-S, ParadiseShared. It's not a bad name for a group selling angel feathers."

"It's not," Eva agreed. But if she came out and stated that at Zeke's trial, who would she be accusing? Adelaide Glory had ascended. Someone must have taken over. She didn't like to think it could have been Victoria.

"So what are you doing to investigate?" Beatrice asked. "Anything more I can help with?"

"Depends," Eva said, narrowing her eyes and staring over the plates at the witch. "Are you offering because we're friends or because you want a feather?"

"I told you, it's both."

Eva sighed. Part of her had really hoped Beatrice would just say they were friends. She liked the witch and help couldn't hurt.

Dashmoor students were already beginning to gather by the tables. Mutters of annoyance passed through them. Last week, Eva and Nathan had been serving lunch by now.

"Form a line," Beatrice ordered. The witch had a naturally commanding voice, and though there were complaints, the others followed her instructions. She leaned closer to Eva and whispered. "Don't tell me Nate's ditched school again. So much for greatness. I know you like him, but he's a lost cause. I mean if he'd bail on you like this—"

"He hasn't," Eva insisted, but even she was starting to

grow nervous. If Nathan didn't show up, she'd have nothing but pastries to sell. The Dashmoor students would get annoyed, and many seemed to love blaming Eva for any inconvenience.

She checked her phone. Nate hadn't messaged since promising to be there by lunch. But if Daniel had gotten worse, then maybe he hadn't had time?

Just as Eva was considering the best way to apologize to a crowd of hungry teenagers, the doors to the cafeteria opened. Nathan entered with Chris behind him. Both carried several large containers of soup.

41
NATHAN

"I'm so glad you made it," Eva said for the fifth time since he'd arrived.

Nathan made the mistake of looking at the angel. Her smile was bright and warm, lighting the room and making Nathan's heart skip.

Why does she have to be so perfect?

Nathan hated himself for what he was about to do.

The massive pot he'd borrowed from the cafeteria to reheat the soup sat atop the table. It had taken several minutes, and lunch was almost halfway through. A line of students snaked toward them. The soup was ready to serve.

But Nathan wasn't sure he was ready to serve it.

"It smells amazing," Eva said, lifting the lid. "Can I try a little before we start?"

She took a spoon from beside the bowls. Nathan grabbed it from her before she could dip it in.

"There might not be enough," he mumbled, reorganizing the cutlery.

"Just give people a little less," Beatrice suggested. Instead of lining up with everyone else, the large brunette stood with her hands on her hips before the tables, as though she were guarding them. Nathan didn't understand what she was doing there. Offering unrequested assistance evidently because in her next breath she volunteered, "I'll help Chris take in the money for you guys. He looks out of his depth."

Chris had managed fine last week, and he looked relaxed as always, but Nathan preferred fewer people around. He'd have gotten rid of Eva too if he could have.

Don't look at her.

He didn't, but his body remained acutely aware of her presence. Their arrangement behind the tables meant the angel was only ever a few inches away.

"Should I help you serve the soup?" Eva offered.

"No, I got it," Nathan answered fast without looking up. "Focus on your pastries."

The first student arrived, a chubby freshman holding his bowl ready. He wore square glasses and offered a broad smile.

Nathan's hand hovered over the ladle. He felt like he might throw up.

Think about Dan.

Nathan poured some of the soup into the boy's waiting bowl. The freshman went to Eva for a tartlet, and the next customer approached.

And that was it. There was no going back.

Nathan's stomach remained clenched for the remainder of lunch, but he dished out all of the soup. In the remaining minutes before class, he helped return the supplies to the kitchen, faked a smile, and thanked anyone who complimented his cooking.

Everything seemed perfectly fine until the next period. Then the food poisoning kicked in.

42

EVANGELINA

Dashmoor High School transformed into a war zone. Teachers gave up trying to keep their students in class. Teenagers in denim jeans crowded the hallways, fighting with one another to enter the bathrooms. Others crouched over trash bins, clinging to them like buoys in a storm. An awful scent filled the air, making even those who weren't affected by the sudden illness retch.

Eva pinched her nose as she walked toward the principal's office. Nathan slunk ahead of her. His chin dipped and his shoulders hunched as though hoping to escape notice despite his height. But everyone glared as they passed. Eva could guess why.

They all ate our food.

Eva had made the connection as soon as the first three had run from English class. The faces crowded in the halls only confirmed it.

This was not good.

Nathan and Eva climbed the steps to the second floor

and followed the passages to where Principal Davis waited in his office. His secretary ushered them in without fanfare.

The principal's bald head glinted in the light from the window behind him. Sweat stains dampened his armpits. When he saw them, he raised two thick eyebrows and exhaled with enough force that the hairs of his mustache trembled.

Eva scampered into one of the two chairs before him. Her fingers twisted in her lap, clasping and unclasping as though debating whether or not to pray. She'd been to the principal's office before, but always of her own volition. She'd never been summoned.

Nathan dropped into the remaining seat, stretched his legs, and rested a hand casually over the back of the chair. "What's up, Davis?"

The principal's jaw clenched at the casual tone, but his gaze settled on Eva. "We have a crisis on our hands. You assured me there wouldn't be any problems, Miss Heaven. But this could be a disaster."

"I'm so sorry, sir!" Eva felt terrible. "Something must've gotten into one of the dishes somehow."

Principal Davis held up a hand. "Obviously your food stand has come to an end."

"Please, it's just one unfortunate incident!" Eva clasped her hands. Their lunch stall was her best way to guide Nathan to greatness. The guardian phone even agreed. "People are really enjoying it, and we've raised so much money for the hospital. The PR for the school will be great."

"Not if we get sued by parents. You don't have the proper permission to be selling this food."

Eva's hands fell to her lap. "But you said—"

"I would never have agreed to let you sell food on

campus had I realized that it was being prepared in your houses," Principal Davis said.

It was true that they hadn't discussed where the lunches would be prepared, but Eva thought the food being homemade had been implied. And Principal Davis never asked. Perhaps to give himself an out for this exact scenario.

"It's unsanitary precisely for this reason," the principal continued. "Now what am I to say when a parent calls wanting to know why their child was able to purchase contaminated food?"

"I'm sorry, sir, it was an accident."

Principal Davis snorted as though it made no difference. "There will be repercussions. Serious ones, Miss Heaven. And they won't just fall on my shoulders."

Eva's chest tightened, locking the air inside. She'd never gotten into trouble with a school principal. What could she do? Keep apologizing? But that didn't seem to be helping.

Tears rose to the corners of her eyes.

"Stop blaming Eva," Nathan snapped. He leaned forward, placing his arms on the principal's desk. "This isn't her fault. It's mine."

"Oh, I have no doubt," Principal Davis said, with a half-sneer. "But ultimately, I agreed to this arrangement with Miss Heaven—"

"It was my soup that made them sick."

"We don't know that," Eva said quickly. She appreciated what Nathan was trying to do, but he needed to be whatever the guardian phone deemed *great* in under a week. It would be better if Principal Davis blamed her.

But Nathan continued. "I do know. I did it on purpose." His eyes flicked to Eva and then quickly away. "I gave the school food poisoning."

The principal's fists curled on his desk. "I beg your pardon, Mr. Ward? Are you confessing to purposefully poisoning your classmates?"

"No, he's not," Eva said, shaking her head and silently begging Nathan to stop.

Why would he lie about something so serious?

"Yes, I did. Just me," Nathan insisted, still not looking at Eva. "So only I should be punished."

"Gladly, Mr. Ward. Consider your expulsion effective immediately. Gather your things and get out of Dashmoor."

"No, you can't—" Eva started to protest. But a sudden thought, quick and unexpected, stole her voice.

Nathan wouldn't let me try the soup.

He'd pulled the spoon from Eva's hand when she'd attempted to taste it. What if he'd done that so that she wouldn't contract food poisoning?

But why? If he was callous enough to infect everyone else, why would he make sure that I didn't get sick?

"Gladly," Nathan said, slamming Eva back to the present. He grabbed his bag and walked out of the office, not even turning to glance at her one last time.

43
EVANGELINA

Ten minutes later, Eva raced through the still crowded hallways. Nathan couldn't have just left. He had to be somewhere. She had to find him.

Her mind had been scrambled in the principal's office. She wasn't used to getting in trouble, and it had led her to over interpret things. But Nathan must have been lying to protect her. Because Eva knew Nathan. He wouldn't poison their classmates.

But Principal Davis believed it. He was happy to scapegoat Nathan and avoid the blame. Before Eva could leave, he'd stopped her to offer unsolicited advice. She needed to be more selective about which boys she gave attention to. Mr. Ward might seem charming and cool with his *devil-may-care* attitude, but she'd soon realize that he was a delinquent and a troublemaker. He'd always had something dark and wrong with him, and now he'd committed a criminal offense. Principal Davis intended to involve the police. When they asked Eva about the incident, she needed to say: *It was Mr. Ward's idea. He lied to me about having permission from the principal.*

Eva had nodded blankly, but she couldn't say any of that. It wasn't true. The principal only wanted to save his position, not caring if it meant condemning his student to prison.

Nathan needed to recant his story. There had to be a school board or an administrator, someone above Principal Davis, who they could go to for help.

Eva spotted a blue baseball cap outside one of the classrooms. "Chris!"

Other than his long nose being wrinkled in disgust, he appeared fine. But he'd had the soup.

From a special bowl Nathan set aside.

That didn't mean anything. Eva kept being paranoid. She pushed it aside and rushed toward him.

Chris' face relaxed as he turned to her. "What happened with Davis? He's not expelling you too, is he?"

Eva shook her head, a lump rising in her throat. She scanned the area behind Chris, expecting to see Nathan leaning against a wall. "Where is he?"

"Nate left. Said goodbye. He actually gave me a hug." Chris laughed, but his eyes looked tense and worried. He leaned closer, lowering his voice. "There's a rumor going around that this was on purpose."

So fast?

Eva's chest tightened. "I have to find him."

"No, I wouldn't—" Chris shouted, but it was too late.

Eva took off down the hallway, hurrying toward the school's entrance.

Something soft hit the side of her head. A putrid scent accompanied it.

Eva covered her mouth to stop from gagging. With her other hand, she reached up and felt something wet stuck in her hair.

A sticky brownish yellow substance stuck to her fingers. It took Eva to a second to figure out what it was.

Vomit. Someone else's.

A voice shouted from the hallway. "It was that bitch from Cassel! She thinks she's so much better than us, she poisoned us!"

Oh no.

Dashmoor students, faces green and paled, turned to Eva. They pointed. Those whose stomachs had settled enough—and some who likely hadn't eaten the soup but wanted to join in on the public humiliation—stalked toward her. Another projectile launched into the air. Then another, and another.

Eva raised her arms in a desperate attempt to block them.

Her classmates' voices grew louder, accusing her of any number of horrible things. Eva wanted to defend herself, but every time she opened her mouth, another projectile came. She pressed her lips tight for fear of tasting someone else's puke.

It was no use. The humans here hated her. And she'd lost Nathan.

Tears pooled in Eva's eyes. Her body trembled. And in her panic, her wings burst free.

The projectiles stopped. Someone gasped. A thud sounded as another passed out from shock.

Oh no.

Eva stood in the center of the hallway with at least a hundred eyes on her. There was nowhere to run.

Wings, go back in. Go back in.

Eva closed her eyes, desperately praying. But she couldn't calm herself enough to hide her wings. Her secret was about to be discovered by a horde of very angry teenagers.

A hand wrapped around Eva's arm and yanked her across the hall and into a classroom.

"You're welcome."

Something tugged on her wing. Eva spun around at once.

Beatrice had saved her. Sort of. The witch also seemed to have been trying to pluck a feather to reward herself.

"Humans tend to mob angels in a mass of sudden fervor. If they don't faint from shock," Beatrice said, grinning as she pushed a desk in front the door. "You're lucky I was here."

Outside, someone had started weeping. A voice shouted that their sickness was a curse from God. Silhouettes gathered beyond the opaque window of the door. But between shock and sickness, they didn't seem to have noticed where Eva had gone.

"Thank you," Eva whispered, retreating to a corner of the classroom. Her body shook. How had everything gone so wrong so quickly?

The guardian phone squawked inside the pocket of Eva's feather jacket. It was a new sound and not a good one.

She pulled it out. The screen flashed at her with red letters: *WARNING!*

Beatrice crept closer so that she could see the screen. "Is it upset about something with Nate?"

YES. The answer flashed in response to the witch's question.

"Wicked!" Beatrice joined Eva, leaning in to get a closer look at the phone. "I didn't realize it could hear us. What else can it do?"

Eva wasn't in the mood to explain more about the

device. If it was worried, there had to be a reason. She could think of only one.

"Can I guide Nate to greatness if he gets arrested?" Eva asked.

NO.

Eva's chest tightened. "What about if he's just expelled?"

The screen blanked as though in thought. Then, the flashing red *NO* returned.

That was it then.

Eva slid down the wall, collapsing to the floor. The tips of her wings brushed the tiles. They cramped in the tight, uncomfortable space, but Eva was too stressed to dismiss them. And she didn't deserve the comfort she'd feel from stretching them either.

I failed.

The Fates had seen greatness in Nathan. But Eva had messed up. She'd robbed him of the future he deserved.

And it wasn't just Nathan she'd doomed.

Eva curled forward, wrapping herself into a ball. She burst into tears.

"Nate's getting arrested and expelled? Because of some soup? That's a shitty deal," Beatrice said, kneeling beside Eva. "But it's not your fault. Nate's always been one mistake away from expulsion. And prison's not that much of a stretch given the delinquency. I mean, statistically speaking—"

"Shut up," Eva snapped.

The comment caught both her and Beatrice off guard. They stared at one another.

More tears pooled in Eva's eyes. She blinked. "I'm so sorry. I shouldn't have—You're being really nice. I didn't—"

"No, I'm sorry. I didn't mean it like that. I know you like

Nate." Beatrice wrapped her arm over Eva's shoulders. It would've been easy for the witch to steal a feather. But she didn't try.

Somehow, that made Eva feel even worse. She wiped her eyes, fighting to hold back the tears. "It's not just Nate. It's my family."

Eva pointed to the countdown, still taunting her, at the top of the guardian phone. Between her tears, she tried to explain, but her thoughts felt scattered. She kept pausing to sniff and wipe the snot from her face.

"Farrah won't let me testify if I fail. Because Irena will tell the judge I'm a failure who deserves to lose my feathers. And Zeke won't have anyone to defend him. So he'll become an irin too. And so will my parents. And then me. And instead of being great, Nathan's whole future will be ruined. And his brother won't have anyone to take care of him. Which is going to be horrible. Because he's really sick. And—and—and I've ruined everything."

"No! You haven't even failed yet," Beatrice said. She pointed at the countdown on the guardian phone. "There's still time or that wouldn't be there anymore. Right?"

Eva wiped her nose with her feathery sleeve. Another minute dropped from the countdown.

Irena said the device would disappear when my assignment had ended.

But Eva still held the guardian phone in her hands. Beatrice was right. There was still time to fix things.

Eva sprang to her feet, wings spreading across the classroom and almost knocking over the witch. "You're a whiz at potions, right? Could you make a forgetting spell?"

"Probably," Beatrice said, avoiding Eva's wings as she pushed herself upright. "But I don't think forgetting your problems is going to help you here."

"Not for me, for the school. We could wipe this day from everyone's minds, right? That way Nate wouldn't be expelled or arrested. I could still guide him to greatness!"

"You want enough to wipe the memories of everyone at Dashmoor? I mean, human memories are easier to affect, but that's still a lot of potions. I can't afford all those ingredients. Unless..." Beatrice trailed off, but Eva could guess what the witch had been about to say.

White feathers shimmered on Eva's stretched wings.

Lose one and lose them all.

But Farrah claimed that was propaganda. She'd seen otherwise. Which made sense if there was an entire black market for angel feathers like Beatrice said.

Eva reached out. Her fingers brushed against the soft down.

She thought of Farrah pressing the guardian phone to her head, pretending it was a gun. *Your feather or someone's life?*

Images flashed through Eva's mind: her brother, trapped in an iron cell beneath the earth. Her parents locked in a spotless house and stewing in silent fights for the rest of their lives. And Nathan—whose lashes fluttered and made Eva's heart race—thrown into a police car, screaming out to his little brother as he got taken away.

Eva had to save them, even if it damned her.

Her grip tightened around a feather, and she pulled.

44
NATHAN

Nathan swung his backpack over his shoulder as he stepped out of the bank. He'd expected ten thousand dollars in cash to weigh more. But the teller had passed over only a few small stacks of bills. Perhaps he should've asked for the money in ones.

This payment was the largest and the last. And all he'd had to do was poison his classmates and get himself expelled.

The memory of everyone throwing up in the halls weighed heavier than the cash as Nathan walked toward his apartment. When G had produced the bottle and told him what she wanted, he'd almost refused. But she'd offered more than just money.

She'd offered Daniel a chance.

If Nathan could go back in time, he'd make the same choice. After all, his classmates would be fine in a few hours. He'd tested the poison on himself to be certain. It had been an unpleasant few hours, but he'd recovered by this morning, just like G had promised. The concoction shouldn't have worked any differently on humans.

There was no reason for Nathan to feel regret.

Yet guilt whispered in his mind, torturing him with the image of Eva's face. She'd looked so worried when he'd left. And how would he explain things to her? Either he'd have to claim to have poisoned their classmates as a joke or admit that he'd been paid to ruin her plans. Both meant she'd hate him.

The thought made Nathan's chest ache. Maybe it would be better to slip away without saying goodbye to her. With the money in his bag, Nathan had every intention of moving himself and Daniel to a new apartment. Somewhere that round-faced strangers in purple cloaks wouldn't come looking for them.

Nathan was so unfocused, he almost bumped into his neighbor as he stepped into the apartment.

Eric stood by the mailboxes. His sweat-stained t-shirt clung to his stomach, and he had crumbs in his beard. Despite his appearance, Eric was a decent neighbor. Didn't change his Wi-Fi password, didn't throw loud parties. Dependable.

"Did you leave Dan upstairs?" Nathan asked, trying to keep the annoyance from his tone. He'd begged Eric to watch the eight-year-old last minute. If their neighbor had stepped out to grab his mail, Daniel could survive.

"Yeah, he's with your friend."

Nathan's blood turned cold. "What friend?"

"A blonde," Eric said, flicking through his mail without looking up. "You so popular you need more details than that?"

Nathan bolted up the stairs. Had G returned? Why? He'd done everything she'd asked. He'd messaged and told her. Nathan reached his apartment, shoved his key into the lock, and hurried to push open the door. "Dan! Are you—?"

His breath caught.

The contents of the brown envelope G had left spilled across the coffee table. Daniel examined a lanyard with a photograph of himself at the end. Eva sat on the couch less than a foot away. Her hair fell in damp waves over a blue t-shirt. In her hands was a letter.

45

EVANGELINA

Eva barely noticed the door open. She kept staring at the letter.

Daniel Ward had been accepted to a medical trial for unknown magical illnesses at Castor's Care Hospital. He could report for testing next Monday. His treatment would be covered by ParadiseShared.

"Why aren't you at school?"

Eva's head snapped up at the sound of Nathan's voice. He stood in front of his door, backpack tossed over one shoulder, hair artfully falling in his face. The sight would have made her heart skip less than an hour ago.

Not now.

After giving Beatrice her feather, Eva had abandoned her vomit-covered jacket and bag, slipped through a window and gone straight to find Nathan. Well, almost. She'd taken Beatrice's advice and made a quick stop at a café's bathroom to wash the vomit out of her hair. But she'd wanted to find Nathan and apologize for letting him take the heat for what happened, let him know she was going to fix everything.

When Eva had knocked on the door, Daniel came running. Eric had been relieved to let someone else take over. They'd let her in, and she'd seen the envelope on the coffee table. Normally, she wouldn't have pried, but there'd been no mistaking the sender: Castor's Care Hospital. As its name implied, it treated the city's magical inhabitants.

Daniel's name had been written in the center. When Eva showed it to him, he'd ripped it open and shaken out the contents. The admission letter had fallen face up. Eva shouldn't have looked, but when she saw the name *ParadiseShared,* how could she turn away?

"Who are you, Nathan?" Eva asked, trembling as she stood.

"What do you mean? I'm me," Nathan said, running his hand through his hair. His eyes flitted toward the kitchen, obviously nervous. His lashes—

No, Eva refused to notice those now. She closed her eyes, holding back tears. She couldn't cry, not about this, not in front of him. Nathan didn't need to know just how much this hurt.

"Why do you have this?" Eva demanded, shaking the letter.

Nathan hesitated before shrugging. "Dan got accepted into a medical study."

"I did?" On the floor, Daniel's eyes lit up. "Are they going to cure me?"

For a second, Eva's heart softened, and she almost smiled. She hoped the hospital did, no matter who'd funded it. But a human child wouldn't be accepted to a magical treatment facility. Just like an average person wouldn't have ties to ParadiseShared.

"You've been lying to me this whole time," Eva whispered, wrapping her arms around herself in an effort to hold back the tears. "I knew you were connected to Zeke somehow, but I didn't think—"

Eva swallowed a sob before it could escape.

"Dan, go to your room," Nathan ordered.

"But—" Daniel started to object, but a look from his older brother sent him scurrying.

"Eva, I don't have any connection to your brother, I swear." Nathan reached forward as though he intended to comfort her.

Eva stumbled back, and her sob burst free and transformed into a scream. "How stupid do you think I am? ParadiseShared funds your study and I'm supposed to think you have nothing to do with what's happening to Zeke? To my family? Do you work with Hyde Leonard or Adelaide Glory? Did they recruit you to steal angel feathers?"

"I don't know any of those names. I swear. Please, Eva, can we just talk?"

His eyes were so sweet, so sincere. It wasn't right. A boy as attractive as Nathan shouldn't get to be a liar. He'd break too many hearts.

I kissed him.

Worse, Eva had liked it. No, she'd loved it, had indulged in the memory of it every night since.

How could she have been so naïve?

She needed to leave before she made more of a fool of herself. Eva reached for the door, but Nathan wrapped his fingers around her wrist.

"Please, Eva," he whispered her name, so sweet and soft it was like a prayer.

And just like that, pathetic and hopeless as it was, Eva hesitated.

46
NATHAN

The truth poured out of Nathan in a flood of words. He couldn't look at Eva as he admitted that he'd been paid to ruin her plans and poison the school. Her judgement would sting worse than his own.

Throughout his explanation, she stood before the door, arms crossed and body trembling. Part of Nathan wished she'd interrupt, but she didn't. Not until the end.

"Irena Elysium," Eva said, voice blank and listless. A strange, agonizing giggle escaped her. "That's who you're describing. Middle-aged, blonde curls, round face. She paid you to ruin my assignment. She never wanted me to succeed."

"I'm sorry, Eva," Nathan said. He didn't recognize the name, but he'd obviously helped someone who wanted to hurt her. And that made Nathan an absolute ass.

"Do you know why I've been trying to make you great?"

Nathan shrugged. "You're a plucky young angel who set out to prove no one was beyond saving?"

"I'm your guardian angel."

Nathan snorted. "That's bullshit."

Eva's face transformed. It radiated with a cold fury that did nothing to diminish her beauty. "Why would I lie about that?"

"I—" Nathan started, but he caught himself. She wouldn't. "But that's not possible."

"Are you human, Nate?"

Nathan's insides twisted. Throughout his explanation, he'd avoided addressing that issue. Because maybe—just maybe—Eva could forgive him for being an ass to help Daniel. But once she knew what he was, that would be the end. She'd want nothing to do with him.

He'd never see Eva's smile again, never see her face light up as she spotted him, never hear her laugh, or feel how soft her hands were when she touched him.

Nathan wasn't ready for that. He didn't want to lose Eva. He couldn't, because—

"We're angels too," a soft voice spoke from the corridor.

Nathan's head whipped around. Daniel had snuck out from the bedroom and now stood, peeping at them from the corridor, with his bear dangling from his hand.

How much had he heard? Daniel shouldn't be burdened with the weight of things Nathan had done.

"You can't be angels," Eva whispered, some of her usual warmth returning as she looked at Daniel.

"Yes, we are," he insisted.

"No, we're not," Nathan said. He lowered his head, squeezing his eyes shut. "But I used to be."

Nathan didn't look up, but he could feel Eva's eyes on him, waiting for him to say more. But whenever he reached for the word, it died on his lips. The only thing he could do was show her.

Nathan closed his eyes and forced his body to relax to an extent that felt almost unnatural. His wings unfurled with a clatter. The bones scraped against one another, rattling and aching. Nathan hated the feeling. But he stretched his skeletal wings and forced himself to look.

A small, desperate, pathetic part of him dared to wish that Eva wouldn't run, that she'd see the truth and stay, that the warmth might flood her expression once more as she understood.

"You're an irin," Eva whispered the word that Nathan couldn't. Her voice trembled with shock and fear, perhaps revulsion.

And then, just as Nathan had feared, she fled.

47
EVANGELINA

Eva's feet pounded on the pavement. She should slow down. A regular human couldn't sustain this speed for such a distance. It would raise suspicion if someone noticed.

But Eva didn't care about rules right now. Everything was wrong.

Nathan was an irin.

It was impossible. The Sanctum taught that angels came to Earth to guide its inhabitants. They weren't assigned positions as guardians of each other. That wouldn't make sense. And a fallen angel was still an angel.

But Eva had seen Nathan's wings.

A shiver went through her as the image flashed in her mind. The skeletal frame stretched like a spider web of bones, featherless sinew scraping like nails across a board. The alabaster sheen stole the light from the apartment, darkening the air to create its own dull glow. With his high cheekbones and dark features, Nathan looked both beautiful and horrifying.

Desire and despair had crashed through Eva. She'd been

torn between rushing to Nathan or bursting into tears, so she'd split the difference and run.

Nathan had lost his feathers. He'd never be able to fly back to their true home. His body here would die, and he'd be as mortal as the humans.

There was nothing Eva could do to save him.

Irin had been doomed by their sins. They couldn't be guided to greatness.

Irena set me up to fail.

Bright red flowers blossomed in Eva's view as she approached Ladybug Park. Excited laughter rose from the playground where a group of small children climbed over the slides. A couple, strolling on the paths between the gardens, nudged one another and pointed.

Eva slowed and wiped her face, conscious of her tears. She couldn't risk attracting attention and having her wings pop out now. Beatrice had her jacket. The witch had said she'd use it to help hide Eva's feather.

I should never have given it to her.

Saving Nathan from expulsion wouldn't solve anything.

The muscles in Eva's legs cramped in protest now that she'd stopped running. She'd pushed her body to its limit.

Exhausted, Eva dropped to the grass, letting her knees and palms catch her before she ended up with a face full of mud. The strolling couple turned to look, but they didn't stop to check if she was okay.

Good. The tears dripped from Eva's lashes onto the grass.

Is this part of the plan? Me crying in the middle of the park?

Eva would've screamed if she had the energy. Instead, she pushed herself onto her knees. Something bulky pressed against her thigh: the guardian phone.

She pulled it from the pocket of her leggings. The device

flashed its large red *WARNING*. In the top right corner, the clock continued counting down.

"Did you know that Nate wasn't human?"

Beneath the *WARNING*, a folder opened with details about Nathan Ward. His species remained listed: *human*.

"You're wrong," Eva said. "You made a mistake. Nate's an irin. I should never have been assigned to him."

A new screen appeared beneath the warning letters: *All goes according to God's plan. There are no mistakes.*

"So you knew Nate wasn't a human?"

The incorrect information reappeared.

"He's an irin," Eva said. An unfamiliar surge of frustration made her clench her hand into a fist around the phone. She shook it as though she might be able to knock something around in its wiring and make it understand. "Nathan Ward has been excommunicated by the Sanctum. I can't make him great. By law, I'm supposed to avoid him."

Triggered by the word *great*, the device flashed its usual list. Another talent had been added.

Nathan Ward is great at lying.

The new information hadn't erased the rest. Nathan remained great at making Eva blush, great at distracting her, great at kissing. Each bullet point felt like a cruel little jab in Eva's chest.

"I know I liked him. I don't anymore," Eva said. She couldn't because it would be extraordinarily stupid to have feelings for an irin who'd lied to her for weeks. Even if he'd been manipulated by Irena, even if he really didn't have connections to ParadiseShared, even if...

He did it to save his brother.

The guardian phone squawked. Eva looked down, expecting a summons. But the device only wanted to add a dramatic flair to its continued warnings.

"Change the list," Eva ordered. "Or shut up. Or turn off. Or something."

As if flashing and buzzing while displaying a list that broadcast Eva's feelings wasn't bad enough, the device started to vibrate. Its warning flashed. The numbers on the countdown glowed.

Eva couldn't take any more. The guardian phone probably wasn't even real. Irena must have created a fake device with faulty information.

This whole time, instead of helping Eva, it had been tracking her movements.

In a moment of fury, Eva flung the device across the park. It crashed into a tree, dropped to the ground, and disappeared into a patch of flowers.

"Good. I hope you broke," Eva shouted after it, earning more concerned looks from nearby humans. She didn't care. She felt lighter without the bulky phone. Maybe she could finally breathe and think.

Irena had set her up to fail. She'd funded Daniel's treatment with money channeled through ParadiseShared. She had to be behind everything. Maybe Adelaide Glory had worked with Hyde Leonard until her ascent, then Irena had taken over the operation.

It sounded absurd. Strait-laced, hyper-punctual Irena Elysium allied with a criminal to sell angel feathers?

But Nathan's description had matched—round cheeks, small nose, blonde curls. And, as Eva had learned, she wasn't a good judge of character. If Irena had been acting in their meetings, she wouldn't have noticed.

"Evangelina Heaven."

A hand clamped around Eva's shoulder. Its heat numbed her bone.

She turned, and her face collided with a thick, dark

forearm. She tilted her head back to find a broad man with a shaved head and serious expression. A single dark blue feather dangled from his right ear.

One of the Powers.

Eva's heart stopped. She had to remind herself to breathe.

The Sanctum's internal enforcers didn't just wander around parks.

"Why are you here?" Eva's throat was dry. "I haven't—"

She cut herself off. Eva wanted to say that she hadn't done anything. But that wasn't true. She'd given Beatrice a feather.

"You're wanted at The Sanctum," the Power informed her. "I would suggest you come without resistance. It wouldn't reflect well if you made a scene in front of these humans."

Eva nodded. He removed his hand. And a moment later, she stood, legs wobbling.

The Power stepped forward and took her hand in his. To the casual observer, it might've seemed a sweet gesture.

But Eva knew the truth. She'd been worried about Nathan, but she was the one being arrested.

48
EVANGELINA

Despite having wings, Eva had never flown to the Sanctum Headquarters before. It was located in the heart of downtown, and rules dictated flights be kept to the outskirts of the city, where the Castors maintained strongholds.

But the Powers could turn invisible.

Her polite captor had led Eva to an alley, out of sight of the humans, then asked permission to lift her. Once she agreed, he'd scooped her up and carried her into the air.

The colors of Castor's Grove blurred beneath them. Natural pockets of blue and green sprouted and blended with the city's mixed architectural styles. Residential areas full of Queen Anne gables and gothic spires turned to art deco panels and looming skyscrapers.

Eva didn't try to track their location above the city. The enforcer's touch sent a numbing heat through her body, making her limbs limp and weak. But it didn't quiet her mind, which was too bad. Eva might've preferred to have her panic dulled.

Why had the Power come for her? Did he know about

the feather? What about Irena's scheme? Eva had been duped. Maybe the whole Sanctum had been. Should she tell the large man who'd taken her hostage?

The Power dropped her on the roof of the Sanctum Headquarters.

Eva's legs wobbled. She held out her arms for balance and inhaled the cool, clean air. The setting sun cast a pink glow across the city, and a soft breeze lifted the edges of her hair. It felt almost peaceful.

"Fastest you've ever made it." Irena's voice cut through any illusions of tranquility.

Eva's spine snapped straight. Fear and fury battled within her. Did she scream or play stupid?

Why is Irena here? Did she send one of the Powers to fetch me?

The karmic angel marched toward Eva. Despite her circular shape, Irena's limbs jutted at sharp, unfriendly angles. Even her white wings folded themselves into points behind her burgundy suit.

Beyond her, not moving toward Eva, stood a tall man in a white robe. Short gray hair framed his long, clean-shaven face. Massive wings stretched from his shoulder blades. Streaks of gold radiated within the white.

Any thought of confronting Irena died on Eva's lips.

First a Power. Now a Prince of the Inner Sanctum. What was Irena planning?

Eva's pulse raced. Her fingers twisted around one another.

"Don't fidget," Irena said, swatting at Eva's hands. "It makes you look guilty, and I should hate for that to be the case, Miss Heaven."

That's rich. Eva bit back the comment.

Irena continued, "This is Judge Reign. He'll be overseeing your brother's trial."

A lump rose in Eva's throat. The man before her would determine her family's fates. When she spoke, her voice sounded squeaky, "It's an honor to be in your presence, your Greatness."

Judge Reign took a single step closer. He assessed Eva with a pair of gray eyes, so pale the irises almost vanished. "I hear you wish to give testimony for your brother, Miss Heaven." His voice carried a gravitas that could squash a mountain to dust.

Eva started twisting her fingers, then thought better of it. She squeaked again, "I do."

"That is either noble or corrupt. Do you know which I suspect?"

Given that Irena had been talking to him, Eva could guess. She swallowed, trying not fidget.

Judge Reign paced in a semi-circle before Eva. His long robe billowed behind. His movements were lithe and measured so that, were it not for his wings, she would have been tempted to compare him to a large and lethal cat.

"Ms. Elysium has allowed me to review the file on your guardian position," the judge said. "Perhaps you would also be so kind as to lend me the device you were assigned."

He wanted the guardian phone. Did that mean he knew there was a problem?

Irena leaned over and hissed, "That's not a request I would hesitate to comply with, Miss Heaven."

Eva knew that. Even the youngest angels understood that they needed to obey when a Prince of the Inner Sanctum made a request. But there was a slight problem.

"I don't have the guardian phone."

"What?" Irena's voice rose to a level that would've made dogs howl.

"I see," Judge Reign said, placid expression unchanged. "You've failed your assignment. An expected outcome."

"My sincerest apologies, your Greatness," Irena said, lowering her head as she addressed him. "This must be a recent development, or I would've been notified of the device's return to our stores."

"It won't have returned," Eva informed her, and she tried to layer as much meaning as she could into her next statements. "The device didn't vanish. I threw it into the grass."

Steam threatened to blow through Irena's ears. She leaned in and whispered again, "Whatever rebellion this is, Miss Heaven, I suggest you choose a better time."

If Irena wanted Eva silent, perhaps this was the perfect moment to speak.

"However the device left you," Judge Reign continued, "does not change the fact that it is gone. You've been relieved of your guardianship by destiny. Why do you suppose God has punished you in this manner?"

The question made Eva's chest constrict. But she didn't need to be nervous. A Prince of the Inner Sanctum wouldn't be corrupt. Judge Reign couldn't know the truth about what Irena was doing.

But would he believe Eva?

"I didn't fail my assignment," she said quickly, before her courage fled. "Because my assignment never existed. My guardian phone was a fake. I'm not being punished. I'm begin set up."

Judge Reign's face remained unreadable.

Irena's eyes grew wide and panicked. "Please your

Greatness, Evangelina is a child. She doesn't know what she's saying."

"I'm not a child," Eva corrected her. "And I do. Nathan Ward is an irin. I saw his wings. Irena has been paying him to purposefully fail at anything I try to help him with. He told me so himself."

Irena's eyebrows rose. Her neck snapped to Eva, and she hissed, "Have you gone insane?"

Eva's jaw quivered. She knew this was a risk. Irena had better standing among the Sanctum than any of the Heavens at present. But Eva was telling the truth. That had to count for something.

"Irin aren't assigned guardian angels," Judge Reign said, voice flat.

Eva flinched as though he'd slapped her. Was that all he'd gotten from what she said?

"Irin by their very nature are the opposite of great. They fell victim to the temptations of this world, allying themselves with the basest of its creatures. Your assignment was to guide Mr. Ward to greatness, is that correct?" Judge Reign asked.

"Yes, but I told you, it wasn't a real—"

"Miss Heaven, stop. You've said quite enough," Irena said, covering her face, perhaps to hide any flashes of guilt that the judge might see.

"Please, I'm telling the truth," Eva insisted.

Judge Reign nodded. "Ms. Elysium, you must allow Miss Heaven to speak, or I shall have to ask Mr. Kind to assist you." He gestured to the Power who balanced on the edge of the roof.

Eva had almost forgotten about the large man.

"Continue Miss Heaven," Judge Reign instructed.

Eva relaxed. The judge hadn't dismissed her concerns outright. She had a chance to convince him. Eva didn't have all the facts about ParadiseShared, but she did her best to explain what she believed had happened.

Irena remained mute throughout.

Judge Reign brought Eva to a stop as she began explaining today's incident with the soup. "I don't need your entire life story, Miss Heaven. You are accusing Irena Elysium of dealing in the illegal sale of feathers, consorting with an irin, creating a fake guardian device, and scamming the Sanctum out of hundreds of thousands. I will investigate. You are aware of the repercussions for attempting to deceive a Prince of the Inner Sanctum?"

"Yes."

In a single fluid motion, Judge Reign turned, robes billowing behind him. "Mr. Kind, please escort Miss Heaven to the holding room while we assess the validity of her claims."

"You're locking me up?" Eva didn't understand. "But I'm not lying. It's the truth."

The Power grabbed her shoulder. Panic shot through Eva, and her wings broke free. Their sudden appearance caught Mr. Kind off guard. He released his grip and stumbled backward.

Irena and the judge both turned toward Eva.

"Are you attempting to flee, Miss Heaven?" Judge Reign's pale eyebrow rose in a dramatic arch. "I don't believe you'd get far."

Eva shook her head. But she was too scared to defend herself.

"Miss Heaven loses control of her wings sometimes when she gets overwhelmed," Irena replied, without looking at Eva. "I doubt this was intentional."

"A curse from our Lord," the judge said, lips curling into a small frown. "A bit of advice, Miss Heaven. Use your time in the holding cell to pray."

49
NATHAN

Nathan waited beside the gray Dashmoor gates. Given his expulsion yesterday, he had no good excuse for his presence if Principal Davis caught him loitering outside. Chris could have met him at a nearby park.

A sliver of blonde danced at the edge of Nathan's vision. His head whipped toward it.

Some sophomore Nathan had never spoken to before walked out the gate. She caught his eye and gave him a thumbs up. "We're on your side!"

Weird. She must've mistaken him for someone else.

Nathan leaned against the wall and combed his hair out of his face, feeling foolish.

I'm here to meet Chris. No other reason.

But it was difficult to keep lying to himself when every passing blonde wearing a white t-shirt made his heart rate spike. It wasn't an accident that Nathan had suggested meeting by the gate Eva always used.

What am I thinking? Eva never wants to see me again.

The look on her face when she'd seen his wings had

haunted Nathan's dreams. He might never recover from the stabbing pain her rejection had wrenched through his chest. But how could he blame her? Nathan knew what he was. He hated his wings too.

Another blonde. Another rise and crash of Nathan's hopes.

What am I even going to do if she appears? Apologize again? Beg for forgiveness? Tell her I love her?

Not that last one.

That was only in his mind because Daniel had suggested it before Nathan left him with Mrs. Taylor. Which made no sense. Nathan had told his brother numerous times that he was going apartment hunting, not searching for Eva.

But Nathan had found a place faster than he'd feared. It was a small one-bedroom above a coffee shop near Castor's Care. Ten thousand covered the deposit, with enough left for rent, bills, and food for the next couple months while Nathan found a job. He'd signed the lease on the spot and found himself with hours left until Mrs. Taylor needed to leave. So, he'd come to see Chris. Only Chris.

"There you are!" A girl spoke from behind Nathan.

It wasn't Eva. He knew that, and yet Nathan was still disappointed when he turned and found Beatrice. She had her hands on her hips and an annoyed expression on her face.

"Do you have any idea how difficult you are to find? And I don't normally have a problem finding people."

Nathan rolled his eyes and turned back to the road, pretending not to be watching the students exiting from the corner of his eye. He couldn't imagine why Beatrice would be trying to find him. They weren't exactly friends.

"If you're hoping to see Eva, you're going to be disappointed. She's not at school today."

Anyone else and he might've dismissed the comment. They could've been sick. But Eva wouldn't catch a cold like a regular human, and she'd never skip school.

"Is she okay?" Nathan asked. Worry made his voice loud.

"No, or I'd be incredibly annoyed with her. Do you have any idea the amount of work I put in to get you unexpelled?"

"What are you talking about?"

"I got you back on the student roster at Dashmoor. And kept you out of jail too. Davis wanted to call the police. So, no need to drop to your knees in gratitude or anything dramatic, but a thank you might be nice."

Nathan still didn't understand. "What's wrong with Eva?"

"She got arrested. Ironic, isn't it?"

Nathan's body went numb. How could Eva be arrested? She was an angel. She'd never do anything wrong.

Except accidentally consort with an irin.

Oh God. Nathan felt suddenly sick. He licked his lips. "Who arrested her?"

"The Sanctum," Beatrice said, waving her hand. "You know how angels are."

"Not all of them. Eva's not—" Nathan cut himself off as he realized what she'd said.

"Thought so," Beatrice sang the words with an unnecessary level of smugness. She grabbed Nathan's arm before he could protest and pulled him away from the gate. She was surprisingly strong. "You can buy me a drink for all my kindness. We have a lot to discuss."

———

"An irin," Beatrice tested the word as she tapped her fork against her chin.

She'd dragged Nathan to The Purple Porcupine and shoved him into one of the booths at the back. Chocolate cake crumbs littered the plate between their mugs. They'd ordered a slice to share, but Beatrice had eaten most of it while Nathan explained his side of the story.

"I didn't think guardian angels were assigned to other angels. Or do you not count as one anymore?"

Nathan winced. Beatrice's tone was curious, not callous, but he didn't love the question. And truthfully, he found the matter perplexing himself. "She shouldn't have been assigned to me."

"Agreed. I always thought it was a mistake." Beatrice sipped her matcha, and her nose wrinkled in distaste. "No offense. I just never thought you were destined for greatness. But I didn't know you were a fallen angel with a sick brother. I mean, I just assumed you skipped class to smoke weed with Chris. And I was probably a bit jealous too. I mean, I still think Eva should've been assigned to me if we're looking for someone destined for incredible things."

Beatrice talked like words were a limited resource, and she was an oil baron. Nathan zoned out most of what she said after *mistake*.

"It must've been," he admitted. "Excommunication means ostracization from the Sanctum. Other angels only interact with us when its unavoidable. They're definitely not supposed to get close in any way."

The memory of Eva's lips made Nathan buzz. He recalled the feel of her body pressing against him in the darkened booth, his fingers tracing over her thighs.

"Shit." Nathan buried his face in his hands. "Do you think that's why they arrested her?"

"It's not impossible. Maybe Eva was punished because of whatever was going on between you two!" Beatrice sounded almost happy about the idea.

But this was Nathan's nightmare. What if after Eva saw his wings, she'd been so disgusted that she'd run to the Sanctum to confess her sins? What if they'd overreacted and imprisoned her? What if it cost her everything?

"They can't—they can't take her feathers over a mistake, right?" Nathan reached for his coffee, but his hand trembled too much to hold the mug.

"You tell me. I'm not exactly an expert on angelic law. I'm just reading the tabloids." Beatrice pulled a magazine from her bag. The name *Witch Whisper* glowed in pink cursive above a photo of a woman with matching lips. Judging from the sleeves on her dress, she was a witch.

Beatrice opened the magazine and turned it so that Nathan could read. The section was titled *Hottest New Gossip.* Under normal circumstances, he would've rolled his eyes at something so inane. Now, Nathan poured over every sentence, searching for a mention of Eva.

And there it was!

About halfway down the page, the article mentioned *Ezekiel Heaven's sister,* who had been taken into Sanctum custody for questioning on an unknown matter. That didn't stop the magazine from speculating. Their writers offered a number of theories, most of which involved Eva either being complicit in her brother's crime or cooperating with the Sanctum to turn him in. All sounded equally like nonsense until near the end.

One source claims that the sister had been working as a guardian angel. Her performance is under review, and it appears she's even more corrupted than her brother.

There it was. In writing. Eva was in trouble, and it was Nathan's fault.

"Shit, shit, shit," Nathan muttered, tightening his fist in his hair. He should never have agreed to foil Eva's plans. He could've found another way to get a treatment for Daniel.

If Eva loses her feathers, I—

"We have to do something. We have to fix this."

"Glad to be included," Beatrice said, looking far too relaxed given the situation. "But I'm surprised you're not more pleased by this turn of events."

"Eva's locked up, and it's my fault? Why would that make me happy?"

"Because if they take her feathers, then she'll be like you, and the two of you can…" Beatrice waved her hands. "I mean, you obviously like her."

Precisely why Nathan didn't want anything bad to happen to her. He crossed his arms and scowled at the witch.

Beatrice didn't seem to notice. She was rolling the tabloid back into a cylinder. "And it's not definitely your fault. It could be mine too."

"How?"

"Let's not get caught up in irrelevant details. The point is that Eva is in trouble, and we need to save her."

50

EVANGELINA

The door to the dark cell swung open for the first time since Eva had entered.

Finally. Judge Reign must have confirmed that she'd been telling the truth. The Power must have been coming to release her.

Eva leaped to her feet and rushed forward. Mad as it was, her instinct was to wrap Mr. Kind into a massive hug.

The Sanctum had provided a bookshelf, with several appropriate texts for those in temporary holding, but no clock. Eva had been measuring time in meals: rice and beans, cold oatmeal, green pea soup. Dinner, breakfast, and lunch made it close to a day since she'd been taken into custody. Plenty of time for Irena's plot to be uncovered.

But it wasn't Mr. Kind who entered.

"Farrah?" Eva stopped short as the door swung shut. She rubbed her eyes. The clammy sensation of being under the earth had done strange things to Eva's thoughts. She'd hallucinated several visitors: Irena coming to mock her, Zeke arriving to tell her they were all free, Nathan visiting to—well, they hadn't talked in that particular fantasy. He'd kissed her and then transformed into a shadowy menace, and instead of shying away, Eva had fallen into him. Then her skin had started itching and she'd struggled to breathe as she grabbed the blankets in her cell and struggled to reorient herself.

But the wild haired angel before Eva wasn't a figment of a panicked imagination. Farrah's glasses slipped to the end of her nose. Her tie was askew. For once, she'd left her mountains of paperwork elsewhere.

"What are you doing here?" Eva asked.

"I honestly don't know," Farrah muttered. She blinked, less accustomed to the dim light. "I guess that if I'm helping one Heaven sibling, might as well damn myself by helping the other. But I don't know how much I can do for you now, Eva."

"I don't need you to do anything. Just get Judge Reign to investigate. He'll find—"

"That Irena Elysium is an upstanding member of the Sanctum with all her feathers perfectly intact. Can you say the same?"

A cold, clammy sensation crept across Eva's skin.

"Judge Reign saw your wings," Farrah continued. "He thinks there's a feather missing."

Eva's clamminess turned to dread. "Nathan was going to get arrested. I thought—"

Farrah leaped forward and pressed her finger against Eva's lips. She glanced pointedly to the door.

Eva understood. Someone might be listening.

"I'm telling the truth about Nathan," Eva said, switching topic. "He's an irin. Someone set me up."

Farrah sighed and lowered her hand. Her dark eyes glowed like pools of honey in the dim light. "I looked at the irin records. There was a Karina Warden, who was excommunicated with her infant son, Nathaniel. The Sanctum lost track of her. Given the descriptions, I assume that's your charge and that Karina changed their names."

"That proves I'm right," Eva said, grabbing Farrah's hands and squeezing in excitement. "So why are we whispering?"

Farrah glanced at the door again. "Because I took the matter to Judge Reign. I think he already knew."

Eva's blood turned cold. "You think a Prince of the Inner Sanctum is covering up illegal feather trafficking?"

"No! Of course not!" Farrah's voice grew loud for a moment. "You need to let go of your obsession with ParadiseShared. Your brother did something stupid. It is what it is. You can't go around accusing respected angels of being involved in criminal activity to clear his name. No, I think Reign had already figured out that your charge was an irin. The only person who seems shocked is Irena."

"She's acting."

"Irena Elysium doesn't have the imagination to act. If someone is setting you up, it's not her."

"But Nathan saw her. He described her perfectly."

Unless Eva had put the suggestions in his mind. Had she led him with her questions? Or had Nathan been lying again? Why was she so quick to trust someone who'd betrayed her?

"Why are you helping me, Farrah?" Eva asked, studying the older angel. It couldn't just be guilt about Zeke. In the car, she'd talked about an angel who lost their feathers. Was it Farrah herself? "What were you doing with Hyde Leonard? Did you sell him something?"

"Of course not," Farrah hissed, eyes widening. She licked her lips. "I talked to Hyde because he claimed your father had approached him."

"That's not true."

"I didn't say I believed him. I don't think he'd ever met your father. But he certainly wanted me to think that he had, and to give up on your family's case."

Eva's brow furrowed. Why would Hyde Leonard care about the Heavens or Farrah?

"Did you lose three of your feathers?" Eva asked the question so softly she barely heard her own voice. "Please, please, tell me the truth. I need to understand why you're helping me."

"It wasn't me, Eva." Something seemed to crack in Farrah's voice. She glanced at the door, then grabbed Eva's arm and dragged her into the small bathroom that adjoined the cell. Farrah turned on the faucet and drummed her fingers against the wall. When she spoke, the words came fast. "It was my mother. She got assigned a difficult charge while working in the Guardian Division, ended up thwarting some demon's plan. He must've wanted revenge. He tried to kidnap me."

Farrah paused and licked her lips. Her tapping grew more erratic. Beneath the running water, her voice bordered on inaudible.

"He shifted his face to look like my father. I was four-teen and a moron. Didn't notice. My mother's assistant was watching me. She realized something was off. She called my mom and—"

"Your Mom saved you," Eva finished.

"With a kitchen knife."

Three stabs. Three feathers. That's what Farrah had said in the car. But if that was true, she was trusting Eva with a massive secret. Angels didn't kill, not even demons. If the Sanctum learned the truth, Farrah's family would be excommunicated.

"When we realized what had happened, my mother got mad—" Farrah cut herself off. Fear burned in her honey-colored eyes as they focused on Eva. "Listen, if you did something wrong, and I'm not saying you did. But *if* you did. When Judge Reign questions you about a missing feather, you need to lie."

51
NATHAN

"This is a terrible idea," Nathan muttered, scowling at the pair of skyscrapers. The Sanctum Headquarters rose toward the clouds. Panels of dark glass blocked within from inquisitive eyes.

"How?"

Nathan glared at Beatrice. "Because they're not going to let us just walk inside."

"Why not? Angels are kind and trusting by nature. They're not suspicious high-security freaks like the vampires," Beatrice said, inspecting her outfit. She'd opted for traditional witching attire. Her black dress bore a high collar and long bell sleeves for hiding potions. The only things missing were a pointy hat and a broom.

But at least her dress suited her.

"If angels are so trusting, then why am I disguised?" Nathan asked, gesturing to the shirt she'd forced him to wear. On top of being black and too thick for the current weather, it featured lace embellishments on the sleeves and collar. The threads poked Nathan's skin, making him itch.

Coupled with the dark trench coat, he felt like a black hole attempting to make a fashion statement.

"Because irin and demons are pretty much the only ones that angels won't allow in. So you need to look like a warlock." She adjusted Nathan's hair, then leaned back and considered. "You should've worn the eyeliner."

"Not a chance." Nathan suspected his disguise was mostly Beatrice messing with him. "Where did you even get these clothes?"

"Jacket is Albert's, and I borrowed the shirt from Oliver."

Nathan recalled both Beatrice's brother and his friend. They'd been in his class last year at Dashmoor. "Does Oliver know you *borrowed* his shirt?"

Beatrice ignored Nathan's question. "Let me do the talking when we get inside."

"Do you ever not do the talking?" Nathan muttered, but he shut his mouth as he followed her in.

Nathan must have been in the Sanctum Headquarters before, but he had no memory of it. The inside had always been a mystery, safer ignored behind its dark glass. He didn't know what was within, and he didn't want to.

Or so he'd told himself.

Stepping into the Sanctum hit Nathan like a child stepping into a fairytale. Light shone through the windows, flooding the room with sunshine. A glass orb rotated in the center, catching the rays. It swallowed the white light and spilled out a rainbow. Over thirty feet above, murals of angels flying in a golden city had been painted onto the ceiling.

Castors walked around the massive entrance. An elf with pointed ears carried a stack of paper. A fairy with pink, dragonfly-shaped wings stared at her phone while a mountain nymph with cracked, pebble-covered arms attempted to make conversation. And all between them were angels with white feathers that caught the rainbow hues.

Nathan's chest ached. This could have been his life.

"State your business, please." An angel stepped before them. A vibrant explosion of silver curls coiled around his head. The tops barely reached Nathan's chest. But the angel's wings stretched into a gate, blocking their entrance.

"We have an appointment in the building," Beatrice lied.

Silver-curls offered a bright smile. His dark eyes were big and trusting. But he didn't lower his wings. "What's the name of the person you'll be meeting?"

"Farrah," Beatrice said.

"Last name?"

"Ah…" Beatrice faltered. Eva had mentioned a Farrah in connection with her brother's case, but she'd never given a last name. "Farrah Peace?"

Nathan fought the urge to slap his forehead. Beatrice had just guessed a name that sounded angelic, hadn't she?

Silver-curls kept smiling. "And you two are?"

"Beatrice Blackwell and—"

"Oliver Wyrmwood," Nathan lied. Beatrice had told him to pretend to be her brother, but no one would buy that they were related. Granted, no one would mistake Nathan and Oliver either, but it was a closer match.

"Very good, very good." Silver-curls nodded. "A witch and a warlock, then, is it? You know, Mr. Wyrmwood you have an odd aura about you."

Nathan shrugged and glanced at Beatrice, hoping she'd respond to that comment for him.

"I don't believe we're scheduled for a renewal of our magical protections," Silver-curls continued. Despite the angel's cheerful smile, Nathan suddenly got the sense that this was not going well for them. "I'm also not familiar with anyone by the name of Farrah Peace working in this building. Perhaps one of my supervisors—"

"I may have the last name wrong," Beatrice interrupted. "Maybe it was...Beauregard? Or Wellwish? Farrah Kindthoughts?" Beatrice kept guessing. "Farrah Prayer?"

Oh God. Her ideas were getting worse. They should cut their losses and leave now, before—

"I can help these visitors, Haniel," an unfamiliar voice issued the offer like a command.

Nathan's head lifted toward the speaker. His breath caught as their gazes locked, and Nathan found himself staring straight into a familiar pair of round blue eyes.

———

Irena Elysium led them toward a large glass elevator. Her black kitten heels clicked as they entered. Blonde wisps curled beside her temples. Dark makeup did little to hide her rosy cheeks. There was no question. Nathan was staring at G's face.

And yet—

"Are you taking us to the basement?" Beatrice guessed, reaching for the button.

Irena slapped the witch's hand away and pressed the number 5. "I should, but I doubt you'd appreciate the trip."

She had a sharp voice, deeper and more annoyed than her face would suggest. Had she faked the high-pitched, almost girlish lilt she'd had with him? Or was she forcing it lower now? Maybe, but her voice wasn't the only discrepancy.

Her body is wrong.

The large shoulders of Irena's suit couldn't disguise her natural plumpness. Her stomach and chest would've brushed against a purple robe. G had been slender and willowy.

The elevator dinged and opened to a corridor with soft white walls spaced so wide that an angel could stretch their wings without their feathers brushing the sides.

Irena led them down the passageway toward a massive glass-walled office with industrial furnishings. A blue-haired nymph, with rivers coursing across the skin of her arms, sat behind a desk. She smiled as they approached.

"Hold my calls," Irena ordered. She stormed into the glass office and held the door for Nathan and Beatrice. Once they entered, she jammed it closed and crossed to a high-backed seat.

Nathan glanced around for another chair, but there was a conspicuous absence.

"I never thought I'd have an irin in my office, Mr. Ward," Irena said. She remained standing with her fingers steepled on her desk. "But do you know the Sanctum's motto?"

"Uh..." Nathan gaped at the scowling face before him, still struggling to disconnect it from G's own.

"Spread the light," Beatrice answered for him.

Irena huffed. She opened a drawer and rested her hand on something within. "I meant its unofficial motto."

Nathan didn't care about mottos, official or unofficial. His mind kept spinning. "Do you have a twin?"

Irena frowned. Her eyes cut to Nathan. "Have you seen my face before, Mr. Ward?"

Nathan had no idea how to respond. Irena wasn't G. The more he saw of her expressions, the more certain he became. But they had to be connected in some way.

"Why has Eva been taken into custody?" Nathan asked instead. "She had no idea what I was. You shouldn't punish her."

"How kind of you to lecture me on what I should and shouldn't do," Irena said. "You know, the penalty for an irin seeking to involve themselves in Sanctum matters is to have the last sliver of their divinity stripped. I've never seen it, but I'm told it's unpleasant."

Her tone was blunt and cold. Something told Nathan that it wasn't an overflow of empathy that had stopped her from reporting him so far.

"And I'm sure there are repercussions for a witch who attempts to sneak one in," Irena added, lips curling in distaste as she looked at Beatrice. "Ones it might benefit you to face, Miss Blackwell."

Despite the obvious threat, Beatrice grinned. "You know who I am?"

"I reviewed Evangelina's list of classmates at Dash-moor. Your name stood out." Irena's eyes returned to Nathan, and for a moment, her stern expression slipped. He caught a hint of concern beneath. "Your name didn't strike me. Had I been more thorough, perhaps. But I was lax, and so here we are."

Irena sighed, opened a drawer, and took out a rectangular brick of a device: Eva's other phone. Nathan recognized it at once.

"I was certain it would have disappeared. And yet..." Irena's voice grew soft. She turned the device in her hand, almost as though she'd forgotten the teenagers were there. Then, she clicked her tongue, looked up, and extended her arm. "Take it, Mr. Ward."

The option of refusing didn't occur to Nathan until he'd already reached for it.

Idiot, what if she'd boobytrapped it or something?

But Irena didn't seem the type to engage in deception. "Miss Heaven believed that I had tampered with the device. I admit that I lack the skills to know if someone else did. Certainly, it is not entirely accurate in its information on you. And what it's chosen to track is *curious.*" Her eyes darted to Nathan. He swore he saw a flicker of amusement. "Regardless, the Fates granted Evangelina this assignment. So long as the device remains, she hasn't failed. You should give it to her."

Nathan didn't understand. "Why don't you give it to her?"

"Because Miss Heaven is beyond my assistance now. I'll be prosecuting both her and her brother. And Evangelina has already intertwined me in the narrative more than is healthy."

"What?" Beatrice's head snapped up. She'd been staring at the device in Nathan's hand with an almost greedy expression. The witch obviously wanted to get her hands on it, but this news bothered her more. "Are you saying Eva is on trial?"

"The time is set for right after her brother's own." Irena shot the witch another disgusted look. "A feather was discovered missing from one of her wings. She confessed to giving it to someone but refuses to provide a name."

Nathan's hand tightened around the phone. He glared at Beatrice, who stared guiltily at the floor. There was no way Eva would've given the witch a feather. The Sanctum considered it a crime. Eva was too good. Beatrice must've stolen it and had Eva cover for her.

Dammit! This was worse than the Sanctum arresting Eva for kissing him. They had an actual case. Nathan needed to do something. He needed to save her.

"Where is Eva?" Nathan demanded. "You have to tell us so we can give her the phone."

"It was never a secret, Mr. Ward," Irena said. She glanced away, and for a moment, she looked pained. "Evangelina is being tried as a criminal. The Sanctum transferred her to Ironvault earlier this afternoon."

52

EVANGELINA

"**I** *told you to lie, Eva. Why didn't you listen?*"

Farrah's hissed whisper echoed in Eva's mind. They'd been allowed a few minutes to confer before Mr. Kind carried Eva off. Farrah's eyes had been red, but she hadn't cried.

Eva had. Tears had streaked across her face like she'd been caught in a torrential rain. She hadn't expected that the truth would land her in Ironvault with its dark walls and heavy chains.

But she couldn't lie, not to a Prince of the Inner Sanctum. It would be deceitful and self-serving. Eva couldn't consciously make a decision she knew to be morally wrong.

Judge Reign had questioned her himself, pacing before her like a panther. When he asked about her missing feather, she'd confessed: *I gave it away. It was a mistake, but I thought it was the right thing in the moment.*

Eva refused to provide more details. She couldn't implicate Beatrice. And if she admitted that part of her concern had been for an irin—No, that wouldn't go over well.

Olivia waited for her at Ironvault. She shackled Eva's

wrists with a stony expression. "Follow my directions. Any attempts to run will be harshly punished."

Eva's pulse pounded in her ears as she marched through the black-walled corridors. Dim lights flickered overhead. Instead of the visitor's room on the first floor, she climbed several flights of steps.

Olivia unlocked the door to a windowless cell. She whispered, "You'll like this one." Then, sealed Eva within.

The guard's statement felt overly optimistic, even to Eva. Black iron cast everything in heavy shadows. A toilet and sink in the corner offered little in the way of amenities, and the narrow bed lacked the plush blankets that the Sanctum had provided. But at least Eva was above ground, and she had space to spread her wings.

Eva stretched, letting her feathers brush the walls. The darkness turned them gray and sent a chill racing up her spine. Eva folded her wings at once, fell onto the uncomfortable mattress, and let out a sob.

"Psst." The iron wall beside her reverberated as though being tapped. "Eva, is that you?"

Her head snapped up. She knew that voice. "Zeke?"

"When I told you to visit again, this wasn't what I meant."

Eva pushed herself upright, kneeling on the mattress so that she faced the wall. "I thought they were keeping you underground."

"Someone must like me." Zeke's grin was audible. "Though when Liv offered to put us in neighboring cells, I thought she must've been joking. I mean, my little sister doing something to get in Ironvault? You wouldn't even take extra chocolates from the buckets on Halloween."

"They have signs that say to only take one," Eva reminded him, smiling at the familiar argument. Then her brow furrowed. "Did you refer to our guard by a nickname?"

"Did I?"

Eva groaned. No wonder they'd ended up next to each other. Did her brother ever take a break from girls? "You can't date the guards, Zeke."

"Of course not. There's no law against flirting though."

Poor Olivia. She must've started interacting with Zeke more after Eva's visit. Girls often fell head over heels for him. But he always lost interest when things grew serious.

"Liv said you gave away one of your feathers. Did you do that for your charge, the one who you were blushing about last time?"

Eva pressed her hands to her cheeks, grateful for the wall. "Olivia's definitely not supposed to give you all that information."

"That's totally a yes, isn't it?" Zeke's chuckle echoed through the wall. "You're so predictable. Guess that means you took my advice and kissed him. Did you two start dating? You're only ever reckless for the people you love—"

"Nate is an irin," Eva snapped, glaring ineffectively at the wall. She didn't know why her brother had jumped to love. No one said anything about love. But maybe she did— No, maybe she had—Ugh. Her brother fell silent and, unable to resist, Eva added bitterly, "Guess Olivia didn't mention that."

"Someone set you up too," Zeke whispered.

It was the first time someone had recognized that without Eva having to explain. Tears slipped down her cheeks. She pressed her hand against the wall, ignoring the biting chill of the iron. Eva wanted to be as close to her brother as possible. Because of all people, Zeke would understand.

Eva told him everything about her attempt to investigate ParadiseShared, and Irena bribing Nathan. Zeke listened, only interjecting on occasion to let her know he was still there.

When she finished, he sighed. A thud against the wall suggested he'd dropped his head against the iron.

"Adelaide Glory, Victoria Celand, and Irena Elysium running a feather racket?" Zeke whispered. "I don't think anyone's going to believe that, Eva. I barely believe that."

"I don't know what else to think."

"That there's something deeper at play. I told you the reason ParadiseShared stood out was because it looked like all the documentation had been written by a single person."

"But the scheme would require multiple people. Victoria to clear the charity. Adelaide to approve the payments. And Irena's obviously running things now."

Zeke was silent for a moment. "You said that the person visiting your irin wore a purple cloak. Adelaide Glory wore a big jacket and gloves when she approached me. I thought it was weird, but when I asked around, people said she often got cold, so I dismissed it. But when someone's covered up like that, it can be hard to tell..."

"You're hinting at something. Just say it."

"Maybe it's one person in make-up and different wigs. But they can't hide their body, so they have to get creative with the outfits. I always thought Adelaide sounded a little too trembly. Like an imitation of an old lady's voice instead of the real deal."

Eva chewed the inside of her lip. Could Nathan's benefactor have disguised themselves to resemble Irena? Maybe. Eva hadn't seen the woman herself. But if that were true, it could be anyone.

"How do we save you then, Zeke?" Eva whispered, eyes watering again. She blinked, wondering when she would finally run out of tears.

"You mean how do we save us."

No, I don't. A pang shot through Eva's chest.

She'd given away her feather. The Sanctum would find her guilty, and they'd be correct. Whatever punishment awaited, Eva deserved it. Her parents and brother did not.

"I already messed up and accused Irena. Judge Reign won't believe me if I say ParadiseShared is a front. And he won't believe you either. We'll need to give him a name."

Even then he might not listen.

Eva didn't voice that fear aloud.

Zeke hummed. It was the sound of his mind working. "Did you find out who reported me to the Sanctum?"

"Yes, but—"

"There's no but, Eva. Who was it?"

"It was Farrah."

53
NATHAN

"Ugh." Beatrice groaned as she ended her call to Ironvault Prison. "Their visiting hours are atrocious!"

Nathan's head jolted upright. He'd been studying the guardian phone since they ducked into the city's public library. The location had been Beatrice's suggestion given its proximity to the Sanctum Headquarters. Nathan hadn't visited before, partly for that same reason.

Beatrice had convinced the librarian to give them access to a private study space with some story about an art history project. It allowed them to speak without being shushed or overheard. Not that Nathan was in the mood to talk to the witch.

"We can go see Eva on a Sunday afternoon, at which point her trial will be done. Or we can go in the middle of the day during the week," Beatrice complained. "Honestly, it's like they don't want people to visit."

They probably didn't.

But those hours suited Nathan fine. "What time tomorrow?"

"Between eleven and one. I'll have to skip school."

"You don't need to come. You've done enough," Nathan assured her, returning his attention to the device. It felt bizarre seeing his own face half-smiling back. "If this thing was tampered with, what's the point of returning it?"

"I don't know. But it's really cool. It answered Eva's questions. Want to see?"

"No." Nathan twisted so that the witch couldn't grab the device.

Beatrice huffed. Without invitation, and despite the table being long enough to seat twelve, she took the chair right beside Nathan. "Do you know why Eva gave me her feather? She wanted me to save you! This thing kept giving her warnings." The witch leaned forward and tapped the image of Nathan's face. "It said she'd fail if you got arrested and expelled. She wanted me to wipe everyone's minds so that your little stunt with the soup never happened. So you're at least as responsible for her situation as I am."

"You think I don't know that?" Nathan snapped. Eva had believed in him, and he'd let her down. But something in the witch's story didn't make sense. He'd checked his school account on route to the Sanctum at Beatrice's insistence. She wasn't lying about Davis cancelling Nathan's expulsion. But it wasn't that simple either. "If you wiped everyone's mind, why am I still suspended for selling contraband?"

"You really think I'd sell an angel's feather to bail you out? Maybe to save Eva. But I figured out a different way to help." Beatrice paused. She stared at Nathan, evidently waiting for him to ask what it was.

He didn't.

Beatrice continued anyway, "I spread a rumor that the cafeteria had slipped something into your soup because they were jealous of your success and that Davis was scape-goating one of our own instead of the Cassel transfer. Then, I got everyone who'd ordered the soup to sign a petition saying they wouldn't sue the school once your expulsion was revoked."

"Jesus Christ, you did that in a day?"

"I'm very persuasive. Plus, glimpsing Eva's wings made half of Dashmoor suddenly believe in mercy. Luckily, no one's pieced together what she is. Humans have an absurd talent for explaining away supernatural phenomenon. Practically wipe their own minds," Beatrice said. "Now, we can't visit Ironvault this evening, which means we get extra time to play with Eva's phone."

Nathan stood, lifting the device out of Beatrice's reach. "If you have Eva's feather still, you can return it. Maybe the Sanctum will forgive her."

"No way! Did you see how strict that Irena lady was? They'll still hold it against her, and I'll lose my chance to perform a miracle." Beatrice jumped up, still angling for the guardian phone. "The way I see it, our best chance of helping Eva is—"

"Convincing the Sanctum that she's innocent?"

"Well, yes, obviously. But I was going to say that Eva needs to succeed in her assignment."

Beatrice couldn't be serious.

"Eva's assignment was fake. Someone tampered with this thing." Nathan waved the device. "There's no succeeding."

"Seriously? You can't find a way to be great? For Eva?"

Nathan ran his hand through his hair and dropped back into his chair. Of course, he'd try for Eva, but how? "I don't think selling food and giving the proceeds to charity is going to make the Sanctum reconsider."

"Agreed. And I don't think Davis will let you sell anything ever again. But see this countdown on the top of the screen?" This time, Nathan didn't pull the device away when Beatrice touched it. "Eva thought her assignment was connected to her brother's trial. I think it's connected to her own."

Nathan watched the seconds decrease near the top of the screen. Maybe Beatrice was right, but—

"How the hell am I supposed to achieve greatness in the next three days?"

"Not a clue," Beatrice admitted. "Do you have any talents besides cooking?"

Nathan would have said no. But the guardian phone flashed, and a list appeared spelling out the answer for him.

Nathan Ward is great at:

- *Making the seniors at Dashmoor High hate Evangelina Heaven*
- *Being hot*
- *Cooking*
- *Taking care of his brother*
- *Making Evangelina Heaven blush*
- *Kissing*
- *Distracting Evangelina Heaven*
- *Lying*

Nathan's eyes widened. He didn't know if to be flattered or amused. Then his eyes fell on that last bullet point.

Is that really what I'm good at?

"Maiden, Mother, and Crone! You and Eva kissed?" Beatrice grabbed the phone before Nathan could stop her. She looked way too excited. "Where? When? How?" A sly expression came over the witch's face. She rushed out of reach with the device. "Phone, tell me everything. What happened between Nathan and Eva? Does he like her?"

"Seriously? How old are you? It's not going to—" Nathan started to object until, to his horror, an answer appeared on the screen.

54

EVANGELINA

E va almost tripped as she stepped into the visitor's room at Ironvault. The shackles on her feet bore only partial responsibility.

When the guard had informed her she had visitors, Eva assumed it would be her parents. Given how they'd reacted to Zeke's capture, she'd also assumed that they'd come to disown her. She'd braced herself for their disappointment and rejection as the guard—a tall man with thick eyebrows, who her brother was not flirting with and therefore had no inclination to offer Eva details—escorted her through the corridors.

Eva hadn't prepared to see Nathan, sitting on a dark chair with one arm over it as though he were posing for a magazine cover. His dark eyes locked onto her the moment she entered.

He's gorgeous.

Eva's heart sped up, and her thoughts evaporated. She stumbled, barely catching herself before she fell flat on her face and embarrassed herself.

What is wrong with me? I shouldn't be excited to see him!

It took a second chair scraping for Eva to realize that Nathan wasn't alone.

Beatrice sat beside him. She grinned and waved. The witch had styled herself with the red gloss Eva had selected for her.

Despite her current situation, the sight made Eva smile. "What are you two doing here?"

Neither Beatrice nor Nathan had a chance to reply before the guard began issuing directions. The rules hadn't changed: hands on the table, no touching. But now, Eva couldn't disobey, even if she'd wanted. Manacles locked her wrists to the table and her ankles to the floor. Her skin itched beneath.

"I want to start by saying how very sorry I am," Beatrice said. She kept her hands on the table and leaned in. As always, she had her words in order. "I had no idea this would happen, or I never would have asked for, you know—"

"It's fine. I forgive you," Eva said. She meant it. "It was my choice. Not yours. Did it—uh—work?"

Silly question. It must have, or Nathan would be the one in a prison cell. Eva risked glancing at him. Nathan had rested his fingers on the edge of the table, as though afraid to get too close. His leg bounced, knee tapping the underside of the metal. He met her gaze and froze.

"Eva," Nathan whispered her name. She'd forgotten how much she liked hearing him say it. "I'm so—"

"Stop." Eva cut him off before he could apologize. She was beginning to understand why her friends had come. Both felt guilty.

A flicker of disappointment stung Eva's chest. But she

was being silly. Why else would Beatrice and Nathan visit? Had she hoped they'd come just to see her? Either way, them apologizing felt wrong.

"You were trying to help your brother," Eva said, forcing herself to hold Nathan's gaze without letting her attraction melt her mind back into goop. "I wish you'd trusted me as a friend and told me the truth earlier, but I can't hold any of it against you."

Beatrice snorted. "Oh please, a friend?"

Nathan's eyes shot toward the witch. He looked annoyed.

Eva's cheeks heated. She should've known better than to call them friends. Nathan felt guilty about the role he'd played in her failure because he was a good person, not because of any friendship. She might have thought of him that way, but he'd been lying the whole time.

"We came because we want to help you," Nathan said. "You can't lose your feathers."

He sounded so earnest. It made Eva's heart speed up again.

What is wrong with me? Nate's an irin.

But Eva would be too soon, so that might not be as effective at stopping her feelings as she wished.

"I deserve my fate," Eva admitted. Her fingers twitched. She wished she could scratch under the manacles, or even behind her neck. In fact, everywhere felt itchy now.

Was this what Zeke felt like when I visited?

At the thought of her brother, Eva had a sudden epiphany. "But if you want to help me, I think I know how."

———

"So you're saying that this Farrah Downes—That's her last name, huh? I would not have guessed that," Beatrice said, going on a slight tangent before continuing, "She inserted herself into your brother's case by volunteering to help, noticed and reported finances being siphoned from this phony charity, and you saw her with Hyde Leonard. But you still need more evidence? This is what reasonable doubt is based on."

"It's an angelic trial," Nathan said, eyeing Beatrice again. "There's no doubt, reasonable or unreasonable. They don't believe they can make mistakes."

"Then what is Eva being tried for?" Beatrice sounded like Zeke, in more ways than one.

Eva chewed the inside of her lip, twisting her hands as much as she could within the shackles. The evidence against Farrah sounded obvious when listed. Zeke felt confident. Eva felt like a fool.

How many times had she considered that Farrah might have ulterior motives only to dismiss them? The assistant always seemed to have an explanation. She'd overheard Irena scheming. Hyde Leonard had approached her. A horrifying moment from her childhood had transformed her into someone who believed in the power of forgiveness. If Farrah had invented it all to play on Eva's sympathies, it had worked!

She looked genuinely nervous telling me about her mother.

But maybe there had been some truth to the story.

"It wasn't a wig and makeup," Nathan said, ignoring Beatrice's last question and leaning closer to Eva. "I'm not an idiot. I'd have noticed if that were the case."

"If only we lived in a world where magical disguises were possible," Beatrice muttered, rolling her eyes. "Honestly, angels should never investigate."

Eva would've preferred that. She wanted to trust people, not be searching for evidence of betrayal. "You said you could disguise me if you had the right demon's head. What if Farrah had one?"

"Then all she'd need is a witch smart enough and willing enough to cast a spell and—poof! She's Irena Elysium," Beatrice said. "At least until the potion ran out. She'd need a fortune to keep buying them though, and anything permanent would be unstable."

"What if she had an angel's feather to use in the spell too?"

"Oh that would change everything!" Beatrice sounded almost excited as she explored the hypothetical. "You could stabilize the skin. Maybe turn it into a mask..."

The witch kept going. Eva's stomach turned. She'd expected the response. But she'd still hoped for another.

"Look, Farrah's too young to have done all this on her own," Eva said, cutting Beatrice off before she started listing more horrifying ingredients. "Her mother must've been involved too. But I don't know how the Downes are connected to Adelaide Glory or Victoria Celand. Maybe you two can find out. I can give you Victoria's address."

Beatrice typed it on her phone before the guard caught her and reminded her to keep her hands flat. The witch played it off like she'd forgotten. Her excuse went on so long, the guard got bored and turned away again.

"Now," Beatrice whispered, leaning over and elbowing Nathan without lifting her hands. "Come on. While he's *not looking.*" She mouthed the last two words, flicking her eyes to the guard.

Eva frowned. What were they planning?

Nathan slipped his hand into his pocket and produced Eva's guardian phone. He slid it across the table.

The guard glanced back over. Eva managed to maneuver her hands just enough to block the device from his view.

"How did you guys...?" Eva left the question hanging.

"Irena," Beatrice said. "She seems to think that, rigged or not, your assignment isn't finished."

Eva didn't know what part of that made less sense. The idea that she was expected to continue being a guardian angel to an irin while locked in Ironvault, or that Irena Elysium wanted her to smuggle the device into her cell.

But the countdown remained at the top of the phone's screen. Maybe it could still be useful. It might be possible to have it reveal who'd tampered with it.

"You'll need to..." Eva fluttered her wings, once again trusting Beatrice and Nathan to interpret what she meant. Her hands were shackled and hiding places were limited in the gray Ironvault jumpsuit.

Beatrice winked. She stood up, but instead of placing the phone behind Eva's wing, she went to the guard.

"I've always been curious about what it's like working here," the witch said. "You must get all the best gossip on the prisoners."

Eva pursed her lips, holding back a smile as Beatrice continued chattering at the guard, who eventually caved, turned, and started answering the witch's questions.

Once his attention shifted, Nathan seized the opportunity. He lifted the guardian phone again, leaned forward and pushed it behind Eva's wing. His fingers brushed her feathers.

Heat shot through Eva at the contact. She turned and found Nathan's face less than an inch away. Their eyes met, and his lips parted, softening his features. They hadn't been this close since—

"Hey, what are you two doing? Butt in the chair," the guard barked.

Nathan complied faster than he ever had for the teachers at Dashmoor.

Eva's face heated. She clenched the muscles in her wings, pressing them tight against her back to hold the guardian phone in place.

Nathan was an irin. He'd probably been affected by the sight of Eva's feathers. What excuse did she have for how she'd reacted to feeling his fingers brush her wing?

"Did you know the two of them kissed?" Beatrice said, drawing the guard's attention back to her. "Nathan won't tell me when. But Eva thinks he's great at it."

Oh no! Eva's eyes widened. Was Beatrice implying —?

Nathan's eyes flicked to Eva. He gave her the faintest hint of a smile. There was a definite sense of smugness. He'd seen the list.

"I didn't write—Those just appeared," Eva started trying to explain, but Beatrice was still speaking. And it was difficult to compete with the witch's voice.

"What I personally want to ask though," Beatrice said. "How does Nathan feel about Eva? I mean, he won't say, but there's definitely an answer *somewhere*."

The smirk vanished from Nathan's face. He glared at the witch.

The guard sighed with overt exasperation. "I think you kids have visited long enough." His tone oozed with obvious annoyance, but it wasn't malicious or distrusting —more like one of the teachers at Dashmoor when they caught students making out in the halls. Eva tried not to over interpret that.

At the guard's command, Nathan and Beatrice pressed their backs against the wall while Eva was freed and then re-shackled with portable chains. The guard escorted her through the passageways and back into her cell.

Eva held her wings close the entire time, feeling the weight of the guardian phone against her shoulder.

55
NATHAN

Nathan's knees hit the back of the seat as the car rolled toward Downtown. Beatrice had hailed a taxi the moment they left the Haunted Woods and given the driver the address Eva had provided. Nathan appreciated the witch's assistance, and her footing the bill, but he wished she'd be more selective about how she offered her *help*.

"I'm just saying, you didn't have to make it weird with the guard," Nathan muttered.

Beatrice snorted as she reapplied her lip gloss. "You two were obviously doing something. Better he thinks you were trying to make out. Besides, how do I know you weren't?" She grinned. It looked borderline manic.

Nathan rolled his eyes. "You might want to use a mirror."

Beatrice pulled out her phone, looked at her reflection, and wiped her lips over the back of her pink sleeve. She tried applying her gloss again. Somehow, she managed to talk while doing it. "Anyway, we both know that's not the comment that upset you."

Nathan crossed his arms, feeling his jaw tighten. He didn't want to discuss this in the backseat of a cab. Or ever.

"It doesn't matter, you know. Eva likes you. She'll obviously ask the device what you think of her. That would be the first question I'd pose to it if I were in her shoes." Beatrice laughed as she closed her tube of lip gloss.

Nathan's face burned. He wished Beatrice had never seen any of the information stored on the guardian phone. She'd had a hundred questions. For Nathan and the device. But despite all her curiosity, Beatrice still didn't get it.

"Eva doesn't like me," Nathan said. "Whoever set her up just messed with the device."

"Oh please! You know Eva likes you. That list is completely accurate. She turns pink just talking about you, and you won't give me details, but you obviously kissed, and she obviously enjoyed it."

"No, she wanted to be *friends* after," Nathan hissed, wishing the cab driver would turn up the music. He hated feeling like a stranger was listening to this conversation. "Besides, not everything on that list was good."

"I'm pretty sure she got over you embarrassing her in English."

But that wasn't the entry Nathan meant. It was the last one.

Did Eva really think he was a liar? Of course, she did. Seeing it in print stung, but what else would Eva have thought? Nathan had lied to her. About everything. Even his feelings.

"What time do you think we'll be back?" Nathan asked, changing the topic. "I want to let Chris know. I'm going to owe him like a hundred meals."

"He's happy to help, you know," Beatrice said, and her voice was surprisingly gentle for a moment. "I mean, watching your brother gives him an excuse to skip school and stay on a couch playing video games all day."

Nathan would've defended his friend if the comment didn't align with Chris' own response when he'd been asked to babysit. But it wouldn't be fair to expect Chris to watch Daniel all the time. The lease Nathan had signed began yesterday. He'd moved their few belongings into the small apartment. It felt good to go somewhere new without the memories of his mother's drunken rants. Even stuck in bed, Daniel kept grinning about the new place.

But we can't stay, not if we clear Eva's name.

ParadiseShared was paying for Daniel's trial. The money would vanish if they exposed the charity as a front. Nathan couldn't return to Dashmoor, care for Daniel, and get a job to cover their expenses.

"What exactly is wrong with your brother?" Beatrice asked. She made an effort to lower her voice, but the witch seemed incapable of a proper whisper.

Nathan shrugged.

"Fine, let's talk about you and Eva. Were you guys at Dashmoor when you kissed? Did you take her under the bleachers?"

"Of course not, we—" Nathan caught himself. "Let's focus on helping, Eva, okay? What do you think we're looking for when we get to this address?"

———

Beatrice kept knocking long after Nathan had given up. The address Eva had given them was for a large, two-story house in an expensive area close to downtown. It featured white coral stone walls and large glass windows, with the blue curtains drawn. Nathan didn't think anyone was home.

"Maybe we can break in," Beatrice suggested, eyeing one of the windows.

She wasn't thinking of smashing it, was she? A witch should have a more elegant, magical solution.

Beatrice reached for a rock on the lawn.

Nathan put his shoe on it before she could grab it. "I don't think angels are going to accept evidence obtained illegally."

"Well then, what—?"

"Just wait!" They were at a residential house. The owners had to return.

Nathan leaned against the coral stone wall and pulled out his phone. The Wi-Fi network was unlocked.

Definitely an angel's house.

Nathan messaged Chris and got an update on Daniel.

Beatrice joined him by the wall. But patience wasn't her strong suit. Or maybe she just couldn't bear silence. She managed to distract herself with her phone for less than ten minutes before creeping closer and spying on his.

"Your brother's a lot younger than you. Was he an angel too?"

"No," Nathan admitted. He didn't like the way the witch's eyes kept flicking between the rock and the window. "Dan was born after our excommunication. Now can you stop prying into my personal life?"

"Would you rather talk about your feelings for Eva? The ones the device—"

"Please, shut up." Nathan slapped his palm over his face. Now he was considering smashing the window.

"I thought angels flew down from the heavens," Beatrice said, though her tone implied a healthy dose of skepticism.

"Dan's not an angel."

"But he's not human. You wanted to get him treatment at Castor's Care."

"He's got wings, okay?" Nathan snapped. "But no feathers. Just bones. Like—"

Nathan cut himself off as he noticed a pair of brown-haired teenagers—a boy and a girl—approaching. The two must have been siblings. They shared the same square faces, with prominent cheeks and matching gray eyes. The purple insignia of Cassel High School had been sewn onto the pockets of their white button-down shirts. They whispered to one another, eyeing both Beatrice and Nathan.

The boy jogged up. He smiled and tossed his hair out of his eyes as though he'd practiced the motion in a mirror. "Can we help you with something?"

He'd addressed the question to Beatrice.

Nathan answered. "Depends. You know someone called Victoria Celand?"

———

"So you're Eva's charge," the girl—who'd introduced herself as Leah Celand—grinned as she handed Nathan a glass of water. Her eyes swept over him, checking him out without any pretense. "There goes your chance Max."

"I thought you wanted nothing to do with Eva while her trial was happening," Max responded. His tone remained light and cheerful, but he shot his sister a notice-ably un-angelic glare. "What could possibly have changed your mind?"

"Ignore him," Leah said. "I'm avoiding Eva because we

were advised to. For her sake. No one said we needed to avoid her charge." Leah took a seat on the couch.

The Celand twins—at least, Nathan assumed they were twins—had invited Nathan and Beatrice into the living room of their house and insisted on getting them drinks.

Nathan sat on the edge of a cream armchair. He balanced his glass on his knee, but he had no intention of drinking something from a stranger who Eva had sent them to investigate.

In the chair beside him, Beatrice took a massive gulp. She better not expect Nathan to carry her out if she fainted from some magical drug.

"Who advised you to stay away from Eva?" Nathan asked.

"I don't know if we should say," Leah admitted. "It felt like she was giving us advice outside of her role."

"Was it Irena Elysium?" Nathan guessed. "Wearing a big purple cloak."

The Celand twins' eyes widened at once. A look passed between them. Nathan was right.

"How did you—?" Leah started to ask, then changed her mind. "She visited shortly after Zeke's arrest and warned us. Eva didn't believe her brother was guilty, but Irena said she'd get in trouble too if she kept defending him, told us we needed to give Eva space until after the trial. She thought it would be safer that way."

Of course. G—or Farrah, or whatever her name was—couldn't risk Eva convincing anyone to look more closely into the arrest. She'd disguised herself as Irena, visited the Celands, and persuaded them to keep their distance. The angels probably didn't even question the advice.

"You said you're a Wyrmwood warlock, right?" Max asked. He had yet to take a seat, but stood by a fancy drinks cart to the side of the chairs. "How'd you find out that you were Eva's charge? Are you the one who stole her feather? Why are you looking for our mother?"

So angels had some sense of suspicion after all. Nathan didn't know if to be annoyed or reassured.

"Max, stop—" Leah said.

"No," her brother snapped. "We all know Eva didn't just give away her feather. She'd never do that."

"She might if she was in love," Beatrice said.

Nathan's chest tightened. He didn't know if it was guilt or hope. He glared at the witch.

For once, her voice had gone unnoticed. The Celand twins were loud when they argued.

"Yeah, but you can't accuse him of stealing it just because he's a warlock. That's so offensive!" Leah said.

"You just think he's attractive. He's obviously up to something. We don't even know what Eva's task was. Maybe it was to keep him from casting some sort of terrible curse. And who is she?"

Max gestured to Beatrice, who hopped up at once. "I'm Beatrice Blackwell—"

"And she's here because she's madly in love with me," Nathan said, speaking over the witch for a change.

The comment was outlandish enough that Beatrice fell silent and glared at him. But he was pretending to be Oliver Wyrmwood, and quite frankly—given her comments to Eva —Beatrice deserved this.

"Look, I didn't steal Eva's feather. But you're right. Someone did," Nathan lied, standing as well. Although Leah had been nicer to him, he addressed Max. "Eva sent us looking for information on someone called Farrah Downes. Is there any connection between her and your family?"

"I don't know anyone by that name." Max answered so fast, it was obvious that he hadn't thought about it.

Nathan hadn't convinced him to help. Dammit. Maybe he should've let Beatrice do the talking after all.

No, I can get through to this guy.

Because they had something in common. Nathan had recognized it the moment Max accused him of stealing a feather.

"You like Eva too, right?"

Max crossed his arms. His gray eyes narrowed in definite suspicion. "I've known Eva since we were kids. We're close."

There was a very clear implication in that word. Nathan's jaw clenched. He bit back a sarcastic congratulations. How close had Eva been to this guy when she'd been making out with Nathan in a restaurant booth?

But Max Celand wasn't the enemy. And if he liked Eva, could Nathan really blame him?

"I get it," Nathan said. "You wouldn't be so angry about someone hurting Eva otherwise."

"I'm angry about it too," Leah piped up. "And I'm also close to Eva. We're best friends."

"Never heard her mention you," Beatrice muttered.

Nathan glared at the witch. This was not the time for either of them to get competitive.

"Look, Eva sent us to your address. She obviously trusts you both to help her," Nathan continued, letting his gaze sweep between both Celand twins.

As he suspected, however, it was Max who broke. "I've only heard the name Farrah in passing," he said, sighing and glancing at a bookshelf on the opposite wall. "But I do remember someone with the last name Downes."

56

EVANGELINA

"Have Nathan and Beatrice made progress?" Eva asked the guardian phone, holding it above her head as she lay on her cell's mattress. Its screen provided the only light. The guards shut the electricity off eight hours each day, allowing darkness to consume the prisoners. Without windows, it was the only way to measure time in Ironvault.

The device searched its files, then flashed its response: *YES*.

Eva squealed.

"That sounds like good news," Zeke's voice came through the wall. "Did it answer?"

"Uh huh!"

"That's good. Guardian phones only track what they consider relevant to the assignment."

"Really?" Eva squeaked, cheeks growing hot. What did that suggest about its previous observations?

"Obviously," Zeke said. He'd wanted to be a guardian angel for years and had asked anyone who'd answer about what it involved. He'd probably flirted his way into information about the phones. "Didn't you ask Irena how it worked?

He made it sound like Eva's lack of knowledge was her own fault. "Irena wasn't exactly keen on answering my questions."

"See if it knows anything else. Nathan had it in his possession for a while, right? The devices link to people. It might know more now."

That felt like a long shot given how unhelpful Eva had previously considered the phone, but she asked, "Can you tell me what they found out?"

To her surprise, the phone searched its files and pulled up a new one titled: *Nathan Ward's Investigation into Farrah Downes (on behalf of Evangelina Heaven)*.

Eva read the brief description. It wasn't much, but it seemed significantly more useful than the information the phone had provided before. Either its time with Nathan had improved its ability to analyze him, or Eva should have tried chucking it against a tree from the beginning.

Of course, it could also be whoever tampered with it messing with me. Could Farrah know if we're onto her?

"What's it say?" Zeke pressed.

"Farrah's father worked in the Charitable Division. He wasn't in the same department as Victoria, but he reported to Adelaide."

"That's got to be it!" Zeke slapped the wall. "Adelaide set up ParadiseShared on her own, looped in Farrah's father, and then he passed it on to her."

Maybe, but Eva didn't see how they'd prove it to Judge Reign. She slipped the device under her pillow and let darkness swallow the room. "If Farrah tampered with the phone, do you think she can see its notes?"

"Would make it tough to keep tabs on you otherwise,"

Zeke admitted. He hummed for a moment. "Do you want to write a message for her to see? Or are you worried about her realizing that we're onto her?"

"I—" Eva sat up. "I can write messages?"

"Of course, just tell it to switch to manual mode. Have you not done that?"

Eva grabbed the thin pillow and buried her face, muffling her groan. If the guardian phone had different settings, why hadn't it come with instructions? "I could have been deleting its observations this whole time?"

"You could've tried editing them. The phone won't delete anything it thinks is important. At least, that's what I've heard. But why would you want to delete notes that could be helpful to your assignment?"

Because I'm quite certain the device was programmed to mess with me.

"Ugh. It's too late anyway. He already saw them." Eva sighed and dropped back to the mattress. Her head thudded against the phone. Ouch. She pulled it from beneath her hair. Her touch had activated the screen. Nathan's face smiled back at her.

Eva's cheeks heated. She felt strange staring at his picture while lying alone in the dark.

Well, not entirely alone.

"When are you going to stop stalling and ask the device what you really want to?" Zeke's voice came through the wall. His amusement was obvious.

Eva shoved the phone back under the pillow.

"The guards think you made out with him in your meeting today," Zeke continued. "And since he had to announce his species to get inside, they've now convinced themselves you sold your feather hoping to get caught so that you'd have an excuse to be with an irin because you two have bonded and fallen desperately in love." Zeke laughed like the idea of the guards discussing Eva's relationship with Nathan wasn't unbelievably mortifying.

"It's not like that. We're just friends, if we're even that much."

"Ask the phone and find out. It's clearly tracking your relationship."

Eva's cheeks heated. She should never have told her brother what Beatrice had suggested. But there was no one else to talk to in Ironvault.

"Are you scared to find out that he doesn't like you or that he does?" Zeke's tone turned serious. "Because, if we can't save ourselves, then it's easy. You can be with him. But if we can prove what Farrah did—the Sanctum won't let you keep your feathers and be with an irin."

Eva sighed, wrapped her thin blanket around her, and stared into the dark. If she thought there was any chance of saving herself, maybe she would worry about that. But Eva knew she was doomed.

The main reason she'd avoided asking the guardian phone about Nathan's feelings was because it felt like an invasion of his privacy. Shouldn't he tell Eva himself?

And maybe, a small part of her was afraid that she wouldn't like the answer.

But Eva couldn't admit any of that to Zeke.

"Let me guess," she said instead, rolling toward the wall. "You want to give me some brotherly advice. Tell me to prioritize myself over a boy."

"I want you to keep your feathers. I want us all to keep our feathers," Zeke admitted. "I know sometimes I question the Sanctum's teachings, but I've always believed we'd fly home at the end of our time here. Dying sounds—do you think reincarnation is real? Like, maybe if our souls were trapped on Earth, we'd reincarnate into some other species? It might be cool to be a dragon. What would you be?"

"I don't know." A sob rose in Eva's throat. She'd never wanted to be anything else. She buried her face into her wing, letting the tears fall onto her feathers. Their softness had always brought her comfort. She'd better enjoy the feeling while she could. Because in two days, Eva's feathers would be gone.

57
NATHAN

Nathan tapped his heel against the floor of the Ironvault meeting room. His heart grew louder with every approaching footstep. Eva would arrive soon. She'd have looked at the guardian phone, and—

Focus. That's not why you're here.

Nathan glanced at the book on his lap. The guard who'd escorted him, Olivia, had already checked it and cleared it to come in.

The footsteps grew closer. Nathan turned. He tried to keep his expression casual. Then Eva appeared.

Confinement had robbed her hair of its bounce. The waves hung looser and more disheveled over her shoulders. Instead of a feather dress, a gray jumpsuit pulled in at her waist, accentuating her hips in a manner that had likely been unintended by whoever designed the Ironvault's prisoner attire.

Her eyes landed on Nathan. A brilliant smile spread across her face. "You came back."

How is she still managing to glow?

It took Nathan a moment to find his voice. "Uh... yeah. Obviously."

"Where's Beatrice?"

Ouch. Wasn't he enough?

No, don't be stupid. That's not how Eva meant it.

"She'll be here soon. She had a test this morning, or something." Nathan shifted in his seat, studying the book on his lap while a guard chained Eva to the table. Beatrice's excuse had seemed flimsy. Nathan suspected the witch wanted to give him a chance to talk to Eva alone. Whether that counted as kindness or cruelty on her part, Nathan couldn't say.

"Great. I'm really glad you came," Eva said, her fingers stretched toward him, then curled back. She couldn't reach, and touching wasn't allowed.

Nathan rested his hands as close to her own as he dared. "We found out—"

"Farrah's dad works in the Global Charity Division. I know. *Something* told me."

"Oh." That answered Nathan's question about if she'd been interrogating the device. He swallowed, trying not to think about the guard still listening by the door. "What else did it tell you?"

"You found out more?"

"No, not really." Nathan's stomach tensed. He'd expected Eva to bring it up. She must have read how he felt about her. The stupid phone had happily displayed it to Beatrice. Nathan doubted it would have his back.

So if Eva knew, what did it mean that she was avoiding the topic?

"We met your friends," Nathan said, studying a point on the wall behind Eva. "Max seemed cool."

"Max is great," Eva agreed.

Nathan offered a small, curt smile. He hadn't wanted her to agree with that statement. But some masochistic part of Nathan couldn't stop himself. "He likes you."

"No, he doesn't. I mean, he used to. We dated for like a month when we were fifteen, but then we kissed, and it was obvious there was nothing there. We realized we worked better as friends and ended things."

A pang of jealousy shot through Nathan's chest. However, it was accompanied by a sudden, unexpected empathy for Max Celand. "That a common pattern with you after you kiss a guy?"

"What? No, I've only kissed—" Eva broke off, pink spreading across her cheeks. There was something endearing about how easily she blushed. She never hid behind a mask of indifference. "You know I didn't feel nothing when we kissed."

"Because I'm a great kisser?"

Eva's blush grew brighter. Despite the restraints, she managed to shuffle in her chair, before finally blurting out. "Because I obviously like you. I couldn't date you while I was your guardian angel especially not with Zeke on trial, but I thought maybe afterward—But then we talked in the café, and you made it clear. I get it. Our kiss meant more to me than it did to you."

"No, it didn't," Nathan snapped back without thinking. His neck grew hot. But Eva knew that wasn't true. "You know I lo—"

Nathan caught sight of Eva's blue eyes, watching him with such open sincerity that the word died on his lips. A loaded silence hung between them.

"I think you two need to be alone for a couple minutes," the guard, Olivia, announced, stepping forward. Her voice made Nathan jump. Somehow, he'd forgotten that she was there.

Nathan stared at the ceiling while Olivia unlocked Eva's restraints. What the hell was happening?

"I trust you'll be angelic in your comportment." The guard smiled and winked before walking back toward the door. She stepped into the hallway and closed it behind her.

Nathan's heart stopped. "Is she allowed to do that?"

"The guards can use their discretion. I don't think they consider an angel a high risk." Despite being unlocked, Eva remained seated. Her eyes—a color the sky would envy—pierced into Nathan. "What were you about to say?"

"Come on." Nathan crossed his arms and leaned back. "You know."

"No, so say it. How do you feel about me?"

"I—You do know. You read it." Nathan stood. The book fell from his lap. Nathan ignored it. Unable to meet Eva's eyes, he paced behind the chair and recited the sentence that had burned itself into his memory. "Nathan Ward's feelings for Evangelina Heaven *colon* love." He held up his hands to represent the brackets that followed. "In denial." Words out, Nathan spun, clinging to the back of his chair as he faced Eva. "Can't you just let me stay in denial? It's a hell of a lot easier that way."

"You love me?"

"You know I do!" Why did Eva sound so surprised? Unless, she hadn't understood Beatrice's suggestion, and she never checked. Oh God! That meant Nathan had just—but he couldn't put the words back in his mouth. "Any guy would fall in love with you, Eva. You're sweet, and kind, and stunning. When you smile, you literally glow. And you have this natural warmth. I think you're the only person I've ever missed only seconds after seeing. And—"

Nathan didn't know how long he would've kept going if Eva hadn't stood. She stepped forward and wrapped her arms around his neck. Feeling her body against his wiped all the thoughts from his mind.

Eva rested a hand on his cheek, fingers brushing over the bone and sending sparks shooting across his skin. Then she pressed her lips to his.

For a glorious minute, Nathan lost himself in Eva. His fingers curled around her hair; his leg pressed between her thighs. He tasted her, pulling her tongue into his mouth and biting at her lip. Despite her confinement, Eva's mouth remained sweet. She moaned. Soft and breathless. And too short, like she'd cut it off prematurely. Nathan desperately wanted to hear her make that sound again. He needed to.

Until he felt her feathers.

Eva's wings must have broken free while they kissed. Nathan grabbed her waist and felt them, soft and perfect against his skin. Eva couldn't lose them. He wouldn't let her.

Nathan broke their kiss. His hands dropped to his sides.

Eva's arm remained around his neck. She leaned back and studied him. Nathan studied her as well: the twitches in her brow, slight tremble of her lips, and the question in her eyes. He understood it as perfectly as if she'd communicated with words.

"We can't be together," he said, putting his hands on hers and pulling them from his neck with an agonizing pang. "They'll take your feathers."

Eva's lips twitched. Her smile was as sad as Nathan had seen it. "Maybe you missed it, but they're already going to." She gestured to their current surroundings: the lone table and chairs, the dark, iron room. "But they'll release me afterwards. I can't give away feathers I don't have. Zeke is the one who committed an actual crime. He's the one who needs saving." Eva's eyes landed on the book that had fallen onto the floor. "What's that?"

"It's like the Sanctum's version of a yearbook, I think," Nathan said, pushing his hair back. "The Celands had a bunch. This one is from six years ago. When ParadiseShared first formed."

"Their dad is the Sanctum's photographer," Eva said, bending to pick up the fallen book. She returned to her original chair, though she angled her body so that she faced away from the restraints as she flipped through.

"Here. This is the page that shows Farrah's father." Nathan leaned over and skipped ahead. He pointed to an image in the corner where an angel with unruly curls smiled uncomfortably alongside his coworkers. "And that's Victoria's department up here." Nathan tapped a larger picture on the opposite page. "With Adelaide Glory, right?" The photographs weren't labeled. He and Beatrice had trusted the Celand twins to identify the angels.

"Yes, and that's Zola Astrum." Eva touched the image of a red-headed angel, who stood beside Victoria. Despite their proximity, something in the women's posture suggested they weren't friends.

Nathan frowned. He didn't recognize the name. "Were we supposed to look for information on her as well?"

"No, but maybe we should have been," Eva said. She chewed her lip as she studied the page. "We need to see who's really in that cloak. I might have a plan. But it'll take both you and Beatrice. Do you know if she kept my jacket?"

58

EVANGELINA

An hour later, Eva gave her friends one final smile before Olivia marched her down the hall. The guard had been unbelievably generous. Eva hated to ask more, but if her plan was going to work, she needed to be certain.

"I know visiting hours are done," Eva whispered, leaning back so that the werewolf could hear. "But would I be allowed to make a call?"

Olivia nodded. "We have phones for prisoners. Coin operated. I could lend you a few, but you'd need to know the number."

"I do. At least, I know one."

Instead of leading Eva upstairs, Olivia shoved open one of the doors. On her first visit, Eva had assumed she was surrounded by cells, but the first floor held no prisoners. Instead, the doors hid additional corridors and secret rooms. This one held a path. At the end, a row of five phones stood beside each other.

"I don't know why we have so many," Olivia admitted.

"We almost never let prisoners in here at the same time. Too high risk. Getting switched to guarding you and your brother has been a dream. I wish all my prisoners were angels. Do you know your Sanctum initially labeled Zeke as highly dangerous. We were spooked until you came to visit."

"The Sanctum has different ideas about danger," Eva admitted, sitting at the first phone.

"I'll say." Olivia dug in her pocket and produced a few coins. She passed them to Eva. "The person on the other end will need to agree to the call."

"Oh." Eva's chest tightened. Olivia hadn't mentioned that before. But Eva had already sat down. She might as well find out.

Hand trembling, Eva lifted the old-fashioned receiver and pressed it to her ear. The numbers had been written on buttons. They beeped as Eva pushed them.

Ring. Ring.

Silence.

A lump rose in Eva's throat. Would he—?

"State your name," a robotic voice ordered.

"Evangelina Heaven?"

More silence.

Then, her father's voice. "Eva?"

Tears pooled in her eyes. "Dad! You answered."

"I—" Cyrus hesitated. "I don't know what to say to you, Eva. Or your brother." Pain laced his voice. He sounded on the verge of crying.

"I'm sorry, Dad," Eva whispered, blinking back her own tears. He'd had such high hopes for her as a guardian angel. She'd let him down.

No, if I save Zeke, the Sanctum might leave Mom and Dad alone. They can't be implicated in my crime, only his.

Eva took a deep breath and closed her eyes. "Dad, I need to talk to Farrah. Is she with you?"

Cyrus sighed. "Give me a minute."

Eva counted thirty-seven seconds. Then, Farrah's voice came through, stressed and uncertain but not unkind. "Has something happened?"

"Many things. Listen, I know this conversation might be recorded, but that story you told me—"

"I can't discuss that on the phone."

"I know. But I just need to clarify something. What did you mean when you said that your mother got mad?"

———

"I can't believe you spoke to Farrah," Zeke said. He was pacing his cell. Eva could hear his footsteps through the wall.

"I had to. I wanted to be certain." Eva leaned against the cold iron. It stung her wings, but she'd gotten accustomed to the feeling. The moment she'd gotten back to her cell, she'd knocked, and told her brother everything she'd learned.

"Are you?"

"No," Eva admitted. "But it makes sense, doesn't it? I mean if one person did all this, they needed access—"

"I'm not arguing about that," Zeke cut her off. "But are you sure Farrah doesn't suspect?"

"Positive."

Zeke continued pacing. "Your plan relies on a lot of things going right."

"But they could go right."

Zeke didn't respond.

"I have faith," Eva said, turning toward the wall. "Besides, what do we have to lose?"

Zeke sighed. His footsteps finally stopped. "You'll need to send a message on the guardian phone. Tell it you're switching to manual mode."

Eva pulled the device from beneath her pillow and followed her brother's instructions.

"It won't save anything that's a lie," Zeke warned. "Your phrasing has to be perfect."

"I'm aware." It had been Eva's idea. She took a deep breath, closed her eyes, and began to dictate a message.

59
NATHAN

Nathan trudged through the Cursed Woods with Beatrice a few feet behind. The witch had arrived at Ironvault with an hour left for visitation. And it had barely been enough time to go over everything.

They'd stayed until even Olivia, who must've been the nicest prison guard in history, insisted that visiting hours had ended. Eva had smiled as she left, still managing to glow despite her surroundings. Nathan saved the image in his mind.

Next time he saw her, the goodbye would be permanent.

Beatrice had been quieter than usual. They were nearly out of the Cursed Woods, and she'd only pointed out six plants. Nathan was almost worried.

At the end of their visit, Eva had whispered something to Beatrice. Nathan had no idea what, but he swore both their eyes had flicked to him.

"Did Eva say something about me?" Nathan guessed, pushing aside a branch. He held it up for the witch to follow.

"I don't know. What would she have had to say?" A smirk flickered across Beatrice's face as she stepped in front of Nathan. "Are you two officially together?"

"No, and we never will be."

Beatrice stopped, forcing Nathan to do so as well. The witch frowned at a wet patch of earth. Was she about to launch into a diatribe about some worm that lived in the mud? Their first journey through the Cursed Woods, Nathan's head had threatened to explode from the witch's barrage of facts. It was a wonder Beatrice retained as much information as she did.

But no worm facts came. Instead, Beatrice spun toward Nathan. "I left you alone with Eva for over an hour, and you still didn't work up the courage to talk about how you feel?"

"This has nothing to do with my feelings for her," Nathan said. But as soon as he heard the words, he knew they were wrong. "Actually, it does."

He loved Eva. Which was why he couldn't let her lose her feathers.

"I saw what happened to my mother after her excommunication," Nathan admitted. Kay had spent the last eight years regretting her decision and numbing herself in an attempt to forget what she'd lost. It wasn't just the loss of her husband that had sent her over the edge. "Daniel," Nathan whispered. He loved his brother. He didn't regret Daniel's existence. But his mother did. "If Eva lost her feathers, she'd never have angelic children. She'd have to give birth. They might be—"

"Sick?" Beatrice guessed, and her expression softened.

Nathan nodded. "Born with bones for wings. A constant reminder of what Eva's lost. I—I can't have that happen to her. She has to keep her feathers."

"Nate, that's actually sweet," Beatrice said it as though

she'd made a startling discovery. "But I don't think that's your call. Or mine. Or even Eva's. She admitted to giving away one of her feathers. Angels don't take that lightly. How would we change the judge's mind?"

She shrugged as though it were hopeless. But Nathan already knew. He had a plan of his own.

This whole time, Eva had been guiding him toward something, so how could Nathan save her? The answer was obvious.

"I'm going to do something that I'm great at."

60

EVANGELINA

"Mom and Dad are here," Eva whispered, peering through the one-way mirror door that led to the Sanctum's courtroom. The space had been designed to force the accused to face themselves. Massive mirrors covered the walls and ceiling. Only the floor had been spared.

Cyrus and Magdalena Heaven had chosen seats at the front. Both wore white. Beside them, Farrah had chosen a pale purple that matched her glasses. For once, she'd tamed her curls into a bun.

"They were probably ordered to come. They'll be arrested next," Zeke said, adjusting his collar. He faced the interior of the small dark room. They'd been deposited within a few minutes earlier by the same Power who'd collected them from Ironvault that morning. The massive angel had been as stone-faced and silent as Mr. Kind.

"Don't say that," Eva whispered. "This is going to work."

"I trust the plan," Zeke said with a hint of a smirk. But it didn't last. "The Sanctum I'm less confident in."

The comment bordered on heresy. But that would be the least of Zeke's offenses.

This will work.

Eva had to have faith. She closed her eyes, offered a short prayer, then slipped the guardian phone from where she'd tucked it behind her wing.

"Did Beatrice give Nathan my feather?"

The device searched and responded with a list of things currently in Nathan's possession. Eva's feather was the final bullet point.

Good.

Eva pressed her face to the one-way glass again. A marble seat had been carved and anchored to the wall above. But Judge Reign had yet to arrive. In the meantime, strangers filtered in eager to watch an angelic trial. Some wore lanyards indicating they worked for newspapers.

A few faces were more familiar. Leah and Max sat with Eva's other friends near the back. Irena stood by the prosecutorial podium in the front. Maddie sat a few feet away, sorting through papers.

Everyone's eyes flicked to the judge's empty throne as they waited.

"Did Beatrice speak to Irena?" Eva whispered. The guardian phone made no attempt to search. It tracked Nathan and Eva, not an irrelevant witch. The lack of information made Eva feel blind. But wasn't that a crucial component of faith?

A gasp from the courtroom made Zeke join Eva at the door. Judge Reign entered from the ceiling, swooping towards his marble throne. The gold streaks in his white wings reflected in the many mirrors, like a thousand stars had flashed into existence. He sat upon his throne and raised his hand. "Let the judgement of Ezekiel Heaven begin."

Eva had just enough time to squeeze her brother's hand before the door opened, and Zeke stepped into the courtroom.

———

Zeke was going to lose.

He'd presented his case with his usual charm. For a moment, Eva imagined her entire plan might be unnecessary. Zeke was innocent. That would be enough to save him on its own.

But then Irena had taken flight. She'd questioned Zeke, noted that he'd been told to dismiss his concerns about ParadiseShared by a superior and pulled up a long record of previous heretic statements. The karmic angel really had been tracking him for years.

Judge Reign was a pale statue on a marble throne. Nothing betrayed his opinion.

But the crowd had been swayed. Eva could hear it in the way the whispers changed. Magdalena buried her face in her husband's shoulder. Farrah patted her arm.

Eva clasped her hands, closed her eyes, and whispered, "Please."

An alarm sounded. Heads raised. The audience turned to the mirrored ceiling and walls, searching for the source.

The main doors to the courtroom burst open. A short angel with silver curls flew into the room, bowing in apology as he approached Judge Reign and whispered something.

If it worried the judge, it didn't show. He lifted his arm,

commanding silence. "We will take a short recess," Judge
Reign informed the audience. "It seems an irin has broken
into our Sanctum."

61

NATHAN

Nathan waited in the basement of the Sanctum's building. Breaking in had been easy. The Celand twins still believed him to be Oliver Wyrmwood. They'd vouched for Nathan, and he'd walked in without incident. He felt almost guilty.

But Max would have the last laugh. By the end of the day, he'd have a better shot with Eva than Nathan ever would.

Why is that what I'm thinking about right now?

Nathan pressed himself further into the corner, counting the seconds as the alarm wailed. If the Sanctum wanted irin to keep out so badly, they should put up wards like they did for demons. But perhaps protective magic didn't consider *lack of feathers* indicative of a different species.

And besides, Nathan technically did have an angel's feather.

He reached into the lining of his coat and brushed his thumb against the soft white vane as he continued counting. Nathan assumed the wailing had to do with him. A message alerting the Sanctum to his break-in had been pre-scheduled to send shortly before the alarm began. Hope-fully, the angels would trust that he'd broken into the Guardian Division as claimed. Nathan didn't want the wrong person finding him too fast. Not until the right person did.

"What game are you playing at, Nathan?" A familiar voice spoke from behind a pile of boxes.

Nathan snapped upright, kicking himself away from the wall where he'd been leaning.

So much for playing it cool.

But Nathan would finally see G's real identity. That would be crucial. Had Eva's guess been correct or—?

Victoria Celand stepped out from behind the boxes. Nathan recognized her face from the photographs. She had the same gray eyes and dark brown waves as her children.

No, not Victoria.

"You're wearing another mask," Nathan guessed. Otherwise, why would she bother with the purple cloak?

But shit. They'd assumed that G wouldn't risk bringing the mask into the Sanctum's Headquarters. Would the plan work if she didn't reveal her actual face?

G smiled with a familiar sense of smug amusement. The mask disguised her features, not her mannerisms. "I'm quite familiar with human recording devices. And memory extraction spells."

"You understand technology and magic. Congrats," Nathan covered his discomfort with sarcasm. "Suppose that makes sense since you used to work in the Guardian Division. You were there when they first came out with the phones, right?"

G raised an eyebrow, expression torn between exasperation and amusement. "Are you hoping to record a confession?"

Nathan shook his head. They didn't have hidden cameras, but G's precaution might ruin things all the same. "Guess you won't do me the courtesy of explaining why you went to so much trouble to set the Heavens up. Shall I hazard a guess myself?"

G's eyes narrowed. She twisted her head, peering around the basement, likely to check for hidden devices or to confirm that they were alone.

Nathan suspected they were. The alarm masked the sound of footsteps—whether that worked to his advantage or disadvantage remained to be determined. But he stalled by explaining Eva's theory.

"You had access to the list of Ezekiel's heretical statements and thought he'd be an easy target for a feather. But you misjudged. He started digging into your schemes and almost uncovered you. If he'd succeeded, your operation would've been ruined. You needed to discredit him first. And that included targeting his family since they were the ones most likely to believe him."

G smiled. "Seems like I could've saved the Heavens a lot of suffering if I'd just sent a cute boy to beg Eva for a feather instead."

Nathan's jaw clenched.

G must've noticed. She laughed. "I got her message. She's ready to become an irin and run off with you. Meanwhile, the phone tells me you have romantic notions of saving her. So why are you selling her feather? You're not planning to use the money to start a new life with her."

"No, but I'll still need to take care of my brother."

"Ah yes, the boy who shouldn't exist. Your mother told Hyde all about it when he found her outside a club last year.

I thought she'd lost it from all the drugs at first, but I'm glad he kept her information. You've proved a useful ally in the Heavens' downfall."

Nathan's stomach twisted. He couldn't even defend himself against the claim.

"Let's talk price," G said.

Already?

Had G said anything damning? Even if she had, who would've heard? Nathan needed more time, more information.

"Another ten thousand," she offered.

"Not enough."

"Fifteen then."

Was that the going price of an angel's feather? It sounded both too low and too high. Either way, Nathan needed to extend this conversation. He shook his head. "We could reveal your identity. Ruin your whole operation."

"The Sanctum won't listen to irin. You aren't even allowed in this building. I'm only offering fifteen thousand because part of me actually likes Eva. What do you keep looking for?"

Dammit. Had Nathan been that obvious? He couldn't let G grow suspicious, not yet, not until he had proof.

Like the mask.

Could Nathan get it?

"I don't exactly want to get caught selling you a feather," Nathan lied. Then he took a risk. He slipped his hand into the lining of his jacket. "Don't you want to confirm it's the real deal."

G's eyes narrowed. "I know it is. The guardian phone doesn't lie."

"You got it to say I was human."

"Prior to its programming being finalized. It has to

believe anything it adds to be the truth," G said, but her voice wavered, cracks showing in her confidence. "Let me see it then."

Holding the feather, Nathan extended his fist without stretching his arm fully. He needed her to come closer.

G inched forward. She lifted her hand to take the feather.

Nathan let it drop to the ground. He grabbed G's wrist, managing to wrangle it through the cloak's oversized sleeve. She wriggled in his grip.

"What are you doing—?"

Blue flashed within the shadows of the sleeve. G slipped her arm free, leaving Nathan clinging to loose fabric. But it made no difference. Her hand had never been his target.

G screamed as Nathan's nails sank into the flesh beneath her chin. For a moment, he worried he'd made a mistake. Perhaps Eva had been wrong. Victoria Celand had been the villain this whole time.

The soft flesh turned hard and leathery. Nathan pulled and stumbled back, holding a blank white mask. Three strands of hair hung from the center of its forehead: gray, blonde, and brown. That last one had been wrapped between the eye holes and tied.

G turned, shielding her face as she reached for her hood. The action limited her peripheral vision. She likely didn't see when Irena and Beatrice appeared several feet away, almost as though they'd poofed into existence. A dark green scarf hung around both their necks.

"Did you get all of that?" Nathan asked, waving to Beatrice.

Irena's wings whipped forward with a sudden force. The weight of the gust knocked G to the ground. The hood fell back, revealing a nymph in her mid-thirties with bright blue hair. Nathan had seen her last time he'd entered the Sanctum: Maddie Lake, Irena Elysium's assistant.

Eva's hunch had been right.

She'd explained her theory to Nathan and Beatrice at Ironvault yesterday. If one person was behind Paradise-Shared, it must have been someone with a very specific set of capabilities. They'd known how to tamper with a guardian phone, been familiar enough with both Victoria Celand and Adelaide Glory to successfully impersonate them, and they had a method for finding angels willing to sell feathers. True, they'd made a miscalculation with Zeke, but Eva's brother wouldn't have been chosen at random. The Justice Division kept a list.

Angels could transfer divisions. But so could assistants.

"I should've known you were too clever to be satisfied with your position," Irena said, lips curling in a sneer.

Maddie started to protest. Excuses flew from her lips. Irena advanced on her assistant as though she heard none.

Nathan watched until Beatrice tugged the mask from his hand. She shoved the scarf into it instead and stamped on his foot.

"Run, stupid! Eva made me promise that you wouldn't get caught. Irin aren't allowed in the Sanctum, remember?"

Nathan wanted to argue that his presence had just brought a criminal to light. But Beatrice was right.

He couldn't get caught. Not yet.

Nathan grabbed the fallen feather from the floor, tied the scarf around his neck, and vanished from sight.

62

EVANGELINA

Mr. Kind escorted Eva from the dark room through a narrow tunnel. Her heart pounded, but she had no reason to be afraid. Her plan had worked! Maddie had been captured, and Nathan had left the Sanctum without being apprehended. The guardian phone had reported as much when the alarm stopped.

The short passage led to a better-lit office space that must've been hidden somewhere adjacent to the court-room. The white furniture within appeared sleek and well-maintained, but there was little in the way of personal touches.

Judge Reign sat behind a long white desk, wings half-open behind him to reveal the golden streaks. Before him, stood three others.

Zeke held himself straight-backed and focused, but his hand kept tapping against his thigh. Across from him, Irena scowled at the wall, arms crossed tight against her chest. Between them Farrah faced the judge.

"Maddie wouldn't do that. She's not a bad person. She's —" Farrah shook her head, breath catching as she struggled to face the reality of what had happened. Eva couldn't blame her.

"You investigated the matter, Miss Downes. How did you fail to see the inconsistencies that Mr. Heaven spotted?"

"Because—I told you—" Farrah floundered for a response.

"With all due respect, Judge Reign, no one in the Sanctum noticed anything suspicious about Paradise-Shared," Eva said. "Zeke's superiors expressly told him to dismiss it. Are you going to interrogate all of them too?"

Four heads whipped toward Eva.

Farrah looked shocked; Zeke mildly impressed. Even Irena's scowl softened. Judge Reign's face expressed as much as a slab of granite.

Eva took a deep breath and stepped forward. It wasn't bravery that allowed her to confront the judge. She'd already accepted her fate. What more could Judge Reign do?

"Farrah assumed the similarities in writing style across ParadiseShared's information to be the result of translation," Eva explained. "Which they could have been."

"If the articles had been translated," Irena muttered.

Eva nodded. Maddie didn't speak Thai. Perhaps she'd learned the basics enough to fool Victoria Celand's assistant when she'd pretended to vet the fake charity, but the nymph couldn't have written with the fluency of a native speaker. Despite basing ParadiseShared in Thailand, Maddie had needed to compose the documents in English.

"I'm not here to pick apart the schemes of Madeline Lake," Judge Reign said. He lifted something on the desk before him. Eva hadn't noticed it at first. The white mask blended with the painted wood. "She is not an angel. Her crimes are a matter for a different court. I want to under-stand your involvement, Miss Heaven."

Isn't it obvious?

"Zeke almost unraveled Maddie's scheme. She needed him excommunicated, and she couldn't risk anyone remaining who might be sympathetic to his claims. So she set out to sabotage my family."

"She's the one who told me that Hyde had approached Irena with a claim that he'd met with Cyrus," Farrah admit-ted, voice soft.

"Which I dismissed as a likely lie," Irena added. "But Mad—Ms. Lake played a pivotal role in Miss Heaven's guardian angel assignment. She delivered the phone to my possession and monitored it on my behalf. I admit, I shouldn't have accepted her offer. But I've always found technology frustrating, and I trusted Ms. Lake. She's always been a highly competent assistant."

Of course she had been. Maddie must've been excep-tionally clever to pull off what she had. And a good actress. She'd seemed so sweet every time Eva spoke to her.

"The best assistant," Farrah whispered. Her gaze turned to Eva. Farrah didn't speak, but recognition bloomed in her eyes. She must've understood now why Eva had called her yesterday.

Seeing Zola Astrum standing beside Victoria Celand in their department's picture had caused something to suddenly click in Eva's mind. Maddie had mentioned working for one of Irena's friends prior to taking her current position. It wasn't the most solid evidence. But Irena's exacting personality made her neither popular nor overly fond of most people. Only a small circle could be considered her friends, and the timing for when Zola had joined Magdalena's department matched exactly with when Maddie had started in the Karmic Department.

ParadiseShared's existence required two people to sign off on it: Victoria and Adelaide. Someone of a similar build, in the right position, and with the ability to transform their face could have impersonated both. Zola would've gone on that same trip to Thailand, so would her assistant.

But what about the mask?

When Farrah said her mother had gotten mad, Eva assumed she'd meant angry. But that didn't make sense. They'd been talking about after the demon had been killed. Panic and dread would've been more likely than fury at that point.

Which meant Farrah had been about to say something else and caught herself: *My mother got Maddie.*

The truth had come out during their conversation on the phone. Maddie Lake had worked for Farrah's mother. She'd been the assistant in the story. She'd helped clean up the mess and cover everything up. When she'd handed in her resignation a year later, the Downes family had been disappointed, but not surprised. They thought she deserved a fresh start and provided a glowing recommendation—no doubt why Zola had snapped her up.

That was why Eva had thought Farrah and Maddie seemed close. Because they were.

But Farrah had never considered how witnessing an angel kill and lose their feathers might have affected Maddie. The nymph must have started to question the Sanctum, and its claims: *lose one feather, lose them all.* Maddie knew the truth. She knew angels could be corrupted and survive. Why wouldn't she try to profit from selling them?

Originally, Maddie had probably skinned the demon's

face and pocketed the feathers for a rainy day. They'd have been worth thousands to witches. But over time, the idea for ParadiseShared must have grown until she couldn't resist. She'd used her time in the Global Charity Division to establish its existence and funnel herself the money required to begin the operation. Then, Maddie jumped to the Karmic Department to find potential sellers.

"I'm afraid you have all misunderstood my question," Judge Reign said.

Eva frowned. She'd forgotten what he'd asked. But he didn't repeat. Instead, the judge lifted the white mask, holding it before him for the others to see.

"Demon-forged magic reinforced with angel feathers to bypass our wards. Its permanence suggests a grotesque perversion of our immortality. And a clear illustration of why laws on feathers must be strict." Judge Reign's lips turned down in disgust. He rested the mask on the desk and turned to Zeke. "Mr. Heaven, I am dismissing your case." His unreadable gray gaze turned to Eva. "Your involvement, however, must be addressed."

63
NATHAN

Nathan slipped through the doors at the back of the courtroom. Mirrors stretched the floor into an unending walkway. A hundred spectators multiplied into thousands. Nathan felt grateful for the witch's scarf around his neck. It would've been impossible to hide if he'd been surrounded by his reflections, and he couldn't risk being recognized until he was ready.

Irin couldn't interfere in angelic matters.

Nathan had made sure someone spotted him running out of the building. Then he'd slipped into an alley and tied the magic scarf Beatrice had borrowed from some other witch. It made him vanish from sight, making it easy to stroll back to the Sanctum. The angels assumed he'd fled and took no precautions to thwart an invisible return.

Once Nathan revealed himself, however, his punishment would be swift. And likely painful.

Nathan pushed the thought aside as he proceeded down the aisle. An anxious blond couple held one another near the front. They must've been Eva's parents, Cyrus and

Magdalena Heaven. Empty chairs surrounded them. Nathan took one at the edge of their row.

A mirror near the back of the courtroom swung open. A familiar face stepped in. Irena took her place near the front, gray suit unwrinkled. No one would guess she'd captured and detained her former assistant within the past hour.

Behind Irena came two people Nathan recognized from photographs: Farrah Downes and Ezekiel Heaven. The former took a seat near the front, next to Eva's mother while the latter stood before a marble throne.

Gasps came from the crowd as stars flashed in the mirrors. Nathan blinked, trying to clear his eyes. Overhead, an angel with gold flecked wings swooped from the ceiling. Eva had described him—Judge Reign, a Prince of the Inner Sanctum, and the man who would ultimately decide her fate.

The reflections meant no one could hide their response to his entrance. Most people, including Nathan stared openly as the judge folded his wings and took his place on the throne. Eva's mother, however, didn't even glance up.

"Dismissed?" Her voice grew loud, and she wrapped her arms around a startled-looking Farrah in a massive hug.

Nathan held back a smile. Guess he knew where Eva's sense of personal boundaries came from.

Cyrus pulled his wife back into her chair. They didn't speak, but some exchange occurred, and Magdalena's face grew suddenly anxious. She turned back to Farrah, still loud enough for Nathan to overhear, she asked, "What about Eva?"

Farrah shook her head.

The sound of Magdalena's sob wrenched Nathan's chest. Had his mother cried when he'd been condemned with her? Maybe. Kay hadn't always been as cold and indifferent as she'd grown.

The judge dismissed the case against Ezekiel Heaven *in light of new information brought in by Ms. Elysium.* Nathan hadn't expected recognition for his role, but the statement seemed lacking. What about Eva's contribution to Maddie's apprehension? Shoot, even Beatrice deserved to be mentioned.

Murmurs of confusion swept through the onlookers. But Judge Reign appeared unaffected by public opinion. Without further explanation, the newly acquitted Ezekiel Heaven joined the front row. He sat beside Farrah, not his parents though his mother leaned over to take his hand.

Nathan missed the rest of the interaction. The judge had announced his next trial, and Eva had entered.

The room fell silent, probably in awe. Despite spending days imprisoned, Eva had never looked more radiant, or more angelic. Blonde waves cascaded over her shoulders and between her wings. A long white dress clung to her hips. Its hem brushed the floor. Her eyes landed on her parents, and she smiled.

Nathan's chest tightened. Eva looked far too happy for an angel facing excommunication. But that was her charm. She would've smiled through an earthquake.

Eva took her place in a carpeted square of floor directly before the judge's seat. He stared down his nose at her. "What charges do you bring against Evangelina Heaven, Ms. Elysium?"

Irena flew upward, positioning herself slightly below the judge. "Your greatness, Evangelina Heaven is accused of succumbing to the vices of mortality. She has confessed to giving away one of her feathers. We have a witness to the crime, a witch: Beatrice Blackwell."

The judge nodded to a large angel with blue dusted over his white feathers who stood in one of the corners. Another door opened in the mirrors and Beatrice entered, practically skipping. The sleeves of her pink dress hid her hands in the traditional style of the Castor's Grove covens.

Nathan clenched his fists. He'd expected Beatrice's appearance. She'd gone to Irena and offered to confess in exchange for admission to the Sanctum. It had been part of Eva's plan. After all, Beatrice had needed to be close to Irena when the alarm sounded. Otherwise, they would never have gotten the karmic angel to the basement to witness the exchange between Maddie and Nathan.

Still, Beatrice's confession would damn Eva.

"Miss Blackwell, you informed me that Evangelina Heaven freely gave you one of her feathers," Irena said, flying lower to speak to the witch. "Please, repeat your story to Judge Reign."

Before Beatrice could open her mouth, Nathan pulled the scarf from his neck. His sudden appearance shocked those in the audience, but Nathan didn't draw the judge's attention until he shouted, "I stole Eva's feather!"

64

EVANGELINA

At the sound of Nathan's voice, Eva spun. He couldn't be there. She had to have imagined it.

But she hadn't. Nathan stood in the front row, right beside the aisle, only two seats shy of Eva's own father. He wore jeans, an old brown coat, and a collared shirt that failed at the formality angelic courts preferred. For once, he didn't lean, but kept his back straight, head tilted up to stare at the judge.

Eva's heart stopped. *What is he doing?*

Defiance burned in Nathan's eyes. But he couldn't be at an angelic trial. Having him return to the Sanctum had already been a risk. He'd been supposed to flee to safety immediately after.

Gasps rose from the crowd. Onlookers didn't typically make declarations. Nor did the judge typically leave his seat.

Gold glinted in the mirrors, and the shadow of wings passed over Eva's head. Judge Reign flew lower, stopping to hover only a few feet above Nathan.

"Who is this boy?"

Irena answered, "Nathan Ward. Originally named Nathaniel Warden before he lost his feathers."

Murmurs moved through the crowd.

"Show me your wings," Judge Reign ordered.

Eva held her breath. Nathan needed to run, not reveal himself further. She had to get him out of here.

"Miss Heaven, do not leave that square," Irena hissed, flying lower and positioning herself so that her wing blocked Eva's path. "Please, for once, take my advice."

Eva might've ignored the warning and pushed past Irena's blockade, but she was already too late.

Bones rattled and scraped as skeletal wings spread behind Nathan, dark and mesmerizing. The room knew what he was.

The crowd's conversation rose from a whisper.

"I will have silence in my courtroom," Judge Reign commanded. His deep voice filled the massive space. He turned his pale gaze back to Nathan. "I am already aware that you are in possession of Miss Heaven's feather. You obtained it from the witch, Beatrice Blackwell. I have reviewed the transcripts on the guardian phone given to Miss Heaven. Allow me to recite—"

For a split second, Eva worried Judge Reign intended to go over the list of Nathan's talents. It would've been the least of her problems, but she didn't relish the thought of an entire crowd hearing how much she'd enjoyed kissing her charge.

But Judge Reign didn't repeat anything the device had recorded. Instead, voice flat, he quoted word-for-word the message Eva had typed, *"My fate is sealed. I'm prepared to become an irin and be with Nathan. But we'll need money. If you don't want him to reveal your identity, meet him in the basement at the Sanctum Headquarters. You'll know when. We want to sell you my feather."*

It sounded bad when read without additional context. Eva watched her parents exchange a look before their eyes fell on her. She wished she could go to them and explain, but Irena's wing cautioned her to stay in place.

Judge Reign continued to study Nathan with his pale gaze. "The device believed all these statements to be true. Do you deny that Miss Heaven wanted her feather sold to a woman she knew to be a criminal?"

Eva's eyes widened. Was this why Nathan had returned? Did he think the truth would save her? It was so sweet, she could've cried.

But it won't matter.

Nathan's lips tilted up. He slipped his hand into his coat, pulled out something small and white, and held it up to the judge. "This is the feather that we wanted to sell. You can have it if you'd like."

Judge Reign made no move to take it. "That is not an angel's feather."

"Technically, it is," Nathan said. "It's a feather from Eva's jacket. Beatrice plucked it and gave it to me at Eva's request."

"I could've said all that if he didn't steal my spotlight."

The sound of Beatrice's voice right beside her ear made Eva jump. She turned and found that the witch had snuck across the front of the courtroom to join her on the square. Eva had been too focused on Nathan to notice.

"I told you he needed to leave right away," Eva whispered. Judge Reign discovering Nathan had been exactly the scenario she'd wanted to avoid.

"I didn't know he was going to pull this stunt. Although

I did suspect," Beatrice admitted. "He's in love with you. He's not going to let you lose your feathers."

Eva squeezed her eyes shut. She loved Nathan as well, but he and Beatrice didn't understand. Nothing they said could convince Judge Reign to release her.

Because, ultimately, the truth was not on Eva's side.

65

NATHAN

"Evangelina Heaven is missing a feather from her left wing," Judge Reign said. When he'd flown to Earth, he must've found a body carved from rock instead of human flesh. Despite the depth of his voice, his lips barely moved when he spoke. "Whatever ploy she invented to fool Madeline Lake does not alter this fact."

"I know—" Nathan started to explain, but the judge continued.

"Evangelina Heaven confessed to giving away the feather of her own free will. I bore witness to her confession myself. This is a simple matter."

"No, it's not." Nathan's fists clenched. "I told you, I stole it."

"The feather from Evangelina Heaven's wing?"

Nathan crossed his arms and glared at the judge. "Yes, Eva's actual feather. She didn't give it away. You can't blame her for its loss because I stole it."

"And why would Miss Heaven lie?"

"To protect me."

"Actually, she's protecting me!" Beatrice shouted.

Nathan's eyes flicked to the witch's reflection in the mirror. She waved from behind Irena's wing.

"I stole Eva's feather," Beatrice said. "I plucked it when she wasn't looking."

"I stole the feather," Zeke declared, standing with a smile that made the lie a bit too obvious.

Nathan stifled a groan. He'd intended to save Eva by finally putting one of his talents to *great* use. Lying had been on that list. He hadn't intended to start a whole thing.

"I stole the feather," Max Celand shouted from the back. His sister's voice followed, "No, we stole it." Then more voices, likely from other angels who'd been Eva's friends.

Then Cyrus stood. "I bet the woman who framed Zeke stole the feather."

"Yes, Madeline Lake!" Magdalena agreed, leaping up too. She pointed to Irena. "Her assistant."

Irena clicked her tongue in obvious exasperation. "The entire courtroom can't have stolen the feather, and I don't see why Evangelina would lie to protect Ms. Lake."

"Maybe because Eva didn't realize and was afraid it had fallen out by itself," Farrah suggested, standing as well. "You'd condemn her for that too, wouldn't you? Any angel would be afraid. But even if Eva did give her feather away, isn't the fact that she told the truth evidence of her not succumbing to human vice? She doesn't deserve to be punished!"

Murmurs of assent swept through the crowd. But Judge Reign didn't seem the type to be swayed by public opinion. Throughout all the outbursts, he'd kept his pale, unnerving gaze on Nathan. Perhaps he feared an irin might corrupt the others if he turned his back for a second.

Or if he blinks. Does he ever close his eyes?

"Ms. Elysium, it is your job to argue against Evangelina Heaven," Judge Reign said, finally glancing toward the karmic angel. "But you must also present me with facts. Is it possible that Miss Heaven's feather was stolen?"

Oh God, did that mean his decision would come down to what Irena said? Nathan watched the round-faced woman with her semi-permanent scowl.

Irena frowned. "Evangelina's wings pop out when she's surprised or overwhelmed, making her feathers an easy target. You saw it yourself, I believe. So, yes, technically, it is possible."

Nathan held back a grin. That sealed it. The judge would have to find Eva innocent.

But the gold-feathered angel didn't return to his throne. "There is also the matter of Miss Heaven's guardian angel assignment. You are her charge, Mr. Ward. But irin cannot be involved in Sanctum matters. This is forbidden."

Nathan's eyebrows rose. The judge couldn't be serious. "You can't blame Eva for that. The whole thing was a trap."

"You claim there was a mistake?'

"Obviously."

Finally, the judge turned. He set his pale gaze on Eva. "What's your assessment of the situation, Miss Heaven?"

66

EVANGELINA

Despite this being her trial, almost no one had been watching Eva until now. Irena flew higher, putting more distance between them. It meant that Eva was no longer trapped—or shielded—behind the karmic angel's wing.

Judge Reign repeated his question, "Do you agree that your assignment was a mistake?"

In the mirror, Eva saw people nodding: her brother, her father, Max and Leah and her former friends near the back. They all wanted her to say yes, to save herself. Irena's head gave the slightest twitch.

Does she want me to say no?

Nathan's wings remained visible. A dark light clung to the bones, making the air seem to tremble around him. But he stared at Eva, his brown eyes wide and pleading. His lashes fluttered. And she could see the desperate wish within their depths.

How could I ever regret meeting him?

"It wasn't a mistake," Eva said, not because it was what anyone wanted her to say, but because it was the truth.

"Maddie tampered with the phone and set me up to fail, but I don't believe my assignment was a mistake. I was meant to be Nathan's guardian angel."

For the first time, Eva swore Judge Reign smiled.

"I've made my decision," he announced. "Evangelina Heaven has not fallen to the vices of this earth. Everyone is free to leave."

Eva gasped. Her smile started to spread, but it quickly froze as Judge Reign turned back to Nathan.

"Except for you, Mr. Ward. Irin cannot involve themselves in Sanctum business. You will have to come with me."

———

Eva tried to follow as a pair of Powers escorted Judge Reign and Nathan through one of the courtrooms' hidden doors. But before she'd taken even two steps, Zeke grabbed her arm and pulled her back.

"We did it, Eva! We can keep our feathers!" Zeke enveloped her in a giant hug.

Their parents arrived, wrapping their arms and wings around them as well. Zeke scoffed and shot their father a look, but then he leaned in. Their mother's head fell on Eva's shoulder. Magdalena made no effort to hold back her tears.

"I knew you would be found innocent," she whispered.

"I didn't," Cyrus admitted. "But I'm sorry for doubting you both."

At another moment, Eva would've been relieved to have her family all together again. Now, she felt trapped in a mass of feathers.

I get to keep mine.

Eva could never be upset about such a thing. But what did that mean for her and Nathan? They could never—

The future doesn't matter. I need to help now.

Where would Judge Reign have taken him?

Eva extricated herself from her family, allowing her brother the chance to accept their parents' apologies himself. She studied the mirrors on the walls and saw her own anxiety reflected back. Where had the door been?

"I do not approve of the stunt your charge pulled back there," Irena said, heels clicking as she landed on the floor. She folded her wings. "And I don't believe for a second that Judge Reign didn't see through those lies. Obviously, your feather wasn't stolen."

"But it could have been. You said so yourself," Beatrice said, skipping toward them with a broad grin. "And Nathan's lies gave the judge an excuse to dismiss Eva's case. Can't take an angel's feathers just for lying. You'd all lose them."

Irena's eyes narrowed. "I believe you might want to keep studying angelic law, Miss Blackwell. You have a poor grasp of how it works."

Maybe Beatrice wasn't an expert, but her assessment didn't seem inaccurate either. Eva had confessed. If Nathan hadn't introduced the idea of her feather being stolen, Judge Reign would've had no reason to inquire.

He saved me, just like he wanted.

Something cawed from the pocket of Eva's dress. How had she forgotten about the guardian phone?

The countdown flashed across its screen, larger now. One minute left until her assignment ended.

Eva had to hurry. "How do I find Nathan?" she asked.

Behind the countdown, a map appeared.

67
NATHAN

Nathan pushed open a white door at the top of a long staircase. The sky spread before him. He paused, and a hand shoved him forward. Nathan stumbled onto the rooftop of the Sanctum Headquarters.

The door swung shut behind him. Nathan pulled on the handle. Locked.

Had the guards marched him to the rooftop and trapped him? Was this how they stripped the last of his divinity? By letting the sun burn it from within?

That seemed far-fetched. Nathan rolled his shoulders, turned from the door, and crossed to the rooftop's surrounding ledge. Castor's Grove spread before him. Black tarmac roads divided the city into carefully planned square grids. But bizarre, mismatched buildings sprung like wildflowers between, showing no concern for architectural cohesion.

"Are you afraid of heights, Mr. Ward?"

The sound of the judge's deep voice made Nathan jump. He spun to find the statuesque angel perched at the corner of the roof.

Judge Reign's wings stretched behind him, gold streaks sparkling in the sun. Exposing them outdoors in the center of the city would normally be considered illegal—or at least reckless. But the Sanctum's towers stretched almost to the clouds. Nathan doubted anyone on the street could see them when they were so high up.

"Should I be afraid?" Nathan asked.

"Most irin are. It's the sudden realization that you could fall and die, I've been told."

"Ah. Right." A bead of sweat formed on the back of Nathan's neck. He pushed his hair back, trying not to glance over the roof again. He wasn't afraid of heights, but maybe, right now, he should be. "Why did you bring me to the roof, sir?"

The judge stepped from the ledge. His gray eyes stared into the clouds. "It is a highly unusual situation we find ourselves in. No irin has ever been permitted access to Sanctum proceedings nor assigned a guardian. It cannot be allowed to stand."

A lump rose in Nathan's throat.

Don't look down. Don't look down.

Nathan couldn't even make out the cars from this distance. They were blurs of color on the tarmac grid. His stomach turned. He took a deep breath and tried to play it cool.

"You already said that, sir."

The judge moved closer.

Oh God, he's going to push me off the roof.

That must've been how they stripped irin of their divinity. Death.

"That's not how I'm to be addressed. I serve as a judge, but I am also a Prince of the Inner Sanctum. Do you know the correct honorific for an angel of my status?"

Nathan searched his memories, heard his mother muttering curses. "I apologize, your Greatness."

The judge's pale lips twitched. "It seems that our Lord has used Evangelina Heaven as his vessel to guide you to me." He stepped forward again, moving like a lion ready to pounce on a gazelle. "Turn around."

Nathan considered resisting. It felt wrong not to fight. But he suspected those guards remained on the opposite side of the door. He couldn't escape. So, Nathan closed his eyes and prayed as he turned toward the ledge.

He could feel the judge standing behind him. It was the perfect position to shove someone to their death.

"Your wings, Mr. Ward."

So that Nathan could attempt to fly with bones? Or maybe the judge would bind them in some way. Most irin probably summoned theirs on instinct when they fell. Might be better not to have the humans below find a corpse with skeletal wings.

Screeee. The familiar scraping cut through the wind as Nathan obeyed. His wings clattered and ached as the bones unfurled, knocking against one another.

The judge slapped Nathan's back, right between the shoulder blades.

This is it, I'm—

Wait, what was he doing? The force of the judge's slap should have propelled Nathan forward and sent him tumbling to his death. So why did Nathan feel as though he hadn't moved?

He opened his eyes.

Warmth flooded Nathan's body, radiating into his wings. The bones hummed with a strange, low vibration. At the edges of Nathan's vision, a dark glow transformed into golden rays.

White feathers grew within.

Nathan's mouth fell open. His head swung left-to-right, then back again. Outstretched behind him was a pair of proper angel wings.

The judge moved his hand. The golden light vanished. But the feathers remained.

"You... healed me," Nathan whispered. He couldn't believe it. He'd thought the judge had intended to kill him.

Nathan spun to thank the angel with the unreadable face, but he found the roof empty.

How did he—?

The handle of the white door trembled. A moment later it burst open and Eva rushed through. Tears made the blue in her eyes sparkle. Her cheeks appeared flushed as though she'd exerted herself. But when she looked at Nathan, her smile burst across her face. Dressed in white, standing in the glow of the sunshine, she'd never looked more radiant.

"The guardian phone led me up here, but then the guards refused to let me through until it vanished, and I thought I was too late, but you have feathers!" Eva ran to him and wrapped her arms around his neck. The force of her hug nearly sent Nathan over the ledge after all.

He steadied himself, grabbed her waist, and spun her around, carrying them both toward the center of the rooftop. "You guided me to greatness after all. Just not my own. The judge healed me."

The tips of their wings brushed. Eva's smile grew bigger. She was the most perfect thing Nathan had ever seen.

And his presence wouldn't doom her.

Nathan lifted his hand to Eva's face. He traced from her cheekbone down to her chin. His skin warmed where he touched her.

Eva's eyes shone. Her massive smile remained, until she closed the space between them.

Their lips met with a soft uncertainty as though both sensed that this time their kiss symbolized something more permanent, something possible. Nathan wanted it. He pulled Eva closer, wrapping his hand in her hair. Their wings curled together, feathers intermingling and blending until it was impossible to tell where one began and the other ended.

Eva melted against him. Any sense of hesitancy vanished. Her fist gripped his hair while her other hand roamed across his shoulders, fingers running along the ridge of Nathan's new plumage. He held her close, exploring the curves of her hips, letting his hands slide over the soft silky fabric of her dress, feeling the heat of her thighs beneath.

For a perfect moment, nothing existed beside Eva.

Then, the witch's voice, loud as ever, yanked Nathan back to reality. "Holy crap! I thought maybe—" Beatrice broke off to take a deep breath. "—you'd need help. So I followed, but—Nate, are you wrapped in Eva's wings or—?"

Nathan would've been happy to ignore Beatrice and let her keep talking for another few minutes, but Eva pulled away. The blue still sparkled in her eyes. She giggled and lowered her arms, unwrapping herself and her wings from Nathan.

"Maiden, Mother, and Crone! You got your feathers back!" Beatrice shouted. Referencing the witches' pagan gods seemed a curious choice given her current location, but Nathan had never been one to preach.

Nor could he find it in him to be as annoyed with the witch as he might have liked. She'd interrupted his moment with Eva, but for the first time, Nathan felt confident that there would be other moments, perhaps even an eternity of them.

"Aren't they gorgeous?" Eva said, smiling and gesturing to Nathan's feathers.

"The judge gave them back," Nathan said, neck heating at her compliment. Still, he grinned as he flapped his wings. "Or maybe he regrew them."

"So it is possible," Beatrice said, and a dangerous look glinted in her eyes as they roved over Nathan's new feathers. "Can I have one?"

Nathan snorted and folded his wings. He assumed the witch was joking.

"No, seriously," Beatrice said, placing her hands on her hips and staring at them both. She lowered her voice. "I have an idea, but I'm pretty sure I'll need two."

68

EVANGELINA

"He has feathers for five seconds and gives one to a witch?" Zeke whispered. "You two really are a good fit."

Eva elbowed her brother to get him to shush. Daniel didn't know that Nathan had his feathers back yet.

The little boy sat on a stool before a large cauldron in Beatrice's basement. Nathan stood behind him. He kept one hand on his younger brother's shoulder and the other on his back. He said he wanted to make sure that Daniel didn't fall off, which was likely true. But Eva suspected Nathan also wanted to see what the witch was doing.

"The Sanctum is going to have so many opinions about this," Zeke said. Despite barely escaping excommunication just yesterday, he sounded excited by the prospect.

"If the Sanctum is upset about us helping a sick child, then they'll be the ones in the wrong," Eva whispered. "Not us."

"Suggesting the Sanctum could be wrong? Heresy," Zeke teased, lowering his voice further. He and Eva stood in a corner by the stairs, guarding the entrance from any of

Beatrice's family. "I'm sure just visiting a witch's potions den marks us as immoral. Though I'm not sure this counts as one. Think being able to see the rafters and pipes helps with the magic?"

Eva gave her brother her best glare. Beatrice had referred to the unfinished basement as a potions den. And it must have been. Bottles of strange ingredients lined the walls. Eva read one labeled *Fairy's Hair* and decided to stop looking lest she discover something more unsavory. She didn't need the reminder that the witch would happily use pieces of them as ingredients. The feathers were bad enough.

But it won't be bad if she succeeds.

"You didn't have to come, you know," Eva said.

"You wanted me to stay at home with Mom and Dad? Alone?" Zeke pressed his hand to his chest as though wounded by the suggestion. "Do you realize how awkward things are?"

Eva smiled. She did. But their trial had been only yesterday. It would take time for things to go back to normal, but they would eventually.

"Is it supposed to bubble like that?" Daniel asked, peering into the cauldron. Beatrice had just added something that made the liquid rise up and pop.

Nathan shushed his brother. The witch had warned them not to distract her. She'd never tried a spell like this before.

Beatrice didn't react. She flourished her hand within a long black sleeve and pulled out two white feathers. They glowed in the dimly lit basement.

Across the room, Eva caught Nathan's eyes. She recognized the determined set of his jaw. He needed this to work, but he struggled to believe it would.

That was okay. Eva gave him a reassuring smile. She would believe for them both.

Beatrice dropped the feathers into the liquid. The color changed to a shimmering rainbow-like sheen. Bubbles burst and released stars into the air. In a matter of seconds, most of the potion had evaporated.

"Is that supposed to happen?" Zeke whispered.

"Yes," Eva answered with complete certainty despite the fact that Beatrice hadn't told them what to expect.

"Now, you drink it," Beatrice said, dipping a small glass into the cauldron. What little remained of the potion filled it.

Daniel glanced at his older brother.

Nathan nodded. "It's medicine."

Daniel reached for the glass, cupped it in both trembling hands, and raised it to his lips.

An agonizing scream pierced the basement.

Nathan grabbed his brother's shoulders as Daniel started to convulse. Fear flashed across Beatrice's face. Even Zeke stepped forward.

Eva remained still.

Daniel's wings burst from his back, black bones rattling and hissing. A dark glow surrounded them. And then, feathers started to sprout—black as ink.

The little boy stopped shaking.

"Dan? Are you okay?" Nathan leaned over, gripping his brother's shoulders.

"I'm so sorry, I didn't know—" Beatrice started to apologize, but Daniel's voice stopped her.

"Nate, I have feathers," he said. A smile exploded across his face. He leaped from the stool, spreading and flapping his wings in the basement. "I feel—I feel—I feel amazing!"

Nathan grinned.

"Careful, or you'll knock over my ingredients," Beatrice said, but she didn't sound annoyed. If anything, the witch looked relieved.

Eva wrapped her arms around Zeke's neck, forcing him into a hug as they watched the little boy rejoice. As much as she wanted to go to Nathan, this wasn't her moment to be with him.

Daniel continued stretching and flapping and spinning in a circle. Nathan scooped his brother into his arms and showed him his own healed wings. The little boy's smile grew so big it threatened to stretch off his face.

Beatrice crept closer to Eva and Zeke.

"Pretty impressive magic," Zeke noted. "Maybe you should've been the one to receive a guardian angel."

"No, because Beatrice didn't need our help getting there." Eva released her brother and hugged the witch instead. She whispered in Beatrice's ear. "You are the best friend I could've ever hoped to find at Dashmoor!"

Beatrice grinned. "I told you I could want a feather and a friendship." She glanced at Nathan and Daniel, then back to Eva. The witch lowered her voice, "I didn't mean for the wings to be black though. Is that acceptable among angels?"

Eva looked at the little boy, flapping his wings in his older brother's arms. Warmth filled her chest, and her smile grew bigger. "It is now."

69

EVANGELINA

TWO MONTHS AFTER THE TRIAL

"Try it now." Eva dipped her finger into the cupcake batter and held it out.

Nathan turned from the pot on the stove in her family's kitchen. His head tilted as he studied her outstretched hand. He smirked and fluttered his lashes in the way that always made Eva's heart flutter with them. "Interesting way to present it. Couldn't find a spoon?"

Eva's cheeks heated. Which was ridiculous! She shouldn't still blush so easily when Nathan teased her now that they were officially together.

"Fine, I'll sample it myself." Eva sucked the batter off her finger, holding Nathan's gaze.

His smile grew. "Not really any less suggestive."

"Maybe that's the point," Eva said. She wished he'd blush in response too, but Nathan's skin was darker, and he never got flustered by her comments in the same way. She'd have to keep trying. "Here. Taste it."

Eva stepped forward and wrapped her arms around Nathan's neck to pull his lips to hers. She slipped her tongue—flavored with the batter—into his mouth before pulling away.

"Not sure." Nathan grinned, and wrapped his arm around her waist, pinning her in place. "Let me try again." He pulled her lips back to his.

"Is that what they mean when they say made with love?" Zeke asked as he came around the corner.

Nathan sprang back, and Eva swallowed a laugh. That was one way to get him flustered at least.

Whenever any of Eva's family appeared, he grew nervous. It was cute, but unnecessary. Her parents and Zeke all liked Nathan, and they already considered both him and Daniel to be part of their flock.

Zeke pulled up a stool on the opposite side of the kitchen counter. He wore a button-down shirt that perfectly matched his eyes, and the beard he'd insisted on keeping had been neatly trimmed.

That's his date outfit.

"I thought things ended between you and Olivia," Eva said.

"There was never a *thing* to end," Zeke insisted. "She's a werewolf. One kiss is all it takes for them to imprint. We knew it wasn't meant to be."

"Uh huh." Eva knew all that. But it hadn't stopped Zeke and Olivia from meeting several times after that realization. Their former guard was incredibly sweet. She always came in. So why did Zeke's answer feel cagey. "Are you going on a date with someone else?"

"No." Zeke scanned the kitchen. "How am I smelling

like fifty different foods?"

That was an exaggeration, but only a slight one. While there had been no chance of Principal Davis allowing Nathan and Eva to keep selling lunches at school, they'd found a new charitable project. Since the trials, the stigma had fallen from the Heaven family. The angels who'd distanced themselves all rushed back to make themselves friendly again. Cyrus' employees had returned, and Magdalena had regained control of several local charities. She'd tasked Nathan and Eva with providing meals for one of the homeless shelters. The Sanctum bankrolled the cost of the ingredients. So, Nathan and Eva got creative.

"Any baked goods yet?" Zeke asked, rising off his stool. He walked further into the kitchen, inspecting the island countertop where Eva worked. "I want to steal a couple."

"As in two?" Eva asked, swatting her brother's hand away as he attempted to dip it into her batter. "Are you sure you're not going on a date?"

Zeke inhaled. "Are you using lavender?"

"You are going on a date!" Zeke never asked about Eva's recipes unless he was avoiding the topic. But if he wasn't meeting Olivia, then who— "Is it Farrah?"

"We're meeting to discuss oversight in the financial division. It's not a date."

But Zeke was wearing his favorite shirt. Eva grinned. "You should kiss her and see if there's something there."

"That's terrible advice. Who would be dumb enough to listen to that?" Zeke succeeded in stealing some of the batter. Instead of tasting it, he flicked it onto Eva's forehead, laughed, and turned away. He patted Nathan's shoulder before leaving the kitchen. "Save a plate of whatever you're making for me to have for lunch tomorrow, Nate!"

"You're not homeless!" Eva objected. But Nathan gave him a thumbs up. He always caved to Zeke. And truthfully, there was always extra food. The Heavens eating the leftovers was better than them going to waste.

"Do you guys have any mint?" Nathan asked, turning from his pot to lean against the stove. He looked comfortable again now that Zeke had left.

"It's up here." Eva crossed to the cupboard and reached up, standing on the tips of her toes to reach the spice rack. "Thought you'd know your way around our kitchen by now."

"I do. I just wanted to watch you get it."

Eva turned and found Nathan grinning. Heat rose to her cheeks again.

"Entering the house!" Beatrice shouted from the front dor. A few moments later, she called again, "Entering the kitchen!" The witch appeared, holding one hand across her eyes and the other over Daniel's own. "Safe to look?"

"Why do you always do that?" Daniel giggled from beside her.

"Because she's a moron," Nathan muttered, turning back to the bubbling pot and giving it a quick whisk.

"You're welcome for the free babysitting," Beatrice said, taking a seat on the stool that Zeke had just vacated.

A smile flashed across Nathan's face, but he didn't turn to let the witch see. The two seemed to enjoy bickering with one another. But they'd become friends too. How could they not have given everything Beatrice had done for them?

"We went flying in Castor's Forest today!" Daniel announced, bouncing on his toes as he stood beside his brother. "There were no humans, so I got to practice. And I flew upside down! It was awesome!"

As Daniel grew excited, his wings burst out, jet-black

feathers shimmering as he stretched them. Since they'd grown, the strange sickness had vanished from within him. Beatrice really had managed a miracle.

"Careful, Dan!" Nathan said, as one of the little boy's black wings bumped against the bowl of cupcake batter.

Eva caught it just in time.

"You're as bad as the cat," Nathan said, ruffling his brother's head. "You have to keep your wings under control inside."

Daniel turned to see Eva clutching the bowl he'd almost knocked over. He offered an apologetic smile as he retracted his wings. "Oops. Sorry!" He looked so guilty.

Eva smiled. She knew what it was like to have wings with a mind of their own. She grabbed a spoon, dipped it in the cupcake batter, and called Daniel over. "You can make it up to me by tasting this."

The guilt vanished. Daniel licked the spoon. "Yum! Don't bake it. We should eat it just like this."

"Agreed," Beatrice said, appearing with a spoon of her own and tasting it before Eva could stop her. "We saw Zeke when we came in. He looked nice. Who's he meeting?"

"Farrah."

"Really?"

"To discuss oversight in the financial division."

Beatrice snorted. "What's that code for?"

"If you're hanging out in the kitchen, you're helping. Not gossiping," Nathan said, throwing a towel to Beatrice. "Someone needs to do the dishes before Magdalena sees this mess."

The witch feigned offense, but Daniel offered to help, and the two took up their posts by the sink. Nathan chopped and stirred. Eva measured and mixed.

They did keep gossiping though, Nathan included,

despite his initial objections. At least until Chris arrived. Then their conversation shifted to school and more human-appropriate topics.

"You're joining my campaign after I help you with this, right?" Chris said, scratching beneath his hat before he took up the task of peeling garlic. He grinned at Eva. "You've turned him into too good a man, Blue Eyes."

"A great man," Eva corrected, wrapping her arms around Nathan. "But he always was."

"Stop, you'll make Nate blush," Chris joked.

"I wish," Eva admitted. "I'd love to see Nate flustered for a change."

Chris' eyebrows rose until they touched the edge of his hat. "Did you miss the weeks of him drooling over you and pretending otherwise?"

"I think I did. Tell me more."

"Eva, come help me find something in your pantry," Nathan said, grabbing her wrist. He scowled at Chris, who appeared to be holding back a grin. "You should focus on peeling if you want me to have any free time this afternoon."

Eva giggled, but she didn't resist as Nathan pulled her into the pantry.

A mewl greeted them. Halo rubbed against their legs.

"Always someone," Nathan muttered. He scratched the cat's head before shooing Halo into the kitchen and closing the door.

"What are you looking for?" Eva teased. She felt quite confident Nathan just wanted to avoid whatever joke Chris had been about to make.

Nathan leaned down and kissed along the side of Eva's neck. His eyelashes brushed against her skin, making her breath catch. His lips trailed higher. Eva shivered as he kissed her jaw before finally reaching her mouth.

"Found it," he whispered.

Nathan deepened their kiss, and Eva sank into him, letting his leg press between hers as her fingers tangled in his hair. He tasted like the honey and spices he'd been cooking with.

"We know what you're doing in there!" Beatrice shouted.

Eva and Nathan broke apart as Daniel's voice responded, "What are they doing in there?"

"Your brother's trying to hide the fact that he's drooling. Pantry doesn't have good light," Chris responded quickly.

Nathan slapped his palm over his face.

Eva bit back a laugh. "We should probably go back out."

"Probably," Nathan agreed, but he didn't move right away. Instead, his hand brushed Eva's cheek. The simple gesture sent heat coursing through her again. "Come to my place for dinner tonight after this? Chris can campaign with Daniel, so it'll be just us for a change."

Eva stared into Nathan's warm eyes with their gorgeous lashes. The heat made her cheeks flush again and her heart pound, but she smiled. "That sounds perfect."

NOTE FROM THE AUTHOR

Thank you so much for visiting the magical city of Castor's Grove!

If you enjoyed *Angel's Feather*, please tell your friends, or leave a review in the place where you purchased it. It would mean so much to me!

Please visit Plotworks Publishing to explore more of the Castor's Grove universe! Sign up for my newsletter and get a discount!

You can also follow me on Instagram: @aj.renwick

The Castor's Grove Universe consists of several stand-alone novels about the many creatures living in the city. In the future, I hope to explore the angels again, particularly the significance of Daniel's black wings. However, he has some growing up to do before we revisit him.

In the meantime, you can read *Orphan's Egg* to learn about the Knights who wish to destroy magic, *Changeling's Dagger* to meet a shifter, or *Dragon's Wisp* to discover more about—well, you can guess which creatures!

Or, if you enjoyed Beatrice's character, you can read her

story and learn more about the witches in Castor's Grove.
Turn the page for a preview of *Banshee's Breath*—

CASTOR'S GROVE

BANSHEE'S BREATH

a young adult
paranormal
romance

A.J. RENWICK

BANSHEE'S BREATH

None of the Blackwells were dead yet, but it was only a matter of time.

Their banshee had shrieked on Friday morning.

For most covens, the herald of death would've been a somber occasion. The Blackwell Matriarch had decided to throw an impromptu party.

"Tabitha does know that she's the most likely to die, right?" Beatrice asked as she climbed out of the van. Her short pink heels sank into the mud and the hem of her new dress brushed against the grass. "I mean, she's over a hundred and thirty. That's old! Even for a Matriarch."

On the driver's side, her brother Albert groaned in response and slammed the door. Visiting the manor always put him in a foul mood and having to squeeze into an old suit of their father's did nothing to improve it. At least his tie was a vibrant red.

Beatrice's dress was new, but gray, with sleeves a tad too long, even by witching standards. Unfortunately, the options had been limited in the plus-size section of the store, and her attempts to convince the dress to turn pink had failed. Clothing had a tendency to resist magical impressions.

"Or maybe that's exactly why Tabitha's gathered us here," Beatrice theorized as she trudged toward the driveway. "The banshee visited her dream and confirmed that her death was imminent."

Albert beat her to the back of the van. He lowered the ramp to allow their grandmother, Gigi, to wheel herself out.

"And now, Tabitha wants us all to tell her how great she is and heap praise on her while she's still alive instead of waiting until her funeral," Beatrice continued.

"Of course, you'd think that," Albert muttered, staring down and tugging at his too-tight shirt as though he could force the buttons to lay flat over his stomach.

"It's not the worst theory," Beatrice said, ignoring her brother's comment. "I mean, that's what happens in King Lear. Granted, that doesn't end well, but only because—"

"Darling?" Gigi reached the bottom of the ramp with a loud *thunk.* She rolled her weight and the wheelchair onto the drive and crooked a finger toward her granddaughter.

Beatrice leaned over. Loose brown waves fell over half of her face. With the long sleeves, she couldn't even quickly tuck it back behind her ear.

Gigi grabbed Beatrice's lips and pressed them shut between her index finger and thumb.

Albert let out a loud and uncalled for cackle.

Beatrice would've stuck her tongue out at him if she could, but she had to settle for an annoyed glare instead. *And he calls me immature?*

"Don't run your mouth. Not tonight. It's too important." Gigi released her grip and continued wheeling herself up the drive.

What does that mean?

Beatrice desperately wanted to ask, but she knew the question would only give her brother ammunition to mock her, so she clamped her mouth shut and decided to remain quiet until they reached the manor.

Four of the Blackwell servants met them at the bottom of the stairs. They carried Gigi to the front door. A broomstick would have simplified the issue, but their Matriarch detested anyone flying through her house, and, for all its wealth and glamor, the Blackwell Estate was not wheelchair accessible.

The property consisted of fifty acres of woods, sectioned off from the surrounding city by large black walls. Enchantments ensured that the humans of Castor's Grove could look at the monstrosity of wealth in their city and somehow think nothing amiss.

Several houses existed on the estate: a massive greenhouse, old windmills, smaller homes for less preferred relatives. Among all the buildings, however, the Blackwell Manor was the crowning jewel. It rose out of the trees like a castle from a gothic fairytale. It boasted four towers, seven stories, and over a hundred rooms.

Beatrice had never stepped foot beyond the first floor.

Nor would she tonight.

The party was held in the Manor's ballroom, which was large enough to hold Beatrice's entire house. Constellations shifted on the ceiling. Gargoyles in the form of dragons, griffins, and misshapen cherubs prowled above the stone pillars, their eyes glowing in the flickering light of the torches on the walls. A grand piano in the far corner filled the room with a waltz. Witches and warlocks danced in the center on a wooden floor or stood on the edges, observing and sipping champagne.

As always, Beatrice and her family were the last to

arrive. They were the only ones who didn't live on the Estate.

"Oh look!" A high-pitched, nasal voice stage-whispered from beside the door. It was their distant cousin, Debby, making a point of talking to her sister loud enough for them to hear. "The Barely-Blackwells are here."

Beatrice's jaw clenched. It wasn't fair. Just because her mother wasn't a Blackwell didn't mean she wasn't an equal member of their coven. She was ten times the witch either of her cousins was.

"Are you talking to us?" Albert scowled as he marched toward them. Even in his ill-fitting suit, his broad chest and pulsing forehead vein made a menacing display though he was more likely to lose his voice screaming than hurt anyone.

Beatrice went to follow her brother, happy that they were on the same side for a change.

Gigi grabbed her arm. "He can handle them. Come, push me further in. And keep an eye out for anything unusual. Our Matriarch loves a performance. Do you see anything?"

I thought I wasn't supposed to speak.

With some effort, Beatrice swallowed the retort. Compelled by her own curiosity, she followed her grandmother's instructions and studied the members of her coven as they strolled through.

In the far corner, whispering and ignoring Beatrice as usual, were her first cousins: Rett, Gabriel, and Elle. The two brothers seemed to be fawning over the fair-haired girl, probably praising some potion she'd brewed. Everyone believed Elle to be the most talented young witch in their coven.

Which was ridiculous. Beatrice's spells were twice as powerful. Where was her admiration and praise?

Apparently going to Linda. The middle-aged woman wore a tasteless red-sequin dress, which made her shine like a bleeding disco ball in the center of the dance floor. Her feet stomped on her partner's toes, but he smiled through the pain, ravishing her with compliments. As Tabitha's successor, that was all Linda ever heard from the other members of the Blackwell coven.

Meanwhile, they stared at Beatrice with their noses upturned like she hadn't showered.

"I don't see anything worth my attention," Beatrice informed her grandmother. "You should've let Albert bring Oliver."

It was only a joke, meant to ease the strange tension that Beatrice sensed building in her grandmother, but it drew an exasperated sigh from the old woman.

"You need to rid yourself of this childish crush you've developed on your brother's friend. Oliver Wyrmwood is a snake and the last thing that should be on your mind tonight."

Really? Because daydreaming about Oliver seemed a lot more pleasant than interacting with her coven.

"I don't like him," Beatrice lied, glancing around out of habit to ensure that her brother wasn't standing nearby. "But he is cute. You can't argue with that."

Or perhaps she could because *cute* was an understatement. Oliver had been built like a Greek statue and dipped in bronze. He had broad shoulders, short dark curls, and a jaw to make hearts melt.

Oliver had befriended Albert when they first started middle school, and a year later, Beatrice had fallen hopelessly in love with him.

Her first day of sixth grade in a human school, she'd made the mistake of talking to her classmates about magic. They'd all thought she was crazy and teased her all the way until lunch. She'd probably have been bullied for the rest of middle school.

But Oliver stepped in to save her.

He'd marched over and informed them all that he believed in magic too and that he could show it to them. He plucked a white lily from the earth and turned it black before their eyes. The other kids gasped and ran off shouting.

Oliver gave her the flower, and Beatrice's heart had skipped a beat.

She still had the lily, preserved by an enchantment and hidden in the basement.

"It's not his appearance that bothers me, it's his character." Gigi's voice, soft but annoyed, pulled Beatrice from her memory. "You're a romantic. And Oliver Wyrmwood is no Prince Charming."

Beatrice gasped. It wasn't what her grandmother had said, she'd heard Gigi's thoughts on Oliver a hundred times before.

Something had just touched her arm.

Beatrice looked down in time to see a bluish-gray blur, streaking across the floor and bouncing onto others. It must've been Bean, Tabitha's familiar. Beatrice had always liked him more than their Matriarch.

"I found what's out of place," Beatrice announced, a smile spreading across her face. "Do I win a prize?"

Gigi frowned at her, clearly confused.

But before Beatrice could say more, a loud cough echoed through the ballroom. It brought a stifling silence.

The piano ceased; the dancers froze; conversations died mid-sentence.

A platform rose from the back of the room. The Matriarch stood in its center, a small old woman, buried in a thick layer of black fur. Red heels peeped under the bottom and her face, like a pale moon, rose from the top.

Behind Tabitha, Linda's sequins assaulted the eyes of anyone who happened to glance in her direction. She smiled and waved as though she was a contestant in a beauty pageant.

Beatrice immediately averted her gaze to the third person on the platform. It was Wilburn, the coven's lawyer. His sharp green eyes glared down at the rest of the Blackwells in the room. They landed on Beatrice, and his scowl darkened.

"My beloved Blackwells." Despite her shriveled appearance, Tabitha had the powerful voice of a career woman in her forties. "These past seventy years, under my leadership, our coven has become the most powerful in Castor's Grove. Now, I suspect that I am about to die."

She paused, waiting for any murmurs of dissent. None came.

"And so, I must leave you in the hands of a new Matriarch. One who can guard my legacy."

Linda's smile broadened, and she moved as if to step forward.

"The most powerful witch amongst us."

Linda's foot froze in mid-air. Not even she was conceited enough to believe herself the most powerful of the Blackwell coven.

"That's right. I'm dispensing with this city's ridiculous notion of female primogeniture and returning to the old ways. The title of Matriarch will pass to the most powerful witch."

Whispers filled the room. Heads began to turn. Most went to Elle.

Only Gigi's went to Beatrice.

"She will step forward upon my passing." Tabitha tapped her cane for silence once again. "You will know her by the card she carries in her sleeve."

The Matriarch looked out across the room. Her eye caught Beatrice's gaze, and her lips curved into the slightest hint of a smile.

Or maybe that was Beatrice's imagination. She did have a tendency to let it run wild.

But she couldn't resist indulging in the fantasy, at least for a moment, that the Matriarch had seen something special in her.

Heart pounding, Beatrice's hand searched for the pocket that had been sewn into the too-long sleeve of her dress. Her fingers latched around the compartment, and she froze.

There was something inside.

PLOTWORKS PUBLISHING

And now turn the page for a peek at another A.J. Renwick series, *The Warlock's Homeowners Association*, a comedic suburban fantasy!

the

WARLOCK'S
HOMEOWNERS
ASSOCIATION

presents...

**BOOK
ONE**

SUB
DIVISION
BATTLES
OF THE
DEAD AND UNDEAD

A.J. RENWICK

SUBDIVISION BATTLES OF THE DEAD AND UNDEAD

On a cold night in the middle of June, at exactly 10:57 pm (though when the story was retold, the time would be changed to midnight for dramatic purposes), a dead man strode into The Clover Motel.

A brown messenger bag hung from his shoulder, and beneath his arm, he clutched a black chrysalis. It shimmered with iridescent light and radiated with the heavy heat of the underworld.

Bartholomew Whitlock wasn't dead in the traditional sense, or even the untraditional sense. His heart still beat. His breath was steady. He had no desire to moan, hold his arms stiff before him, or eat brains. His death was a metaphorical one.

Gone was Bartholomew Whitlock, exalted among the Acquisitions Department of The Bearded Syndicate, in his place was—

"Bartholomew Bartlow?"

Rebecca Willis, the woman stuck working the night shift at the motel's front desk, peered at the identification card through a pair of pink-rimmed spectacles. Had she looked closely, she might have noticed a curious sheen on the plastic, like it was turning brown in a pattern of lines and dots. But the news was reporting on a plane crash, and Rebecca took a morbid delight in listening to tragic stories, even if only so she could inform her husband the next day and chide him for his lack of empathy when he remained indifferent. She was eager to get this new guest checked in so that she could get back to the television.

Still, she attempted to make what she considered polite conversation as she typed Bartholomew's information into the old computer. "I'll bet school was tough for you."

Rebecca cracked a sympathetic smile and looked at the man before her desk.

He stared back, dark eyes serious beneath a pair of thick black brows that matched the curls on his head. His lips were drawn in a tight thin line. "No," he said, "I was an excellent student."

Rebecca stared at him. There was something unsettling about his voice. In the moment, she couldn't place what it was, but when she recounted the meeting later, she'd realize. Though Bartholomew's face was smooth, not a day over thirty, he spoke like a radio-announcer who was pushing seventy.

"No, I meant— Right, well..." Rebecca waved her hand in dismissal and continued entering the information. "And do you know how long you'll be staying with us, Mr. Bartlow?"

"Who? Oh that's me." He nodded. "No, not yet. But I'll need a pet-friendly room. I'm about to get a cat." For some reason, he shifted the black chrysalis in his arm as he spoke. An arc of light shimmered around it, as though it were wrapped in a rainbow.

Rebecca blinked. She'd never seen anything like it,

which wasn't surprising. Most people, even magical and undead ones, hadn't.

"Very good, Mr. Bartlow. Pets are only allowed in rooms on the first floor. We have one still available." The Clover Motel in fact was mostly empty, but Rebecca had been instructed to say otherwise by her boss, who was under the mistaken assumption that the lie gave the establishment an air of desirability. "We'll keep your credit card information on file until then. Wi-Fi password and information are in a binder on the side table when you go in. Room is right down the hall, second on the left. Here's the key."

She dropped it into Bartholomew's waiting hand. Like the rest of his body, his fingers were long and thin. Unlike the rest of him, they had a tendency to twitch like the limbs of a dying spider. They curled around the key with a snap.

He turned, took two steps toward the hall, and stopped. His fingers flitted into his pocket and retrieved a green bill.

As a habit, Rebecca's interest in guests ended the moment the room key was exchanged. She'd already begun switching the computer tab back to the news. However, the glint of green caught her eye.

It wasn't often that guests bothered to tip her.

And it wasn't a one-, or five-, or even a ten-dollar bill that Bartholomew was crinkling in his fingers. Rebecca recognized Benjamin Franklin's shiny forehead, and even if she hadn't, the two zeros beside it could have only meant one thing.

Bartholomew had her interest once more.

He rested the hundred-dollar bill on the desk. "If someone with a beard shows up, tell me."

"Absolutely!" Rebecca grabbed the money before Bartholomew could change his mind. She would have responded just as eagerly to a ten.

Of course, she would have been just as inefficient if he'd given her a thousand.

Two bearded men would visit the motel in the next week, and Rebecca would inform Bartholomew about neither. Not due to malice, but because the entire encounter slipped from her mind, replaced instead with facts about the night's disaster.

The private plane had exploded mid-air, killing three individuals: the pilot, co-pilot, and a single unnamed passenger. His face flashed across the screen: a man in his thirties with a black beard, long, slicked back hair, and dark eyes that seemed strangely familiar.

I bet he'd be handsome if he shaved, Rebecca thought, and then immediately imagined a new, and incorrect, face for the deceased passenger, which drew more than a little inspiration from the hero on the cover of a romance novel that currently waited beside her bed.

It would be years before she realized that she'd rented a room to a dead man, or even remembered Bartholomew's request. And even then, it would be only for a second before a bearded man plucked the memory from her mind.

PLOTWORKS PUBLISHING

Visit Plotworks Publishing to continue exploring the Castor's Grove universe—and find many other titles too!

ABOUT THE AUTHOR

A.J. Renwick is a lover of all things fantasy, from mermaids and unicorns to vampires and dragons. She writes young adult paranormal romance with strong plots, dual points of view, and happily ever afters.

When she's not writing, A.J. Renwick enjoys reading (duh!), baking (some things more successfully than others), and spending time with her three dogs (the Dragon Squad).

You can find out more about her at Plotworks Publishing.

www.ingramcontent.com/pod-product-compliance
Lightning Source LLC
Chambersburg PA
CBHW030554020726
47494CB00005B/1608